# TENDER CONQUEST

Hannah didn't have a free hand to slap him so she kicked him instead, hurting her big toe. She hardly felt it, though, because Jake kissed her then and all she could think was why had he waited so long.

His mouth was hard but sweet, and she opened to him like a flower. He responded by grasping her braids and pulling her head back. Arched over his arm, she hung on to his shoulders and let him conquer her tender mouth. Then, as he pulled away from her, his hand reached to loosen the laces on her shirt and Hannah was sure she would explode.

He lifted her toward him, and as they kissed, he pressed against her. Then he looked into her passion-filled eyes. "I've wanted you every minute of every day since I first saw you." His thick voice licked over her with tiny tongues of flame. "And I promise you, you're going to feel the way I do. You're going to want me more than you've ever wanted anything before in your life."

# RENEGADE HEART

## MARJORIE PRICE

and published by:

Kensington Publishing Corp.
475 Park Avenue South
New York, NY 10016

**ZEBRA BOOKS**
**KENSINGTON PUBLISHING CORP.**

# Chapter One

Afraid she would scream, Hannah bit down hard on her fist. She barely felt her teeth sink into the sparse flesh. She didn't want to look at the leap of flames or hear the shrieks of the dying, but she couldn't turn her head. They were her friends and she couldn't help them. Savages on horseback circled the bonfire that had been five covered wagons, their insane yelps voices from Hell.

Five wagons weren't enough, everyone had warned. Five wagons would only invite attack either by Indians or by bands of renegade soldiers still on the prowl after the end of the war. Both would kill, rob, rape, and burn, everyone had said. Everyone was right.

She pressed her slight body to the ground, knowing her survival depended on stillness even as every impulse of her soul urged escape. She owed her life to that stubborn insistence on her own way that made her mother call her Headstrong Hannah. Uncle Simon used the same term. Hannah knew she exasperated people, but in this instance being headstrong meant she was still alive. So far.

She cowered lower, deathly afraid the pale gleam of her skin would show up in the glare of the unearthly blaze before her. Would the Indians search for her? Had some scout seen her sneak away to forbidden privacy before the attack? The biting wind that had pelted them with dust and dirt all day was hot now. It tossed burning pieces of cloth and wood into the night.

Hannah moved frightened fingers over her body, assuring herself that she was whole. Her dress was soaked, even her hair. How had she gotten wet? She had been carrying a bucket of water to the seclusion of some bushes, intent on getting a bath. She remembered the bucket, its weight and promise, but not throwing herself to the ground or dropping the bucket. Evidently she had done that at the sound of the attack. She remembered the curdled shouts and screams though. She would remember those forever. Wet, her gray dress looked black. It would blend into the shadows better that way, but what about later? Would she survive now, only to die of exposure?

Her mind circled helplessly. Marcie. Marcie was dead. She had only been with these people for sixteen days, but already she loved Marcie and little Jonathan. Oh God. Little Jonathan. She commanded herself not to think about the Torvolds, but to *think*. She had to. She had to move back from the carnage. Any minute now the grass and bushes around her could catch fire and roast her where she cringed.

Perhaps someone else was alive and hiding as she was. Willie. She choked back a sob at the thought of Willie, her guardian and protector for this junket. Uncle Simon would kill Willie if anything happened to her! Then she realized that Willie was certainly dead, too. Fresh tears blurred her eyes and she stumbled, catching herself by grabbing an outcropping of rock.

After that, Hannah moved back by careful inches, afraid to go faster. She could still hear the Indians though they no longer rode rings around their destruction. Some chased horses, others slaughtered the few milk cows. Most, however, were gathered in a tight circle just beyond the still-burning wagons. Hannah could see the outline of their raised arms and weapons as they flailed at something in their midst. A cow?

6

At their guttural cheer as the group broke apart, Hannah shrank deeper into the shadows. Opposite her, firelight shone on the blunted face of one painted Indian. He raised his hand in triumph, displaying a dripping scalp. Not a cow, Hannah saw, gagging reflexively, a person. A person! Another half-naked figure bent to the ground. When he rose, he had Willie's domed beaver hat, the one Willie was never without. He clapped it onto the murderer's head.

Hannah never knew what they did next. She turned away blindly and ran from the horror. Back, her mind told her, and she obeyed. Stumbling, crashing, she flailed her way through bushes and branches and rocks. She fell, got up, ran, fell again, but on she went, running to keep herself from screaming. With no air in her lungs for screaming or even for running, she threw herself forward and fell one last time.

She saw rocks tumbling past her face, jumbled with slapping leaves. When the world stopped suddenly, leaving her gasping, she looked up into a ring of hard brown faces, one an unpainted Indian. Not the Indian who had killed Willie—she saw that clearly—but an Indian. The others were dirty white men in tattered Union-blue uniforms. She stared, hearing only the drumming of her frantic heart and her rasp for breath. They stared back, faces blank with surprise.

The nervous whinny of a horse broke through to her battered senses, the impact of the sound like a cannon's boom in her mind. She had to steal one of the horses. She had not spoken, nor had the men. She edged up. Hands reached for her. She shook them off, her mind only on the horses. When she was on her feet they gave her room, magically falling back to let her stand.

If she'd been capable of thinking beyond her goal of the horses, she would have wondered why they let her stand, why they gaped at her so. Time was distorted.

What took only seconds seemed to go for an eternity while she willed breath into her chest and strength into her legs. The world dipped at her first tiny movement, but it steadied, seemingly held in place for her by the raptly watching men.

The horses stood well away from where the men silently circled her. Now that she was stronger, she feinted at another small collapse as if she might fall. When she didn't, they eased back from her again, one organism she seemed to control by her will. She waited, then sprang from the circle, heading straight for the horses.

"Get her!"

Hannah heard the harsh command as she broke free. Still, she ran, never acknowledging that her goal was impossible. She launched herself toward the back of a black horse as if her feet had wings to lift her to its height. Instead, her legs were shackled by the dragging weight of a man's body that carried her down under the slashing metal-shod hoofs. With her last bit of strength she threw up her arms to protect her head, then fell into darkness, strangling on a scream of protest.

In her dream Hannah rode Lucky Jim's coppery back, the hunter green velvet of her riding habit bouncing at the horse's side. She knew the picture she made as the rush of air teased out tendrils of auburn hair from under her feathered hat. Daniel had told her often enough that she was a vision of loveliness. She believed he meant it. And why not? He loved her and wanted to marry her. Of course he thought she was beautiful.

Others of her set, girls as rich and pampered, worried that one or another of the men who courted them loved their wealth more than their persons, but Hannah never did. No matter what Uncle Simon cautioned, she knew Daniel Veazie loved her. She had never loved or even liked another person in her whole life who failed to love her back. Why should she question so ardent a man as Daniel?

Daniel wasn't the only man who pursued her; he was simply the only one who appealed to her. He was handsome, charming, debonair, smartly dressed, even ambitious. And Uncle Simon couldn't complain about Daniel's ambition or about his relative poverty. Not really. Simon had been poor once himself. It was no disgrace, as he himself often said. Ambition and hard work had won Simon Sargent an empire that extended far into the uncivilized and unsettled West on thin iron rails, so it was no sin for Daniel, also, to be ambitious. Besides, Hannah would have scorned a man who had no fire in his belly. With Simon for her model of manhood, how could she feel otherwise?

Because Uncle Simon had lost both his wife and his sister Josie, Hannah's mother, he had made Hannah his personal reason for living. Whatever she needed for happiness, or even wanted for amusement, was hers. Like himself, she had lost so much with the death of both her parents that he could deny her nothing, not even Daniel Veazie. Prudence decreed, however, that he give Veazie only the same opportunity for the exercise of his ambition through the combination of hard work and intelligence that he himself had used. Simon Sargent gave no handouts, even if he saw that it angered the younger man in time.

At first, though, Hannah and Daniel had been happy. Or at least Hannah had been happy. Gently, if indifferently, Daniel initiated her into the mysteries of the marriage act. She had been warned by her one already married friend not to expect great pleasure, but still Hannah had been disappointed in some vague way she scarcely understood. She was also puzzled to find that Daniel, who had wanted her so desperately before mar-

9

riage, quickly lost interest in her once she was his.

Within the first year she became pregnant. Her hope that having a child would please and interest Daniel died within days. Though her body raged with hungers she could barely credit, Hannah accepted Daniel's explanation of his absence from her bed. Naturally, she would do nothing to harm her baby.

The birth of her beautiful son, David, brought Hannah only one disappointment. Daniel showed no interest in his child beyond an initial, short-lived pride in his sex. And no revived interest in her either. Quickly giving up all pretense of husbandly concern, Daniel announced that he was leaving Knoxville, Tennessee, for the wider world of New York. He was going and he was not coming back. Scandalous as it was to be deserted by her husband, Hannah had no desire for divorce. Her married status kept other fortune hunters away and she was content, even happy. She had David to care for and to love.

David was four years old when he got the sore throat that led to his death. Within days he lay burning with fever—scarlet fever, the doctor called it. But giving the disease a name was all he could do for the child. No matter how much money his great-uncle possessed, no matter how earnestly his mother prayed, little David died. Stripped of everything that gave her life meaning, Hannah wanted to die, too.

She returned from the funeral, dry-eyed and stiff, a husk of a woman, held upright by willpower. She went directly to David's room, seeking comfort from the place where he had lived—and found it had been emptied of every possession. Every toy, every piece of clothing, every stick of furniture had been carried away from the house and burned during the funeral. The doctor had ordered it done to protect others from the disease, she was told. It was accepted medical practice. To Hannah, it was the final indignity, the ultimate violation of David's young

10

life. It meant she had nothing left of David but a curl of his strawberry blond hair she wore in a locket around her neck. It shocked her into the rage that probably saved her sanity even as it seemed to threaten it, mellowing after days of near madness to mere inconsolable grief.

It was months before she could realize that Simon also grieved, and too long after that before she could reach out to him either to give or to seek comfort. Between them they made a bad job of it, but finally Simon presented her with a way to fight back to life. By chance he had learned that a cousin of Hannah's, Elizabeth Farrell, lived in the Nebraska Territory.

Elizabeth was married to a settler in Fort Kearney, outside of Omaha, the growing railroad center and jumping-off point for the last leg of the transcontinental railroad. Simon had met and liked her husband Calvin. Between them, they decided that Elizabeth, who was expecting her first child in a place far from her origins, needed Hannah's companionship as much as Hannah needed someone to care for. The fort, in Simon's view, was as safe as any frontier community could be, especially since civilization in the form of the railroad was already on its doorstep in Omaha City.

At first Hannah protested going. She knew Simon depended on her love, as she did on his. How would they fare without each other? But then she understood. They both needed change, something to shake up their lives. She especially. Simon needed to know she wasn't at home brooding every time his business took him away. She had tried without avail to resume the social pursuits that had filled her life before marriage. She was no longer that untried girl, happy just to play at life. She needed something more. In Nebraska she could help Elizabeth, whom she remembered fondly, perhaps hold a child again, even if not her own.

Simon solidified her determination to go by assuring

her that she could always come back—which she knew—
and by telling her that her extra eyes and ears there close
to the building of the railroad would be useful to him.
She would go under her own name, he said. No one but
her cousin would ever connect Hannah Veazie to Simon
Sargent and his wealth. That was the way he wanted it.

Before she left, Hannah took one more step. She
removed her wedding ring and made her travel arrangements as Hannah Hatch, using her maiden name. Without little David, there was nothing to bind her to Daniel
anymore. He was gone. Her marriage was over. Perhaps
someday she would divorce Daniel, but until then she
would not carry his colors any more than she would
Simon's. If she was to make a new life, she would do it as
herself, Hannah Hatch. It was a plain and unremarkable
name, the name of the spinsterish schoolmarmy woman
she felt herself to be at twenty-five. She considered the
name eminently suitable for the person she had become—
her own person at last.

Pain knifed through Hannah's head, hot and sharp.
Frightened, she tried to move and made it worse. With a
whimper of protest she waited for relief. Finally it came.
The pain was still there, but now it pounded with subdued force just behind her eyes.

Knowing better than to lift her head this time, she
moved only her hands. They were under a rough blanket
against her bare abdomen. At her breast she found a
buttoned garment that lay open. She brought the edges
together carefully. She couldn't manage the buttons, but
just knowing they were there comforted her. One arm, her
right one, was bound with a wide cloth bandage. Touching the bandage didn't hurt, but moving the arm did. She
decided to lie still after hearing her own groan of pain,
embarrassingly loud.

Suddenly she realized she wasn't alone. She opened her eyes and stared up into a man's shadowed face. He moved his hand above her face and she tried to escape deeper into the taut surface beneath her. The effort renewed the hot stab in her head and added another on her back. "Oh, no," she said thickly.

"Are you awake? Can you see my hand?" It was the voice of a Yankee, as hard and forceful as the hand he displayed. "How many fingers can you see?" he asked.

"Three." With her eyes adjusted to the dimness, she could see that his gesture was not threatening, and some of her fear subsided. "Where am I?"

"In my tent."

"Tent?" Her eyes searched beyond his head. "You're a soldier. A Yankee."

"Was," he said firmly. "Are you going to hold that against me?"

Hannah tried to take in the fact that he seemed to be teasing her. Before she could talk anymore though, she had to moisten her dry lips. Even her tongue was dry, too dry to do any good.

"You're thirsty," he said. "Be right back."

In the moments he was gone, Hannah decided she liked his decisive way of speaking. It engendered trust. The gentle way he lifted her head and shoulders so she could sip water from a tin cup helped that trust along. He supported her head in the crook of his muscular arm and lowered her slowly back to the cot when she had taken all the water he permitted.

"You took most of your lumps on your head," he told her matter-of-factly. "Your head must really hurt."

"It does." She couldn't think of nodding. "What happened to my arm?"

"The horse's hooves cut your arm and back. They're bandaged, but you'll feel them more as you spend more time awake."

"Thank you."

"What's your name, ma'am?"

"Hannah."

"Hannah what?"

"Hatch."

"Did you . . . um . . . lose any of your family in that attack?"

"Family? No." The question brought back vivid pictures of the Indian and Willie. Tears filled her eyes the way groundwater rises into dug soil and she struggled to control them.

"You were alone?"

"No. I had a . . . friend." She tried to think how to explain what Willie was to her, what he had been since she had gone to live with Simon as a ten-year-old girl. It wasn't fair to call him a servant, because he was so much more than that. "He was . . ."

"Never mind. You don't have to explain."

His harsh tone alarmed her and she reached for his arm with her left hand, grasping him urgently. "You weren't with them?" she demanded. "You weren't one of them?"

"The attackers, you mean?"

"Yes. I saw the Indian."

"You saw no Indian."

"I did," she insisted, ignoring his flat denial. "There was an Indian with the soldiers around me." Her eyes narrowed to fix on his features. She was trying to remember if she had seen his face in that fearsome circle. "You were there." She didn't know that, but she said it as if she did.

He didn't deny it, but said, "You've taken several blows on your head."

Hannah saw that it was useless. If he had been one of the attackers, she wouldn't be alive now. "You're renegades." She made the statement as neutral as possible, yet it still sounded like an accusation.

"Yes."

"What's your name? I know you're the commander." She knew it was his voice that had shouted out the order to get her as she had tried to run. Without a doubt he was also the one who pulled her down.

"My name is Jake Farnsworth."

"Thank you for taking care of me, Captain Farnsworth," she said.

"I'm sorry it was necessary," he answered gravely. Then he smiled. "Please call me Jake."

"Jake." She tried it and smiled back. "It fits you."

"A hell of a lot better than Jacob, I'll tell you."

In spite of the pain she laughed.

"Go to sleep, little Hannah Hatch," he said gruffly. "I'll be back later with some food. You'll be hungry."

"How long was I asleep?"

"It wasn't sleep. It's been three days, but you'll be fine now."

Hannah had to believe him. "Thank you, Jake."

When he was gone, she didn't sleep as immediately as she would have liked. She took in as much of the tent as she could see without moving her head. It wasn't much. Probably there was little to see. She'd never been inside a tent before. It was barely big enough for Jake to stand up straight in the middle, with sharply sloping sides.

She was much more interested in thinking about Jake Farnsworth. His face fascinated her, she realized now that he was gone. Like his voice and hands, it was hard, but capable of surprising gentleness. He wasn't handsome like the men she knew in Tennessee, nor was he charming. He had only once smiled, and that so slight she might have missed it. Perhaps his teeth were bad; perhaps he was self-conscious about some disfigurement like that. His courtesy couldn't be faulted though, she decided, remembering that "ma'am" in his address to her. He'd cared for her, given quick sympathy and understanding

15

along with a gruff kind of tenderness she found oddly appealing.

Then there were his eyes, so startlingly blue in that tough dark face. She found herself thinking of them as she drifted off to sleep.

And woke to find those same eyes peering down at her. Had he spoken to her? She had responded to something, to some call from him, perhaps only the weight of his attention. She smiled and said, "Hello, Jake," her voice husky with disuse.

"It's morning, Hannah. You must be famished."

Hannah noted that again he had anticipated her needs.

"Do you think you can sit up?"

"I'd like to try."

"Good girl. Be right back," he promised.

Already Hannah had learned to count on that. He was quickly back with a cup and bowl, which he put down on a box at the side of the cot. Her head swam as he lifted it onto his arm and she bit her lip to silence an outcry. He slid behind her to prop her limp body with his sturdier one. "Hang on," he warned, his eyes watchful. When she made no sound, his expression of approval was all the reward she needed.

"First a drink," he directed. "Just a sip. Take it slow."

She followed his advice unthinkingly, her mind busy absorbing the feeling of his welcome support at her back. All the textures around her were rough and hard—the blanket, the shirt she wore, even his body—yet she was comforted by them all. She felt safe. That was it.

Gratefully, she accepted his help with the spoon when the stiffness in her bandaged arm made feeding herself awkward. The porridge was lumpy and thin but little worse than what they had eaten on the trail. She stopped herself from thinking further along those lines and just ate till the food was gone. Finishing with the cup he offered, Hannah sighed. "Thank you. You're a good nurse."

A puff of air at her ear reminded her how close his face was to hers. Somehow she had concentrated on the pleasant warmth of his body embracing hers like a human chair and had forgotten his face. "You may not say that when I'm done changing those bandages. It'll hurt like hell, but it has to be done and we might as well get it over with while you're already up."

In spite of herself, Hannah stiffened when Jake reached around her and opened the front of the shirt she wore. It wasn't buttoned, but she had made sure it overlapped before she sat up. She had been holding it closed with her left hand. He sat behind her, his chest to her back, positioned to have a clear view of her chest from above her shoulder.

"I'm a nurse, remember?"

What could she say? He had certainly been the one who undressed her and put her into this shirt. To object now because she was conscious would be foolish, though she wanted to. That was the crux of the matter. She was entirely *too* conscious, of him and of herself, of his masculinity and of her femininity. Awareness pulsed in the air between them as he whisked the shirt from her left arm and eased it off from the bandaged right. Though she never felt that he achieved the impersonality of a physician, Jake gave her the shirt to hold to her breast as soon as he could.

Soon she was clutching it for reasons beyond modesty. The bandage on her back was no problem. He pronounced the cut well on the way to healing and replaced only the inner pad. Her arm was another story. It hurt all the way from her shoulder to her elbow when he pried the stiffened bandage away.

Hannah concentrated on clenching her fist around the cloth of the shirt so she would not cry. She felt his sigh of relief once that was done, then the quick intake as he

17

reacted to something else.

"That's what I was afraid of," he muttered, more to himself than to her. One big hand flattened on her bare back, startling her more than the flare of heat on her arm as he touched the wound itself. "Sorry," he said, taking his hand from her arm but not her back. Vaguely, she realized she wanted that hand to stay. It pressed her into a more upright position, lingering warmly against her skin. "Can you sit by yourself a few minutes? I have to get something."

"Yes." She could sit by herself, of course, but she didn't like it. She missed Jake's warmth and, curiously, found that she felt more exposed without him behind her. She had little time to think about that, for he was quickly back.

"Can you sew?" he asked, catching her mentally off-guard as he did some painful things she refused to watch. She could have looked at her arm but chose not to.

"Sew? You mean cloth?" she asked stupidly.

"Yes, cloth—as in your dress. Obviously, it got cut up pretty badly or you wouldn't have these wounds. The sleeves could come off, I suppose, though it might look odd, but the back has long slits. Maybe you could sew them."

She realized gratefully that he was using the conversation to divert her from his treatment of her arm. "I suppose I could. I don't have a needle or thread though . . ."

"We do . . . somewhere . . ." Jake's voice trailed off to a distracted mumble, warning her that he was about to do something that would really hurt.

It did, but because she had been warned, even inadvertently, she was able to stifle her cry, though not her tears. They leaked out and ran down her cheeks. She wanted them gone but couldn't give up holding the shirt to wipe them away.

18

"You're a hell of a soldier, Hannah," he said.

High praise, she felt, and smiled.

"Sorry about my language. I forget myself."

"I don't mind. You sound like my uncle." Simon, too, usually apologized.

"Ah. Then you're not all alone in the world."

"No, I have a cousin in Fort Kearney. That's where I'm headed."

"Where did you come from?"

"Knoxville, Tennessee."

"That explains the drawl then."

"I don't drawl. I really come from Ohio. I was born there."

"Maybe, but you've a Rebel sound to you now. How long have you lived in Tennessee?"

When he began rewrapping her arm, she found it hard to think. Jake noticed and asked, "Am I hurting you now?"

"N-no." It wasn't pain anymore, just sensation, and when he turned her head so he could look at her, she was suddenly drowning in confusion.

He brushed the remnants of tears from her face, his eyes concerned. "How long?" he asked, letting go of her chin.

"What?"

Jake smiled then, showing her there was nothing at all wrong with his teeth. They flashed white against his weathered skin in a grin of purely masculine amusement. "How long have you lived in Tennessee?" he repeated.

Hannah looked down at the heavy blue shirt she had bunched at her breast, blushing like a schoolgirl because he had seen how addled she was. "Um . . . it's been fifteen years now."

He chuckled. "Long enough to turn Rebel."

"I wasn't. I mean, during the war." She wanted him to understand she bore him no enmity for his uniform.

19

"People warned us starting out with the wagons that there weren't enough of us. That Indians or renegade bands of soldiers would attack."

"Well, it certainly wasn't your decision," he said, dismissing her from responsibility.

"I mean, that's why I was afraid and tried to run away. I thought you were with the Indians." She didn't mention again that an Indian had been in his group. It wasn't necessary now.

"You had reason to be afraid—one woman falling like that into the midst of a group of men—not to mention what you'd escaped from." He shook his head ruefully and took the shirt to help her dress again. "How did you escape, by the way?"

Answering him helped her over the shock of finding herself suddenly, though briefly, naked before him again. As she told him about her aborted but well-timed attempt to get a bath, she thought how much more of her body Jake had seen than even Daniel had.

"Then that's why you were soaked to the skin," he said. "I wondered how that happened. It made getting your clothes off the devil's own job. That and the blood from your cuts. Your dress is clean now though. You can have it back anytime."

"And the needle and thread," Hannah reminded him as he eased her back to the cot.

She tried not to collapse, but she barely heard him say, "Later," before she was dead to the world. Though she woke sporadically throughout the day, sometimes at Jake's urging to eat or take sips of water, she spent most of the time in deep, peaceful sleep.

It was dark in the tent when she heard Jake move around as he prepared for sleep. It was his tent, yet she never really considered where he made his bed. The important thing was that he was always near, always available. Beyond that, she had no interest in knowing.

20

She was safe in her dreams of Tennessee.

But after a while her dreams changed and became frightening. The sound of Lucky Jim's hoofbeats merged with the pounding pain in her head and became one with her thundering heartbeat. She was riding, being chased by unseen demons, circled by yelping figures with fantastic faces. Beyond the faces another circle of flames danced, fed by winds that tossed the bodies of people from the wagons. She could see only their faces, distorted and huge, then each face became the hideously painted Indian. He raised his arm in triumph again, and Hannah cried out, "No! No, don't!"

For the first time since she had been in the tent, she pushed herself upright, uncaring that her arm hurt and her head wobbled. Strong arms reached around her instantly and let her cling. She whimpered, still in a netherworld between waking and dreaming, clutching at Jake's bare back.

"Sh, sh, Hannah, it's all right. You're safe."

"No," she protested weakly.

"It was just a dream. A nightmare. There's nothing here to hurt you." His deep voice soothed and gentled her. His hands stroked her hair back from her face and dried her tears as fast as they fell.

"It was awful. So real! I couldn't get away . . . they were killing the people . . . little Jonathan . . . and Willie. Oh God! It was *Willie*'s scalp! His *scalp!*"

"I know, I know. But it's over and you're safe. You're here and safe."

Hannah soaked up the words, trying to make them real. His arms and hands were real. He surrounded her, gentle but strong, stroking and soothing, giving comfort and warmth. She was so cold. She shivered and shook, unable to stop as long as the images controlled her mind.

"I'll never be able to forget," she whispered, her throat raw and convulsed.

21

"No, but the horror will fade in time."

Hannah knew that, but just now it didn't seem possible or even right. If she forgot, then who would remember what they had suffered? She shook her head sadly.

Jake took the gesture for denial and pulled her face out of his neck. He framed her jaw with one big hand, insisting, "It will, believe me."

She tried to smile with trembling lips. "I know, but I'm so scared." She forced her way back to the security of his chest, her good arm tight around him, pressing into him, burrowing to safety. The hard thrum of his heart beneath her ear was as wild as the beat of the horses that rode through her dream. As soon as she closed her eyes, comforted, the Indians were there in her mind again, circling, slaughtering. . . .

"Oh, Jake," she whispered, sobbing again.

He peeled her from his chest and struggled to free himself from her clinging hands. "Hannah, I have to get my pants . . ."

"Don't leave me! Please!"

Jake got up, his back to her. Before he could take one step to his cot in search of his clothes, Hannah followed. Though she saw the long unbroken line of his bare back, only the fact that he was leaving registered. She swayed on her feet, unsteady but determined to be with Jake. He sensed her motion and turned in time to catch her as she fell. He lifted her to the cot, following her down, his pants forgotten.

"Jake, don't go." She pleaded with the tightness she saw in his dark face, wrapping her arms, even the sore one, around his torso.

"Hannah, I . . ."

His hesitation made her frantic. She had to keep him with her. She pushed her hand down his corded back to his waist, clinging and pressing against his warmth.

"Sweet merciful . . ."

22

Hannah didn't know if he was praying or swearing. It no longer mattered. What had begun as a bone-deep need for comfort and closeness had become something else, something Hannah had never felt before. Not like this. His breath came in hard, fast pants against her throat. His hands, those caring, healing hands were all she felt as her wounded back took first her weight, then his. His mouth was hot on hers, swallowing the sound of her low moan. His lips fastened hungrily on hers.

The hard demand of his body shook her, raising a glimmer of sense, but then her world narrowed to nothing but Jake. Every sense, even pain, left her. His mouth devoured her breasts and his hands roamed over her hips, stomach, and legs.

Frenzied now, Hannah clutched Jake with both hands, unmindful of the hot pain in her injured arm. "Jake," she pleaded brokenly. Her head was spinning, her mind fixed only on Jake. Her hands coursed his broad back with clumsy force. Unerringly, her awkwardly stiff right hand scraped the one spot high on his back where the horse's hooves had cut deeply into his flesh. He howled in surprised pain as the bandage ripped free.

Swearing viciously, Jake wrenched away from her and sat up. Hannah followed as if drawn up to him by strings.

"I'm sorry, I'm sorry," she whispered. "Your back . . ."

Vaguely, she realized his injury confirmed her belief that he had been the one to tackle her, but her mind was too full of her sudden loss to focus on it. She tried to replace the bandage she had dislodged, tried to soothe him and draw him back to her, but he pushed her back with rough efficiency and tore from the cot. Within seconds he was gone from the tent as well.

23

# Chapter Two

It wasn't pain that sent Jake stumbling from the tent; it was fury. Cursing himself, Hannah, and the world in general, he batted open the tent flap, belatedly hauling on his pants as he went. If he'd had the sense of a jackass, he told himself, buttoning them up, he'd have worn them to bed. Certainly he'd have had them on before he went near Hannah. He slapped at the cloth in disgust, as if it, not what it covered, had betrayed him.

He had known she was trouble from his first sight of her, soaking wet and wild-eyed with fright, falling into the midst of his men like a juicy red apple from the top of a tree. If ever a moment had been ripe for trouble, that one was. If he hadn't grabbed her, she would have been raped a dozen times over and left for dead. However much the men condemned the carnage inflicted on the rest of her company, Hannah herself would have been fair game.

Besides himself, only Many Buffalo, of all the men three, would have tried to help her. But he would have had the impossible task of stopping them physically, for a command to them from an Indian meant nothing. Of the rest, Jake considered, Colby and Zeb would both have abstained, though for different reasons. Colby because he was the much-married father of a girl close to Hannah's age and Zeb because he had no appetite for women. Neither of them, however, would have saved her life.

Wonderful, Jake congratulated himself sarcastically. So you saved her life just to enjoy her in private. He raked his fingers through his hair, considering and rejecting going back inside for his shirt. He didn't think he'd ever want to go in there again. Cold air was just what he needed.

If only he could get rid of her. But how? That pitiful little train of wagons shouldn't have been anywhere near here. Miles off course, they'd been a disaster about to happen. It was a miracle Hannah had survived the attack; another miracle in the form of a passing wagon train willing to take her on was hardly in the offing. He couldn't afford to send a man with her back to Tennessee, or even to the nearest outpost. Further, he couldn't guarantee that two lone riders would make it back to safety. Short of killing her outright—which had a certain appeal right now—he was stuck with her and she with him until he and the men completed their job.

Her uncle, whoever he was, had to have been crazy to send her off to Nebraska that way. But perhaps he hadn't. It was a "friend" she lost in the attack, not her uncle. Jake, above all men, knew what being a friend of Hannah's came to. Damn. He hadn't meant that to happen. He had treated her like fine china, like a *sister*, for God's sake!

And he had been tempted right from the start. What man faced with such a lush body wouldn't be? That wealth of rich brown hair shot through with fiery strands of red, like chestnuts in the sun, would make a saint weep. Seeing it spread out on his cot day after day had worn him down. But he'd bandaged her arm and back, given her his shirt, even fed her—all without touching her soft skin even once like a man. Until she threw herself at him. She'd lost her "friend" from the wagon train and, obviously, he had been elected to be the replacement.

What galled him was that he had been completely taken

25

in by her show of modesty. But that's all it was, a show. Under those shy blushes and softly drawled words she was nothing but a whore. Probably she had no cousin in Fort Kearney and no uncle in Knoxville either. Well, she wasn't going to latch on to him. Thank God for the reality of pain. Without it he'd have taken her just the way she wanted.

From now on, he would stay far from Hannah Hatch. He had no room in his life for a woman like that. He had a daughter who needed a decent mother someday, but that day was far away. First he had to get this job done, pay his debt to Many Buffalo, and collect the rest of the money he'd been promised. Then he could make a home for Caroline before she grew too old to need one anymore.

Jake had only to think of Caroline and the harsh planes of his face softened. She was nine, a child still, but a child who promised to grow into loveliness. Like her mother; like him, too, in ways he liked to think would give her some of the strength a woman needed in this rough land.

The only thing he regretted in his life was his determination to bring Grace west with him from the comfort and security of settled Pennsylvania. He had counted on two things outside himself to keep her going and both had failed him. The first, her hardy German stock, had been more myth than reality; the second, her love for him, had faded to a strange kind of indifference once she'd been uprooted from the good things of life she had cherished. Away from Pennsylvania—the East she'd loved—she had shrunk almost daily, finally drained by the child she'd carried until she was ready to be finished off by the rigors of birth.

Caroline had her mother's blond prettiness grafted onto his own toughness. Female though she was, he had seen her in times of stress employ both her reasoning and her courage, even physical courage. Unwittingly, Jake was reminded of Hannah, whose courage had sent her running to steal a horse and try to escape men she believed were allied with the murderers of her companions. Faced with that circle of men, she had picked out Many Buffalo and made a mental connection—not hard to do, perhaps—but how many women would have used their brains after a fall like that? Not many. Grace would have fainted, or run screaming back to the burning wagons.

Whatever else she might be, Jake had to acknowledge that Hannah Hatch had the mind and spirit he wanted Caroline to develop. He was honest enough to admit that. Of course, he wanted Caroline chaste as well, but he was certain a woman, the right woman, could be both chaste and courageous. The challenge of the West and the life he wanted for Caroline didn't have to mean a choice between death or disgrace. Grace had died, Hannah had disgraced herself; it was going to be his job to see that Caroline fell into neither trap. A big job, but one he was eager to undertake. The coming years would be crucial for Jake. He had to have Caroline with him. But first he had to finish this job and get the money to fund his new life.

Because Grace had died in his care, her parents would not readily relinquish her daughter. Jake would have to wrest her from them, not a prospect he liked in view of his gratitude to them for giving her a home when he could not. That problem, too, lay in his future.

Over and over his mind returned to the more immediate problem of Hannah Hatch. One part of himself chided that his physical frustration, so easily cured, was the only problem. It wasn't true. Little Hannah Hatch had landed herself right in the middle of a situation as flammable as prairie grass in August.

She had survived the attack of white men who had been hired to pretend to be Indians in order to scare away settlers and change the routing of the railroad from a

27

course already set and determined. What they had done would not affect the decision, no matter how many innocent lives they sacrificed, but unless they were stopped, the attempt would go on. Jake and his men were trying to stop the harassment before it ignited an all-out war against the Indians. He himself had no special loyalty to either side of the railroad issue. Though he despised the slaughter he had seen, he fought them for the money he could earn. And for Many Buffalo.

Jake's loyalty was to Many Buffalo and his small band of peaceful Indians, the Pawnee, who were being blamed for massacres like the one Hannah had survived. He would have helped Many Buffalo anyway if he could. It was only coincidence, and an ironic one at that, that the best interests of a wealthy Eastern railroad man should be the same as those of Jake's Indian friend. This way, he did his duty to an honored friend, the man who had once saved his life, and got paid for it too, handsomely.

Admirable intentions aside, Jake had yet to prove he could do the job at all. So far he'd done little. Except for Hannah, the people in those wagons were no better off for his presence nearby. He could tell himself as many times as he wanted that random acts were the hardest to defend, but he couldn't make himself feel better. He couldn't forgive himself for being too late to help those people.

At first, saving Hannah had seemed to compensate his conscience in some way. Now he knew the word for her was complication, not compensation. If she turned those molasses-and-honey eyes on his men, she would ruin more than his troop's hard-won discipline. The deck was already stacked in favor of their failure, and Hannah's interference could mean certain defeat. The men knew they wouldn't be paid for failure, but if Hannah became the prize, many would count the money well lost.

Not he though. Hannah Hatch was not going to keep

him from providing for his daughter and making a decent life for them both. He had too much to lose. He couldn't let any woman ruin this chance.

Jake stood at the edge of the campsite, peering into darkness as total as the blankness of his mind. Determined as he was, he was no closer to knowing what to do with Hannah than when he'd first stumbled from the tent. She had to stay. He knew that as well as he knew he had to stay away from her. But how to keep her from the men, or vice versa, was a mystery. He crossed his arms over his chest, then uncrossed them to plow the fingers of one hand through his straight black hair before he crossed them again. He heaved a sigh and turned to go back when a movement to his right sent his hand to reach for a gun that wasn't there.

"You'd be dead a hundred times over if I'd had a mind," Colby growled.

Jake spread his hands in a resigned, exasperated gesture and laughed soundlessly. "For sure."

"She better?"

Jake discarded several answers that came to mind. "Enough."

"She staying?"

"The whole way."

"Your choice," Colby acknowledged.

"No. Not my choice, necessity. Short of killing her there's nothing else we can do."

"Give her a horse and send her off?"

"Another name for killing her," Jake answered.

"What about hiding her in Many Buffalo's village? Wouldn't he keep her?"

"If I asked, but I wouldn't. I couldn't do that to her. Or to him." Jake pushed the idea aside relentlessly; it was too attractive.

"Him, I understand. If we fail, her presence there would bring him more trouble, but why should she mind?

She'd be as comfortable there and a damn sight safer."

"She wouldn't see it that way. In her mind it was Indians who attacked their wagons. The man she was with was scalped. She saw it."

"Spotted Pony in action, eh? Too bad. Have you told her the rest of them weren't Indians? Maybe she'd understand."

"I haven't said a thing and I'm not going to. I don't care what she thinks."

Jake's vehemence raised Colby's eyebrow questioningly. "What are you going to do with her?"

"Not what you think!" he snapped.

"You know me, Jake. I don't think. It makes my head hurt every time I try it."

Jake laughed at that and clapped his friend's shoulder. "You on watch?"

"I was when you came out. Jethro relieved me and I came to see if you were all right."

Jake sighed. "Jethro. God, I hope he doesn't shoot both of us when we go back."

"He'll be fine. He's just eager. Got a lot to make up for because he missed the big battles of the war, the lucky sod."

"I hope you're right. He scares hell out of me. All heroes in the making do."

"You should know," Colby jibed. "Just keep him away from the lady. He might get carried away."

Jake chose not to refute Colby's designation of Hannah as a lady. If the men knew her eagerness to be bedded, it would only make controlling them harder. The protectiveness of even the lustiest man toward a woman he believed to be pure could be a powerful inhibitor, Jake knew. He would use it and any other deception he could think of to keep the lid on his men and Hannah Hatch. Carelessly, he told Colby, "I'll have Zeb guard her. He won't get carried away."

30

Laughing together, the two men walked through camp. Jake gave Jethro a nod before he turned in for the rest of the night. He would be gone before Hannah woke. Let her make what she could of Zeb. He'd enjoy watching her try her wiles on him.

Hannah woke to a curious sense of interior silence. She was warm. Too warm. But her head no longer pounded. That was the silence. Cautiously, she turned her head, something she couldn't remember doing for a long time.

Sunlight, tinged greenish by the filter of heavy canvas above, gave the tent an underwater look. By the open tent flap Jake's cot, like hers, stood bare of even a blanket or cloth. She, however, was covered to her neck by a heavy blanket, the source of her warmth. In fact, it was wrapped so securely around her she had difficulty freeing her hands. Under the blanket she had the usual shirt, but it wasn't really on her, just tangled with the bandage on her arm.

She sat up, shocked by a sudden, humiliating memory. Blood rushed to her head, bringing a momentary rush of pain that ebbed away quickly. Swaying unsteadily with her feet still encumbered by the blanket, Hannah would gladly have traded the clarity of her memory for the familiar, blurring headache.

She couldn't have.

She had.

No. It was a dream, a nightmare. She remembered dreaming, then shaking and crying as her dream turned on her. Surely what she remembered with Jake was part of that fevered nightmare. She wouldn't have clutched at him so and begged . . . God. She had.

Hannah pulled the shirt around her and tried to make her trembling fingers fit buttons into holes. The effort brought sweat to her face as her right arm protested each movement. Her left hand was so clumsy she exclaimed aloud in frustration.

Her cry was quickly answered. The empty tent flap filled with a blue uniform. Hannah clutched the blanket again to her chest and stared in confusion. However much she dreaded to face Jake Farnsworth, he was at least someone she knew. This wraith of a man was a stranger to her. He was as dark as Jake, but bushily bearded, with unkempt hair that curled wildly about his face. With an eye patch and head scarf he would make a perfect pirate, Hannah thought distractedly. His black eyes met hers without softening recognition or sympathy; like shiny shoe buttons, they reflected her startled image.

"Who are you?" she asked, so apprehensive her voice shook.

"Zeb. I have your breakfast if you're awake."

Since it was obvious she was, Hannah didn't know what to say. She stared, tongue-tied and dumb, wanting to ask about Jake, but unwilling to mention him. What if this man knew what she had done?

As her glance fell from his, the wiry soldier started back through the flap. She spoke up sharply, surprising herself as much as Zeb. "Please," she called out. When he stopped she said, "I feel so dirty, Zeb. Is there somewhere I can go to wash? I'd like to be clean when I eat."

"Can you walk?"

"I think so." She stood up to prove it, the blanket draped in front of her inadequately. Looking down, Hannah saw her legs bare from the knees and tried to drag the blanket in front of her. While she struggled, Zeb crossed to her and took it from her. Her eyes widened in shock, but he merely put it around her shoulders, folded to cover her length without encumbering her feet. It was all done so efficiently and impersonally she couldn't object.

"Try a few steps."

32

She did, then turned with a happy smile. "I knew it. My head doesn't hurt anymore either."

"You kin have some soap I got," Zeb said gruffly, leaving her to follow him out.

Hannah stooped with exaggerated care to keep the blanket in place while she went through the flap, but outside she straightened and inhaled deeply. After the stuffiness of the tent, fresh air was like ambrosia. She filled her lungs gratefully, looking around. Yellow sunlight poured like honey over the tents and surrounding bushes. The campsite consisted of nine tents set in an approximate circle. Only the sound of some twittering birds disturbed a curious stillness. Zeb was nowhere to be seen. After days with the wagon train Hannah could see the permanence in this camp.

Zeb pressed a narrow slab of brown soap into her hands, following it with a gray piece of rough toweling. "You ain't going to fall down?" he asked.

She wondered if he was hopeful or just skeptical. "No," she assured him.

With a curt nod, he started off briskly, never looking back to see how she fared. She let him go without protesting his pace, proud that she did so well. She kept the way in mind for her return, clambering barefoot after him over rough stones. He waited at a stream for her, his black eyes watchful as she looked around.

"You kin be here private if you don't try to run away."

"Run away? Why would I do that?"

Zeb didn't answer, but apparently she had. "Come back when you're hungry."

Hannah waited till he was gone before she dropped the blanket and sought out some bushes away from the stream. For some reason she was certain Zeb wasn't lurking nearby to watch her. She knelt by the water, testing its temperature. It was cold, but not shockingly so. She would be able to bathe and wash her hair. Though

33

Zeb's soap was nothing like the French milled soap she was used to, she was grateful for it. Even lye soap was better than the lingering odor of smoke and sweat.

Hannah found a place in the stream deep enough so she could sit on the rocky bottom and still be safe from the surprisingly strong current. She didn't know how to swim, but she liked the feeling of water around her. She was careful to keep her upper arm dry and free of soap so as not to disturb the bandage.

Just the thought of her own bandage filled her face with deep, hot color. Only the fact that she had hurt Jake, tearing a similar bandage from his back, had kept him from taking her. She couldn't forget that. Or understand it. She had never been so forward in her life—and with a man who was no more than a tattered renegade soldier. Kind, he might have been, kind enough to win her gratitude surely, but not her body offered up as if she were nothing but a prize or the spoils of battle. The war had been over since April, but these men, whoever they were, apparently didn't acknowledge that.

Hannah was glad to wonder about the men because it took her mind from her terrible shame. But even thinking that brought her back to it. How would she face Jake Farnsworth again? It galled her to think she had disgraced herself before someone like that, someone little better than an outlaw. What if he took it for granted that she was a woman of no morals? He had stopped only because of his pain. Tonight he might expect her to take up where they had left off. And why not? Hadn't she pursued him even after he pulled away?

Granted, she had been concerned about his wound—she remembered resticking the plaster onto his back—but she had also begged him not to leave. Even the cool water of the stream couldn't make her forget the primitive way she had burned for him. Was it just her terrifying experience? Or was she becoming uncivilized out here in the

West?

Holding her wet hair aside to wring it of water, Hannah waded back to shore. She wouldn't wash the shirt because that would leave her nothing but the blanket to wrap in. Perhaps she could get her dress from Zeb. Even torn it would be more comfortable and less revealing than a man's heavy shirt. What was it they called this cloth? Shoddy? It seemed appropriate somehow. If she could sew her dress first, then she could launder the shirt for Jake. She didn't want to be beholden to him for anything more. Not now.

She sat on a rock and spread her heavy hair over her shoulders to dry. It made an enveloping curtain that would cover her even if Zeb decided to investigate her whereabouts. Comforted by that, Hannah wondered where the rest of the men were. Were they off raiding and looting? They hadn't been responsible for her troubles, but that didn't mean that wasn't what they did. What else was there for ragtag soldiers to do out here?

And where was this place anyway? Looking around told Hannah nothing. The stream and the countryside looked like the site of every camp they had made with the wagon train since leaving Omaha City. Were they very near where the wagons had been attacked? She would ask Jake tonight. Or perhaps it would be wiser to ask Zeb.

When her hair was no longer dripping, Hannah redonned the heavy shirt and took up the blanket. She would put that back on once she was near the tents. She walked slowly, more tired by her slight exertion than she could believe. Her legs wobbled, forcing her to take frequent rests. Her stomach stirred at the prospect of food, even more lumpy porridge, then growled noisily when she smelled beef stew over the smoky wood fire. She sank gratefully to a fallen log near the fire as Zeb put a bowl of it into her hands.

"I'm in heaven, Zeb," she sighed after the first hot

spoonful of broth. "If I'm not, don't wake me up. I don't want to know better." Even the abundance of salt couldn't mask the rich flavor of onions and beef that went straight to Hannah's hunger. There were hunks of potato and something hard she guessed was turnip.

Zeb gestured to strips of jerked beef she hadn't noticed drying on a nearby bush. "You kin thank those murdering fools for the beef," he said. "Just when we were low on supplies, too."

It took Hannah a second to make the connection. When she did, she gagged. Her mind told her the beef had nothing to do with Willie and the others, but her stomach fought her will to keep the food down. Seeing her problem, Zeb slapped a piece of cornbread into her lap. She focused her attention on the untroubling bread and used it to soothe her abdominal agitation. Zeb took back the stew without comment, adding it back to the pot.

"Thank you, Zeb. You've been most kind." The fierceness of his expression was at odds with her words, but Hannah could think of no other way to put it.

And still he wasn't finished. He brought a bundle of clothes to her, thrusting the whole into her lap with the lack of ceremony Hannah already recognized as his usual custom. Her dress wrapped other garments, her pantalettes, petticoats, and chemise, she supposed. It wasn't until she got to her cot again that she saw the small sewing basket, her stockings and shoes, and a man's cotton shirt. As she fell back into exhausted sleep, she worried that she hadn't shown Zeb enough gratitude. Thanks to him she had been spared having to face Jake. She was also bathed, fed, and clothed again. How could she ever thank him enough?

Over the next several days Hannah had ample opportunity to thank Zeb. He was the only person she saw. From that first night when she heard the men return to camp but didn't venture forth, even in her meticulously mended dress, the pattern was set. Only Zeb came to her tent, and then only to bring her food and drink when the men were there. The cot she thought of as Jake's remained empty. She heard his voice, among the others or, occasionally, raised in command, but she didn't see him.

She told herself her isolation was self-imposed, and at first it was. The idea of seeing Jake, either face to face or in the company of his men, had no appeal for Hannah. It was at least two days before she could think of him without embarrassment. Any questions she asked the laconic Zeb were carefully phrased to exclude any sign of interest in him. Not that he would have satisfied her curiosity anyway. He told her practically nothing about their location (yes, it was near the remains of their wagon train) and absolutely nothing about what the men did away from camp.

Fascinating as it was to speculate on these matters and on Zeb himself, gradually Hannah tired of her gratitude. She was alive and apparently safe. But when could she leave? She had regained her strength, proving it by the number of jobs she took over from Zeb. She baked bread after showing Zeb how to fashion a rude oven for the wood fire. She mended clothes for the men, not even knowing their names, regarding it as occupation for her idleness rather than service as such.

Slowly but steadily, Hannah's pride began to assert itself. Even if she had made a humiliating mistake with Jake, she was not going to cower forever inside her tent, making a prisoner and slave of herself. She was through hiding.

That night, five days after her nightmare, Hannah made her first appearance at supper. She timed her entrance carefully, waiting until the meal was in progress but not giving Zeb time to finish serving and remember her. She had braided her hair into one heavy coil down

37

her back, the best she could do with no hairpins. Her dress was clean and as neat as she could make it without a sad iron. Her back was straight, her head high—and her stomach a quivering mass of butterflies.

Dumb silence struck each group of men she walked past to reach the end of the serving line. The struggle to hold on to her dignity forbid her the luxury of looking for Jake, if only to avoid him. Trying to appear as if this were something she did every day consumed her attention completely. She picked up a cup and bowl and spoon by instinct.

"Ma'am?"

Startled, Hannah raised her eyes to look into soulful brown eyes under a forelock of hair the same soft color. Her mouth was so dry she had to wet her lips to make them work. "Yes?" she managed.

"I'd be pleased for you to take my place, ma'am." The boy's voice—for boy he was, Hannah saw—came dangerously near cracking under the strain of his earnest message.

"Why, thank you." She smiled, making an effort to be natural. She had been about to decline the invitation in an attempt to be inconspicuous when she had realized with a sudden return of her native good sense how fruitless that hope was. One woman, no matter how plainly dressed and circumspect, was going to be conspicuous in the midst of so many men. Better she should accept his civility graciously and not cause him to become insistent and drew more attention to them. And they were getting attention, Hannah saw. It made the air vibrate around them.

Ignoring Zeb's dark look as he slapped a combination of beans and beef into her bowl, Hannah asked the young man, who now followed her, "What's your name, soldier?"

"Jethro, ma'am. George Jethro."

38

For an instant Hannah was afraid he was going to drop his bowl of beans and salute her. Certainly his attention to her was total. "I'm pleased to meet you, Mr. Jethro." She inclined her head. "I'm Hannah Hatch."

"Just call me George, please, Miss Hatch."

A feeling of motherly concern washed over Hannah. He was so young and eager. Would little David have grown up to be like George Jethro, a boy playing as soldier far from home? She wanted to ask him where he was from and why he was here with these rough men. But before she could utter another word, Jake's voice lashed over them. "Jethro! Go see to the horses!"

For one mutinous moment Jethro seemed to consider refusing to leave her side. At the silent entreaty of her eyes, however, he barked out his, "Yes sir!" and headed for the horses.

Jake's message was not lost on the other men. No one spoke to her or looked directly at her during the course of the meal. Conversation among the men was muted, their remarks even to each other stilted and awkward. Hannah sat on the ground by herself, too angry to think straight and too proud to leave. Only her determination not to let him see her anguish kept her upright. She ate every tasteless bite of food and drank the vile brew in her cup, making sure her hand didn't shake. Jake Farnsworth was not going to get the best of her.

When the men began drifting to their tents, casting sidewise glances at where she sat, a rock in an eddying stream, she got to her feet stiffly. She put her utensils with the others, toying with the idea of offering to help Zeb clean up. But Zeb wasn't cleaning up, two others were, and Hannah knew speaking to them wouldn't help anyone. Jake would double their work load and make her the further brunt of his anger.

Engrossed in her own depressing thoughts, Hannah turned from the deeply shadowed clearing to go to her tent—and walked straight into Jake's back. She hadn't seen him at all, but she knew he wouldn't believe that. Without apology, she lifted her head high and caught up the bottom of her skirt in the unmistakable gesture of someone stepping around something unmentionable in the path. In the dying light around them she could easily see the look of fury in his eyes as she swept past to the privacy of her tent.

She had only a moment to savor her triumph. Jake was behind her before she had straightened to her full height on the other side of the flap. That height suddenly seemed unimpressive when Jake glared down at her. And glare he did.

A primitive sense of triumph rose in Jake as he saw Hannah's eyes widen in apprehension at his appearance behind her. She had surprised him by appearing at supper; now he was surprising her. Something in him was out of control, but then it had been that way since he had first laid eyes on her. Her smile into Jethro's infatuated calf eyes had made his blood boil. Just when he'd begun to believe he had the situation well in hand, she upset everything by not staying out of sight as he wanted. Worse, she put him in the wrong with her damnable dignity and ladylike demeanor when he knew she was anything but a lady.

On the surface, of course, she hadn't done a thing wrong. He had avoided telling her she was confined to the tent, hoping she would do the sensible thing. As any decent woman would. But not Hannah. Now he faced exactly the unpleasant confrontation he wanted to avoid; furthermore, he was facing it without first getting himself under his usual self-control.

When Hannah said nothing, but merely raised her elegant eyebrows in lofty inquiry, Jake was forced to plunge into the meat of his command. "You are not to present yourself again before my men." There. That was

40

clear enough.

"Present myself? What do you mean?"

"Mean?" he echoed, dumbfounded. What did she mean, what did he mean?

"Yes."

Hannah didn't yield an inch with that icy word. She stood, haughty and self-contained, even a trifle impatient, waiting for his explanation like a schoolmarm for the answer to a question. Her attitude said she expected the answer to be wrong. Jake was enraged.

"The meaning is perfectly clear. You are to stay inside this tent whenever my men are here."

"For what reason?"

"Because I said so!"

"I take it then that you took offense to my attempt to save Zeb work?"

"Save Zeb work? And how did you do that?"

"By getting my own meal instead of being waited upon. It's difficult to see why that should upset you."

"Zeb doesn't mind," he snapped, wondering distractedly how Zeb and his preferences had gotten into this discussion. "A decent woman wouldn't need to have this pointed out to her," Jake ranted, on the attack at last, "but you are one woman in the middle of a troop of soldiers. Most of them have been weeks and months without a woman. If you continue to prance around here like you did tonight, I can't be responsible for your safety!"

Hannah's face drained of color so quickly Jake at first congratulated himself on finally making her understand the reality of her situation. Then her color flooded back, and he belatedly realized it hadn't been fear that paled her, but temper. But still, goaded though she was, she did not counterattack. She continued to take the high road, trying—all too successfully—to put him in the wrong.

"I've not asked you to be responsible for my safety," she

41

informed him quietly. "The only 'danger' I faced from your men tonight was that of being treated with courtesy by Mr. Jethro, whom you delighted to humiliate in return for his kindness. Perhaps you're afraid I might grow accustomed to being treated with civility."

"Damn right!" Jake roared. "You keep away from Jethro. He's barely dry behind the ears. He's in enough trouble already without making an ass of himself being courteous!"

"I know perfectly well how young he is!" Hannah hissed back at him, pushed now beyond her tolerance. "I was only being pleasant! What do you take me for anyway?" As soon as the words were out, Hannah knew she had opened herself to retaliation. It was not long coming.

Jake smiled in acknowledgment of the question and her fury. In control at last, now that she no longer was, he spoke softly, making his exit with theatrical flair. "Ah yes, that. We both know exactly what you are, don't we? Which is why I'll not 'take' you any way at all."

## Chapter Three

The next night when Hannah heard the men ride into camp, she had still not decided whether or not to brave Jake's wrath and try to eat with the men again. Jake aside, it had not been an auspicious occasion. Though she might have had a diverting conversation with young George Jethro, she doubted its pleasantness would have compensated for the stares of the rest of the men. She wasn't insensible of the delicacy of her position in the camp. The men indeed might be dangerous to her. Would they be less so if they never saw her, as Jake thought, or did mystery—her pointed absence—only add to her allure, as she was inclined to think?

She had pondered the question all day, deciding first one way, then the other. Of course she disliked meekly taking such peremptory orders as Jake's, no matter how well intended, but she wasn't foolish enough to rebel just for the sake of being contrary. On the one hand, she found it hard to believe herself capable of inflaming men to dangerous levels of passion. The men of her acquaintance, even Daniel, had never seen her that way. Of course, these were not the men of her acquaintance. They were Jake's men. He knew them as she did not. Perhaps he knew their true nature and was only trying to save her, as he said.

But then again, perhaps not. His reaction to her brief conversation with George Jethro had been neither reasoned nor sensible. He had behaved like the most jealous and proprietary animal. And what could have been more innocent than their exchange of names? Her gratitude to Jake for his care of her made her want to see him as a benevolent protector with only her best interests at heart. What he did and said made that almost impossible. How could she credit his advice when his behavior was so irrational?

Hannah knew better than to ask Zeb's advice. He didn't offer it either, though she felt the weight of his attention off and on throughout the day. She supposed she was showing him that she had something on her mind, but she didn't try to hide her preoccupation. She had tired of trying to draw Zeb into conversation. He was dependable, even kind in random ways, but he seemed destined to remain uncharted country to Hannah. She knew he had seen furious action in the War of Secession, as he called it. Though he had been wounded and imprisoned, he wasn't bitter. Hannah admired that. His full name was Zebulon Prentiss. He was not married "and never will be," he said with great finality. Something wistful in his face made Hannah question that, but only to herself.

Still undecided, with tension coiled like a snake in the pit of her stomach, Hannah listened to the familiar sounds of the men settling into camp for the night. Their activity seemed protracted. Had they done so much shuffling of equipment every night? Rifles clattered, men joshed each other noisily, trafficking back and forth between their tents and the clearing until Hannah thought she would go mad. Would they never settle down to their meal so she could find out what she would do?

Hard as it had been to walk among them last night,

tonight would be worse. She would be actively defying Jake's stated order. There would be consequences. What form would his punishment take? She couldn't imagine. She was already a virtual prisoner. What more could he do? A lot, her mind told her. He could turn her out into the country unprotected. He could literally imprison her. Regardless of her denial last night, she *had* asked for his protection, at least tacitly. She had accepted his care and relied on him, the devil she knew among a host of unknowns.

She paced between the cot and the tent flap, three strides each way, her agitation growing as finally, inevitably, the sounds outside told her the men were lining up to eat. Another time she would have smiled to hear her bread so loudly praised, bread she had pounded to tenderness by pretending it was Jake.

Zeb accepted the praise as indifferently as he took their complaints, never letting on that it was she who was responsible for their recently improved fare. That was the condition she had imposed upon him, along with the offer to teach him what she had learned about food in her uncle's kitchen. Zeb accepted the condition without taking her up on the offer, saying what she did looked like too much trouble. In return for her help, he taught her all he knew about what she had come to think of as survival cooking. Since he knew a lot, Hannah considered the exchange more than fair.

As she faced the cot, she saw a shudder pass over the skin of the tent and whirled in time to see Jake unfold his length behind her. Not in time to hide the leap of fright in her eyes, however. Had he read her mind? For an eternity she stared into the brightness of his eyes, too dry of mouth to utter a sound even if she'd known what to say.

"I brought your supper," he said, holding it out to her.

He *had* read her mind, and outsmarted her. Reluctantly, she took it from him, still staring stupidly. As soon as he saw her grip was firm on the plate and cup, he ducked back under the flap and was gone.

Damn him!

Hannah marched to the opening, her purpose clear at last. No matter what the consequences, she was not eating alone in her tent like a punished child. She bent to go through the opening, only to collide, tin plate to tin plate, with Jake, now coming back with his own food. She backed up all the way to her cot, her mind a forest of questions.

"May I join you?" Jake asked.

His smile was so breathtaking that Hannah couldn't bring herself to give voice to any of the sarcastic rejoinders in her mind. She sat, too quickly for grace, compensating by waving her cup in parody of invitation. "Please do," she said airily.

She expected him to sit on the second cot across from her. The tent was too small for her not to feel the impact of his presence no matter where he sat, but from that distance she might have been able to breathe normally. Instead, he put his cup on the overturned box still beside her cot, took her cup to put next to it, and sat down on the packed earth floor, practically at her feet like a huge pet dog.

When he began to eat, Hannah fixed her eyes on her food and did the same, determined not to sit staring at him open-mouthed any longer. He had surprised her, but that didn't mean she had to lose all her native wit.

Jake ate like a hungry man, not shoveling the food to his mouth and gulping it down half-chewed, but with forthright appreciation for the satisfaction it afforded both in taste and appeasement of his appetite. Though he wasn't a bit like the gentlemen she had known in Tennessee, neither was he rude and unmannered.

No matter how she tried to block her awareness of him, he filled her senses to the exclusion of everything else. He

46

brought to the confinement of the tent the sharp outdoor odors of horses, smoke, and fresh air. His big, wide-knuckled hands on the utensils made her own hands look pale and weak. Even at rest he exuded a power she had seen in no man before. It was a physical attribute, as much a part of him as his heavy black hair, white teeth, and blue eyes, but based on competence, not physique.

Power was not strange to Hannah. Uncle Simon had it in abundance, as did most of the men with whom he associated. Jake's was different though. It was *his,* not something he possessed; part of him, not an acquisition that could be taken from him; physical, not mental or monetary. It stirred her—*he* stirred her—in a way she could not understand or ignore.

When he had dealt with the food, Jake put the plate on the box and took up the coffee. He didn't drink it, just held it before him, looking at her over the rim. He made an impatient noise in his throat, then sighed gustily. "Hannah," he began, then had to say her name again as his unused voice croaked. "Hannah, I have to apologize . . . no, I *want* to apologize for what I said to you last night."

"That's what this is?" she blurted. "An apology?" Relief made her giddy. "I thought this was my last meal before I was to be hung." She had exaggerated for effect; still, she was surprised by his reaction.

"Christ!" He thumped the coffee onto the box.

Hannah drew back, making her fork rattle against the plate. Jake plucked them from her hands to the now-cluttered box.

"I really am sorry, Hannah." He pushed his hand through his hair and raked her with a fulminating stare. "I haven't known how to handle this whole situation. It was easier when you were unconscious."

"You could always knock me out," she suggested, testing his humor. She hadn't forgotten that he had teased her. From the exasperated look he sent her, he wasn't accustomed to getting back what he gave out. She laughed then. "All right, I won't tempt you further."

A deep flush began to creep over Jake's countenance, confusing her. Had he thought she was serious? Lord, but he was an enigma! She watched him down the coffee in a series of Adam's apple-bobbing swallows and silently pushed her cup his way. "You don't want it?" he asked.

She shook her head, studying him openly. He didn't squirm, but she could tell her gaze made him uncomfortable. She decided to be merciful. "I appreciate your apology, Jake. I really do." Seeing the softening of his mouth inspired her to go beyond graciousness to honesty. "I feel very much lost here. I know I'm a burden to you and I don't know what to do about it."

"There isn't anything anyone can do. Believe me, I've tried to think of something. You're here and you have to stay until our job is done."

"What job?"

"I can't tell you—wouldn't if I could either, so don't waste your breath asking."

"I don't understand, Jake. The war is over. Are you settlers? You said you didn't have anything to do with the attack . . ."

"We didn't. You can be sure of that, but I'll tell you nothing else and neither will anyone else if he wants to survive."

"Jake! You wouldn't kill someone for—"

"Just don't ask, Hannah. I mean that."

She didn't doubt him. The coldness in his eyes and voice were frighteningly convincing. She looked away and swallowed hard. "How long will this job last?"

"Weeks."

"Weeks! But my cousin expects me. Her baby will be born before I get there at this rate."

He smiled harshly. "Were you going to deliver it?"

Hannah blushed in a rush of confusion and embarrassment. "No, of course not, but my uncle will worry. They'll worry."

"It can't be helped."

She saw that. Though she was disappointed, fussing would only make things worse when Jake's opinion of her was already low enough. He had apologized; now it was up to her to confront the real issue between them, especially now that she knew she had to stay.

She began hesitantly, her throat painfully constricted by emotion. "You had reason to say what you did last night. I know you'll find this impossible to believe, but I've never behaved like that before in my life." She paused to run her tongue over her parched lips wishing she could reclaim her coffee, then tried to force herself to go on. She couldn't look at Jake, just at her clenched hands in her lap. A nervous laugh startled her as she confessed, "I was going to try to pretend I had no memory of that . . . occurrence. It seemed the only way to go on. I was frightened, half in the nightmare and half awake. You were kind and—"

"Enough!" Jake hadn't yelled, but his vehemence jerked her head up in surprise. His eyes were pained, and when hers met them, he looked away. "I was there. I remember."

"Yes. Well." Agonized, Hannah stared as he closed his eyes. Was he repulsed? Angry? Though she hadn't thought out what she had expected to gain from her confession—apology—whatever—she couldn't have done it at all if she hadn't hoped it would at least clear the air between them. Sick at heart, she realized she had only made things worse.

"I had another reason for coming tonight," Jake said, suddenly brisk and businesslike. "Can you ride?"

"Ride?"

"Ride," he repeated. "On a horse?"

49

Mystified, Hannah was hesitant. "Yes, I can ride a horse. Why do you ask?"

"We're breaking camp tomorrow. You'll have to go with us."

In spite of what he'd just told her, she found herself asking, "Do I, Jake? Please, you know you don't want me with you. Can't you just let me go? All I have to do is follow the Platte River and I'll meet another wagon train. I'm well enough to be all right now. I could take some of the jerky. It's summer and there are fruits and berries . . . walnuts even. I've seen the trees. I'd be all right."

Jake met the tumble of her words with stony silence and an arched black eyebrow. In her excitement to plead her cause she had risen to her feet, but so had he. He stood like a wall in front of her. "You don't have the sense God gave an angleworm," he pronounced.

Deflated, Hannah stepped back. She was more annoyed with herself than with Jake. Hadn't he just finished telling her she had to stay? Why had she babbled on like that? Desperation was making her stupid.

When Jake piled her plate on his, she grabbed up the two cups, eager to help. He took them from her with a quelling look. She sank back onto the cot and watched with dull eyes as he left, his mouth in a grim line. Though she sat in a disspirited heap, she told herself she was making progress. Last night she had cried after he left. At least she hadn't done that.

She was still sitting there a few minutes later when she heard Jake return. As he lifted the flap he said, "We should get you a door. It's not polite the way I keep barging in here." He carried a lantern to the box, straightening to smile down at her.

As before, Hannah's heart lifted at his smile and her face grew one to match it. "I can usually tell your footsteps," she told him shyly. Did that smile mean he was no longer annoyed?

50

Jake put a bundle into her lap. "Try these clothes on for size."

Hannah investigated, holding up first a pair of breeches, then a pair of pants. "But these are men's pants," she protested.

"We don't have a sidesaddle for you. You'll be more comfortable in these, and safer. We don't want you to be distinguishable from the men."

"Who would see us?"

"No one probably," he answered, then he sighed. "Hannah, could you just try them on without asking a million questions? Please?"

Stung, she retorted, "Just as soon as I have some privacy!"

Though Jake was polite enough not to remind her that he had seen her body more than once, his raffish grin as he left again did it for him.

At first Hannah tried to fit the pants up under her dress and petticoat, but there was so much cloth she was awash in the stuff. She took off the dress and petticoat to stand staring at the two pairs of pants. It was impossible to guess which pair was likely to fit. In both cases the waists were huge. How would she keep them up?

She pulled the breeches on over her shoes and held them up. If she held them to her waist, two inches of the bottom of her pantalettes showed. The pants on the other hand, covered up her shoes as well as her legs. They would also have trailed along the ground had she not rolled them up. She stood there, holding the top of the pants, trying not to laugh.

She was so absorbed in the dilemma of the pants that when Jake spoke at the tent flap, asking permission to enter, her answer was the laugh she'd been holding back. It died in her throat when Jake looked down at her. His face was a blunt mask of fiercely controlled desire. She spread one hand protectively across the front of her chemise, afraid to let go of the pants lest they fall to her ankles.

"Jake, I can't wear these. Look at me!"

Reason said telling him to look at her was insane, but her demand brought his eyes back to the big picture, and it was such a ridiculous one that he began to chuckle. "Quite a challenge you present, Miss Hatch. I didn't tell you I was a tailor before the war, did I?"

"Were you?"

"No, I sure wasn't," he muttered, circling her slowly. "I'm not sure even a real tailor could help you."

Hannah let the pants fall in exasperation, kicking them off over her shoes to fling them at Jake. She hadn't indulged herself in a fit of temper like that since she had found herself alone in the world at the age of ten. It felt extraordinarily good, she decided, glaring at Jake.

Hannah had forgotten her earlier modesty, but Jake hadn't. The surge of desire in his body told him how much he preferred her natural, spontaneous behavior. Even her temper. After that speech of hers he didn't know what kind of woman she was. She was either innocent, badly frightened, and out of her element, or she was the best damned actress in the world. Right now he didn't care either way. He wanted to finish undressing her, bury himself in her slim body, and stay there forever.

He caught the pants and retrieved the breeches from the cot. "Were these any better?"

"They showed my underwear," she said to his boots. "Show me."

Her eyes glittered. "It looks to me as if I'm already doing that!"

Jake banked the fire on his own temper. "Just put on the breeches."

She held them in front of her. "There's no use. See where they come?" She bent to indicate their length, showing him instead the shadowed fullness of her breasts.

At least that was where he looked.

"Maybe you could roll them up."

"And show my bare legs?"

Any second she was going to begin screeching at him loud enough to be heard in every tent. "All right, all right," he soothed. "Put the shirt on with these pants. That will plump out the waist. With the legs folded up it will have to do."

"We're riding all day?"

"Isn't that what you did to get this far?"

Hannah considered that. "Not on horseback, and not wearing heavy clothes like these. I would have died."

Without thinking, he laughed. "You were smart enough not to be done up in a corset, at least."

"Jake!"

"That was a compliment," he teased, expecting a fiery answer. Instead, she smiled with a mysterious but mischievous gleam warming her eyes. Knowing better, he couldn't resist saying, "I wonder if I want to know what you're thinking right now."

Her smile blossomed fully, plumping out her cheeks like a child's as she hauled the pants up and tucked in the shirt. The effect was so awful it should have disguised her loveliness, but it didn't. The flash of her teeth reminded him that this was the first time he'd seen a real smile from her, one that didn't apologize or ingratiate.

"I don't mind telling you what I'm thinking," she said with patently false sweetness. "I'm thinking how I would fix you up in women's clothes—corset and all! Just to help you escape from some rapacious fiends who were pursuing you, of course." She pretended to look him over. "I think you'd look stunning in blue muslin—to match your eyes." Then her eyes dropped to his chest assessingly. "You'd need a *lot* of stuffing though."

He folded his arms over his chest and gave her costume the same attention, sliding his eyes down her stiffly held body. "You need a hat big enough to hold your hair and a belt to hold up the pants—unless I decide to use it on your impudent backside instead!"

Hannah's smile only grew mor challenging. "You can't control my thoughts," she told him. "They're my own."

"And so are mine," he said, smiling back. "You might think about that while you're riding tomorrow." Judiciously, he chose that moment to duck outside the tent for the night.

At first, Hannah did no thinking at all the next day. Never at her best in the early morning, she had a lot to cope with long before the sky was bright. Jake woke her early, insisting that she dress in the men's clothing and pack her own few possessions to carry with her. Her tent had to be struck with the others and loaded onto the pack mules. Breakfast was a hurried affair, mostly coffee Hannah didn't want. She put some leftover bread into her pack to eat on the road.

She was nervous about riding the horse Jake had for her. She had never ridden astride, and certainly she had never had to keep up with men on the move before. Her first bad moment came when she saw her tent collapse to be folded away. She had come to think of it as her refuge, and now it was gone. She remembered many similar occasions in her life as she stood by the nervously prancing horse, trying not to get in anyone's way.

From the time she had left Ohio in Willie's care, a ten-year-old wit no parents, being taken to live with an uncle she had only heard of, she had been wary of being uprooted. Now it seemed that this whole trip to Fort Kearney had been a series of partings, some of them wrenching. Though Uncle Simon himself had seen her off, she had been filled with misgivings at having to part from him and the security and comfort of his home. Change was fine in theory, she decided that day as the train rumbled, belching black clouds of smoke; reality was too much like seeing all you hold dear fading from sight behind you, while before you lies a vast unknown. Knoxville wasn't the small farm in Ohio and she was now grown up, but leaving was the same.

Hesitantly, Hannah patted the big roan's shivering flank. She reminded herself sternly that she had managed just fine so far and she would continue to do so. After the railroad with its noisy, jerking motion and dirt, she had next gotten used to the steamboat up the Missouri River to Omaha City, then to the wagon that had carried her here. Each change required adaptation. Each had excited, pleased, and frightened her by turns. This was no different, she told herself. She was alive, she was whole, and she was going to stay that way.

Jake boosted her to the back of the horse without noticing her blush as she swung her leg across the animal's wide back. When he was mounted, he nudged close to her to say, "Show me how you hold the reins." Nodding approval when she did, he instructed, "Don't be afraid to be authoritative. This is a man's horse. He's used to rough treatment."

Hannah nodded grimly, deciding then and there to treat the horse to the first taste of humane handling in its hard life. "What's his name?" she yelled above the tumult of neighs, brays, and curses.

"Name?" Jake half turned in the saddle to look back at her. "Call him what you want!" he shouted. "I told you, he's no damn pet!"

Prophetic words, Hannah soon decided. Her humane handling lasted through twenty minutes of hell on horseback. She had no time to think about the strangeness of her clothes or to worry about what the men thought of having her along. She had to fight to stay in the saddle, but fight she did. Her arms, shoulders, thighs, and knees ached and turned to jelly. The few glances she managed at

Zeb, who rode ahead of her, indicated that her struggle was extreme. Zeb sat in the saddle as if it were a rocking chair. His horse merely followed the one before, plodding docilely, while her beast plunged and tossed, trying to rid himself of her tenacious self.

When Jake pulled up beside her, she could barely spare the energy to spear him with a malevolent glare. He took the reins, abruptly halting them both. "I thought you said you could ride," he accused.

Hannah tossed her head so hard her hat bobbed up and resettled down over her eyebrows. Having to push it up to see spoiled the effect of her gesture completely. Her frustration almost made her cry. Almost. She smiled instead. "Why don't we just change horses for a while and see how we both do?"

Jake eyed the horse and her tight, red face. "He's used to a strong touch," he commented, choosing his words with care.

"I repeat my offer."

Jake pried her hands from the reins and swore at the welts he saw. "Damn fool," he muttered. "Why didn't you yell?"

He reached behind him for his heavy packs and threw them, none too gently, onto the horse's back behind Hannah's small one. Instantly, the horse eased and settled, the transformation visible from relaxed ears to stilled tail.

"Well, I'll be damned," Jake said. "He's just not used to such a light load as you, I guess. Who'd have thought it?"

Hannah shook her head in wonder. "Certainly not me! I just thought he was the devil incarnate."

"Do you still want to change?"

"No. I'll try it this way. I hate to have a horse order me off its back."

"I'll bet you do, but if he gives you any more trouble, we'll change." When she nodded, already reclaiming the reins and preparing to ride again, he asked, "Have you given him a name yet?"

"Many," she said, laughing, "but none I'd want to repeat now."

Though the rest of the morning was easier, her initial bout with her mount had taken its toll of Hannah's strength. By the time they stopped to rest and water the horses, she wasn't sure she'd be able to stand on her own. She hung onto the stirrups, waiting for her head to clear before she tried to walk to the shade. Zeb led the horse away and Jake helped her to the ground. He brought her some jerky, bread, and water, joining her under a cottonwood. Too tired to chew the tough meat, she satisfied her thirst and rested her head against the tree.

"I'm sorry to put you through this, Hannah," Jake said. His voice came to her from far away.

"I'll be fine. Just rest awhile . . ." She felt him lower her to the ground and pull off her hat to use as a pillow. Her heavy shirt was in her pack now, leaving only the light cotton shirt as cover. She slept until Jake lifted her and began to carry her to the horses, then she fought back to wakefulness.

"Put me down, Jake. I can walk!" She was horrified that he was carrying her in front of the men. The wildness of her struggle finally got through to him and he stopped to set her on the ground.

"You're riding with me this afternoon," he said. "I wish we could put it off till tomorrow, but we can't."

"I'm riding by myself," Hannah told him. "Where's my hat?"

He pulled it from his belt and handed it over. "You can barely walk."

"The horse does the walking. I just have to sit there, and I will." She rolled her hair into a fat sausage to coil on top of her head and stuffed the hat over it. Her first few steps were awkward, but she fought off Jake's helping

57

hands and walked to the roan's side. She had to accept his boost, but she did everything else under her own power. Jay, as she had decided to call the horse, accepted her without question this time. Buoyed by that, she set her sights on the middle of Zeb's back and got in line again. When Jake ordered from behind her, "Pull your hat lower. Your face is getting burned," she obeyed without hesitation or resentment.

The thinking she had not done in the morning she did now. To keep herself alert, she consciously looked around her, at the countryside, at the men and their equipment. If they weren't soldiers or looters, what were they? Where were they going? They followed, roughly, a riverbed. Was it the Platte River? Were they going toward Fort Kearney?

The next time Jake came abreast of her she asked, "Is that the Platte?"

"Sometimes," he answered.

What kind of answer was that? "What do you mean sometimes? Either it is or it isn't."

"The Platte has tributaries. Some of these are streams."

They had forded some small streams, she knew. "Is this part of the Oregon Trail?"

"Could be."

"Jake! You're being obscure."

"In case you didn't know, Hannah, the Oregon Trail isn't a roadbed yet."

"Of course I know that. It's what our wagon train was following."

"Your wagon train was miles off course," Jake said scathingly.

"Really?"

"Really. Why else do you suppose you were ambushed?"

Hannah absorbed that news silently. It confirmed a suspicion she had harbored, but hadn't been able to verify. After all, what did she know of trails? Their leader

58

had been hired in Omaha City. Though he purported to be an experienced guide, he had never inspired confidence in Hannah, especially once they were away from settlements. "We were too small, everyone said."

"That too," Jake confirmed. "But you were in the wrong place."

"And where are we now?"

He didn't smile. "In the right place." Before she could ask another question, he faded back to follow her or to check on the mules bringing up the rear. She didn't turn to see which, not wanting to give him any satisfaction when he gave her so little.

Their stopping place was a copse of willows and box elders, as secluded as the ravine where they had been before. Wearily, Hannah wondered what had been gained by the move. Not enough to compensate for her ravaged muscles that protested every motion, she was sure. Because it hurt as much to sit as to walk, Hannah got the soap and towel she'd inherited and told Zeb she was going to bathe while the men were busy making camp.

Her last glance before she was claimed entirely by wooded peace and the gurgle of water caught Jake characteristically working with the men. He might be the commander or whatever the term was for his actual rank, but he wasn't the kind who shirked performance for mere direction from the sidelines. In that he was like Uncle Simon, not Daniel. Obliquely pleased with that observation, Hannah continued along the course of the stream, searching for a deep section.

When she realized she wasn't going to find a natural bathtub without going too far, she worked her way back close to camp, settling for a portion of the streambed that was well screened by bushes instead of deep. She had to lie down full length in the slow-moving water in order to get wet all over. The odd sensation, not quite floating, not quite lying down, pleased her. She pretended she was swimming, wishing she really could. Water so shallow was more comforting than bracing, she found, and she was reluctant to wade ashore after her hair was well rinsed. She compromised by sitting in the soothing water while her hair dried sufficiently not to soak her clothes when she dressed.

Tired as she was, Hannah still had no reason to hurry back to the camp. She was wary of Jake. However much she admired some things about him, she didn't feel easy or comfortable around him. His temper was too uncertain. If her tent wasn't ready, she'd have to make herself inconspicuous there. It was easier to do that here by the stream, so she sat, immobile and nearly insensible, listening to the patterned hoot of an owl.

Since she had begun living in the wilds of the Nebraska Territory, since leaving Omaha City in fact, she had begun to appreciate the outdoors as more than just something she moved through to get between one place and another. Here there was a natural pattern to each day. Like the call of the owl, it was repetitious, but soothing in its rightness and immutability. She found she liked things she'd never known or had forgotten since leaving Ohio. Nebraska reminded her of Ohio, in fact. It was flatter, but the air and light were similar—very different from Tennessee, where the great Appalachians held sway. Here the sky was endless over limitless tall prairie grass, broken only along the narrow watersheds that were so blessedly abundant.

Soothed by her thoughts and the quiet around her, Hannah was never sure whether or not she actually dozed off to sleep sitting next to the stream. Disoriented, she recalled herself with effort, roused by a prickling feeling of unease. Ten feet from where she sat, three Indians walked with careful purpose in a single line. Instinct held her in place, frozen with fear. She saw their faces in profile only briefly, blunt and hard and expressionless beneath heads shaved of all hair except for a front-to-back ridge that stood stiffly erect. They wore only animal skin breechclouts and necklaces strung with what looked like small beads, their coppery bare limbs gleaming as they moved.

Hannah stared until they disappeared, then started to her feet. After a few following steps, she came to her senses. Though they had been completely silent, nothing in their demeanor indicated stealth. They walked from the campsite, not toward it. She tried to remember the faces of Jake's men around her the night of the attack. One had been an Indian, but was he one of these? She couldn't be sure. Her perspective had been different then. This time she saw details of dress she hadn't noticed before. Had that Indian worn such a ruff of hair? She didn't know. Jake had tried to make her believe she had imagined seeing that Indian. But these? Three of them? She couldn't have dreamed them; she wasn't that imaginative.

She walked slowly back to camp, wondering whether or not to tell Jake what she had seen. What would he say? Would he try to make her disbelieve the evidence of her own senses again? Somehow, she was afraid that he would. It bothered her to think that of Jake because she wanted to be able to trust him. As she reached the first of the tents and saw how settled into routine the camp already was, she had her decision. There was no cause for alarm. Whatever the Indians meant to her, they were not the enemy to this troop. She would let Jake know what she had seen, but quietly, in private. His reaction would be a test for her of just how reliable he really was.

Her decision weighed heavily on Hannah, for she knew in her heart that Jake would fail to credit her seriousness. Where before he had blamed her blows on the head, this time he would say she was tired. She was tired, of course, but not that tired.

Jake wasn't in sight. It was Zeb who pointed out her

tent, standing slightly apart from the others. Had she looked instead of asking, she would have known it by the patched spot to the left of the flap, if not by its placement. Supper was going to be the inevitable beans and dried meat, she saw, deciding to forget food for sleep. Even her appetite was tired.

"Do we travel again in the morning?" she asked Zeb.

He gave her a droll look. "Do you think we go to this trouble for just overnight?"

She looked around. "I don't know. Then we're here to stay? For how long?"

"Long enough," he said flatly.

Hannah made a face at him. "You mustn't confuse me with so much information, Zeb. My head is too tired."

"Then go to sleep. We'll be here awhile. Probably."

Her laugh drew a few quick glances from the men, but most ignored her as she wound her way among them, only her long hair and small size distinguishing her from them.

Her cot had been assembled for her, she saw, thankful to whoever had done the work. A blanket and her pack rested on it. She took out the nightgown she had constructed from one of her petticoats and put it on. It was a laughable garment from the standpoint of fashion, but she liked it. It covered her from neck to knees, leaving her bare arms to poke through the opened side seams. She had adjusted the waistband ties to meet at the front and make it reasonably secure. All in all she was pleased. It protected her skin from the scratchy blanket, yet it was cool when she first went to bed. Nebraska extremes of heat during the day and cold at night made comfort difficult with such a limited wardrobe as hers.

When she looked for a place to put her discarded clothes, she realized she had no second cot or box this time. She put everything back in the pack again, brushed off the bottoms of her feet, and stretched out to rest, her last coherent thought that she had not told Jake about the Indians.

Later she would wish she had sought out Jake immediately to tell him, but by then it was too late. The damage had been done.

Hannah.

had been there.

## Chapter Four

Unlike Hannah, Jake found sleep elusive that night.
Just when he had sent two men to the settlement of
Columbus on the Loup River, Many Buffalo arrived to
warn him of rumors that the Sioux were readying for war.
Their target, his friend told him, was the Pawnee Nation,
at least for now, but Jake knew any Indian uprising could
bring government troops into battle.

The United States Bureau of Indian Affairs had an
undistinguished record when it came to understanding the
subtleties of intertribal warfare. A few voices — no more
admirable — always suggested leaving both sides free to
decimate each other, thus saving the white man's ammuni-
tion, but they never prevailed. As soon as one white
person was killed, the cry changed; and a white person
always died somewhere, and soon.

Jake had sent Colby and Whitcomb to Columbus to
find out who was backing Spotted Pony's marauders.
Spotted Pony was crazy, but the men with him were not.
Their targets, apart from Hannah's little convoy of settlers, had been carefully chosen, their raids carefully
orchestrated. They were putting fear into the hearts of the
small knots of immigrants, especially the Swedes and
Germans from Iowa and Wisconsin who were increasingly
homesteading in the Nebraska Territory. Soon their de-
mands for protection would bring the Army into play — if

the Sioux didn't manage it first.

Lying with his eyes on the tent above him, Jake entertained the thought for one mad moment that the Sioux were in on the plot, too, but he knew better. No one managed the Sioux. They claimed all the land north of the Platte River's meandering west-to-east course across lower Nebraska as their traditional hunting ground. Naturally they took exception to the encroachment of settlers, miners, and railroads into their land. The railroads would strike the final blow, Jake knew, but an uprising would only bring down the might of the United States government sooner.

The large picture for the Indian, Pawnee or Sioux, was hopeless. Nothing could stop the march of settlement across America, certainly nothing Jake could do. What he could do, he hoped, was help just one small band of peaceful Pawnee Indians retain their small spot on earth. It didn't seem too much to ask, for them or for himself. His doubt was vast, however.

Doubt was not all that kept Jake awake. He'd had to force himself into this tent to sleep alone when he knew Hannah was so near. Deliberately, he'd set up only one cot in her tent, knowing he'd have used the existence of a second as an excuse to sleep near her. He remembered her quiet, deep breathing. With a desperation he could scarcely credit, he wished to be able to hear it now.

All day he had watched over her, admiring her determination and gumption, her straight back and small chin. The feeling of holding her in his arms haunted him like ghost pain from an amputated limb. Over and over during the afternoon trek he'd been ready to pluck her from the saddle and hold her against him to let her rest. Each time he approached, she either hurled her damnable questions at him or edged closer to Zeb, as if for protection from him.

His thoughts were so full of Hannah that when he

heard the first sounds from her tent he told himself he was imagining them, hearing what he wanted so he would have reason to go to her. They continued, the protests and cries he'd heard before when she had been trapped in the nightmare that had ended the lives of everyone traveling with her.

He was on his feet, struggling into his pants, before he tried to stop himself, but he did try. It was only a nightmare. She was perfectly safe without him — safer, in fact.

He didn't listen.

Hannah's cries went on from inside her tent, but when he got inside, he heard another voice and saw another form hulking over her cot.

"Ssh, Miss Hatch. It's all right. Wake up now. Oh, please, don't cry!" On and on the cracked masculine voice pleaded and soothed, filling Jake with blind rage.

"Out!" he roared. "Get out!"

"But sir! She's . . ." Hannah's winding arms held Jethro like tentacles. He tried to free himself and tried to help Hannah, succeeding in neither.

Jake grabbed Hannah's wrists and pried her away from Jethro, wrenching her back onto the cot. "Get out. Now."

Still Jethro hovered, torn. "I was on watch, sir . . . I *am* on watch . . ."

Jake didn't watch him leave. Hannah's pale, gleaming flesh and inky black shadows were all he saw, her bare shoulders and arms, her eyes dark and wide in the pallor of her face, her hair tangled and wild. Fury and frustration writhed inside him. He had fought so hard against the demon of desire in himself, only to see her wrap herself around Jethro, whimpering to him.

Hannah was awake now. Wide awake. The nightmare of Indians and murder was gone, replaced by a living nightmare that was much more dangerous. She pushed back from Jake, rubbing her wrists. He was a dark, hard-

66

breathing shape that loomed above her. She put up her hands to fend him off and met the hot, hard surface of his bare chest as his weight came down solidly on top of her, trapping her hands between them. His muttered "Damn you" was a burst of air on her cheek, felt more than heard.

She turned her head and cried out, "No, Jake!"

Again he captured her wrists, taking both in one hand he pressed to the cot above her head. His other hand tunneled into her hair at the back of her neck to pull her head back, arching her body helplessly beneath him. She managed one wild, inarticulate sound before his mouth covered hers, settling over her opened lips with breathtaking finality. His tongue invaded her mouth, bringing the taste of male demand and conquest. The thrashing struggle of her legs, the only part of her body she could move, brought them into intimate contact with his hard lower body. She went still and limp, instinctively choosing to fight him that way.

The bruising pressure of his mouth on hers softened then and became enticing. He let go of her hands, his hand wandering down over her cheek to her neck and shoulder before it closed warmly over one breast. Waves of reaction volleyed over her skin as his tongue flicked against the roof of her mouth to the same rhythm his thumb employed to torment her tight nipple. She moaned and moved her leg against his. Her arms wrapped his shoulders, one hand in the thickness of his hair, the other on his back.

Slowly, reluctantly, he dragged his mouth from hers to nuzzle in the curve of her neck. His ragged breathing warmed her throat as he found his way to her ear. "Hannah."

Just that. Her name, whispered like a prayer, completely undid her.

"Say you want me, Hannah."

She told herself to say no, knowing she couldn't. If he'd been imperious or abject, she would have resisted. But he wasn't. She herself had started this all those nights ago. Her need was as great as his. "Jake, I . . ."

He rose onto his elbows, freeing her body from his weight. Certain he was leaving, Hannah cried out in protest and reached for him.

"Ssh." The sound was between a laugh and a croon. He found the hem of her petticoat-nightgown and lifted it by moving his hand the length of her body. Only the white material was really visible in the dim interior, and then it was gone.

Jake wished he could see her. The sight of her body was permanently etched in his mind from the times he had cared for her, but he longed to see her breasts bloom under his hands. He lowered his head, rooting with his mouth to find the dusky tips he'd dreamed of, wanting to see them wet from his mouth, glistening and distended with her passion. He felt that passion building in her restlessly moving limbs. She gasped when his lips closed over his prize and the sound sent his pulse higher, hardened his body even more. He wanted to take her hand and put it on the front of his pants, but he didn't dare. He didn't know how she would react. Whatever her morals, she had been gently reared. He undid the buttons himself, leaning up awkwardly to kick off the pants.

When he came back to her, she had made a place for him between her legs. He was lost in a fever of need, ridden by his desire to spend himself there inside her. He touched her, stroking slowly from her soft stomach to the tangled door of her womanhood. She was shuddering now. He covered her mouth with his to swallow up her soft panting cries. One thrust and he was smoothly home, but then he had to wait for control as the heat of her welcome nearly undid him. He held her hips still, his hands clamped harshly over the thinly padded joints, then trailed them up to cup the softer roundness of her breasts. The clean feminine fragrance of her flesh filled his starved senses.

For one tortured second Hannah had been reminded of Daniel Veazie, not from a feeling of guilt, but disappointment. He was her only point of reference as to the nature of men, particularly in moments of intimacy. Jake aroused such need in her that any comparison with Daniel seemed profane. Yet when he stopped moving as soon as he entered her, she thought, "Oh, God, no," unwilling to accept that all her tenderness and desire would be extinguished so abruptly. Jake had to be different!

Then he was and she understood that the strength of his own need, not callousness, had nearly overwhelmed him. Exultant, Hannah released her fears. At that moment her senses leaped, hung suspended, and then soared upward in a long fiery spiral.

Jake didn't leave Hannah that night. Though the cot was narrow and hard, he cushioned her head with his shoulder and upper arm, one hand around her to keep her securely against him. She slept dreamlessly, waking only when he roused her to make love again. Each time he had the power to make her forget the sore stiffness in her muscles from the hours of unfamiliar riding.

*Forget* wasn't quite the right word though, Hannah decided, thinking back joyously over the events of the happiest night of her life. Physical discomfort simply melted from her under Jake's touch. With him, her body became a magical creation capable of seemingly endless delight. As Jake's breath played with a tendril of hair at her forehead, she thought of waking him as he had her. Would he like that? Had she given back any of the delight she'd received? She wanted to ask him. His murmured words of love and praise, pleasing as they had been, weren't exactly the confirmation she needed right now.

What did she need? she wondered. A proclamation of love? She would distrust that from him as much as from herself. She had loved Daniel once, or thought she had. Those emotions had been too flimsy to sustain her in the real world. They had been fantasies daydreamed by a child, part longing for the home she had lost with the sudden death of her parents and part yearning for physical closeness. Like this, she realized, leaning into Jake deliberately to feel the instinctive response of his tightening grip. She had been ignorant then. Perhaps she still was. Probably.

The thought didn't disturb her. She wondered if it should, but dismissed the idea at once. She liked herself better now, like what she had become. In spite of losing her parents at an early age she hadn't grown up as soon as she should have. She saw that now. Uncle Simon wasn't to blame, not really. He had cosseted her, of course, but she had needed that. His wealth rather than Simon himself was more to blame. Wealth like that made too many things easy. It made a girl too willing to be deceived by pretty phrases and insincere gestures.

No, Hannah decided with grave finality, she didn't want any smooth words of reassurance from Jake when he woke. She would be content with one of his rare, heart-stopping smiles. Already the deep green gloom of the tent was lightening. She was almost able to see Jake clearly.

Hannah forced herself around to look at him as much as she could without disturbing his slumber. His head had fallen back heavily, giving her a perfect view of the underside of his strong jaw and the column of his neck. The beard that had grated her skin with exciting abrasiveness during the night was well established again to match the fierce, beetling hair of his brows. His chest, though deeply muscled, had only a triangular crest of curling hair perfectly centered between nipples like dark copper coins. His legs were powerful and long; one trailed beside hers like a darker, longer shadow. Beside him she looked white and insubstantial.

"So what do you think?"

At Jake's lazy question Hannah gave a small shriek he quickly cut off with his hand. Her eyes were still wide when he let her go with a chuckle. She put her hand to her pounding heart and gasped, "You scared me to death!"

"That's only fair. Next you were going to count my teeth."

Though her face grew warm, she was haughty. "I was just getting even. You had me unconscious for three days. God only knows what you did then."

"Not near enough," he said, laughing. "I was too busy being an honorable nurse."

"I'll bet." Unconsciously, her hand strayed to her upper arm and covered the scar.

Jake took her hand away and inspected her arm, probing with his fingertips, then kissing her there. "You may not have much of a mark there in time, especially since your skin is so fair."

"I had forgotten about it," Hannah said, suddenly embarrassed and shy of him.

He saw the change in her and drew her face up when she tried to avert it. "Good morning, Hannah," he said pointedly.

Why did his frankness make her self-conscious? She had anticipated seeing Jake clearly, but not *being* seen. "Good morning," she managed, but her hand went to straighten her disheveled hair.

Letting her go, he laughed at her with his eyes. He tweaked the end of one breast playfully. "You look exactly the way you should this morning," he pronounced, still teasing her. "You look beautiful and you know it."

71

Hannah knew nothing of the kind. She wanted to flounce indignantly from his disturbing presence, but first she had to find her nightgown.

Jake watched her search, not hiding his amusement. Finally he relented. "Is this what you're looking for?" He drew the nightgown from under his back. It was crumpled by his weight, but Hannah snatched it up. When her head emerged from the top, he was still watching her avidly. "If you think that's going to protect you, think again."

Heat washed over her. This time embarrassment had no part in her reaction. She watched him with melting eyes as he leaned slowly closer. Her tongue slipped out to wet her parted lips, drawing his eyes quickly to her mouth. When his mouth was inches from hers, he gave a great sigh and said, "Ah, me, duty calls at the worst times." He got up without even kissing her.

Hannah jumped to her feet, determined to wipe the smug grin from his face. She advanced on him menacingly. "Oh, no, you don't, Jake Farnsworth! Nobody gets away with making a fool out of Hannah Vea—"

She stopped abruptly, so amazed at the name habit had popped into her mouth that she didn't know what to do. Though she recovered quickly and ducked to her pack, scrambling inside it for her shoes to throw at Jake, he had seen her confusion.

He caught her shoulders and pulled her upright. "What did you call yourself?" His narrowed eyes scoured her face.

Thinking quickly, she sighed and let her shoulders slump in defeat. "Oh, all right. You've discovered my guilty secret."

"What guilty secret?"

"My middle name."

"V?" His left brow lifted suspiciously.

"For Velma."

"Velma?"

72

"Don't you dare laugh," she warned him. "Tell me, do I look to you like a person who should have been named Velma? And if you say yes . . ." She raised the one shoe she'd found.

Hannah knew she had done well, better than she had any reason to hope for, but Jake still looked unconvinced. She lifted her chin defensively. The defensiveness was genuine at least. It may have been that gesture that finally tipped the scales her way.

He let go of her arms and stepped back. "Velma," he said, testing the name. When he smiled, it didn't look totally natural for a few more heart-stopping seconds, then it did. "As a matter of fact, I think it suits you rather well. Perhaps I'll call you that from now on."

"Jake . . ." She wanted to pretend anxiety over the threat, but genuine regret for her deception made any more pretense impossible. Incredibly, Jake saw that and dropped the subject to draw her into his arms. The sweetness of his kiss was her undoing. She kissed him back fervently, promising herself she would tell him the truth before they loved again. Tonight, she told herself sternly.

Jake's eyes were vaguely unsettled as he lifted his head. Seeing that look, Hannah repeated her vow out loud. "Tonight." She was acknowledging more than her need to confess about Daniel, but she couldn't tell how Jake took it. He nodded, his expression unrevealing as he put on his pants, the only garment he had to wear. She watched him leave, then turned, sagging now without artifice, to put the shoe back into her pack.

A strange sound just outside the tent froze her in her tracks, then sent her flying to the flap.

"Get up, you bastard!"

Jethro.

Jethro stood like a fire-breathing dragon over Jake, who was crumpled at his feet, not so much fallen as folded in half over his stomach. While Hannah peered at them, torn between her fear for Jake and her far greater fear for Jethro—because already Jake was gathering himself to get up again—she put the awful story together in her head. She had forgotten Jethro entirely. Now she remembered. Jake had ordered him away, but how far had he gone?

"Get up and fight!" the incautious Jethro challenged again.

Hannah closed her eyes. Even she could see that he was stupidly vulnerable, standing too near Jake with his legs braced and wide. If she ran out and threw herself . . .

But it was too late. Jake was up and Jethro was down. The impact of Jake's fist sent him flying to land like a flung rag doll.

No one noticed Hannah peeking through the tent flap though now there were men everywhere. She prayed that Jethro would have the sense to stay on the ground, even as she knew he wouldn't. If he had that much sense, he would never have attacked Jake in the first place. The men knew better than to urge him up verbally, but their lust for the continued fight was obvious. Jake waited silently, his muscles bunched and ready, as eager as the men.

Sickened to be the cause of a fight, Hannah still couldn't pry herself from the opening to dress. Jake would not appreciate her interference anyway, but in a nightgown?

"No, no," she breathed. Jethro was getting up. He shook his head, sending drops of blood from his nose spattering to the dirt. His charge at Jake was uncoordinated, a useless flailing of fists. Jake held him off with one hand and sank his fist deeply into his midsection.

Hannah felt the blow in sympathy and curled protectively over her own stomach. Her gasp of pity went unnoticed as Jethro fell onto his face and knees. Jake

74

stood over him for a few seconds, then turned him over onto his back with one bare foot. It seemed a charitable act to Hannah at first because it took the boy's face out of the dirt, but when Jake took a gun from one of the men and leveled it at Jethro, her throat closed over a scream of protest.

"I could kill you right now, Jethro," Jake said in a voice as deadly as the revolver. Hannah couldn't see Jake's face, but she could Jethro's. She saw the slow dawning of comprehension, followed by terror, and found herself hating Jake for his cruelty. "I'm going to let you live—this time—but only because we have a job to do and we need every man to do it. Next time though I won't think twice. So you'd better see there's no next time." He waited for Jethro's agreement, which even Hannah could see was grudging, handed the gun back, and strode to his own tent without a backward glance. Two men picked up Jethro and bore him away.

Hannah stayed on her knees by the now-closed tent flap long after there was nothing to see outside. Over and over her mind reenacted the brutish scene so she could damn first Jethro, then Jake. Who had asked Jethro to defend her virtue? She certainly hadn't, but she knew Jake wouldn't see it that way. He would blame her for the whole thing. Damn men anyway, she thought, painting both men with the same black brush.

She dressed in her own clothes for the day, then rested on the cot until the camp quieted. It would take longer today, she supposed. She would wash the pants and shirts she wore yesterday so she would have them available for the next leg of their journey—if it was a journey.

She had so much to think about she knew she wouldn't doze off no matter how tired she was. And now that she was again alone, she realized just how many muscles ached and why. It was the why that bothered her most. She had accepted Jake last night just as she had accepted his reasoning about her traveling with these men for however long it took them to complete their mysterious job. Now she was determined to think the situation through for herself.

It took all morning to accomplish both her chores and her thinking, but by the time Zeb, whom she had been avoiding, thrust a bowl of warmed over beef and beans at her, she had made her decision. She had no more time to spend on regrets and what-ifs. If she'd gone straight to Jake to tell him about the Indians, all the rest, from her nightmare to the fight between Jethro and Jake, might never have happened. She hadn't, however, and no amount of wishing would change it.

Whatever it was the men were doing here, it was clear to her that she was in their way. Her very presence caused disturbance. Jake had been right to order her away from the men. She'd only said hello to George Jethro and that, plus his misguided sense of chivalry, had nearly cost him his life. Jake would have been a murderer. She couldn't live with herself if she stayed here and continued to cause trouble.

Yesterday had taught her that she could disguise herself as a man and be perfectly safe. Fort Kearney was on the Platte River. All she had to do was follow that river west. She would hide herself at night and hobble her horse to graze. With food, a blanket, and the horse she would take—not Jay, she decided—what could go wrong?

She knew the answer to that question, of course, but she countered with another that was unanswerable. What choice did she have? She was making Jake's life and work impossible. If he didn't hate her already, he would after the next incident. She had to leave.

It wasn't hard to outsmart Zeb. He trusted her. On the pretext of getting greens for a salad, which she actually did get, she selected the horse she would use and carried water from the stream to it so it would be ready to go

76

when she was. There were only two horses left to choose between and neither was Jay. She chose the smaller for her own ease in mounting, hoping it was also the least valuable to the men. She packed all her things, even the blanket, in Jake's saddlebag. Hers wasn't big enough to hold the blanket too. Once she had her pack in Jake's tent as a substitute, she dragged the filled bags to the woods, where she would add jerky and bread before she left.

Despite her scurrying, she found she wasn't tired, just exhilarated. It was exciting to take charge of herself and her own destiny. The letdown and fatigue would come later, she feared, but for now she was absorbed. She had to leave well before the men returned just in case her absence was discovered. She didn't expect to be missed until supper was well under way or even over. Once Zeb thought she was in her tent resting, her getaway would be easy. Her plan was to announce a nap and then watch for her chance to slip away when Zeb got busy. Without a way to sneak under the back of the tent, it was the best she could do. Unpegging the tent in one spot was her backup option, however.

She didn't have to do either. Zeb heard her intention to sleep with profound indifference and strolled off from the campsite, giving her no explanation. Nonplussed, then amused, Hannah didn't hesitate to take advantage of her opportunity. She had already arranged a blanket "body" in her cot to look as if she were there to someone carelessly looking from the entrance. In her heart she rather suspected no one would come near her at all that night. Jake might easily decide to let her sleep. And why not? His day hadn't been exactly wonderful. Why would he want to see her?

She ran to the pack and dragged it off. Getting it up onto the horse was the hardest task, but she managed without causing the horse to bolt. Once she had him ready, she hiked up her skirts and climbed on. Her body

77

wasn't happy to be back in the saddle again, but she was prepared to suffer a bit for her freedom.

And for Jake's freedom from her, she reminded herself. That was as important to her as her own. It hurt to think of never seeing him again. He had saved her life. She wished she could have written him a note of thanks. Then she realized she didn't know if he could read. It made her pause. She knew so little about him really, and he had been her lover for one ecstatic night. She dug her heels into the sides of the horse, urging him onward, determined not to get maudlin about Jake. Once she was at Fort Kearney, she would think about him—not before.

The horse was not responsive, choosing to move at his own pace regardless of what she did. She snapped off a makeshift crop from a willow, but even that failed to impress him with her seriousness. She was under way though, and Hannah felt enormous satisfaction at that and at the fact that she knew where to go to get to the Platte River. Jake had been unhelpful on that score, but she was sure she knew. Yesterday they had left the main river—the one she thought was the Platte—to follow this stream up into the woods. She was reversing that process, then she would go upstream along the Platte. She refused to consider the possibility that that wide, but slow-moving river was not the Platte. It just had to be.

Once she got into the open, she pulled out the hat that was part of her male costume and fixed her hair up under it for coolness and protection from the sun. She meant to stop and change out of the dress as well, but that seemed less imperative than putting as much distance as possible between herself and the camp. Since she had no idea where the men had gone that morning, she could only pray she wasn't in their homecoming path.

Hannah found the river, the one she called the Platte with fingers crossed for luck, and turned to go upstream beside it. From experience, both yesterday's and from her

78

time with the wagon train, she knew she would be forced away from the river occasionally by rough terrain. She told herself she wouldn't get lost as long as she headed west. Jake had told her sand was as much a problem as the ravines and washes that had deviled their wagons at the beginning. In spite of her attempts to keep her spirits high, she found herself more and more anxious the farther she got from the camp and its security. By the time the shadow of her plodding horse was lengthening, her stomach was well tied into a bundle of squirming knots. She would have to look for a place to sleep soon, but as far as she could see ahead was just long prairie grass waving under a flat, though fading, sky.

She walked the horse to the river so it could drink while she considered what to do. As she released the reins to let the horse reach down to drink, she wished she had also dismounted, but it was already too late. Her shoes would get wet now and the horse might not understand being led back out of the water again before it could drink. She looped the end of the rein securely around one wrist and kicked her feet from the stirrups to rest her legs by at least changing her position in the saddle.

Without warning, the horse knelt in the water and began to roll over. No longer rooted to the stirrups, Hannah slid helplessly forward over the horse's head to be dumped into the water. The horse completed its ecstatic, hoof-waving roll in the refreshing water without her, dropping off the saddle bag at the same time. The water was only thigh deep on Hannah, who chokingly fought the soaked but floating weight of her skirts for firm footing and air, only to be dragged by her wrist farther along the bank as the horse prepared to do it all again.

Because Hannah had been preoccupied with her own thoughts as she rode, she had not looked behind her to see the two men on horseback who followed her. Though they had been slowly gaining on her for some time, it

79

wasn't until she had started to walk the horse into the river that they'd urged their horses to a full gallop. They reached her just in time to prevent the socket-wrenching pull of the rein from dragging her under the weight of the flailing horse.

One man freed her hand while the other lifted her to his hip to carry her to dry ground. He put her onto her stomach and pressed strong hands into the small of her back to force the water from her lungs. Next, she got to her hands and knees and gave up the contents of her stomach. When she could breathe enough to speak, she said the name that burned in the back of her sore throat. "Jake." He had saved her again.

She rolled over onto her back weakly, her eyes tightly closed against the condemnation she knew she'd see in the blue depths of his eyes. She was such a failure. She couldn't even run away successfully. Muttered words in a language she'd never heard before opened her eyes in stark fear.

Indians!

She sat bolt upright, staring, a scream stuck in her mouth. The setting sun behind them made it impossible to see their faces clearly as she struggled to her feet. They watched, not helping, but not concerned either. One held the rein to her horse still, a horse she had no desire ever to see again. Their horses would be better, she knew, planning how she would race to them and leap up on the closest to dash away. They had saved her life, they had her dreadful horse, surely they would let her go.

Clinging to her fantasy, Hannah watched for her chance. When one spoke again, drawing the other's eyes, she turned to flee. She took two steps, two squishy, sodden steps, before she was grasped by the waist and lifted off her soaked shoes. This time she got to the horse all right. She was thrown face down across the beast. She fought, kicking and screaming without consideration for

80

the horse, but the Indian was quickly in place to capture her hands and tie them behind her. Though she couldn't escape, Hannah continued to howl and shriek her rage for as long as she had breath to spare from the jouncing motion against her fortunately empty stomach.

Dusky shadows doubled the height of the cluster of tipis Hannah first saw as she was pulled off the horse. The sudden reversal of blood from her head made her stagger. Without her arms for balance she would have fallen but for the steadying hands of the stoic Indian beside her. Other Indians raggedly circled them in what she supposed was curiosity. Reminded of that ring of men in Jake's camp, Hannah tried to see if any of these Indians looked like the one that night. These were mostly women though.

Her abductor spoke to the one woman who approached them openly. Her voice was softer, making the harsh sounds almost musical. The woman got her answer at some length from the Indian male. Whatever he said drew smiles, then outright laughter and knowing glances at Hannah from the women.

Hannah glared fiercely at them all, but that only made them giggle and poke each other. She lifted her chin defiantly and looked off into the middle distance beyond their faces. She had lost her hat in the river and her hair was a Gorgon's head of matted, half-dried tangles from her ride while upside down on a fast horse. She concentrated on not letting her teeth chatter from the cold and tried to think. The second Indian and the wretched horse that had caused her trouble weren't to be seen, she noticed. What did that mean?

She had no time to wonder. The Indian woman with the gentle voice led Hannah to a tipi and lifted the covering skin that served as a door, motioning for her to enter. Again she found it awkward without the use of her hands, but she managed. Hannah found the inside dark,

81

warmer than the rapidly cooling air outside, and as spacious as the tent in which she'd been living. She stood uncertainly, unable to keep her eyes from devouring the nest of fur robes and blankets on the earthen floor.

She turned to look at the Indian woman and discovered that she was alone. Suddenly, that was almost more than Hannah could bear. The woman had looked sweet and kind, and after what seemed ages of nothing but men around her, the company of even an Indian woman was precious to her. She sank to her knees on the robes and fought back scalding tears, telling herself it was just as well. Someone from the wagon train had told her that Indian women were as ruthless as the men, sometimes worse.

The woman came inside holding out garments made of deerskin. More pants, Hannah thought with an odd, sinking feeling. But at least they would be dry. She turned to show the woman her tied hands and shrugged.

The woman laughed and fell to her knees next to Hannah. "I can free you, but you can't go," she said. "Sees Far is outside. See?" She lifted the flap to show Hannah the masculine foot and leg visible just outside.

"You speak English?" That fact was much more important to Hannah than legions of Indian guards outside. "Oh, how wonderful!"

"I am named Bright Star. Black Bear calls me Star, sometimes Twinkle Star." Her nose wrinkled with delicate distaste at the latter, yet Hannah could see affection in Star's expression.

Unable to sort it all out, she rushed to say, "Hannah. My name is Hannah."

Star smiled, but shook her head firmly. "You are Fire Woman. Many Buffalo said."

Hannah was bewildered. "Fire Woman? Who is Many Buffalo?"

"Many Buffalo is Chief and friend of Black Bear."

Hannah sighed. "Please. I won't run away if you undo my hands. I'm too tired." Although she said it sincerely, fully aware that it was all too true, at the same time she didn't hold herself to the promise as she ordinarily would to such a vow. Knowing that she wasn't ready to take on the owner of those feet outside right off anyway, she decided the promise was almost as good as true.

Star nodded wisely. "Black Bear will come for his woman soon." Her tone told Hannah that Star believed she would welcome that bit of news, but in fact it made her head swim. Much as she appreciated Star's attempt to communicate, she was afraid the mention of one more Indian name would start her screaming again. Her impatience died only when Star untied her hands and she was finally able to push her tangled hair back from her face.

Star got up to go. "You dress now."

Once Star was gone, Hannah did. She used one of the blankets to chafe warmth into her chilled body before she pulled on the leggings and shirt. They were surprisingly soft against her skin though she couldn't help but long for underwear too. As with the men's pants, the waist was large, though not by such a great margin. These were garments for a woman, just a woman of slightly different proportions. The mocassins, on the other hand, were a perfect fit.

Hannah was trying out the wonderfully comfortable shoes when Star came back. She held up a comb carved of what looked like bone to Hannah.

"Oh, thank you. You *are* kind!"

Star kept the comb from her, saying, "Let me."

Hannah sat down eagerly, welcoming the service as a long-forgotten luxury. "How did you learn to speak English so well, Star?" she asked, trying to stay awake under the woman's gentle ministrations.

"Many of our village speak English since Beauty Woman's time."

83

Hannah didn't ask who Beauty Woman was. She closed her eyes and rested. When her hair was smooth, Star formed two braids she wrapped with strips of hide.

"Black Bear will like your fire hair this way."

Hannah wanted to ask Star about Black Bear. She sensed that he was important, at least to Star. Perhaps he was her husband, she thought wearily. As she slid lower, letting her cheek rest at last on the furry surface of a robe, the last thing she heard was Star's soft but senseless assurance, "Black Bear will come soon."

# Chapter Five

Streaks of soft light were just showing above the far horizon when Hannah stepped over the snoring Indian outside her tipi and made her way to the edge of the settlement. The needs of her body had awakened her, but now that she had washed at the stream, she considered again trying to proceed to Fort Kearney. Certainly there were horses here for the taking. But though she was tempted, she put the idea aside as unwise.

To steal a horse from Indians who had not mistreated her would only invite pursuit and recapture. Since they spoke English, she believed she could reason with them as long as she didn't provoke them more. Running away from Jake was one thing, this would be quite another. Especially since she had no idea which way to go. Her brief encounter with freedom and independence yesterday had made her aware that there were worse things than being kept from self-determination.

She walked around the village, moving cautiously to avoid discovery. Now that she had decided not to escape, she wanted to look at the tipis and the equipment scattered about outside. How many white women ever got this close to an Indian encampment? Back in Tennessee she would be able to dine out for the rest of her life on just this one story. Who would ever believe that her fierce Indian guard had fallen so deeply asleep?

While she admired a drying rack for jerky, her foot

displaced a pole she hadn't noticed, sending it clattering to the ground. A dog exploded from the shadows to bark at her and, instantly, Indians emerged from silent tipis to surround her. There were not so many of them, but their expressions were grim.

"I wasn't trying to escape," she said, looking from one unyielding face to the next. "I was just looking at the drying rack." She spread her hands in a gesture of innocence. Still they stood; no one spoke.

She tried again. "Look, I could have run away if I'd wanted to. I've been walking around here for twenty minutes by myself . . ." Did they understand English?

Hannah was getting desperate. She began to edge forward, then stopped when the dog, attuned to the air of tension, growled in warning. She had no idea how long she and the Indians stood, squared off in mutual suspicion, but finally a voice from behind her took command, cracking out orders in that harsh Indian tongue. At first the unfamiliar sounds and her fear of what the men were being told to do kept her from recognizing the voice, but as the Indians backed away, leaving her, she longed to run after them, certain their mercy would be kinder than Jake's. For it was Jake behind her. She knew that before she turned to face him.

"So, Velma," he said in a deceptively conversational tone, "we meet again."

"So we do, Jacob," she answered.

"No thanks to you." That sharp tone was more what she had expected. Then he laughed unpleasantly. "What did you do, stick a knife in your guard's ribs?"

"You'll find him snoring peacefully. At least that's what he was doing when I stepped over him earlier. Of course, all this ruckus may have waked him by now."

"Ruckus you caused."

Hannah didn't deny it. How could she?

"And to think I was concerned that you'd be frightened to be taken by Indians," Jake said bitterly. "I should have known a cat like you would land on your feet."

Touched as she was by his admission of concern, which she reckoned had cost him something in pride to say, nevertheless, the rest of his statement goaded her to anger. "I *was* frightened, but they've been kind to me, especially Bright Star." Deaf to the implication in that assertion that he had been unkind, Hannah went on rashly, "In fact, I think she means to play matchmaker. She keeps telling me about someone named Black Bear. She thinks I'll be his woman." That was what she had finally figured out from Star's enigmatic statements, but she was more amazed than Jake to hear herself talking about it so blithely.

Jake faced her with hands resting lightly, almost negligently, on his hips. The stance might have fooled someone else into thinking he was casual, but his grimly amused expression told Hannah she had just dug an immense hole for herself. "So you aspire to be Black Bear's woman, do you?"

Because she had no answer for such a question, Hannah was almost relieved that his hand lashed out to pull her off after him. Almost. From the grip he had on her wrist, she doubted blood would ever reach her fingertips again, but she had to run too fast to protest. When he tired of half pushing, half dragging her, he lifted her to his hip with his forearm clamped around her waist. Something about the position set in motion thoughts she couldn't organize, but recognized as important. The other Indian had carried her this way yesterday . . . the *other* Indian . . .

That was it. Jake was an Indian. He spoke the language . . . his hair . . . his skin . . .

Jake didn't stop until he was at the tipi where she had

slept, where her guard still slept. His rest ended when Jake stuck a boot into his side and dismissed him with a few curt Indian words. He put Hannah onto her feet to scurry inside. She was fast, but not fast enough to avoid the hard swat of his hand to her hide-covered bottom as it was framed in the opening. The sting surprised a squawk from her, and she whirled on him as he stood up inside. He caught her hand before the blow she aimed could land on his smug, laughing face.

Laughing? Hannah was confused.

"Thank you for saving my reputation as a man with that little shriek you just gave. Long River will undoubtedly embellish the tale of your beating so he can distract attention from the way he fell asleep on guard duty."

"My . . . beating?"

"The one an Indian woman would get for stealing a horse and running off. The way you screeched all the way here with Sees Far the whole camp anticipates a good show from you. Of course, an Indian woman wouldn't make a sound, but they make allowances for white women and their delicate ways."

Color washed over Hannah's face. Now she knew what all the women had been laughing at when she arrived. Thank God she hadn't known then! She wouldn't have been able to stand the humiliation on top of everything else just then. It was bad enough now.

"Jake, I didn't steal your horse."

"No?" His black brow arched up imperiously. "Borrowed then?"

"Bought," she said firmly. "I was going to send you the money once I got to Fort Kearney."

"Oh, that makes all the difference in the world," he said, folding his arms across his chest. "How much were you going to pay me?"

"Not very much! That's the worst horse in the world.

88

Worse even than Jay. He, at least, moves along."

"Jay?" Jake wasn't doing well controlling his expression. "Was Jay named for anyone in particular?"

"It's my special name for the devil," Hannah retorted.

"Maybe you just have a way with horses, the way you do with men."

"Jake, I didn't mean what I said before."

"About what?"

He wasn't making anything easy, but she supposed she deserved it. "About that Indian man, Black B—" The rest of the puzzle fell into place. Hannah's eyes widened. *"You're* Black Bear."

Jake inclined his head regally. "So, do you still want to be Black Bear's woman?"

"No!"

"That wasn't the impression I got two nights ago."

"That was different. I was—"

"Don't tell me. You were half asleep and frightened, and I was kind . . ."

"You *weren't* kind! You were horrible!"

Jake grabbed her shoulders and hauled her close. "You'd better explain that remark."

"You were horrible to Jethro. You were going to shoot him."

"Would you rather I beat him senseless instead?" he asked between clenched teeth.

"I'd rather you left him alone."

"So would I, but he didn't give me that choice. He was the one who dropped me, in case you've forgotten. Or maybe you mean you wanted me to leave him alone with you in the tent so he could have been 'kind' to you?"

Hannah didn't have a free hand to slap him so she kicked instead. In the soft moccasins, so wonderful for walking, all she did was hurt her big toe. She hardly felt it though, because Jake kissed her then and all she could think was why had he waited so long?

His mouth was hard and hot, but sweet, like rain on parched soil. She opened to him like a flower, drawing his tongue into her mouth, then pushing at it with hers. He responded by grasping the braids Star had wrapped and pulling her head back. Arched over his arm at her lower back, she wasn't able to be so aggressive. In fact, she could barely stand. She hung on to his shoulders and let him conquer her tender mouth. When she was wrung to total surrender, he bent his head to her neck.

"By God, you'll make a savage of me yet, Hannah," he rasped.

If he meant to frighten her, it wasn't working. "I'm sorry," she said. "I shouldn't have left. I caused you trouble . . ."

Jake wasn't listening. He lifted her off her feet to lay her on the robe where she had slept, but he didn't follow her down. He took off his boots and knit stockings, tossing them blindly aside one by one. She held his gaze, aware every time it wandered from hers down over her body. He threw aside his shirt and crouched beside her.

"Now you."

He removed and discarded her moccasins the same way he had his own footwear, carelessly, all the while watching her face. When his hand reached the laces at the front of her doeskin shirt, Hannah was sure she would explode. Her face burned. "Jake, I—"

"Hush, Hannah, this is my dream come true. Dreams don't talk back." He loosened the tie and lifted her toward him by the shoulders. "You do have to help a bit though. In my dream you were never an Indian."

Hannah raised her arms obediently and moved just enough to let him work the shirt off over her head. Just letting him bare her breasts had tensed the peaks to hardness that pleaded visibly for his touch. His eyes

90

touched, caressed even, but when he reached, it was to take her braids and unwrap them.

"Star said you'd like braids," she whispered.

"Not now." He tossed the hide strips away, his eyes hard on her face. "Were you so eager to please Black Bear?"

"I was happy just to have my hair combed again," she told him honestly. Her hair was still divided into sections, one on each shoulder.

Jake put them behind her and said, "Loosen your hair. I want it free."

She sat forward. When she reached up with both hands to fluff out her hair, he bent to taste one jutting nipple. Her hands halted in reaction as the heat of his mouth made its impact. His left hand took both wrists to hold them at her neck, while his right hand held her waist. The tossing motion of her head did what her hands could no longer do and sent the rich fire of her hair streaming down her back like a flag of surrender.

Strong hands held her imprisoned in a gentle grip that offered her breasts to his avid mouth. His teeth captured first one darkened morsel, then the other, to wash each throbbing point with sweeps of his tongue. The pleasure was so piercingly sweet that Hannah sobbed aloud. He rewarded her cries with nibbles that teased and tormented, then with deeply satisfying pulls of his mouth. Still suckling, Jake slowly eased her back to the fur robe.

With her hands free now, Hannah plowed them into his black hair to try to hold his head in place. For a while she was successful, but finally Jake lifted his head to look at her with heavy-lidded eyes. He took in the flushed warmth of her face and smiled crookedly. "This is what I wanted the other night—to see you like this." He watched his thumbs cover her glistening, softened nipples and watched them poke out again as nubbed buds when his thumbs were gone. "Beautiful."

91

He didn't know that Hannah found just as much beauty in the harsh majesty of his face. Every passionate feeling was etched into the planes and angles of his determined jaw and forceful brow. His mouth, fresh from her breast, had a contrasting softness and vulnerability that moved her profoundly. He was strong, yet he needed her, needed the tenderness she felt. His kiss was different this time, gentler. Sure of his welcome, sure of her response, he could give and not demand. He let her tease him, chasing his tongue with hers, biting it playfully.

As they kissed, his chest rode just above hers, but one of his knees rested between her thighs, a warm presence and promising weight against the tight breeches she wore. He undid the lacings at the waist and reached inside to touch the warm skin of her abdomen. She moved instinctively to accommodate his seeking fingers, twisting until his hand rested, cupping the mound at her very heart. His knee pressed up, driving her legs farther apart.

"Do you feel that ache?" he asked. "That throb? That's what I've lived with since you tumbled out of the bushes at my feet, wet and wild-eyed. That's the way I've wanted you every minute of every day since then." His thick voice, potent as a thunder roll, licked over her with tiny tongues of flame. He sat up and peeled down the Indian trousers, turning them and Hannah's soul inside out. "You're going to feel that ache the way I do," he promised fiercely. "You're going to know what want is."

He tossed aside the pants, paying no heed to her cry as she told him, "I do, I do!" Whatever she felt, his implacable expression said, it wasn't enough. His hands caught at her knees, drew them up, and pressed them apart. Her eyes widened in disbelief as he bent forward slowly. Though he saw her alarm, he didn't stop until his mouth was on her belly. Her relief was huge but short-lived, for he didn't stay there. His fingers stroked first among her sweet curls, then lower until he made his entrance there. Quickly, so quickly she gasped, he replaced his fingers with his mouth. His breath warmed and tantalized, then his tongue flicked at the center of her desire.

The pleasure was unbearable. "Jake," she choked out. "Oooh! What . . ."

Jake took his time. His hands lifted her bottom, holding her up to be tasted, licked, and suckled until her quivers of pleasure quickened to tremors that shook her slender frame. His name was chanted and moaned in a litany he would never forget. Nor would she. Even when she stiffened, he didn't let her go until she climbed all the way up that slippery peak again. Then, finally, when she was sobbing brokenly, he sent her over the edge to oblivion with a tender kiss.

Dazed as she was, Hannah was still aware enough to see that Jake's expression, though pleased, wasn't smug with self-congratulations. She wouldn't have been able to bear that. His words had been fierce; he had been tender and loving. She hid nothing from him, not her wonder, not her satisfaction, not even the tears she couldn't stop.

He kissed them away, catching the salty drops with his tongue. She framed his face with her hands and kissed his mouth tenderly. Her hands dropped to his shoulders, then to his waist. He knelt still between her legs, propped on his arms at her shoulders. The shivers of his skin at her touch gave her courage to follow his belt to the buckle and unfasten it. The wonderful pouched manliness under the straining buttons drew her to free them slowly, one by one, until she could push the pants away and let him spring free. His groan became strangled as her hand went around his fullness. When he left her to strip off the garment, she followed to worship him, her hands on the hard muscles of his buttocks. His hands tangled the long hair he'd insisted on freeing, sifting and lifting the strands.

"Enough!" he cried in time.

But it wasn't. It was the start of more loving that was as protracted and tender as two needy people could make it from their first joining to their final long fall into satiety.

Hannah, whose sleep that night on this same robe as a quasi-Indian had been less than perfect, drifted seamlessly from stunned satisfaction to peaceful slumber. She woke as she had once before in Jake's tent, pulled back to reality by the weight of his attention. She smiled uncertainly; he didn't smile at all, not even with his eyes. Whoever had told her — and she was sure someone had — that blue eyes were bland had never met Jake. Deep thoughts consumed him, clouding the bright clarity she had seen there earlier. She felt the separation from him as a coolness on her skin.

But then he noticed her and asked, "Do you know what they call you here?"

"Fire Woman," she answered, still uncomfortable. "Star told me Many Buffalo named me that."

Jake grinned. "Last night he said he was changing it to Screeching Woman."

Hannah closed her eyes in dismay. "I'm a joke to them, aren't I?"

His answer surprised her. "Life is hard," Jake said gently. "They get their fun where they can, like most of us. If you're a joke, I'm not laughing."

"No," she agreed, hardly comforted. "You're angry."

"I was. I came back early yesterday. I . . . oh, I don't know, I felt badly about what happened. I knew how it would look to you. I knew you'd be upset. I needed to talk to you."

"I'm sorry."

He laughed shortly. "You would have been if I'd been

the one who hauled you out of the river."

"I thought it was you. I couldn't see anything at first; I never dreamed it would be anyone else."

"I was on your trail, believe me. You wouldn't have been able to sit on a horse for a year if I'd gotten to you then. Damn it, Hannah, you could have been killed!"

"I didn't know the horse was so awful, Jake."

"I don't mean the damned horse. You were headed straight for the camp of the men who attacked your caravan. Thank God for the horse, as a matter of fact. It's one I got from this tribe. Sees Far recognized it and then figured out who you were. He knew the horse was a fool for water . . ."

But Hannah was sitting up in alarm. "The Indians?"

"They're not Indians, Hannah. Oh, one of them is, but the rest are white men who dress and paint themselves like Indians. They're hired thugs trying to influence where the railroad goes. Some rich white man is behind it, someone who owns a lot of land he wants to have become more valuable. But if they scare enough white people, the Army will send in troops to slaughter or move out all the Indians around here."

"Jake, that's preposterous!"

"It may sound it to you, but believe me, it's true."

"Jake, I'm not ignorant about railroads. The routes are set already. They've been set for months. A few Indian raids won't change a thing."

"Not for the railroads, I agree. But if the Army turns on the Indians, everything will change for this tribe."

Hannah put her hand on Jake's face. "You're part Indian, aren't you."

"The amount varies from moment to moment, depending on how you make me feel."

She didn't oblige him by smiling. "Tell me."

"My grandmother on my father's side was a Pawnee.

She was called Beauty Woman."

"She's the one who taught these Indians English?"

"She married a white trapper. After he died she came back to the tribe with her two children. My father left when he was young, twelve or thirteen. His sister was killed by the Sioux, but Beauty Woman lived a long life. Her sister, Eagle Feather, was Many Buffalo's grandmother. The Pawnee trace parentage by the mother; their family groups form around the women . . ."

"You mean a male would go to live with his wife's family?"

"Yes," Jake admitted, smiling to see how pleased she was. "You like that?"

"And I thought you said the men here would beat a woman who ran away," she scoffed.

"Oh, they would. For sure. A man who can't control his woman is not to be trusted with warfare or anything else of importance—the buffalo hunt, for example."

"But you said it's a matriarchy."

"I said they trace parentage from the female. That's different than rule by females. The Pawnee are sensible people. Paternity can be faked; only maternity can be proved, so they choose the wise course."

"That's a terribly cynical view, Jake."

"It's realistic. Indians are great realists."

"Then you're only a quarter realist, a quarter Indian."

"Is that too much to suit you?"

"You suit me, Black Bear." She scraped her thumb nail over his whiskery jaw. "You have a great deal more hair than the Indian men of this tribe."

"I come from a long line of hairy missionaries, too."

"Missionaries!"

"My mother's family. Pawnee men pluck their whiskers and even their eyebrows with clamshells. Much as I respect and admire them, I've no desire to emulate their

96

look."

"I should hope not!" Hannah laughed, her hands full of his thick hair. "Do they call you Black Bear because of your disposition or your hair?"

"Both probably, though before I met you I was known as a placid man."

"Placid? I don't believe you." she leaned back to look at him sharply. "You have quite a vocabulary, you know."

"Is that right? And that surprises you?"

"In a way, yes." Though wary of hurting his feelings, Hannah decided to be honest. "Now that I know about the missionaries, it's less startling, but when I was leaving I wanted to write you a note to thank you . . ."

Jake's breath hissed out angrily.

"I'm sorry. I'm probably insulting you, but even if I'd had paper and something to write with, I'm not sure I'd have done it. I didn't know if you could read."

"Never mind that. What burns me isn't being patronized, it's that you wanted to fob me off with a polite little thank-you after what had passed between us! There would have been no surer way to guarantee that I'd ride through Hell to find you."

Hannah swallowed and moved back. "I think you scare me, Jake."

That made him whoop with laughter. "Me? Scare the Fire Woman? The woman who was going to ride all by herself to Fort Kearney disguised as a man from the neck up?"

It was hard to maintain her injured dignity in the face of such ridicule. "I was going to change my clothes, too. I just wanted to get farther away. I suppose I was a little foolish . . ."

His merriment increased until Jake saw she was trying to get up. He pulled her back to his chest. When she continued to fight him, he let go of her, suddenly and

97

perplexingly reversing himself. She got to her feet, but he grabbed up her clothes before she could reach them. He put them under his body, smirking at her. She let him think he had won, then dove into his pants. She would have made it safely outside except for the length of the legs. She had his shirt clasped around her, but she tripped over the too-long pantlegs and fell, half in, half out of the tipi flap. Jake fell onto the bottom half of her, tugging the pants off and pulling her back inside.

Hannah screamed. "Jake! Stop it!" She had seen something above her. "We have company coming!" she shrieked, holding on to the pants for dear life. Jake hauled her, laughing like an insane woman, back inside. Her dignity was in shreds, but she was at least covered, sort of. Jake was not so lucky.

And that was how she met Many Buffalo, who chose that moment to follow her inside. He wasn't as tall as Jake, but he was dressed and erect, not sprawled naked in the dirt, holding on to a hysterical woman's legs. Hannah extricated herself from Jake and wrapped herself in his clothes and as much of her poise as she could find.

Jake gave a deep, agonized groan as he looked up into Many Buffalo's face. "I see you two have settled your differences," he said, his black eyes snapping with hidden laughter. Hannah knew this was a man she liked.

Everything Hannah learned during her stay in the village, which was only the rest of the morning, confirmed her good impression of Many Buffalo and his people. Their camp was temporary, one they maintained in order to help Jake and his men instead of going about their usual summer business of hunting buffalo for the winter.

Unlike many Indian tribes, the Pawnee had permanent homes they abandoned only long enough to hunt the buffalo, which was their staple food. Their normal homes were sod huts large enough to house all the members of at least one extended family, grandmother down to the smallest baby. Like the white settlers who had followed them onto the prairie and imitated their housing, they planted fields and cared for the land they inhabited. Like the white settlers, too, they wanted to live in peace, preferably on the upper Missouri River where they had always lived. Barring the chance to do that, they would even resettle away from the river in order to have peace.

Hannah followed Jake or Bright Star, who she learned was Many Buffalo's wife, around the camp, entranced by what she saw. Though there were many children, she never heard one cry or even fuss. Babies were carried everywhere, and small children were so constantly and well attended they had no need for tears. It shamed Hannah to think how smug she had been about white superiority in the face of this evidence. She had only to think of the wailing children on the wagon train, or even her own beloved son, David, to realize how much better mothers these women were than any she'd ever seen.

Though her own clothes had been returned to her, cleaned and dried, Hannah wore the doeskin pants and shirt when she left. Jake had told her she should not try to return Bright Star's gift for fear of insulting her. Even Jake's pack, the one the horse had dropped into the river, had been returned to her, while she had given nothing to her hosts. She fingered the thin gold chain of her locket, subdued by her inability to part with the only thing she could have given Bright Star for her kindness. Though she had tried, she hadn't been able to bring herself to give up her only memento of David.

She rode in front of Jake at his direction while the horse she had stolen followed on a lead from Jake's saddle. After they had left the village behind, Jake commented encouragingly, "You're very quiet."

Hannah sighed, feeling the weight of all that remained unspoken between them. The more she knew about Jake, the less she wanted to tell him about herself. Except for David, she had lived selfishly her whole life. She was married to a man she would never see again. If she wanted to divorce him—and now she did, if only to be free of the feeling of guilt thinking of him engendered—how could she do that without finding him?

She had to tell Jake about Daniel, but how? He would hate her, disrespect her—and she wanted his respect so very much. She wanted much more than respect, of course, but without that nothing else was possible. If she told him about Daniel and assured him she would get a divorce, would he think she was trying to trap him into marriage? He hadn't even said he loved her. Probably he didn't. He had a mission to accomplish. She was at worst an impediment to that, at best an attractive nuisance. He took what she offered as any man would; to dream of something more from him only invited disappointment. If she were smart, she would go on as she had begun, telling Jake nothing about herself. If she were smart—but when had she ever been that?

Jake's forearm tightened around her waist, prompting her to speak. "I feel so guilty, Jake," she began softly. He had to lean forward to hear her, making it harder to break the amity between them with unwelcome words. "I misjudged you so badly. I thought you were some kind of outlaw, preying on innocent people, and here you are, practically a saint or a knight . . . righting wrongs."

"Hey, hey," Jake interrupted. "Whoa there right now and back up!"

His horse stopped obediently, making them both laugh. Jake kneed the horse forward to a better stopping place and swung down. It was too early in their trip to rest, but Hannah slid down to join him rather than argue. For the first time in days, rain clouds were gathered in the sky and she knew he stopped only because of her.

He held her shoulders between his palms. "I'm not an outlaw, Hannah, but I'm no saint either. What I am is a mercenary, plain and simple—a hired soldier. I believe in what I'm doing, but I'm doing it for money, lots of it, and so are my men."

"But you're helping Many Buffalo . . ."

"Incidentally. He doesn't sentimentalize this and neither should you. I'm doing this for money. Only for money."

Offended by his tone, Hannah challenged, "Are you trying to tell me you'd be on the other side for the right price?"

He considered the question. "Against the Pawnee, no. I couldn't, I guess. But that's as far as my scruples go."

"You would attack innocent people the way those men did for money? Are you trying to tell me that?"

"Hannah, I've been a soldier, I *am* a soldier still. Other soldiers are fair game. Innocent people aren't, but they still get hurt in a war. The issues aren't as simple as you want them to be."

"I know that. I also know you wouldn't have killed the Torvolds and Willie, not for any amount of money."

"Any amount of money?" He grimaced. "Don't tempt me."

"I will. I will tempt you. Suppose I offered you twice what you're getting now to abandon this job and take me to Fort Kearney?" Then she thought, no, that was too easy. "Make it back to Tennessee, to Knoxville, *and* I'll pay your men double, too."

"You don't have that kind of money."

"My uncle does. I can deliver on my promise, I assure you." She was totally out of control now, her original point lost. All she had wanted to do was prove to Jake that he wasn't a mercenary, wasn't a man without principles. Instead, she was showing him a part of herself she had heretofore kept hidden. Already she could see it was too late to try to stuff what she had revealed back under the rug again. He had seen Simon Sargent's spoiled niece in action and it wasn't a sight Jake would easily forget.

His eyes narrowed to hostile slits as he looked at her. It was too late to back down. She wouldn't anyway, even if she were as bereft of worldly goods as Jake had thought, but the ring of truth in her manner was deafening. Her own arrogance sickened her. It was everything she knew and despised as corrupting. And how little it had taken, she mourned, to make her show her hand, just the tiniest challenge to something she believed, even if it was about Jake and not herself.

"This isn't just bluster, is it?"

"I never bluster."

"No, of course you don't. You don't have to."

Stretched on a rack of tension, Hannah found herself waiting for Jake's explosion of anger. It was inevitable, and she wanted it over. Perhaps she wanted to see if she would survive. She didn't think she would—at least not as she was now.

"Who is he?" he asked quietly, prompting at her blank look. "Your uncle?"

"Simon Sargent. You may not have heard of him . . ."

"I have." Calmly, he continued to regard her with grave and detached interest.

She felt compelled to say something, to explain. "He's not a famous rich man—"

He cut her off. "Famous enough. He's a railroad man."

To say more would be too . . . something. Obvious? Apologetic? She wasn't going to apologize for Uncle Simon or even for her outburst. She had done enough apologizing to this man. And for what? For wanting to leave his virtual imprisonment?

102

Even as she railed to herself, Hannah knew she was just keeping up her spirits while she waited for Jake's attack. But when it came, it was so unlike what she had expected that she didn't recognize it for what it was.

"And your 'friend' Willie? Was he rich, too?"

"Willie?" What had dear old Willie to do with this?

"Your lover. You haven't forgotten him already, have you?"

Hannah didn't know whether she would laugh or cry. Proper, sweet, funny old Willie as her lover was a picture for hilarity, but what Jake's accusation told her about how he thought of her put laughter beyond her. His stance, poised and balanced, elaborately casual, told her he expected her to fly at him. Instead, she stepped back.

"You really are a swine, Jake," she said. "Willie was the best friend a ten-year-old girl could have. When my parents died, he came to Ohio to escort me to my new home in Tennessee. Uncle Simon always felt guilty about not coming himself, but it was the best thing he could have done. Willie wasn't young even then; he was just young at heart, and the heart he had overflowed with love.

"He did magic tricks, not very well, but his skill or lack of it wasn't the point. He took coins out of his ears and scarves out of his hat. He had a domed beaver hat he wore all the time. I always thought it was because he was bald. I found out he wasn't when that Indian—"

"Hannah, for God's sake! Stop. I'm sorry." He reached for her, but she moved back. Her eyes blazed at him, but she didn't even brush away the tears that streamed down her face. It was as though she didn't know they were there. Jake pursued her, his arms open. "Please, Hannah, let me—"

"No. You're wrong about Willie, Jake, but not about me." Her chin went up by at least three inches as she glared defiance up at him. "I couldn't have you think badly of Willie. But now that I know what you think of me it makes everything easier. I didn't know how to tell you. I—I worried that you might have grown fond of me . . . a little . . ."

"Hannah, don't do this."

"I have to, Jake. You have to know. I have to tell you. I'm worse than you think, even. I'm married—not widowed, not divorced—married."

She didn't look at him after that, not even long enough to see the stricken look of pain on his face. She walked to the horses, untied the lead from his, and mounted to the back of the stubborn horse she had stolen the day before. Jake followed, his face as dark and storm-ridden as the sky above them.

# *Chapter Six*

Jake allowed Hannah's poky horse to set the pace for the rest of their return ride, only now and then directing her path. He had reason to hurry, but neither the impending storm nor the time lost to chasing Hannah moved him to do so. He told himself he was coldly furious. Instead, he was an emotional leaf, blown first this way, then that, by feelings from anger to hurt to disgust and back again. He understood the anger and disgust, but not the hurt. How could a person such as Hannah hurt him?

Jake's entire moral code came down to one immutable law: a man's word was final; a woman's, too. A promise was binding. And what was marriage if not a promise? He gave his word only after consideration and lived with the fruit of his decision, whatever it might be. Caroline was one of the pleasant ones, but even her life and his responsibility for it wasn't without adverse effects. She had more or less cost him his wife's life and certainly changed the direction of his. Without the need for money for her, for instance, he wouldn't be here in this present mess.

If Grace had not died in Caroline's infancy, Jake knew he would still be with her, faithfully married, if not happily so. The past few days with Hannah had forced him to reconsider his brief time with Grace. Because of the woman who rode ahead of him, straight-backed and stubbornly proud even when she was dead wrong and knew it, he had reluctantly admitted to himself that, by dying, Grace had freed him from a sorry, mismatched marriage. She had not been tough enough for the life he had chosen, the only life he knew. He had been patient and sympathetic with her tears and fears, especially at first. Whined complaints, though, were another thing, too wearing to be borne after a while.

Hannah's forthright passion, too, stood in marked contrast to the contrivances that had passed for Grace's love. She had never, not once in their three years of courtship and marriage, met his desire with her own as Hannah had. Loving his wife had been a bewildering and often humiliating process, more an act of negotiation than passion, whereby he won favors or incurred subtle punishments according to the ever-changing whims of an increasingly unhappy woman.

Jake had consoled himself that Grace was a gently raised good woman. Apparently, such women did not give up "niceness" even to lie down with their husbands. For a time, early in their marriage, he had looked upon their sexual dance as a challenge. Grace kept him on his toes. He had to continue to woo her. Finally though, he had realized that for all his wooing he would never win her, not really. In her eyes, he was like the West she loathed—rough and unrefined. His man's body and his need of hers degraded her. Coming to know that as truth had delivered a lethal blow to Jake's love for Grace. But even so, were she alive, he knew he would be with her, married still. He could not have left her to fend for herself, and though Grace might have left him anytime to return to Pennsylvania and civilization, she would have needed him to help her accomplish it.

Hannah, on the other hand, had no such constraints. She had left her husband—whoever he was—*and* civilization behind without compunction, like the most callous male adventurer. Her story had never made sense to him. In his experience, decent women didn't travel west just to visit a cousin. What he had supposed, that she had been Willie's mistress, hadn't pleased him, but it was something he could understand. He no longer believed in that relationship — her explanation had been totally convincing on that score. Now that he knew she was wealthy, he understood that she didn't live by any of the rules he did. Her values were different. Feminine creature though she was, she lived the life of her class, lived as a man might, taking pleasure as she chose — husband or no husband.

Jake tried to tell himself that understanding the situation helped. He had always wanted to *know*. In this case the knowledge hurt, but he would get over that. He had never trusted her. He had wanted to, though, and that bothered him. He would have to be on guard from now on.

They reached camp well before the rain began. In his absence Zeb and John Christopher had made necessary preparations for weathering the storm, but most of the men were still out, as were Colby and Whitcomb. Jake frowned at that news, unaware that Zeb attributed it to the sight of Hannah going into her tent.

"She all right?" he asked, following Jake's glance.

"Did you doubt she would be?" he countered sarcastically.

"Naw, but *you* did," Zeb reminded him.

"Not anymore."

Zeb had supper ready early, such as it was. After having been well fed by Bright Star, Jake had little taste for Zeb's cooking. He had less appetite when the men came back to report that their quarry had moved again, this time back toward Omaha City. Two men were trailing them, one to report their next camp, the other to maintain surveillance. Nevertheless, the change meant they, too, would have to go back east. Jake thought their destination might be Bellevue, six miles south of Omaha. That town was still the choice of many as the eastern starting point for the Union Pacific line, not Omaha. Doubtless whoever was behind the pseudo-Indians held land in Bellevue. With track to be laid any day now, Jake was sure the group would make a big move soon or risk losing even the appearance of possible victory.

Even after the rain began, sending all but the guard to seek cover, Jake sat down under a tree. He had ordered his cot moved to Hannah's tent yesterday before he went after her, so there was no question in his mind where he would sleep. Still, he didn't move.

He didn't expect Hannah to object, nor would he change his arrangement if she did. After Jethro's attack, he was taking no chances. She was not going to become a source of contention among the men. Now that he knew she was married, she was safe from his attentions as well. He couldn't undo the past, but could see that it never happened again. At least he could try.

On that equivocal note Jake went inside. Colby and Whitcomb would not be here tonight with their report from Columbus. Tomorrow he would have to decide whether to wait for them or leave Many Buffalo to act as liaison. If he left a man here to wait for them, his force would be strung out all over the map. Sighing tiredly, he shrugged off his worries with his damp clothes. The scratchy blanket would serve as his hairshirt; deservedly so, he decided.

He didn't have to check the cot to be sure Hannah was really there. Her soft breathing might be drowned out by the sound of rain on the tent, but she moved restlessly under her blanket. Maybe she longed for a buffalo robe bed the way he did. Though he put the thought firmly out of his mind, he still smiled to remember the blanket dummy she had put in the cot to fool him.

He wondered why she had left her husband. Was he a

brute? Someone who beat her? Ruefully, he laughed at the thought. No, more likely he was too easy on her. He had only to think of the chase she'd led him and his sympathies were all with her husband. Probably he just couldn't keep up with her, much less keep one step ahead as he would have to. A woman like Hannah, armed to the teeth with money, would be a handful.

He cursed softly at the evocative word. It brought to mind—too vividly—his morning with Hannah. His body remembered the sweet feeling of riding with her in front of him. His arms felt empty without her. He rolled the blanket up and held it, trying to fool himself into falling asleep.

It didn't work. Nothing did. Even the steady tattoo of rain on the drumhead of their tent failed to soothe. It didn't help that Hannah was just as restless. He heard every toss of her head and every turn of her body.

When she got up, Jake held his breath. He heard her struggle with the cot and whisper a fierce "Blast!"

He sat up, muttering, "What the hell?"

"Never mind. Just go right on sleeping."

"What are you doing?"

"Moving my cot."

"Why?"

"Because the rain is coming in on me."

He held the blanket in front of him and looked for his pants. She stood facing him between the cots, well within reach. She had on the nightgown thing while he looked like a fool, hiding behind a blanket like a frightened virgin. "Just a second and I'll do it."

Hannah put his pants into his hand and waited. "Why do you have the oldest, most disreputable tent, Jake?" she asked.

The asperity of her voice irked him. "I didn't know my 'companion' was going to be a great heiress, or I'd have arranged things—"

109

Her slap caught him bending to pull on the second pantleg. He caught her hand and pulled her so she fell against him. "Don't ever do that again!" he warned.

"Don't *you* ever allude to my wealth again!"

"I'll allude to anything I want!"

"Then you'll take your chances."

Jake was determined to get the last word. "As will you." He let her go and tugged the cot away from the drip. There was no place for it except next to his.

Hannah glared at him from the end, the glitter of her eyes clearly visible in the dim interior. "Thank you." She didn't sound grateful.

He felt around in the blanket and found the wet spot. "Take my bed. This is too wet."

"I don't care. I'll be fine." She prepared to climb into it.

Again he caught her arm. "Just do as I say. I don't need a blanket."

"Why are you in here anyway?"

"Do you care?"

"Not the way you think!"

"Maybe you'd rather have Jethro."

"What I'd rather have isn't the issue. It never has been. I'd rather be on my way."

"You'll be gone the instant I decide it's safe."

"Safe," she scoffed. "What do you care?"

He pushed her down onto his cot and threw his blanket on top of her. "Maybe I'll hit your husband up for a reward for your safe return. He's rich, too, isn't he?"

Hannah laughed bitterly. "If that's your next scheme to make money, you'll be a long time poor."

"He doesn't want you back? What happened? Did he get tired of sharing you?"

Jake expected her to attack him; in fact, he wanted her to. He waited, tensed to grab her again, but she didn't move. In a strangled voice she said, "Don't, Jake. You don't know . . ."

"Then tell me, damnit!"

"Why should I? You wouldn't believe me. I could tell you anything, any horror story I wanted. You'd never know the difference. We both know I'm just a willing woman you're tumbling for the hell of it. And why not? It's what any man would do."

Her analysis was too close to the mark for his comfort. "Why did you leave him?"

"Forget it, Jake."

It took him a long time to tell her what was the truth. "I can't forget."

"You will, don't worry."

"Please tell me, Hannah. It's like a toothache. I can't leave it alone." He could hear her thinking, deciding. He sat on the side of the wet cot and waited.

"I didn't leave Daniel. He left me."

Her voice was so small he had to strain to hear it through the rain. He wanted to protest at the absurdity of her words, but she had said them unwillingly and he knew any objection from him would drive her back into silence. "When?"

"Before a year was up actually, although it was later before he made it final."

"He told you?"

"Oh, yes."

"For another woman?"

"He married me for my money—actually for Uncle Simon's. I don't really have any, just a trust fund. It's a very nice trust fund, of course—more than I need—but Daniel had his eye on much more than that."

"How long have you been alone now?"

"I haven't been alone. I lived with Simon, thank God."

"How long?"

"What difference does it make?" she asked wearily. "It's been long enough so that I needed a man. Isn't that what you thought?"

Jake fought down his flash of temper, deciding he'd rather have her bait him than sound so whipped. "No, it's not what I thought. How long?"

"It's been four years and four months since he left for New York."

*And how many days?* he almost asked, enraged that she could cite the time so precisely. "You loved him," he accused.

"Yes!" She threw the answer at him, rising onto one elbow to do it. "Have you gotten your pound of flesh yet?"

"I don't know," he said hoarsely. "God, he must be a fool. No man leaves a woman like you."

"You thought I was a whore."

"My thought processes have been worthy of a squirrel's since I met you."

"It's just lack of sleep, Jake. You'll get over it."

"Why didn't you divorce him?"

"Why? So someone else could try to win the pot of gold?"

"That's foolish. You're a desirable woman."

"Is this a proposal, Jake?"

"You're trying to irritate me."

"Am I succeeding?"

"Yes!"

She turned away from him onto her side, arranging the blanket over her shoulders to sleep. "Good night."

Against his will, or perhaps subject to it—it was hard for Jake to tell—his hand pulled the blanket down and turned her back to face him. "You can't just go to sleep."

"No, I probably can't, but I'd like to try."

"Do you love him still?"

"Who, Daniel? Of course not." As she pushed herself up to face him, the blanket fell into her lap. The pale skin of one shoulder gleamed like ivory, almost as pale as the white nightdress. "I can't expect you to think much of me—"

"I think of nothing else," he interrupted, totally serious.

"I don't mean that. I refer to your respect, or lack of it, for me. Whatever you think of me, well, it doesn't really matter. But I know myself, and I wouldn't even look at you if I still loved Daniel. Hard as it may be for you to understand, Jake, love does die sometimes. It gets killed off.

"I was a young, very green girl when Daniel courted me. I thought I knew him well because that courtship was a long, very proper process. I saw a lot of him. Nevertheless, I know you better already than I ever did Daniel. I never saw him tired and sweaty or angry or . . . anything human. Our life was one long dinner party, one cotillion after another. He wasn't *real*, not to me or even to himself. He didn't know me either. The process of courtship served him no better. He didn't know how stubborn I am or anything!" Almost sputtering, she wound down slowly.

"Then divorce him."

"I don't even know where he is. I've never cared."

Jake wanted to believe her. He almost did. Almost. That Hannah knew exactly how long Daniel had been gone was one obstacle; another was the obvious strength of her feelings. She was proud and stubborn, both qualities that would make a husband's defection unforgivable. That, he understood. Worse, he feared she could mistake the novelty of being denied something she wanted for love itself.

She wouldn't be the first person to pine for what she couldn't have, Jake told himself cynically. He needed to look no further than himself for an example of the species. What had Grace been to him but the embodiment of the unattainable, the perfect lady? And Hannah herself, for all her warm accessibility, was in reality even more remote from him. In a sensible world a man like himself would never talk to, much less hold, a woman like Hannah. It had taken the insanity of murder to put him into her path.

"You must hate me," Hannah said, her delicate shoulders slumped in dejection.

"Hate you?"

"I've brought you nothing but trouble."

Jake mulled the expression silently rather than continue to be an echo. He almost laughed aloud at the impossibility of listing all she had brought him. Trouble? Lord, yes; but so much more than that. He shook his head, certain she'd never see the gesture in the murky light. When he tried to pull the blanket up over her again, he encountered her hands. The strength of her grip surprised him. "Rest assured that I don't hate you, little Hannah," he said, interpreting that grip as a demand for reassurance.

Still she didn't let go of his hands even when he tugged gently. Her breath caught oddly, then she pulled on his arms as she fell back on the cot. "If you don't hate me, Jake, would you hold me now? Just hold me? I know you don't want . . . neither do I . . ."

Had she been able to read his mind? He let himself be pulled down beside her, feeling like the luckiest man in the world. She fit herself snugly against him, a kitten seeking out only his protectiveness. He found his reward when she pulled his arms comfortably around her, issued a deep, heartfelt sigh, and went to sleep.

There was no logical reason for the profound happiness he felt in holding Hannah. She was still married, still wealthy, still unattainable. For now she needed him, though, and for now it was enough.

Jake used the short time before he joined her in sleep to make plans. Now that his mission was coming to fruition, he had to give thought to her protection. Though he often appeared to others as faithless, his curiously mixed heritage

114

served him well. It had given him faith in himself and a sure sense of the world. He could only hope that would be enough.

The world Hannah woke to the next morning was as new-washed and fresh as she felt. Even in the depths of sleep she had been aware that Jake held her—aware and grateful. It meant that at some level he cared for her. A man did not provide selfless comfort for a woman he despised. His tenderness had been a benediction that enabled her to feel hopeful for the first time in ages.

At dawn he had kissed her brow and eased from her bed. She had not tried to hold him. Now she dressed in her own clothes and went to wash at the stream, surprised to find no one at all outside. The bottom of her skirt was wet by the time she reached the water, but she didn't regret her choice of apparel. She had dressed to please Jake. She considered making a detour to the horses on her way back but decided against it. She would ask Zeb where Jake was.

She didn't have to. He was coming from the tent wearing a ferocious frown. It disappeared when he spotted her. "There you are."

"Yes. I didn't run away again." She said it lightly, but Jake's mouth straightened anyway. "I didn't see Zeb," she ventured.

"We're alone," he said shortly.

Dear God, what now? she thought wildly. "Oh?"

"He left some porridge. It's probably inedible by now."

"Am I so late?"

His face split into a boyish grin. "I don't know. Maybe you're always a slugabed like this."

"Worse, I'm afraid," she confessed, happy to see his mood improved. "Have you eaten?"

"All I want." His frown back again, he followed her to

the small fire and the pot of solidly congealed porridge. "Back a while ago I thought Zeb's cooking was improving. Now I don't know."

Hannah poured dabs of hot water into the unappealing mass and stirred it to a better consistency. It tasted no better, but it was less salty and almost palatable. "He has his good days and his bad days," she said evenly, not willing to criticize Zeb.

"Then why can't he make bread again?" Jake demanded. "And leave out half the salt?"

She wasn't going to answer that, so she asked, "How did he happen to go with the men today?"

"I sent him."

Hannah said, "Aah," as if he had told her something revealing, but even that bit of sarcasm went unnoticed. Perhaps he was annoyed because of her request last night. "Jake," she began uncertainly, "about last night . . . I wasn't trying . . ." She faltered and blushed, wishing desperately she had never begun such an ill-considered speech. She didn't even know herself what she wanted to say.

The speech had one desirable outcome, however. It took Jake completely out of his dark mood. His eyes began to dance with hardly suppressed amusement. "What weren't you trying to do?" he prodded innocently.

Instead of answering, Hannah got up and disposed of her uneaten porridge. Vile man! The thought made her motions jerky and uncoordinated as she poured hot water into the pot to rinse it. When she finished and straightened up, Jake was there behind her, so close she had to halt to keep from barreling into him.

"You're so pretty when you blush," he teased.

"And I have so much reason to." As soon as Hannah saw the effect of her words on Jake, she wished she'd held her tongue. That was a trick she'd never learned though.

"Don't put yourself down like that," he said severely.

116

"For your information, last night was special to me, so I won't have you apologizing for it."

Special to him? "But, Jake, how could . . . ?" Silently, she answered her own unfinished question. Why did she assume that comfort and closeness would have no meaning for a man? That was as arrogant as Daniel's assumption that a woman could feel no passion.

She took a deep breath and said, "I wasn't apologizing. It was special to me. I needed just what you gave me. You're a rare man."

There were many cutting remarks Jake could make in reply, but he said instead, "This rare man has rare plans for you now, too."

Puzzled and wary, she waited, letting him walk her away from the clearing.

"Have you ever fired a gun?"

"No."

"I'm going to teach you."

She stopped. "Why, Jake? What's happened?"

"Nothing's happened, but I'll feel better if I know you can fend for yourself in certain situations. Think of it as insurance. I have a small revolver you can have. You'll probably never need it, but that's what insurance is, isn't it?"

Hannah could see Jake was determined. She understood. He was her only protection. In his shoes she would also find that onerous. She fought down her feeling of repulsion and tried to learn. The gun was smaller than the one he'd pointed at Jethro, but it only looked small in Jake's hands. In hers it was huge, heavy, and ugly.

"I'm sorry I don't have a derringer for you, but it wouldn't have the range this does," he explained.

Hannah sagged a bit. "Jake, *range* isn't what I need!"

"Yes, you do. You'd use this only to defend yourself at pretty close range, but with this at least you can be beyond arm's length."

"This," Jake told her, was a Texas model Colt Paterson. It could fire five times without reloading, which he showed her how to do with painstaking care, forcing her to do it over and over. When she looked as though she was about to protest again, he gave her an especially severe look and said, "If you're going to have a gun, you must be prepared to use it. A man faced with you and a gun will assume it's a bluff and keep coming."

Hannah absorbed that sickening message and worked harder, as he had known she would. Her upper lip and brow were beaded with perspiration before he was satisfied. And that was just loading the gun!

Firing was worse. He demonstrated that as meticulously as he had the preliminaries, explaining about sighting and the recoil she would feel kicking up her arm. Until she felt it, she didn't believe it would hurt. Jake absorbed the impact easily. It knocked her to the ground in surprise. He pulled her to her feet, patted her bottom bracingly, and told her to try it with both hands. Her target was his Union-blue hat hung on the side of a tree by a twig.

"But that's your good hat!"

When Jake chuckled and told her, "I think it's safe enough," she was tempted to turn the gun on him. She did scowl at him.

Secretly, Hannah thought she would be a good shot. Her eye for distances was excellent, and she had shot a light bow and arrow when a friend's brother had taken it up for sport. He had thought her very good. Of course, he had added "for a girl" to his praise, but that she attributed to his need for superiority. The gun was different though. It was heavy and frightening. Determined to please Jake, she shot at the tree until her arms and head ached enough to make her weep.

Finally Jake took the gun from her limp hands and drew her to the shade of the tree. The unharmed hat taunted her from above. When she could speak again, she said, "I just didn't want to ruin your hat."

"Or the tree," he drawled. When he saw that she was disappointed, he added, "You did very well, actually. Most women wouldn't even try, you know."

"I didn't know I had a choice."

"You could always faint."

"I never faint." With her head back against the tree trunk and her eyes closed, her assertion didn't sound as strong as she had meant it to be. Then she remembered the night of the attack. "Except once," she corrected.

"That wasn't a faint. It was a concussion."

"Whatever."

"You're not going to argue? You must really be tired."

Hannah opened her eyes wide at that. He was teasing, she knew, but was that really the way he saw her? As endlessly contentious?

Jake didn't let her protest. He kissed her softly. It was meant to be a soothing kiss—even Hannah realized that. She hadn't noticed that he was already sitting next to her until he lifted her to his lap. Once she was there, all the pent-up feelings they had been denying sprang forth. The force of it rocked through Hannah like the gun's recoil.

"Jake," she got out between kisses, "Jake . . . ooh, listen. Don't do . . . that."

But he was unbuttoning the prim closing of her dress to free the bounty of her breasts and she had no resistance left. He made room for his caressing, stroking hand, then for his smoothly shaved face. His hot mouth took from her, biting and licking until she throbbed with exquisite pain, her head thrown back in abandonment.

She tried once more to stop him when his hand went under her skirt and single petticoat. The sound she had meant as denial became an incoherent moan as he searched to release the waistband of her drawers.

"I'd tear them off you if I didn't know you have no

119

replacement."

Hannah helped him and let them go to her ankles, moved to laughter by his unlikely consideration. "They are more precious than outerwear. There I have three choices, Indian, man, or woman."

"Woman you are — always," Jake said fiercely. His hand found the proof and claimed it.

With Jake touching her, it was the most natural thing in the world for Hannah to free one leg from her underwear and straddle his hips. While she undid his pants, he took her mouth, his hands framing her face, holding her gently but inexorably for the slow, deep thrusts of his tongue in symbolic possession. Then it was no longer symbolic, but real, more real to Hannah than the earth beneath Jake or the sheltering branches above her. They clung together, arching and plunging as one, united in pursuit of completion. They descended slowly from that great height as small, repeated aftershocks of pleasure surged through first one, then the other.

The awe that Hannah felt was reflected on Jake's face. "If he doesn't want you, I do!" His muttered vow first thrilled, then dismayed her. The sudden drop from the back of the horse into the river had not jolted her more than this disclosure that even in passion Jake continued to think of her long-absent husband.

Trembling, Hannah pulled from Jake to right her clothes. She walked away from him on unsteady legs, trying to think how to make him see the insult in what he had said. It was not purposeful, but to Hannah that fact made it only more devastating.

She turned back to Jake, determined to make him see that she wasn't a prize to be claimed like salvage from a wreck. He stood, half leaning against the tree, to retuck his shirt, but when he looked up, it wasn't Hannah he saw. His eyes went past her as he collected himself, instantly becoming a soldier again. He held the gun now, though Hannah was certain it was no longer loaded. She had not heard anything, but she knew Jake had.

"Things sure have changed around here."

Hannah whirled to face the men behind Jake, but he did not. He looked chagrinned and slowly stuck the gun into his belt.

"A man could walk off with the whole camp, looks like."

Hannah recognized the speaker, an older man, as one of Jake's men, so she began to walk in the direction of camp. She wasn't going to run, at least not until she was sure the men wouldn't be able to see her. Even walking fast, she wasn't able to escape hearing Jake say, "I was teaching Hannah to shoot a gun."

The man who hadn't spoken before guffawed loudly. "Well, it sure was obvious you were teaching her something!"

Hannah ran then.

# Chapter Seven

"So tell me."

Jake had borrowed an empty tent for his interview with Colby and now they stood face to face. He endured Colby's inspection without flinching, knowing the man he most trusted and liked, his best friend, had a lot he wanted to say. None of it had anything to do with his trip to Columbus, and none of it was what Jake wanted to hear. Whitcomb's crudeness wasn't Colby's style, but the result was the same. Colby was worried that Jake had lost sight of his reason for being here.

Jake had no way of knowing if he passed muster, but finally Colby said, "We got a name."

"Does it mean anything?"

"Perhaps. He owns land in Bellevue and some on the Elkhorn. Most of it isn't where the railroad will go, but enough of it is to satisfy a normal man."

"What's wrong with him?"

"Greedy," Colby said succinctly. "Wants to make a killing."

"Looks to me he's already done enough of that. Who is he?"

"Name's Veazie. An Easterner. He was in Baltimore and New York, then in St. Louis. His backers are from those places, but he's the one who stands to gain the most."

"How did you hear?"

"I got lucky. I put out feelers the way you said and he came to me."

"Will he be able to walk away later?"

"He could," Colby admitted. "If he's smart, he could."

"But he's not?"

"He is and he isn't. He's quite the gentleman on the surface, but he's oily, a real bastard. And it's a grudge match to him. He's trying to do in someone else."

"Who?"

"I couldn't get a name, but it's probably one of the people putting up money for us."

"I take it you didn't find out who hired us?"

"No. He's well hidden. Whoever it is, he's rich enough to have lots of people in front of him."

"Or it could be a group," Jake suggested.

"Could be, but with a group someone always talks. I don't know though."

"So what's our guy like? Dapper, you say?"

"Dapper as hell," Colby grinned. "He has a little goatee. He's about my height, light brown hair; quite a hand with guns, they say."

"Would he fight himself?"

"That's an interesting question. He might, especially if he felt cornered. He has a maniacal hatred for Indians. Thinks they're all like Spotted Pony, crazy and stupid, perfect tools for him. It made me wish Many Buffalo could get hold of him."

"How did you leave it with him?"

"I told him I was from Grand Island, that I wanted the Indians gone. Said my beef was with the Sioux, not the Pawnee. He doesn't see the difference. He's like the do-gooders who want to put all the different tribes together on one big happy reservation, only he wants them to kill each other off."

"They may just do that," Jake told him with a sigh. "The Sioux are ready to move against the Pawnee."

"Down here?"

"Not right off. They're too far north yet, I think. I hope."

"God, what a mess! That's all we need." Colby shook his head. "It would suit Daniel Veazie though, and I'd hate to have anything suit him."

Jake started, then went very still. "What did you call him?"

"Daniel Veazie. I told you, Jake. Weren't you listening? For God's sake, man, you've got to pay attention to something besides that woman!"

Jake made no attempt to stop Colby. The name *Daniel* was ringing in his head, setting off one alarm after another. Hannah's husband. Their enemy was Hannah's husband.

"I heard you just fine, Colby. Now leave me alone. I've got to think."

"Maybe it's about time. That's what I think."

Jake sat down on the nearest cot as soon as he was alone.

Hannah's husband. It had to be. The name *Daniel* was common enough, but *Veazie?* And Hannah had once started to call herself Hannah Veazie, he remembered now. He also remembered her guilty look at the time and the clever way she'd covered it up, calling herself Velma. It hadn't rung true even then, but he hadn't pursued it, only teased her once about the name. Dear God, but she had played him for a fool!

But why? That was the question. Was she spying for Veazie? Chasing him? How much of her story was true? Any of it? What about Fort Kearney? Was she going there to meet Veazie? How did she happen to be in that ambushed wagon train? Was that intentional?

Questions—all of them unanswerable—tormented him. He tried to take one question and think it through logically. Her being in that wagon train had to be acciden-

124

tal. There was no way she could have known he and his men were near. She couldn't be a spy. It just wasn't possible—though there was the business of her running away. That could be . . .

Jake shook his head. It didn't make sense. Coincidence only stretched so far. No. The likely story was that Hannah had been left just as she said. Being Hannah, that wouldn't do at all, so she was chasing Veazie out West. With all her uncle's money, she could have found out he was in Fort Kearney. That wasn't hard to do. He probably was there a while ago. He'd probably been all over the area recently.

The one thing Jake knew was that Hannah wasn't chasing Veazie to get a divorce. She was still in love with him after his four years and four months of desertion—if that's what it was. No woman would remember the time so precisely unless she was crazy in love. He might or might not want her, but she still wanted him enough to chase clear across the country after him.

Which meant that everything she had done with Jake was just what he'd first thought it was.

Jake's hands clenched into fists on his knees. He cursed himself roundly for being a fool. Didn't he know anything? No decent woman acted the way she did. How many times did he have to learn that lesson?

A red haze settled over Jake. He got to his feet and strode to Hannah's tent. He saw nothing of the campsite he walked through to get there, so he had no trouble adjusting again to the darker interior. Hannah's back was to the entrance. She looked over her shoulder at him, then turned slowly, dropping her hands from the front of her dress.

"Jake? What is it? You look strange." She started forward, then changed her mind. She didn't retreat, just stood in place, her eyes anxious.

"Just keep on doing what you were, *Velma*."

125

Velma again? Hannah swallowed and turned back to the cot where her nightgown was spread out. She picked it up, fingering the cloth nervously. "I was just going to change and have a rest, but it can—"

Jake's hand clamped her shoulder and turned her back. "Don't let me stop you."

Said another way, his words would have been welcome. Except for calling her Velma, he had said nothing offensive. It was the cold, angry way he looked at her that made her feel wretched. "Jake, this isn't like you."

"No?" His thumbs rode on his belt as he rocked back easily onto his heels. He smiled mirthlessly. "How would you know?"

"Jake, don't play games with me, if—"

"Play games!" he all but roared. "By all means, let's play games, Hannah *Hatch!* And the game we're going to play is this. You're going to take off your clothes—right now—while I watch."

She backed away. "You can go straight to the devil!"

"I'm sure I will—with your help. But first you're going to do what I said."

"I won't."

Jake stepped closer. "Would you like me to rip them off?"

"I don't care," she said, still defiant. But when he reached out, she grabbed his hands. He shook hers off, and she found she did care. She had the other clothes, but this was her only dress. What if he ripped it beyond repair? "Jake, don't! Please don't be this way. Whatever those men said, it shouldn't turn you into a monster. Talk to me!"

"I don't want to talk. I want a strip show," he said, deliberately crude.

His face was as stiff as a mask. She felt she could rip it off with her nails, but she was afraid to touch him. He frightened her. He was trying to. Worse, he was trying to

126

demean her. But Hannah knew something Jake didn't. Only one person could demean her, and that person was herself. Whatever was wrong with Jake was his own problem, not hers.

She held herself steady before his cold gaze. His air of suppressed violence told her better than anything he said that part of him longed for her continued defiance. He wanted an excuse to harm her—if not to harm *her;* then at least to harm something of hers. But the wording of his demand had given her a way to cope with him.

"I see," she said. She was buying a few precious minutes to steel herself. At other times he had made her feel beautiful and desirable. She tried to cloak herself in those feelings now for protection. "In that case you shouldn't stand so close, don't you think?"

Her smile was unnatural, but Jake was too stunned to notice.

His reaction helped her. She pushed him back, inviting, "Why don't you sit down?" It was more like the toppling of a great tree, but it made him less threatening. "Can you sing something?" she asked.

*"Sing?"*

She waved a hand airily. "Never mind. I just always heard they had music at those shows. It doesn't matter. We can pretend."

Suddenly, that's just what Hannah was doing. She took a position in the small space between the cots as if she were a woman who took off her clothes to music for her livelihood. Even the music was there in her head. She didn't sing it though. Somehow she knew that would jar Jake out of his stupefied surprise. As soon as she acceded to his unreasonable demand as if it were a game, the pendulum of power had swung back to her. She wanted it to stay there.

She was careful not to be too theatrical. That fantasy was just for herself. For Jake she was seductive. She

127

looked straight at him as she slowly undid the row of buttons that opened the front of her dress all the way to the flare of her hips. Once that was done, she froze for a moment, her mind a blank. What now? Usually when she undressed, she hiked up the dress and pulled it off over her head. It wasn't pretty though, and she wanted to be pretty. Jake watched every move of her hands with such tight-lipped fascination that she expected him to tell her to stop any minute. He didn't look as if he were enjoying himself any more than she was.

She pushed the dress off one shoulder, then the other, but the thrust of her breasts kept it from falling even when she shrugged. She had to free it. Then it fell, catching only on the lower fullness of her petticoat.

Jake's eyes were no longer on her hands. They had found the puckered tips of her breasts under the shift, lingering like blue flames there at the evidence of her involuntary excitement. She dropped the petticoat and stepped from the pool of clothing to sit and remove her shoes and stockings. The lump in her throat had grown huge, but she tried to smile at Jake, knowing the easy part was behind her. She picked up the discarded clothes, stalling. If only he'd say something to stop her, or just smile at her. But his face looked as if a smile would break it into chunks.

Hannah's fantasy had deserted her, taking her bravado with it. She had nothing left but her determination not to be bested by the complicated man before her—that and fingers that shook when she undid the front of her chemise. She couldn't smile at him and she wouldn't stop. She raised her chin, pulled the cloth from her waistband, and folded back the sides, one at a time, to shrug it down her arms. She turned her back on the hard hunger of his face and picked up what she had just dropped, unsure she could continue.

"Don't stop now."

Hannah was shocked by the sound of his voice. He had looked as though he would never speak again. She froze with the shift clutched to her chest.

"Aren't you going to turn around?"

She didn't move.

"Then keep on like that. Put that thing down and undo the waist. Slowly," he instructed in his thickened voice.

"Jake . . ."

"Don't make me do it for you."

His threat stiffened her spine. She tossed the shift away and undid the waist just the way he had said. She let the pantalettes drift south by agonizing inches, keeping her back to him the whole time. When they were nearly at her knees, she half turned and bent to take out her legs. As soon as she was free, she let him see her body for one brief instant then she used the drawers as cover and grabbed up her shoes to fling them at his head. Neither hit him, but he had to jump up, startled out of whatever mood of dominance she had lulled him into.

She was scrabbling in the pack for something else to throw at him when he grabbed her around the waist. "Leave me alone, you great bastard!" Anger and disappointment roiled in her. She had counted on being able to shame him. She was sure she had, but not enough. His own anger still burned like a live coal, ready to ignite all over again. She fought him all the way down to the cot, amazed that it didn't collapse as they fell heavily onto it.

"You do that so well," Jake said, pinning her with his weight. "Those amateurish little sulks add just the right touch."

"Sulks!" Hannah pushed on his immovable chest. His half-bare forearm pressed across her neck, forcing her to try to tug it down so she could breathe. With most of his upper-body weight supported by that one elbow, he had one hand free to roam over whatever part of her wasn't squashed under him. He made good use of it to make sure she was both aroused and aware of his arousal. She wanted to fight him, but he turned her own body against her. Her only victory—if that was what it was—was a hollow one. She had, it seemed, the same power over him. His roughness turned against his own clothes, and when his great body joined hers, it was once again an act of passion. His anger had found a new target—himself. His departure from her bed was every bit as sudden and mystifying to Hannah as his arrival had begun.

When Hannah emerged from the tent later that day, her cautious creep was met by the utter silence of a deserted camp. Only a squirrel stopped foraging to scold her from a branch as she looked around. Her unwillingness to endure another encounter with Jake had kept her inside as long as she could stand the stuffy tent, but now she was puzzled. She had never been left alone before. What did it mean? Was this another of Jake's harassments? An invitation for her to run away again? If so, Jake was going to be disappointed. She had no intention of being so foolhardy again.

Short of inspecting the tents one by one, or yelling, she knew of no way to be sure she was really alone. Since neither process seemed wise, Hannah walked along to where the horses and mules were tethered. She might be able to learn something there. The three horses and two mules, none familiar to her, told her the camp hadn't been abandoned, but she already knew that. The men had only gone for the day. Perhaps Jake thought his firearms lesson had equipped her for self-preservation. She didn't have the gun, however, so how could it be that? More likely he had simply decided he didn't care what happened to her.

She eyed the horses skeptically, wondering what demonic trait each hid under an innocuous exterior. Except for Jake's mount, Victor, none here had impressed her, but she tried to pick the one she would take this time if she ran away. Though it was only a mental exercise to amuse herself, she planned to notice her choice—a pied brown and white mare with good conformation—in action later. Perhaps she'd ask Jake or Zeb about the horse. It would be a way to learn to be a better judge of horseflesh.

The mare accepted Hannah's pats graciously, ears twitching. "Now why weren't you left here the other day?" she asked with a laugh. "We would get along famously, I'll bet." Then she backed away to return to the campsite.

The other horse had foiled her escape, but she couldn't regret the outcome. At least before today she hadn't regretted it. If she had thought another attempt would end so happily, she would have done it again in a minute, but after Jake's strange anger today she knew that was a dream. They would have no such tender reunion again. From the time the two men had found them together, something had changed in Jake. The older man, Colby, had chided Jake, while the other had been crude. Neither reaction was pleasant, especially for her, but neither seemed justification for the change in Jake.

Back in camp, Hannah forced herself to stop dwelling on Jake and find something useful to do. She went through the stores of food and decided to start supper. She couldn't raise wheat bread in the time remaining, but she could make cornbread and a decent stew. Their store of potatoes, onions, and turnips were low, and what remained was in such poor shape she decided to use them all. Zeb might be angry, but she could see no point in letting good food be lost to spoilage. At least in their bellies the food would be used. She would make the stew thick so it could be watered down to supply two days' provisions if need be. Zeb could decide that.

Once the stew was bubbling, Hannah bathed and

washed her hair and clothes. She dressed in the doeskin pants and shirt while the sun worked to dry her garments spread on bushes. The more she wore the Indian garb, the more she appreciated its simplicity. The pants were more comfortable than the breeches Jake had given her because they were soft against her skin. Lack of underwear seemed scandalous but necessary. If she went back to Knoxville, she wondered if she'd dare be honest about the way she had lived here. Probably not, she decided with a chuckle. Few of her friends there would understand.

She wasn't sure she understood it herself. Why didn't she mind more that she had so little now? This life was hard. She had only to look at her hands to know how hard it was. Her fingernails were frequently ragged, what few were left. The backs of her hands were brown and so, undoubtedly, was her face. Her comb and soap were her most precious possessions, after the locket, of course.

She told herself she didn't mind hardship because she was alive, and being alive at all was miracle enough. That was true, yet it didn't explain her deep satisfaction each time she learned something new or did something that was hard but necessary. She hated to think she would become someone who was incapable of enjoying life's pleasures. Self-denial had never been attractive to her; it wasn't now. What she liked was the challenge. Work was necessary here. It wasn't at all like the boring business of sewing lace onto bed linens that were already overburdened with decoration. That was make-work. Here it was real. She wondered if she would ever go back to Knoxville to live—if she survived.

Certainly she would want to go back to see Uncle Simon again—he of the ginger-colored handlebar mustache and the emphatic eyebrows. How forbidding he had looked to her at first. Later, she had teased him that his fearsome eyebrows were what had made him a rich man, that without the straight line of thick fiery brows, uninterrupted over his nose, the soft heart they disguised would be obvious to everyone. In business he lived up to his eyebrows, but to her and to little David he had been father, playmate, and friend—all in one genial, rotund shape.

What would Simon make of Jake? she wondered. Instinct told her the men would respect each other, but Simon would surely judge Jake primarily by the outcome of this venture for her. If Jake brought her safely through, he would have a staggering reward. Would that please the heart of a self-proclaimed mercenary like Jake?

Tired of thinking about him, Hannah went along the streambed searching out the greens Bright Star had pointed out to her. She gathered what she could carry in her now-dry dress and went to trim off the bitter ends, preparing them for supper. Star had told her the Indian names, but she hadn't been able to retain them. Some she put into the stew, hoping they were the correct ones; others she washed and cut up as a salad of sorts. Even if the men hated greens, they needed them. Beans and jerky were ultimately intolerable as a steady diet, in Hannah's view.

As soon as she heard hoofbeats, she went to the tent. She told herself it was because she wasn't sure who it might be, but she knew she was avoiding Jake. After some time, however, he pushed open the flap and glared at her without speaking. She glared back.

"I was just checking," he said finally. "The last time there was a pot of salad greens waiting, you had run off."

"Not this time, though I was tempted." She said that just to keep him guessing.

He snorted out a laugh and left. She followed him out to tell Zeb what she had done about supper. He was looking balefully at the stew.

"I hope I didn't upset your meal plans, Zeb."

"Naw," he said, grinning at her. "Didn't have none you

could upset."

When she told him about the vegetables, she was surprised to find she had another listener — Jake. He leaned over to taste the stew and told Zeb, "You touch this stuff with anything but a ladle and you're a dead man."

Zeb tried to look offended, but ended up laughing. "Have I lost my job?"

"Don't I wish," Jake muttered. He left without saying anything directly to Hannah. The look he gave her was poisonous.

Zeb patted her shoulder consolingly. "Don't mind him."

"I don't!" she assured him stoutly before he could say more.

Zeb laughed again, his black button eyes gleaming. "Course you don't," he agreed. "Any fool kin see how little you mind him. Almost as much as he don't mind you."

Hannah went back to the tent then, determined not to speak to Zeb again. By the time she came out to eat though, she had forgotten her annoyance with him. Jake was a different matter. She had forgotten nothing about Jake. Every look he gave her was painful. She couldn't even take the pleasure she wanted to from his obvious unhappiness. It was so unnecessary.

Hannah downplayed the men's compliments to her stew as much as possible and left the campfire when the meal was over, regretting that she had not considered that her bit of cooking would show up Zeb. He treated it as a joke on the men as well as on himself, but Hannah couldn't be so lighthearted when Jake scowled at her from afar.

That night for the first time, one of the men brought out a banjo and began to play a medley of popular songs. Songs from the war — even "Dixie" — ballads by Stephen Foster, and hymns mixed without order as either the accompanist or one of the singers made a choice. The voices raised were often tentative, particularly on the verses where the men didn't know all the words. On the choruses they sang out enthusiastically. Hannah, her feet tapping, was on the verge of going back out again to join when she thought better of the impulse.

A second later when Jake came inside, she was glad she hadn't moved from the cot. He shielded a candle flame with his broad hand and put the holder down on the well-trampled earth between them. "He plays well, doesn't he?"

"Yes. Is it Zeb?"

Jake hooted softly. "Zeb? Good heavens, no. He doesn't even dare sing. That's your friend Jethro."

Since it was obvious anything she said would be used against her, she remained quiet. He was stretched as tightly as one of the banjo strings, and after a long pause he sighed deeply and said, "I don't suppose you care to tell me why you kept your cooking a secret?"

Outside, the music ended and the men began to turn in for the night as Hannah considered how to answer him. "It wasn't important. I only helped a little to keep busy."

"Somehow I figured you'd say something like that." Jake bent to pick up the candle and took his saddlebags from the second cot. "We'll be able to keep you plenty busy for a while now. We're moving in the morning again, and not just for one day. Get all the rest you can tonight. You'll need it."

Hannah jumped up to pepper him with questions. She got out only the "where" before he left her, and because he'd taken his pack, she knew he wouldn't be back.

Next morning she was glad she had managed to sleep well even without Jake in the tent. He woke her without ceremony, telling her she was to dress in the cast-off military uniform as before. She nodded to everything, unsurprised until he gave her the revolver she had practiced shooting. It nestled in a holster as he handed it to

135

her. "Wear this and the hat. Zeb will show you the horse you should ride." Before he left, he turned back with a faint smile and added, "You'll be glad to know this one has a name. He's called Ranger."

Now that she was accustomed to the routine of breaking camp and hardened to riding astride, the first day went well for Hannah. Jake was remote but not unpleasant. The second day was more tiring. What concerned Hannah then was the growing tension in the men. She noticed that certain men, Colby and the man who rode with him, disappeared on separate errands, coming back late, with lathered horses to show for their efforts. Pawnee Indians occasionally rode with them, though more often they simply appeared like brown shadows at the edge of their camp to consult privately with Jake. Then, too, their direction this time was east most of the time. After the third day they went primarily north, if Hannah's reckoning was correct. Though she was bone-weary from the constant jouncing ride with its accompaniment of heat, dust, and exposure, she stayed alert both to the surroundings and to the comings and goings of the men and horses. There was even a day when Jake disappeared from their midst.

When they had traveled for five days, Hannah began to feel decidedly uneasy. She wasn't alone in her feelings. Zeb had no more smiles for her and Jake was suddenly all too attentive, though not with the kind of attention she wanted. He confined himself to curt lessons with the revolver and making sure her bedroll—cots and tents were only a memory now—was well away from all the others, with his own positioned as sentinel in the no-man's-land between. Her spot was always as secluded and protected as the topography of their current site allowed. For that Hannah was grateful, but in and of itself it did nothing to allay her mounting anxiety over the following days.

Jake brushed aside all her questions, giving no answers.

Though she was tempted to question someone else, Zeb, for instance, she never did. She felt certain the others were just as ignorant about what was about to happen. Their restiveness attested to that. Though the men talked by themselves in quiet groups, she was sure she would not miss hearing any general announcement. In spite of all that, she slept each night as if she had been bludgeoned by fatigue. In a way she had been, for tiredness and tension were a potent combination.

Because Jake always jostled her awake each morning, when she woke on her own one gray morning she didn't know what to make of it for a few seconds of surprise. Quickly, she sat up and peered around.

She was alone.

Frightened now, Hannah stumbled into her clothes and rolled up her bed. She still had her pack and the gun, but—oh God—her horse. Ranger—where was Ranger? She ran around, looking for some sign that she was mistaken. Jake would come—or Zeb. *Someone,* please, dear God, she prayed.

She could see the charred remnants of their campfire, depressions in the undergrowth where human bodies had slept. She hadn't dreamed the quiet meal last night, the coffee, the horses. Ranger, she remembered. She had to find Ranger.

She stopped running in circles and tried to reorient herself. For a few panicked moments she couldn't find where she had slept and where her bedroll and pack now lay. The sound of her own blood pounding through her head drowned out all other sounds and all coherent thought. She pressed her hands to her face and took deep gulps of air, then she was better. There was an explanation for this desertion. Jake had not left her totally. He had simply let her sleep late for some reason. She would not bolt foolishly. He knew where to find her and she would be waiting. She still trusted his care of her implicitly. He had earned that much from her.

Once she was rational again, she had no trouble finding Ranger. If she'd been listening, she would have heard him moving restlessly in the company of four mules. The mules reassured her more than anything else. The troop would not leave such valuable animals behind, for even after each person had been individually outfitted with provisions, there was still plenty for the mules to carry.

Hannah unhobbled Ranger and led him to her pack and bedroll. She had just finished hoisting those into place when she heard the headlong approach of someone on horseback behind her. For a few seconds Ranger required her attentions just to keep him from bolting, but then she recognized the rider.

"Miss Hatch!" Jethro cried. "You have to come with me. Hurry!"

"What is it? What's happening? Why was I left here?" Hannah faced him, holding Ranger's reins tightly.

"Captain Farnsworth will explain it all. Come on!"

Hannah didn't move. "Why?" she challenged. She knew she was being difficult, even irrational. She had been praying just minutes before for someone to come for her, but now that it was Jethro, she was annoyed. His urgency provoked resistance in her.

"You're in danger here, Miss Hatch. Captain Farnsworth sent me. You have to come!" He advanced toward her without dismounting.

Hannah turned to put Ranger between them, suddenly suspicious. Jake would never send Jethro to fetch her. She knew it. His pawing, rearing horse was upsetting Ranger, and Jethro himself looked to Hannah like the human equivalent of his mount. She circled, keeping Ranger as a buffer while she tried to think.

Gunfire erupted in the distance, and Jethro yelled at her again. Hannah began to try to mount her increasingly alarmed horse. The furious gunplay sounded closer and closer. Hannah got a quick boost from Jethro as he half dragged her into the saddle by one arm. She collected her reins and stirrups instinctively, about to follow Jethro despite her misgivings. The guns had made all that academic.

Jethro wheeled his horse around. "This way!" he shouted.

Hannah tried to turn Ranger. In her panic she gave confusing signals he couldn't follow. He reared instead, almost throwing her. Then another rider pounded past her after Jethro. She followed, sure of herself at last. It was Jake.

She caught up with him in time to see him aim his gun at Jethro and fire. The shots, three of them, were followed by a mighty explosion from behind them. Jethro fell from his horse and Hannah screamed, horrified, as Jake turned on her, the gun still in his hand.

# Chapter Eight

"Jake!" Hannah rose in the stirrups to look where Jethro had fallen. "You killed him!"

Jake put the gun away, his face grim. "I doubt it." He sidled his horse closer to Ranger and, before she could prevent it, plucked her bodily from the saddle, depositing her in front of him as he urged the horse into a run.

This time Hannah wasn't happy to be there. He pushed her ruthlessly forward until she was forced to put her arms around Victor's neck. His own body lay above hers, though not as flat to the horse because of her. All her protests and questions choked in her throat as their pounding pace over the rough ground made breathing all Hannah could manage. Shots continued to ring out around them, and now that she had nothing to do but hang on to Victor for dear life, she listened to them fearfully.

Jake never slacked the jolting pace, but occasionally he lifted himself from her back. Hannah couldn't see anything but Victor's windblown mane and terrifying glimpses of the ground flying by under them. She presumed Jake was looking behind them. Or ahead.

The gunfire seemed to come closer. Jake rose and fired

behind him. The horse lunged on as Jake covered her body again with his own. Now that her mind was clear, she understood that he was protecting her, putting his own body between her and the flying bullets that pursued them. Who was shooting at them? And why?

Just when Hannah was beginning to believe they had outrun their enemy—the volume of shots had definitely diminished—she heard the report of one rifle at closer range than all the others. Jake rose again to shoot, and then, with the sound of another shot, fell back onto her with a thud that took the wind out of her chest.

"Arrggh," Jake groaned.

The sound of it terrified her. Dear God, she prayed fervently, don't let him die! Or fall! she added. If he fell off, she'd never get him back on the horse again. She felt him list to the right and reached behind her to push against his weight, her fingers digging awkwardly into whatever she could grasp. It was only his shirt, but she held fast. His continued moans told her he was alive, but he was no longer directing the tiring Victor. The only bright spot Hannah could find was the lack of continued gunfire from behind. She listened, hoping she was correct. All she could hear was the horse, flagging now, and Jake's rasping breath above her.

"Jake!" Her cry went unanswered. "Jake, oh please, don't fall!"

She could feel him slipping over sideways, and her numbed fingers were powerless to hold him upright. Victor delivered the final blow. The horse, winded and sick of their combined weight on the neck, shook himself from head to heels. Jake slid to the ground, wrenching Hannah's twisted right arm almost from her shoulder socket as she tried to hold him back. Her attempt to keep him seemed to break the force of his fall somewhat, but there was no question in Hannah's mind that Jake had been unconscious before he landed.

Hannah straightened as quickly as her cramped muscles allowed and climbed down from Victor's great height. She was amazed to see that Ranger was still with them, attached by the rein Jake held even as he lay crumpled in a heap at her feet. She knelt to Jake and eased him into a straighter position. He was still breathing with that labored, heavy sound that tore at her so. He was also covered with blood from his shoulder to his waist. Praying aloud, then crying, Hannah sought the wound. She had to stop the bleeding somehow.

It did no good to bemoan her ignorance. She was all the help Jake had. Under all the blood, she found the source—and more blood. It was in the left shoulder where the muscles met over the flat bone. The bone had stopped the bullet, perhaps even been shattered, but all Hannah could do now was try to stop the bleeding.

She found her petticoat in her saddle pack and tore a strip to fold as a bandage and others to tie around him to hold it in place. Fresh blood oozed to the surface each time she had to move him to wrap the ties. The bandage was soaked through when she finished so she tore another strip of cotton and packed that under the ties. It was so tight she could barely get the cloth in place again, but she decided that made it even better. It took a lot of pressure to stop bleeding from so deep a wound. Her job would have been easier with Jake's cooperation, yet she couldn't want him conscious to feel so much pain.

She wiped her bloodied hands on her pants and her soaked brow on the sleeve of her shirt while she tried to think what to do next. The horses probably needed water, but right now they were content to rest. They weren't far enough from the scene of that battle—whatever it had been—to be safe. They had to keep going. But which way? Without Jake, Hannah feared she would only circle foolishly. Better to stay put and see if Jake would recover soon.

She got out her canteen of water and put a few drops on his lips. His tongue came out instinctively to lick at the moisture. She put her face next to his, rejoicing at the sign of life. "Jake," she called with soft urgency. "Can you hear me? Wake up, please, darling. I need you so much. Help me, please." Determined not to jostle him, and entirely unaware of her endearments, she kissed his face, her fingers smoothing and soothing the hair at his brow. He was Jake. He wasn't going to die and leave her. He was too tough for that. That was what she told herself and him, over and over. Hadn't she been told that unconscious people could still hear?

Hot knives of pain in his back made Jake groan and twist. That was a mistake. The pain sent arrows in every direction, up into his head, down his arm and back. God, that hurt! He had been shot. He remembered now. He remembered the impact and his worry that he'd fall off Victor. He must have, too. Victor wasn't soft like this.

Hannah! Where was she? Again he heard his own groan echo through his head. And felt that softness on his face, like — Hannah. Only Hannah was soft like that. He opened his eyes and saw her eyes widen in answer. Tears streamed down over her face. She wiped at them with her wrist, smearing her cheek with blood.

"You're hurt!"

"No. You are." She sniffed loudly. "Oh, thank God, you came back! I was afraid you'd . . . you were going to . . ."

Jake was fully conscious now. "Where are we? How far did we get?"

"I don't know. Not far. When you fell on me, Victor slowed down. He only went a little way. Then you fell off and I couldn't lift you back up. I didn't even try." She sounded apologetic.

"No, of course you couldn't. But I've got to get up. We can't stay here." He clenched his teeth and collected

143

himself for the ordeal of rising.

"I'll help," Hannah said eagerly. "Lean on me."

Using his abdominal muscles as much as possible, Jake slowly rolled upright, then he used his right hand to push off from the ground. He stood finally, then staggered heavily. He would have fallen except that Hannah was there to catch him and prop him up with her body. She reeled under the impact of his weight, but she held firm, her feet planted wide for stability. He clung to her, ashamed of his weakness.

"You . . . poor thing," he muttered. "Am I hurting you? Just one . . . more second . . ."

Hannah said nothing, just held on grimly, willing her legs to hold for him. If he fell again — well, he wouldn't!

He didn't. Before her legs buckled, he eased himself slowly erect to stand on his own. "Bring Victor over here," he ordered tersely.

She hesitated, fearful that he would collapse, but then she sprinted to the horse and dragged him away from his grazing to Jake's side. It was easier for him to lean on the horse than on her. He could really lean and know the horse could support his full weight.

Jake could feel her concern and he rallied. Just as he reached up to the saddle, he felt the tug of something else besides pain. Amazed, he ran his hand over the strips of cloth around his torso. "My God. You bandaged me!"

"Oh, I hope it holds, Jake. I didn't know what I was doing."

"It helps." He felt again, reassured, and gave her a smile. "It helps a lot."

"You bled so much. I don't know whether or not the bone is broken . . ."

"It's not. The pain is different. I can tell." His hand moved as if he would touch her, but he didn't try. "Thank you, Hannah."

She nodded to the horse and asked, "Can I help any

way? God, I wish I were strong!"

"You are. You're the strongest woman I know. I can do this myself though." It wasn't easy or pleasant, but Jake got himself back into the saddle. While he sat and recuperated, Hannah repacked her bag and swung it onto Ranger's back. She pulled him to a rock and used that as a step-up into her saddle.

"Jake? Should I tie you on somehow? Maybe we could loop together our two belts and—"

"It won't be necessary. I feel a whole lot better."

"But riding will bounce you."

"I'll be fine. You've done well. Now it's my turn."

Hannah was more than willing to relinquish control of this expedition. "Do you know where we are?" She wasn't doubting him, just worried.

"I'm pretty sure. We'll see in a few minutes. Stick right behind me." He didn't wait for her agreement and she had to hurry after him. He rode slowly at first, then picked up the pace as he got his bearings both as to the process of riding injured and to the direction he wanted to go. She knew exactly when he recognized the trail he wanted. He flashed a smile back to her and sat easier on Victor's wide back after that. The horse had a smooth gait at the pace they employed, making Jake's ride as easy as possible. They couldn't gallop as before or the horses would collapse, but they pushed forward with urgency.

After what seemed like ages of relentless riding, they came to a river. Hannah no longer speculated whether it was or was not the Platte. It was water for the horses and refreshment for them. She started to dismount, then stopped to look at Jake uncertainly. "Is it safe?"

"For you. I won't try to get down now. Tonight."

Hannah couldn't help but yearn toward the water, but she hesitated to desert him.

"Give me the reins when you're down. Scoot now."

Ranger was already prancing closer to the stream, as

145

eager as she. She slid down and handed up his reins, promising as he had to her long ago, "Be right back." Embarrassed, she scurried to find cover for what she'd had no time to do upon waking. The events of the morning had overshadowed her need; but now it was pressing. She washed her hands and face, leaning over the water, almost mindless with the comfort it gave. Then, feeling guilty that Jake could have no such refreshment, she hurried back to him.

Even if he didn't dare get down from the saddle, Jake was relieved to have a rest. He blessed the overcast sky for saving him from the heat of a typical Nebraska day. While Hannah was gone, he tested himself and the bandage, pleased with both.

She was the most amazing woman he had ever known. Who on earth else would have found a way to stop his bleeding, moving someone as heavy and uncooperative as he must have been?

He watched her scamper along the edge of the streambed, hurried yet innately graceful in spite of the ill-fitting clothes she wore. Until he'd seen her in pants, he'd never considered that a woman could be attractive in pants. Awful as they were, they still emphasized the slender length of her legs and the neat roundness of her bottom. Noting his body's response to his thoughts, Jake had to laugh. If he could feel this way, he was still a long way from death!

She peered up at him anxiously. "You look flushed. Give me your canteen and I'll fill it for you."

He kneed Victor onto the low banking and gave her the flask, watching the way she bent over to reach the water. He led Ranger out so she could get at her own pack. She ripped off some cloth and wet it for him. Now she watched him warily as he washed his face and hands.

"What's the matter?"

"I'm just worried about you. That bullet should come

146

out. You'll get a fever, and I hate fevers."

Her desperate look touched him. It had been years since anyone had worried about him. "I'll be fine. We'll get to civilization soon and find a doctor."

"Are we near a settlement?"

"Not close, but we're on our way."

His easy reassurances didn't begin to touch the depths of Hannah's anxiety. She glanced around nervously. "Should we be out here in the open like this?"

They shouldn't be, but he wasn't going to let her know she was right. It would be feeding her fears. "Relax, Hannah. Lie down in the grass awhile."

"I can't. I'd feel stupid with you perched up there."

"I won't leer at you," he promised, his grin a sample of the look.

Her laugh was unamused. "I know that! Dear God, I'm nothing to look at like this!"

"You think so? Funny, I was just thinking the complete opposite. Those pants have a way of emphasizing some pretty tantalizing aspects of your charm."

"You've just been out in the sun too long," she snapped.

"There's no sun." His wide smile challenged her, but she wouldn't give up her concern.

"Do you think it's going to rain?"

"No, Hannah. It's not going to rain." Part of him was as frazzled as she was. He was worried about everything she was—maybe more so. He knew better than she the reality of their situation. At best it was precarious. But he sat on, smiling down at her, stubbornly trying to lighten her mood. "Give me a smile," he urged. "Please?"

"Jake, really . . ."

"Just a smile?"

It was actually a grimace; turning up her lips didn't erase the strain in her eyes. Nevertheless, he saw that she wanted to please him and was satisfied. She hadn't ridiculed his desire, at any rate.

She had taken Ranger's reins to lead him along to a rock she could use as a step stool to his back. "Don't you want to rest more?" he asked her. "Do some cartwheels? Move around a bit?"

"No, but if I'm hurrying you, we could talk." She looked hopeful. "I need to know what this is all about, Jake. What did Jethro do?"

Jake noted her lack of accusation as she waited next to the horse. He forced himself to be just as nonjudgmental. "You were leaving with him."

"Of course I was. What else was I to do?"

"You could have waited for me."

"After the shooting started? Why didn't you wake me this morning?"

"You looked so tired. I didn't have the heart."

"The heart! So you abandoned me instead." Her tone was bitter.

"I was coming back—"

"Fine," she cut in sharply. "But I didn't know that. You tell me nothing and expect trust."

Jake moved the horse forward, breaking his contact with her eyes. He couldn't stand the accusation there now. "Tonight," he said over his shoulder. "I'll tell you all about it tonight. This is no place to linger."

Hannah ground her teeth in frustration, then made a childish face at his back. Arrogant beast! By the time she was back on Ranger, following Jake, she had restored her usual good humor. The interlude had given her a few thoughts to chew over as she rode, at least one of them most welcome. He had let her sleep out of concern for her well-being, not from indifference as she had feared. That was something—a concession, certainly.

As the afternoon wore on, Hannah could see from the rigid set of his shoulders that Jake was tiring. She moved up to ride abreast and ask, "Shouldn't we stop soon?"

148

"Not here," he said tersely.

She looked around. "What's wrong with here?"

His soft exclamation drew her eyes back quickly. He had stopped to watch something at a distance, a faint line in the expanse of green prairie grass ahead. "That's what's wrong," he told her. "It's a caravan."

Hannah shielded her eyes with her hand. Although there was no direct sunlight, the wideness of the sky, paled by clouds, made anything below it look insignificant. Excitement grew within her. People. Help. She looked at Jake, her eyes shining in expectation of his confirmation that help was at hand. Help for him. His words hadn't penetrated her ride-dulled mind. Now she saw his lips pressed tight, and her concern for him resurfaced quickly. "Are you hurting? Maybe someone there can help. A doctor even?"

"No."

"No? Jake, be reasonable. You need help. Those are people!"

"They're Mormons, Hannah."

"So what? Mormons are people! Don't be absurd!"

"Absurd, am I?" He looked grim. "All right. We'll get close enough so you can see them, then you'll understand. We won't show ourselves."

"Then what's the point? Jake, I mean it. Your shoulder is getting worse every minute that bullet stays in you. Please don't be so mule-headed." She really didn't care for herself, though every human impulse within her urged her to run headlong to these travelers. There were women there, people like herself she could talk to. Obviously, Jake was not so starved for people as she. He had been with men like himself all along, and now he had her. Still, he needed to think of his health, if not her social well-being.

Jake didn't defend his stand, simply moved the horse along in an oblique path toward the extended line of the wagon train. There was no sign from the train that anyone had seen them.

Hannah followed, still resentful but a bit hopeful she could change his mind, though so far she'd had no success in doing so on any issue they'd considered. "How do you know they're Mormons?" she asked.

"This is their own trail west, to Salt Lake City."

"What do you mean their 'own' trail?"

"They generally stick to themselves and avoid the other settlers. They have had some bad experiences. Because of their beliefs." He slanted her a look. "Do you know about them?"

"That the men have several wives?" she tossed back. "Of course. It's their religious belief though. It's their right, don't you think?"

"Of course. Not everyone agrees though. They sometimes find trouble instead of freedom. That's why they follow their own course going west, too. Mormons use only part of the Oregon Trail, mostly where the terrain gives them no choice. This trail is their own, such as it is."

"We're heading for the end of their caravan, Jake. Are you doing that on purpose?"

"You'll see," was all he said.

Soon she did and her heart sank. The last half of the pathetic parade of wagons and carts was made up of women and children, walking in what Hannah could see, even from their somewhat distant watch, was numbed defeat. There were a few carts among the walkers, but they were pulled by children, not animals. Very old women sat in the carts.

Hannah felt Jake's eyes on her as she took in the reality before her. Though she wanted to avoid acknowledging that he was right, she had to look at him. He wasn't gloating.

"But why?" she asked.

150

"I don't know, to tell you the truth. It's their life. Perhaps it will get better once they reach their goal. For now they avoid the rest of the world. They really don't want to visit with us. I'm sorry."

She could see that he was. "I understand. It's just, I hoped . . ." Her eyes filled with inexplicable tears, for them as much as for her hopes. "Won't they stop for the day soon? Those children—some of them are so little."

"Soon, I'm sure, and so will we."

Hannah followed him without comment, her mind's eye still full of that forlorn procession. She didn't speak until Jake arrived at what was to be their resting place. He had chosen well. They had seclusion for the horses and cover for themselves in case of rain, with the inevitable and necessary stream at hand.

"Have you been here before?" she asked Jake instead of showing approval at his questioning glance.

"Here specifically? I don't think so. Why?"

"You seem so sure. Every place you stop is just right."

"You could do the same thing by now. You know as well as I do what we need."

Knowing and providing were two separate issues to Hannah, but she didn't argue. She dismounted quickly to help Jake. All she could do was hold the reins for him, and that he didn't really need. Victor was well trained and quiet, standing more patiently than Hannah ever could. She had chewed a hole through her bottom lip by the time Jake made it to the ground. Helplessly watching his agony was more painful than anything she had ever felt physically.

She unpacked the horses, loosened their cinches, and led them away to hobble them by the water and the tender, fresh grass growing there. She took a while about her task to give Jake privacy, taking some for herself, too. He was walking in the same area when she returned, his gait the careful one of an injured person.

"Just walking out a cramp," he volunteered.

"Food first or the bandage?" she asked to mask her sympathy.

"Water is what I crave, Hannah. Maybe some coffee?"

She scrambled in the packs for a pan and the matches, glancing up once to ask. "Where's a good place for the fire?"

His expression drove all thought of his answer from her. She dropped the pan with a clatter and ran to catch him before he fell. She didn't exactly catch him, only got between his big body and the ground so she cushioned his collapse, making it orderly and less damaging. His skin had a sick pallor that alarmed her.

He wasn't exactly unconscious, more stunned — as if he had been hit over the head. He didn't answer her urgent cries, but sat, his head slack on his neck like a too-heavy flower on a thick stalk.

Water. He needed a drink. She got the canteen and held it to his lips, supporting his head in the crook of her arm. He swallowed what she put in his mouth, but didn't revive. She eased him back to the ground on his good side so she could start the fire and heat water. The wound was the source of all his troubles and to deal with that properly she had to have hot water.

Though the matches were troublesome, everything on the ground was dry and easy to ignite, first leaves and twigs, then larger pieces of wood. She scraped the soft undergrowth to a bare circle of earth as she had seen the men do for each campfire. If Jake hadn't been in trouble, she would have taken a moment to congratulate herself for all she had learned about surviving in the wilds. She started the water from their canteens heating first, then hurried back to peer at Jake. She felt like a large, ungainly moth, plunging back and forth between the fire and Jake, then the stream and Jake. She told herself it was good that Jake had fainted because then her examination of his wound wouldn't hurt him.

But it did. Her first attempts to take off his shirt brought him back to consciousness. "What happened?" he demanded thickly as his head jerked up.

"You just fainted for a second."

"A second? Longer than that, it looks like. You have the fire going." He made it sound like a crime.

"So I do. Now that you're back, you can help me with your . . . shirt." Her voice faded to nothing as he did just that, revealing a thoroughly soaked pad of cloth from which fresh blood oozed to send small rivulets down over the muscles of his back.

"It's bleeding again?"

"Umm, a bit." She didn't know what else to say.

"I broke open when I got off Victor. I felt it."

"Why didn't you tell me?" she demanded hotly.

"What could you do?"

She peeled away the saturated cloth, sickened by what she saw. It looked even worse now. "Should I wash it? I mean, I know I should, but isn't there something more I should do?"

"How bad is it?"

"Bad."

"You're not going to faint, are you?"

Jake's taunting question raised her hackles. *"You're* the one who does all the fainting around here!" she flung at him, incensed that he should question her.

"Good girl," he chuckled softly, reassured by her temper as he wouldn't have been by any avowal she could have made.

When she realized how she had risen to his bait, she sagged, letting him see just what they faced. "Jake, I don't know what to do. I'm not that strong." Irrationally, she was angry at him for being the one who was hurt. He was the leader, the strong one. He had no right to let this happen. If she had been the one shot, he could have

153

carried her safely away from harm. By now he would have had her all fixed up good as new.

"Tell me exactly what the thing looks like, then we'll decide. Start with washing."

His logic made her ashamed of her emotionalism. She got the hot water and prepared a new bandage of petticoat strips.

"Make some coffee while you're at it," he suggested lazily.

"Yes, sir!" Her barked reply reminded her of Jethro, so as the coffee brewed, she asked, "What *did* Jethro do, Jake?"

He groaned loudly, then shook his head at her. "Here she is, a woman who's about to perform major surgery, and she's got to ask questions!"

"What? Perform surgery! Who?" When he just went on smiling at her, she shook her head violently. "Oh, no. Not me, Jake Farnsworth. I'm not doing any such thing!"

"Who else, Hannah?" he asked softly. "It's in my back. I can hardly do it myself. As you've said a thousand times, the bullet has to come out."

"But Jake, I can't! I'm not a doctor. I've got no tools. My hands are dirty!"

He just looked at her, his expression serenely confident.

"Jake, I'll kill you!" she wailed in total misery.

"No, you won't. You'll save my life — again. You've already done it once and you'll do it again."

"I'll ride to the nearest town and bring back a doctor," she promised.

"It would be too late. I've seen men die from wounds like this, Hannah. It happened all the time in the war."

She had a sudden, desperate thought. "You're just teasing me, aren't you? Because I asked about Jethro. This is all just a way to keep from having to answer me." She expected him to laugh and say something like, "It worked, didn't it?"

154

He laughed, but not the way she had hoped. Not with triumph, just resignation. "It could be worse, honey."

That hope extinguished, Hannah stared at him with tears standing in her eyes. "I don't see how," she said miserably.

"Well, it could be in my backside."

# Chapter Nine

While Hannah was still laughing, Jake began to issue orders, orders she had to take seriously. At first she ignored them, but he was as persistent as she was intentionally deaf. She made one last attempt to convince him of his folly.

"Jake, you don't understand. I'm not as good as you are at playing nurse. My hands shake and I get squeamish." Her words rolled off the blank wall of his stony face without effect. When he didn't smile at her mention of his playing nurse, she gave him her final, irrefutable reason. "I'll hurt you," she said in a small, tight voice.

"Will you mind that so much?"

She lifted her chin to keep it from quivering. "Now that you mention it, no. It'll be a pleasure!" But she had to turn away quickly so he wouldn't see that she was lying. She snatched up the two saddlebags and deposited them at his feet. "Find what I need," she told him. "I'll boil more water."

She didn't need the water as much as she needed solitude to get her nerves under control. She told herself it was simple and necessary. She would do whatever she had to. She couldn't let Jake die.

Once reconciled to her fate, she concentrated on the necessary preparations, conferring with Jake about the procedure and their meager supplies. She listened to his every word with rapt attention, aware that once she was under way, he might lose consciousness and leave her on her own. She hoped he would, in fact, especially when she looked at the grisly assortment of tools he had assembled.

He picked up the narrow-bladed knife. "You'll probably have to cut your way to the bullet with this before you can grasp it with these." "These" were sewing scissors, as thin-bladed as the knife, but nevertheless only scissors.

Hannah nodded blankly. There was no purpose served in whining for what they didn't have. Her eyes fixed on the whiskey bottle, then questioningly on Jake's blue eyes. "Courage for you or me?" she asked, trying to smile.

"Neither. It's antiseptic. Even the thread and needle you sew me up with have to be soaked in this. Pour it on your fingers and soak the cloth pad you use to cover the wound. If there's any left over, we'll share and share alike, love."

She carried all but the whiskey away to immerse them in boiling water while Jake prepared himself for the ordeal. She scrubbed and scrubbed her hands with soap and water as hot as she could tolerate. "Don't burn yourself, Hannah. That won't help." One-handed, he was arranging his bedroll, grinning at her as he tugged and pulled the blanket into place.

The moment of truth finally came when Jake was on the bed, waiting for her. She poured off the water, added whiskey, and made sure every surface was covered. Once her fingers were puddled in the whiskey, there was nothing left to do but begin. She took off the inadequate pad of cotton and confronted her task. The blackened circle of skin filled with bright blood that seeped out with every flex of his muscles and every twitch of his nerves. It seemed to small to have caused such damage.

"How's the whiskey supply?"

Hannah wailed, "Oh, Jake, I just got my fingers

157

ready."

He pushed up with his right hand and put the bottle to his mouth for several swallows. The movement produced fresh streams of blood, as the strain on his left side taxed the wound. "Now," he coughed, collapsing. She peered at his face, hoping he was unconscious. One bright blue eye blinked at her. "Please," he murmured, "help me, Hannah. This is good hurt, the kind I need."

She put the knife to the opening and probed carefully. Muscle, flesh, and skin resisted her cautious beginning, and blood welled thickly around the blade. Sure that all she had done was hurt him, she took out the knife. Surely the scissors would serve the same purpose, she reasoned. They were almost as sharp. She worked the ends down the blood-filled gash by feel. Her eyes filled so quickly with tears that she couldn't see what she was doing. It didn't matter. There was nothing to see but the gush of his life's fluid, pouring from the wound.

Jake didn't flinch or scream. She realized she had been waiting for his reaction, worried about that as much as about what she was doing. Once she understood that her tentativeness was only prolonging his agony, she became bold. She probed deeply, praying aloud without knowing she was speaking her thoughts. "Oh, God, help me, help me, please."

The end of the scissors met bone—or was it? She pushed the tip to the side, feeling the limits of the hardness. It moved.

"It's there, Jake. I feel it!"

Grasping it with the scissors' points was something else though. First she had to open the scissors when the press of his flesh around them held them closed. It was a delicate, exhausting process. She could do it only by blocking out her consciousness of Jake as her suffering victim. He cooperated by giving her total silence and physical stillness. She knew such aid was the product of his resolutely controlled will, not insensibility, but she couldn't think about that.

The scissors caught the rough ball of metal, lost it, then grasped it again. She could only draw it out by the most precisely calibrated pressure imaginable. Too much and she would lose the bullet again; not enough would have the same result.

"Oh, God, it's coming. Jake, it's coming!" Carefully, she inched the scissors to the surface, afraid she was rejoicing too soon. Jake needed to know; *she* needed to know. "I've got it! It's out!"

"Don't lose the son of a bitch!" he muttered through clenched teeth as she stared in wonder at the bloodied scrap of metal in her palm. When she looked at Jake again, she saw that he had finally lost consciousness now that his help was no longer necessary. She dropped the bullet next to the pan of tools soaking in whiskey. She had to pour the spirits into the wound and begin sewing up the damage. Grateful that he was beyond pain for now, she dosed him liberally with the alcohol and stitched the jagged edges of skin together. Her prayers, a combination of entreaty and thanks, were incoherent and heartfelt. The whiskey-soaked pad of cotton, backed by more cotton, was last, tied firmly as before. Then she could begin to wash away the blood from his back. She kissed each cleaned area of smooth coppery skin.

"Beauty Woman would have been proud of you, my love," she told his unconscious form. She covered him tenderly with a fresh shirt from his pack, then the blanket, not even wiping away her free-flowing tears.

Now that it was over and he was no longer aware of her condition, Hannah let go of her self-control. She curled protectively around her squeamish stomach, her bloodied hands akimbo, and indulged her need to cry. It was a strangely silent process, as necessary as the operation she had just performed. She had been brave long enough. She never again wanted to extract so much as a splinter of wood from a finger!

She stumbled to the stream again and washed herself. Even her pantlegs were soaked with blood, she found. She took off all her clothes, conscious of the rapidly dying light around her. She'd brought nothing with her to put on, but she didn't care. The clothes soaked while she did the same. She wrung them out with the last of her strength, flinging them onto the banking to dry out overnight. Or not—she didn't care. Her chemise and drawers were easier. Those she carried with her and put on a low branch near Jake. The air raised gooseflesh all over her as she got out her nightgown.

"Now that's the way a nurse should look."

Jake's voice reached her inside the made-over petticoat just before it settled down over her upraised arms. "Jake!" She hurried to kneel by him. "Are . . . are you all right?"

"Very much so, thanks to you."

Hannah's eyes flooded again with tears. "Do you want another drink? There's some whiskey left if you need it."

"Some of that coffee, maybe? You did make it, didn't you?"

"I forgot to give it to you." Then she saw what else she had forgotten, the pan full of bloodied whiskey and cast-aside instruments. Somehow they looked even more gruesome than before.

"Never mind," Jake said, seeing her state of mind. "Help me up onto my side."

"No! You shouldn't move. Please. I'll take care of everything." She put the coffee back onto the dying fire and carried the pan away. At the stream she scrubbed it out and cleaned the blood from everything. She was shaking in a storm of shivers by the time she finished and padded barefoot back to Jake with the tepid coffee.

He drank the few swallows she spooned into his mouth and thanked her, letting his head fall back to the blanket.

"You're cold, Hannah. Bring your blanket here and put it with mine. Let me hold you."

She ached to feel his arms around her. "You'll hurt yourself. I'm not cold. It's just nerves, I think. A reaction."

"I have one, too. I need to hold you. Please."

She needed no other urging. Her tremors were uncontrollable until he pressed the length of his hard body behind hers, his good arm a pillow for her head, the other carefully placed along her side for safekeeping. His breath warmed her ear.

"No more tears, honey. No more fears. You've done it all. Now just sleep, little soldier."


The hotel room, plain, small, and none-too-clean, offended Daniel Veazie's half-opened eyes. It was furnished with only the barest necessities, the bed he slept in, a scarred chest of drawers, and the whore in bed with him. She was the barest of all, he thought with sour humor as he sat up to put his feet on the floor. The woman, Ernestine, immediately rolled over, filling his vacancy and groping the sheets to find him. Repulsed by her odor, a combination of whiskey and cheap perfume, he stood up and made his unsteady way to the chest to dress.

Once a spare man of better than average height, Daniel had begun to spread through the middle. Rich food and abundant whiskey, most of it better than what he had consumed with Ernestine, was taking its toll. He had to tighten his slack stomach muscles to fasten his belt, but as soon as that was accomplished, he relaxed, forcing the leather cinch to slip below his paunch for comfort. Without a glass above the bureau, he struggled to make a neat job of setting his elaborate cravat into proper folds, finally abandoning the project rather than finishing it with his usual flourish. Flourishes were beyond him this morning.

As he was beginning to empty the bureau, a sound from the bed reminded Daniel that he wasn't alone. He dropped the shirts he held back into the drawer and considered Ernestine. She had come to him each night he had been in Columbus, but now he was leaving. He picked up the untidy mass of her clothing, moving slowly — especially bending over — because of his ringing head. He dumped her belongings on the bed beside her and shook her shoulder. He had to step back quickly when her arm lashed out in retribution for his disturbance.

Angered by that and by the resulting clamor in his head, Daniel struck her sharply on the backside and ordered, "Get up." The harsh sound of his voice punished himself as much as Ernestine.

She sat up with an irate squawk, then fell back, groaning.

Daniel pushed her clothes into her face and said, "Get dressed, and hurry up about it." Turning away, he kicked back the top of his trunk and began dumping clothes into it.

He had almost forgotten Ernestine again when she sat up and spoke to him. "What's going on? Where are we going?"

He didn't look at her. "We're leaving."

She made a resentful noise. "I can tell that. What I want to know is where we're going."

Daniel considered telling her that *she* wasn't going anywhere except out of this room and out of his life, but he knew any such announcement would precipitate a scene. He had kept her around for two weeks, mostly out of laziness; nevertheless, on that basis he knew she had already begun to think of him in terms of permanence. Not marriage, of course. She didn't aspire to marriage, nor would she mind that he was still legally tied to

162

Hannah. Ernestine wanted a protector and thought she'd found one in him.

"I have to go to Bellevue."

Ernestine flounced to the edge of the bed with a jangle of bracelets she never took off. "That backwater," she said dismissively. "There's nothing there."

Daniel indulged himself in a smile of triumph as long as his back was to her. Ernestine might be proud of living in Columbus, which she saw as a bustling metropolis, but he knew that in a few years, five at most, Bellevue would eclipse every town in Nebraska for size and wealth.

Bellevue — not Omaha City — was going to be the jumping-off place for the western leg of the Union Pacific's transcontinental railroad. That meant that every piece of construction equipment, every bit of cargo, and every railroad passenger would ultimately have to go through Bellevue to get to the West. And he, Daniel Veazie, not only owned most of the land the railroad needed in Bellevue, but had caused the town Ernestine now dismissed as a backwater to be chosen for that all-important terminal.

First he had bought up the seemingly useless land in and around Bellevue, carefully hiding his interest behind dummy corporations; then he had set about making sure that Omaha City — where everyone believed the railroad would go — was discredited as unsafe. He had made Omaha and the land just west of it seem inhospitable to the white man and his railroad. For months now, wandering bands of hostile Indians had preyed on isolated settlements and wagon trains heading west. No one but he and a few of his trusted aides knew the "Indians" were hired thugs, most of them white men painted and dressed, or undressed, to look like Indians.

Who but he could have conceived of such a thing? It was so simple and so clever.

And it was working even better than he had hoped.

Just the other day rumor of a suspected Sioux uprising had swept Columbus. His sources told him the rumor was true, but that the Sioux's target was their traditional enemy, the Pawnee Nation, not the white settlers streaming west in ever-increasing numbers. To Daniel that only confirmed his belief that the Indians were too stupid to understand their predicament.

Because the Sioux claimed vast reaches of the Nebraska Territory north of the Platte River as their exclusive hunting ground, they resented incursions by other tribes, primarily the Pawnee, into that territory. They didn't understand that the Pawnee, pressed by whites on the east and south, were being forced farther and farther from *their* lands. Instead of all Indians uniting against their common foe, the various tribes continued to wage their petty wars against each other, doing their enemy's work for them. None of them saw that they were doomed.

Given enough time, Daniel was certain the Indians would destroy each other and thus remove themselves from the white man's path. But he didn't have time to wait for that happy occurrence. The railroad wouldn't wait and neither would he. A Sioux uprising on top of the unrest he had caused west of Omaha City would surely bring in the Army—and that would also help force the railroad to take a more southerly route west. Right through Bellevue.

Everything was going perfectly for Daniel.

Absorbed in his thoughts, Daniel paid no mind to Ernestine, who was now dressed. She stood watching him pack a few minutes, her brow furrowed by suspicion. She had not taken care of herself all these years alone by being fondly trusting. She saw Daniel's withdrawal from her written plainly in every move he made.

So he was going to Bellevue without her. Fine. She had no desire to go there ever again. She knew better than Daniel Veazie what was in Bellevue, nothing but trouble in the person of her stepfather, Eben Dawes. It was Eben Dawes who had introduced her to sex at fourteen, then beat her with his belt when she threatened to tell her mother. It had taken her two years to get away from Eben Dawes and Bellevue. It would take a better man than Daniel Veazie to get her back there. But if he didn't plan to take her with him, Ernestine was going to make him pay.

"I gotta go get my things together, too," she announced, putting herself in his way.

"What?" His head came up from the trunk. He focused on her with slitted, unwilling eyes, then said in too-hearty agreement, "Oh yes, of course. Well, run along and pack. We'll stop by for you on the way out of town."

Ernestine wanted to laugh in his face. "I need the carriage to fetch my trunk."

"You can't bring a trunk. We're not going by carriage. It would take too long."

"What's your hurry?" she challenged, adding for good measure, "You're bringing a trunk."

"I'm storing this. We're going on horseback." He closed the trunk and gave her his full attention for the first time. "Of course, if you think that's too hard on you, I'll understand."

*I'll just bet you would,* she said to herself. But Ernestine was too smart to let him see her disbelief. "I'll need money to buy a carpetbag then. I don't have one. And a blanket and . . ."

Daniel took out a wad of bills and peeled off several. Anything to stop her noise, he thought, growing frantic to be rid of her. Looking at her now, he couldn't remember why he had bothered with her. In the harsh morning light she looked coarse and old, far older than she admitted to being, and the red of her hair was as brassy as the streaks of leftover makeup on her face. He had chosen her for that hair color, even knowing it wasn't real. Something about red hair attracted him, promising passion no woman ever showed him. This one was no different than Hannah really. As Hannah had been cold, so was Ernestine, for all her whore's tricks. He wanted her gone.

He got his wish, but only after Ernestine inspected each bill carefully to be sure none of it was the useless Confederate currency. She even came back for more after she got to the door. The size of that roll was too impressive not to give her second thoughts.

In the hall she had third thoughts, and by the time she reached the ground floor, she had a plan for getting more of that money before Daniel Veazie left Columbus. She was so lost in thought she didn't notice the man who passed her on the wide first floor landing. But he noticed her.

"You got rid of the bitch?" he said to Veazie when he was admitted to the room.

Daniel huffed out a disgruntled sigh and explained.

Porter Kell laughed at him. "You're too soft with women. Why should you pay her anything? She's nothing."

Women were a sensitive issue with Daniel. He was fully aware that greater patience with Hannah years ago would have made scrambling around like this in the primitive Western territories unnecessary. Leaving Hannah had been a mistake, not because she herself was anything special, but because of her uncle. Daniel turned away from Kell as he did from thoughts of Hannah's fond uncle, Simon Sargent. He had to be patient now, because then—when it should have been easy—he hadn't been able to abide his wife's foolish chatter. It had been "Uncle Simon this" and "Uncle Simon that" until he'd been ready to choke on his own spleen.

Well, he thought grimly, dear Uncle Simon was about to learn a painful lesson. When his plans for the placement of the transcontinental railroad and depot went awry, Sargent would know better than to cross Daniel Veazie again. As much as Daniel was going to enjoy his own victory, it was knowing that his victory would defeat Simon Sargent that put the apple in the suckling pig's mouth.

Pleased with that image, which he saw complete with Sargeant as the roasted pig, Veazie laughed for the first time. Taking his laugh as agreement with him on how to deal with Ernestine, Kell dismissed her from his mind and began to recite the details of the arrangements he had made for their departure.

Kell had been Veazie's man for two years. In Veazie, he saw the man he wished to become, with minor modifications. He had yet to achieve the older man's polish, but he was working on it. That took time, which he had, and money. Thanks to Veazie and the war, he also had money now.

A Virginian by birth, Kell had recognized the inevitability of war well ahead of the fact and in plenty of time to leave the state. Unlike his soft-headed acquaintances, most of them as poor and landless as he, Porter Kell had had no desire to put his body in front of the Yankee cannons. The idea of fighting to preserve the right of rich plantation owners to go on playing aristocrat had amused him. He valued his life too much to die so that people who would never willingly speak to him could continue to enjoy their fancy dress balls and horse races.

Now that the war was over and the South had lost, he would be able to go back home and pick up the pieces they had dropped. He had several properties in mind to buy, but if none of those worked out, something else would. As soon as this railroad deal went through, he would have money, something the improvident South now lacked. With his luck and foresight, he would soon be well on his way to becoming one of the South's new aristocrats.

Unconsciously, he smoothed the serviceable material of his waistcoat over his chest. Dressed for travel, he presented an unremarkable picture. Unlike Veazie, he didn't stand out from the crowd. His clothes were ordinary, his face clean shaven. He had once tried a beard, but it called attention to his least attractive feature, a spade-shaped jaw that was already too prominent. Because he wasn't tall, he relied on his new Western-styled boots to make up for that lack. Wearing them in Virginia, he thought now, would also give credence to his claim that he had made his money in the West. No one would ever need to know he had been in Baltimore and St. Louis with Veazie.

Kell stood taller as he realized how far he had come toward his goals. Wisely, he stayed away from the women and booze that gave Veazie no comfort in spite of the rigor of his pursuit. This morning, seeing his boss shaky and red-eyed yet again, Kell was glad time was running out on their venture. Veazie didn't know how to wait. He needed action and immediate results or he lost patience and did something stupid. The trip to Bellevue would keep him out of trouble and make him feel he was accomplishing something at the same time.

As if to confirm Kell's assessment of his character, Daniel poured a shot of whiskey and drank it down. "I've had enough of this dump to last me a lifetime," he said as soon as his reaction to the alcohol permitted him to speak.

"Even this place will grow," Kell said equably. He had no love for any of these raw Western towns, including Veazie's precious Bellevue. He only wanted to soothe the man and get him under way.

His remark pleased Daniel, who laughed again. "It will, won't it? Think of it! Civilization will even come to the Grand Hotel of Columbus because of us." His lips curled into a sneer as he named the hotel.

"Tonight you may wish you were back here," Kell

168

remarked, knowing it was true. Veazie rode and handled horses like a man born to wealth, but he so hated being without amenities that he sometimes took out his irritation on the horses.

The liquor had begun to make Daniel's head feel better, and his mood became reflective and almost tranquil. With his plans so near fruition, he didn't mind their present inconveniences. He clapped Kell's back jovially and asked, "Did you ever think back when we were dodging authorities on both sides of the fence in Baltimore and St. Louis that we'd end up here?"

Kell laughed with him, willing to humor him for now. But still he couldn't resist adding a note of reality to the rosy picture Veazie painted. "Back then I thought we'd end up in jail or hanging from the end of a rope."

Daniel refused to relinquish his expansive temper. Talking about his success was one of his favorite pastimes. "You didn't. Not seriously," he argued. "You had faith in me even when Sargent scared off everyone else. I won't forget that any more than I'll forget the tricks that bastard pulled to thwart my every move. When I think—"

Kell urged his arms into the coat he held, interrupting, "Don't think about it now. We have to go." He had heard it all before, including Veazie's promise of undying gratitude. It wasn't a promise Kell intended to rely on. Promises were cheap. He was going to leave Veazie carrying hard cash. *That* he'd be able to take to the bank, not Veazie's windy words.

When Veazie turned back to the trunk, Kell caught his arm. "I told you not to worry about the trunk. I've arranged to have it shipped to Bellevue. It can stay here until the agent sends for it."

But Daniel only retrieved his whiskey bottle and put it into the carpetbag, quelling any comment Kell might make with a look. If he had to sleep on the ground tonight, he was going to have whiskey available.

Kell said nothing. Even his face remained blank because just then a loud thump brought both of them around to stare at the door in surprise. Before they could gather their wits to speak, someone outside began pounding in earnest. Raising his hand in warning to Veazie, Kell strode to open it, his gun at the ready.

The man who fell in at his feet panted with exertion and smelled of horses and rank sweat. "Thank God you ain't gone yet," he said to Daniel.

"Monty?"

"What's wrong?" Kell demanded.

"They got away," Monty told them. "The ambush didn't work, except backwards. We lost more men than them. Farnsworth got away. It was a trap for us."

"Jethro must have given it away," Kell said to Daniel.

"Stupid pup! I told you not to trust him!"

"He was all we had."

"What about Jethro?" Daniel asked Monty. Then, seeing that the man was still laboring to breathe, Daniel took out his whiskey and handed it over.

Refreshed by a long pull at the bottle, Monty answered. "Shot. Prob'ly dead. The Injun got away and some of the others. I come here to tell you."

"The men left will go to the camp outside Omaha," Kell said, thinking out loud.

"I know that!" Daniel spat. "That's where we have to go." Worried now that his careful planning would be in vain, his temper flared. "Did they get their hands on anyone? Did they take anyone?"

"Them?" Monty was confused.

"No. You. Jethro. Did they take any of our men alive?"

"I didn't wait to see after the Injun took off. I come here."

Kell clapped his shoulder in approval. "Good man. Stay here and sleep. The room is yours." Let the hotel worry about evicting Monty, Kell decided, trying to hurry Veazie

170

out. He managed, but not before Daniel retrieved the whiskey bottle to take along.

Ernestine was waiting for them at the front door, her possessions in untidy packages spread at her feet. She called out and waved as soon as she spotted them, unfortunately several seconds before they noticed her. They slowed briefly in surprise, then walked faster. By the time they reached her, they were sprinting. Kell tried to run interference for Daniel, but Ernestine deftly moved to avoid being cut off from her quarry.

"Daniel!" she shrieked. "Where are you running to?"

His pace didn't flag. He saw her determination and knew the possibility of bodily injury as he ran her down wouldn't deter her. But money would. He tore off some bills and threw them, clearing their path to the door.

Then they were gone and Ernestine was left behind. Moving quickly, she gathered up the money before anyone else could get to it. She counted it, added it to the stash in the bodice of her dress, and collected her parcels to carry them away, wearing a smug smile.

She walked rapidly once she reached the street, eager to get to the safety of her room and tuck away her windfall. The money in her bodice was hers and hers alone as long as Hank never found out about it. With him busy waylaying Veazie and Kell on their way out of town, there was no reason for him to discover it, but she had learned to be cautious. He would try to cheat her when it came time to split what he got from the robbery; she expected that. It was a game he played, never knowing she played it, too, and played it well.

And today, thanks to Daniel Veazie, she held the winning hand.


Hannah came slowly awake, prodded by a vague sense of foreboding. She felt responsible for something that weighed her down. The first twittering of the birds called to her, urging her up, but she couldn't move. She turned her head and discovered that Jake had moved over her in his sleep until he was almost on top of her back, pressing her into the ground.

Extricating herself from his weight was a ticklish process. She didn't want to disturb his sleep or hurt his shoulder. Moving inch by careful inch, she eased forward, continuing to prop him up. Inevitably, there came the moment when she had to let go. Jake's shoulder fell several inches when she moved.

He groaned loudly as the sudden drop jarred him. Either the pain or his own protest brought him partially awake. In that state, he moved too quickly, then came awake on a stifled curse.

"Oh, Jake, I'm sorry. Can I help?"

Conscious at last, Jake was able to call on his self-control. Every move was stiff and obviously painful, but he made no further outcry as he struggled up. Hannah helped. At least she tried to.

"Do you want to try standing up?"

"Eventually. Not now." In spite of the early morning chill, perspiration filmed his forehead and stubbled upper lip. Turning only his head, he sought something behind him.

"What do you want?" Hannah asked.

"A tree."

She looked at him blankly. There were box elders and elms all around them.

"To lean on."

While Hannah wished for the strength to rip one from the soil to put it at his back, Jake began a hitching, crablike progression to the nearest support. It hurt her to watch his effort. Once he was settled, she brought the blanket to tuck around him, using the edge to wipe his face. His eyes were closed in apparent exhaustion.

With no idea whether or not he was conscious, she knelt before him and whispered, "What can I do?"

His eyes opened, their blueness startling against the shadows and lines strain had etched in his face. "I'm all right now. I was just stiff."

Hannah was touched that he wanted to reassure her. "Should I check your bandage?" Just the thought of it made her shudder with apprehension.

Jake noticed and shook his head. "Tonight will be soon enough. It feels good."

"I'll bet it does."

"It feels like hell, Hannah, but that's the way it's supposed to feel. I meant the bandage is tight." He managed a smile. "You're cold. Go get dressed and see about some coffee. Maybe this time you can arrange to have it hot."

Even that obvious attempt to annoy her didn't work. She smiled wanly, shaking her head that he should think her so easy to rile. "I'll try," she promised.

It felt good to be busy. She took the doeskin pants and shirt when she went to the stream to wash and dress, knowing the Union Army clothes she'd washed last night would never be dry. She moved them to another bush, where they would catch the morning sun.

A scolding squirrel watched as she started the fire and made coffee. Fingers of light showed above the trees behind Jake, but she couldn't tell whether he watched her or dozed. She wanted him to rest but worried that he might lapse into unconsciousness again.

When she returned to his side to check on him for the second time, Jake laughed her away. "Stop pestering me, will you? I'm not going to die, unless it's from thirst waiting for that coffee."

Hannah's self-control slipped. She tried to scramble up from her knees and get away before she disgraced herself, but he heard the first sniffle of her tears and grabbed her with his right hand. Although she stiffened, she couldn't pull away.

"You're crying."

"I am not!"

He didn't argue, just raked her face with his piercing eyes, searching for the cause of her distress. "Are you hurt?"

The concern in his voice doubled her anguish. "No. Just let me go." She tugged on her arm without effect, reluctant to wrench away and jostle him.

"Sit down." When she didn't yield, he added, "Please, Hannah."

She collapsed more than sat, still struggling with her volatile emotions. Left alone, she could have regained her equilibrium, but under his silent scrutiny, that was impossible.

"You've never cried before," he stated simply.

"Of course I've cried, hundreds of times."

"Not with me. Not *for* me. Even last night you didn't cry. Why —"

"How would you know?" she protested scornfully. "You passed out."

He gave her a wolfish grin and caught one of her tears with his forefinger. "You have a soft heart."

"And you have a soft head." She tried to fling the words at him, but they had no sting.

He laughed. "I think you're right, little Hannah." He leaned forward and kissed her wet cheeks. "All the same, I thank you for your tears. It's been a long time since anyone has cried for me."

Hannah ducked her head from him, getting up quickly before he could see how affected she was. "I'll bring the coffee," she mumbled, turning away.

She felt his eyes on her as she fussed at the fire across the small clearing from him. She wanted to rejoice at this small evidence of vulnerability in him. It was hard

174

though. Whatever it was he felt for her—lust mixed with gratitude—it would never be enough. He was too strong, too independent to need her the way she wanted to be needed. She already knew the heartbreak of giving herself to a man who didn't want all she had to give. She wouldn't make that mistake again.

When Jake had his coffee, she served up the porridge, her mind busy with plans for the day. She would wash and dry Jake's clothes and perhaps line their bed with leaves and moss to make it softer. It wasn't going to rain today, but it would soon. There was a leaden feel to the air that boded badly for them. She would have to make a shelter somehow.

Jake interrupted her thoughts by putting aside his bowl and getting to his feet. She jumped up to help and nearly toppled him over in her eagerness. He cut off her apologies, saying, "Get packed up now. I'm going to wash up and then we'll go."

"Go! But Jake—"

"We can't stay here."

"But surely we're safe now," she protested. "We went so far."

"We're only steps ahead. We're being followed, Hannah. Count on it."

"But why?"

"I can't explain now."

"You can't ride like this. You can't even mount up."

"I did it yesterday. I can do it today," Jake said, walking off toward the stream. Now that he was up and moving around, he felt better. He had lost blood, but his bandages had kept that to the minimum. He could manage, thanks to Hannah. She had more than repaid him for thinking of her yesterday.

Hunkered down by the streambed, drying his face and hair, he had to laugh at that. Since the beginning, he'd done nothing *but* think of Hannah. He could hardly take credit for that. Besides, if he hadn't been obsessed with her, he might have been more on top of the situation with Jethro. Perhaps they could have used him for their own purposes. They could have turned that ambush completely around. . . .

Pointless thoughts, Jake chided. It was done. He had to keep going. They were pursued, probably by Spotted Pony, who could track a bee through the air. Their only hope was that, in his arrogance, the Indian would underestimate them. He probably wouldn't be distracted even if he got drunk, which he frequently did. Jake didn't dare count on that for their safety, because, even drunk, Spotted Pony could follow the trail they were leaving. In this country it was impossible to hide their direction. Even Jake could track through grass and bush, which meant it was child's play for Spotted Pony.

Jake ran his hand over his whiskers, deciding not to take the time to shave. They had to push themselves today. It would rain soon, maybe even today. He and Hannah had to press their only advantage, a slight head start.

As he expected, Hannah was ready. She watched him mount up onto Victor with anxious eyes. A quick look at their abandoned campsite pleased him. Since the evidence couldn't be obliterated, he was glad the story it told about them was false. It looked well used, as if they had lingered long into the day. He could only hope Spotted Pony would buy the story and grow careless in pursuit.

Puzzled by the way Jake looked back at their campsite, Hannah turned to study it over her shoulder. It had been a good stopping place, one she had no desire to leave behind. She was tired of living on the run. She wanted permanence. Every impulse of her being cried out that Jake wasn't well enough to keep going. She wanted to shelter him and care for him until he was strong again. Did he want that, too? Was that what he thought about when he looked back?

They headed east toward the lightening sky. There would be no sun today, just clouds, and there would be no stopping, just more riding, more running. Hannah continued to gaze longingly behind her until the bushy woods were lost in the surrounding sea of green, unwilling to give up her dream of peace and rest.

Finally though, she faced forward and pressed her knees to Ranger's sides, urging him on to follow Jake.

## Chapter Ten

The rain held off until well into the night. Hannah heard it spatter the leaves sheltering their bed and felt a curious sense of satisfaction. She should have been dismayed, since it would be hard going on tomorrow and she was deeply concerned about Jake. Her satisfaction, however, came from the fact that they had anticipated this problem and met it head-on. It gave her hope that all their problems could be handled as effectively.

Tempted simply to burrow closer to Jake, instead Hannah forced herself to crawl out from under the blanket and check to be sure he wasn't getting wet. She retucked his feet, aware that all her moving around had failed to rouse him. She wasn't surprised. He had barely managed to stay awake long enough for her to change his bandage. Except for brief rests, more for the horses than themselves, they had ridden all day, stopping only when sunset extinguished the light. She was tired, but Jake was exhausted.

When she returned, Jake wrapped her tightly in his arms, the only sign he gave that she had disturbed his sleep. His warmth comforted her, making her feel cherished. He was warm, but not too warm. His wound showed no putrification. With so much right, what was the harm in a little rain?

By morning the harm was obvious. The rain showed no sign of easing. Although heavier than when it had started, it had none of the wind-driven ferocity of a localized storm, the kind that would soon pass. The vast Nebraska sky had disappeared into a seamless gray shroud that pressed down from close above, endlessly generating steady, dispiriting rain.

Jake woke first. He had kicked the blanket away, exposing his feet. In pulling them back under the covers, he yanked free of Hannah and brought her rudely awake.

She protested the loss of her dream as much as the jolt to her body.

"Sorry," Jake muttered, sitting up. He tried to tuck the blanket around her, but she followed him up.

"Are you all right?"

"Just wet. The roof seems to leak."

She laughed and moved closer. "In my dreams we were by a waterfall. The sun was shining and—" She broke off with a cry of alarm. "Your feet are like ice cakes!" Before he could stop her, she was on her knees, chafing one bare foot between her hands.

"Hannah, for God's sake, stop it!"

She placed that foot between her knees and reached for the other. "You got wet, Jake."

He pulled away angrily. "And I'll get wetter before today's over. Don't fuss so."

Stung, Hannah stared at him, her eyes wide.

He didn't apologize, but he touched her cheek gently when she drew back in offended silence. "I'm all right. Let's get dressed. Put on everything you can. It's going to be a long wet day."

She didn't argue. In fact, she didn't speak again except to exchange essential information. Jake found he missed her chatter. Even when she fussed, the sound of her voice was cheering. He tried again to get her talking without

179

going so far as to apologize for his shortness. "By nightfall we'll have a roof over our heads if we can make good time."

Although Hannah was intrigued, she didn't want Jake to know. She looked around at the bleak landscape. "I don't see how you know which way to go. Or do you? Which way is east?" she asked resentfully. They were already astride the horses, ready to ride.

"Look at the rain," Jake said.

"I am. What else is there to see?"

"The wind is from the west. We go the way the rain is blowing."

*Blowing* wasn't the word Hannah would have used, although she could see a slight slant to the fall of water. "How do you know the wind is from the west?" she challenged, still unconvinced.

"It's been coming from there all along. Haven't you noticed? It's been at our backs every day. It's the prevailing wind pattern."

"Couldn't it have changed?"

"It could have, but it hasn't."

"How can you tell?"

"By the way the grass grows, for one thing. And I chose our bed to lie east of the bushes. See?" He pointed back to where they had slept, then forward. "We just keep going that way. And anyway—" he paused to grin at her knowingly—"I've been here before."

"Here?" Hannah looked around, bewildered. How could he distinguish this clump of bushes from any other?

Instead of explaining, Jake nudged Victor into a trot. Still annoyed, Hannah followed without asking any of her eager questions. He gave information as sparingly as if she were his enemy. She hated the way it made her feel. Was he protecting her or himself? And how could there be any difference after all they'd been through together?

Too tired to seek those answers, Hannah consoled

180

herself that Jake knew where he was going. She concentrated on imagining the "roof" they would share tonight. She pictured everything from a cave in the bluffs she had seen in southeastern Nebraska to a log cabin impossibly transported from Tennessee. Whatever the structure, Hannah asked only that it be dry, safe, and theirs alone.

When Jake finally stopped and slid wearily from the saddle, Hannah cried out, "Jake! What is it?"

He lifted his head and looked back at her. "We're here."

She looked around, unable to see anything but rain and grass. "But —"

"Come on, Hannah. Get down." He was already loosening Victor's cinch and pulling up the stirrups. Ranger tugged against her grip on the reins and shook his head, demanding that he be allowed to join Victor munching on the wet grass at their feet.

She dropped the reins and dismounted stiffly. As Jake had, she clung to the saddle while her legs grew accustomed to supporting her weight again. She could have fallen asleep right there, but Jake took down her pack and prodded her into action. "Come on. You can rest when we get inside."

Inside? Roused from her stupor, she looked around blankly, then followed Jake. It was all she ever did, it seemed. Why change now? Even when he bent over, she didn't understand what he was doing or why. Then she saw it and stopped dead to stare.

She stood before a huge mound, a house covered with grass. In daylight she would have seen it at once, but the murky, almost underwater gloom of rain and dusk had combined to blend the mounds into the surrounding plain. She dove head first through the low doorway after Jake.

"It's a house!" she exclaimed, her face alight with wonder.

Jake couldn't see her expression in the dark, but the

181

delight in her voice lifted his sagging spirits. He dropped the packs to the earthen floor and straightened. Her pleasure had given him the strength he needed to complete one more job. "Horses," he said to explain where he was going.

Hannah barely noticed his departure. She was totally caught up in her investigation. Although it was dark, she could sense the ample dimensions of the structure. The floor was smooth and firmly packed, the roof inches above her head. Jake would be able to stand in the middle without stooping.

As her eyes adjusted to the diminished light, she moved around cautiously, reaching in front of her for possible obstacles. In the center of the room the floor fell away suddenly into a depression. The fire pit, she realized. Kneeling, she groped the area, hoping to find fuel ready to burn. The smoky odor told her she had the purpose right, but there was no stacked wood waiting.

She moved on, trying to complete the circle before Jake returned. At the thought of Jake she paused to listen for him. It was silent. She couldn't even hear the rain. Unlike the tent, which rang like a drum in the rain, the sod roof silently absorbed water. Yet it didn't leak. The house was damp, but so was she. Her clothes were soaked.

She heard a sound from the entrance and turned. "Oh, Jake, it's just wonderful. It's like a . . . Jake?"

Alarmed that he didn't answer, Hannah scurried back and almost fell over Jake. He had collapsed in a heap just inside the door. She fell to her knees and patted him frantically, trying to find out if he was hurt. Everywhere she touched, his clothes were cold and wet. She knew he was exhausted. All that on top of being shot was injury enough to fell an ox.

He had landed face down on one of the packs. She scrambled in the other for matches. Light was her first priority. Holding the sputtering flame before her, she found enough dried grass near the fire pit to start a small blaze. There was no wood anywhere within sight, but Hannah found something else almost as good—dried buffalo dung. It was the Pawnee's fuel of choice, according to Bright Star. Gratefully, she fed the tiny fire until she was sure it wouldn't go out. She didn't want to waste their precious matches.

Now that she could see beyond her nose, she found that one area had been partitioned off from the rest. The walls were skins, hanging from frames that extended almost to the roof. She carried Jake's pack to this "bedroom" and quickly made a pallet for him out of his folded blanket. His extra clothes were damp, but not wet. Somehow she had to get him changed and bedded down—not an easy task unless he could help.

Leaving Jake resting on his stomach, Hannah unbuttoned his coat and shirt to pull them off. When she touched his chest, she knew she had found the reason for this latest faint. He was burning up with fever.

Hannah knew one thing about fever. It had killed David.

She began tearing at his clothes. His wound had festered after all. He was going to die. She turned his shoulder toward the fire as she undid the bandage with trembling fingers, terrified at what she would find.

It looked the same. Not pretty; not healed. But no worse. Her ragged stitches held. There was fresh seepage of blood and fluid from the wound itself, but the way he had just fallen could have caused that. The reddened swelling around it was no worse, just very hot—like the rest of him. It even smelled the same. There was none of the dreaded sweet, sickish odor that she had heard about during the war, gangrene—just whiskey from the packing and the normal, masculine scent of Jake's skin.

Hannah recovered the wound, feeling both relief and fear. If it wasn't his wound, what was it? Pneumonia?

Was that any better?

Jake began to moan and move restlessly, flailing his arms and legs. She could see tremors ripple the muscles under his bare back. When she put her hands on him, he flinched and tried to roll away.

She spoke to him urgently, calling his name, needing to rouse him enough to gain his cooperation. "Jake, you've got to help me."

He turned his head toward her as if he understood.

She tried to insinuate her shoulder under his arm, but he shrank from her touch. The process got him sitting upright, however, so Hannah felt she was making progress. She continued tugging him and urging him on. When he wrapped his arms around himself, she unwound one and put it over her shoulder. Somehow, the combination got through to him. He staggered to his feet and they lurched off. She steered him to the walled alcove. Before she let him fall onto the bed, she undid his pants and pushed them down.

Once he was down, she took off his boots and the rest of his sodden clothes. She dragged her pack over and found the second blanket, quickly wrapping him in it. His teeth began to chatter noisily as he continued to shake with cold. She rubbed his chilled feet and started to put them on her legs as she had in the morning. But her doeskin trousers were stiff and too cold to give either of them comfort.

Without a second thought, she peeled off her wet garments. Pausing only to throw more of the dried buffalo dung onto the fire, she crawled naked under the blanket with Jake. His arms tightened around her like iron bars, pulling her tight against his overheated body. It seemed incredible that he could also be cold, yet he shook like a man possessed by demons. The heat of his body was at first welcome to her, then oppressive, but she didn't try to move away. It would have been impossible to

184

break his grip anyway.

In time his shaking eased and he felt warm enough to rest. Hannah fell asleep then. But her rest didn't last long. Inevitably the cycle changed. Now he was hot. He threw off the cover and pushed her away, seeking a different kind of relief. She pulled on the shirt she'd set aside for him earlier and put one of the cooking pots outside to collect water. Using his wet shirt, she bathed his face, arms, and chest to cool him down. She spooned water into his mouth and was rewarded when he swallowed. At times he even held a cup and drank to satisfy his raging thirst.

Between Jake's bouts of temperature extremes, Hannah slept either beside him or in his arms, too tired not to grab at the odd moment for rest. When she hovered in that uneasy state between sleep and wakefulness, she worried about Jake. He was so strong, he just couldn't die. But people did die from fevers. She knew that better than most. All through the night she tended him, bathing him, plying him with water, warming him with her own body, hoping to break the fever.

She barely knew it was morning when she dressed in Jake's wet shirt and went outside. The rain fell unabated. Jake was resting, and she needed a change. She had used most of the available fuel already and was worried about getting more. She had no idea where the horses were either. She arched her back and stretched, looking off idly into the rain.

Straightening suddenly, she gave a small cry and broke into a run. Their house was not the only one here. They were in a village. Perhaps there were people!

She found several more sod houses, most bigger than theirs. She found the hobbled horses hidden away behind another sod mound. She even found more fuel. But she and Jake were the only people; the village was deserted. Unwilling to be disheartened by her discovery, Hannah consoled herself that she really hadn't expected to find people.

She took back as much of the dried dung as she could carry tied up in the front of Jake's shirt. Her inspection of the houses had assured her that theirs was the best. It was not only smaller and therefore easier to heat, but the only one with the animal skin partitions intact. The others had all been taken down and carried away.

As she went inside, she wondered if Jake would be able to tell her about this place. She decided that it was the permanent home of a Pawnee tribe. But if so, why had they left?

The smoky air inside was oppressive. Apparently very little smoke found its way out through the hole in the roof over the fire pit. She had noticed outside that she couldn't see their smoke because of the rain. She dumped the fuel by the pit and again retrieved the pan of water from outside. It wasn't perfect, but they had shelter, heat, water, and food. What more could she want except for Jake to recover?

She gave Jake another drink and ate a bit of jerky. Then she made some weak coffee, deciding that hot fluids would be good for Jake, too.

Later, Hannah would recall those few moments of contentment as the calm before a storm. Instead of getting better as the day wore on, Jake's condition grew worse. He became delirious. He shouted incoherent commands and tossed about, his limbs jerking spastically at times. Once he almost knocked her into the fire.

After what seemed hours of turmoil, he grew calmer and she rested beside him, her hand on his still-hot brow. He opened his eyes and peered into her face as if he were really seeing her for once. His tongue worked to wet his lips and he rasped out a demand for water. When that need was satisfied, he sagged back again onto the blanket.

Disappointed that he hadn't said anything more than that, Hannah touched his face. "Jake?" she called softly. "Can you hear me?"

He mumbled and tossed, pushing her away.

She wanted to cry. What if he recovered physically, only to have his mind deranged from the fever? She knew it could happen. David's doctor had warned her it might happen to him. She put the wet cloth to Jake's face and chest again, sponging him down with renewed zeal. She wouldn't let that happen to Jake.

As she turned away to put the cloth back in the pan, Jake took her by the wrist and pulled her toward him.

Hannah was surprised but willing, especially when she saw his expression. She smiled at him with trembling lips. He was better. He knew her. There was a look of such deep affection on his face that tears came to her eyes. She melted against him.

"Caroline," he said on a hoarse choke. "Oh, honey . . ."

*"What?"* Startled, she pulled back from him, shaking with outrage. Strong as he was, he was no match for her at that moment. She had forgiven him for striking out at her, but to call her by another woman's name! And in such a loving voice.

That was what broke her heart. Whoever this Caroline was, Hannah had no doubt that Jake loved her. He might be out of his head, but that only meant what he said was completely honest. A man in his condition wasn't capable of dissembling. Not even Daniel's defection hurt as much as this. And he didn't even know.

She stared at him, wanting desperately to question him, but the moment was gone. He had fallen asleep, his eyes sunk into their shadowed sockets. At another time she would have pitied the strained, sick look of him. Instead, she pulled the blanket up around herself and sat like a stone, watching for the return of that expression.

It never came. She fell asleep waiting and Jake gathered

her back into his arms with neither of them aware of what they were doing.



Late in the night Hannah woke, prodded by a feeling that something had changed. She was stiff and uncomfortable; her left arm, trapped under Jake, had fallen asleep. She sat up, rubbing the pins and needles out of her arm, and looked at Jake. He had flopped onto his back as soon as she moved, and his mouth had fallen open. His breathing was deep and regular and . . . yes, he was snoring!

The homely sound filled the little sod house. It wasn't what had waked her, but now that she heard him, she felt a great sense of well-being—not to mention an irrepressible need to giggle. Somehow, the fact that Jake would hate having her watch him sleep open-mouthed and snoring made the whole thing irresistible. He didn't normally snore; at least she had never heard him before. Her father had snored, however, and hearing Jake took her all the way back to her Ohio childhood. Her mother had sometimes teased her father when he fell asleep in his chair, but more often she only smiled at him gently, with love in her eyes, and told Hannah that snoring was the sign of a man at peace.

Hannah's lips turned up in unconscious imitation of her mother's remembered smile. Even in the dying light of the neglected fire she could see that Jake was finally better. He had slept many times before, but never with his color so natural and his body so completely relaxed.

She got up to tend the fire, adding just enough of the dried dung to keep it going. Dressed in the nightgown she'd improvised so long ago, she padded softly to the door and pulled back the flap. It was still raining, but not, she thought, as hard as before.

"Hannah?"

If there had been any kind of door frame, Hannah would have hurt her head on it, so quickly did she come erect.

"Jake?" She ran back to him and stood looking down at him, her face wreathed in a huge smile. "Oh, Jake, you're back."

"Back? Where have I been?"

She sat down and put her hands on his cheeks. Under the growth of dark whiskers, grown out enough to be soft, his skin was warm and damp—no longer hot and dry.

"You've been sick. I was frightened to death, Jake. How do you feel?"

He laughed dryly. "Like I've been sick, I guess. How long have we been here?"

"Oh, just forever, it seems." When he looked alarmed, she explained. "It's really only been a day and a half. You passed out as soon as we got here. You had a terrible fever, Jake. You were cold, then hot. You were even delirious for a while."

Reminded of that, Hannah drew back from him. That he knew her now didn't make up for that wrenching experience. He knew everything about her, about Daniel and Uncle Simon—everything. But what did she know about him? Very little. She didn't even know what he was doing out here in the wilds of Nebraska or why he had been shot, much less who Caroline was. He had saved her life once and cared for her when she needed it. Now she had returned the favor. That made them even. She didn't begrudge him anything she had done, but now that he was better, she would have to keep her distance from him.

Jake sensed her withdrawal immediately. "I'm sorry, Hannah. I must have given you a pretty bad time."

Even though she had been the one to initiate this retreat from intimacy, Hannah resented the polite distance of his formal apology. It wasn't like the Jake she knew. That

Jake would rather be drawn and quartered than forced to apologize. "You have no reason to apologize, Jake. You were sick."

And she was going to cry if she had to go on talking to him like a courteous stranger. Her piece said, she moved to get up, suddenly uncomfortably conscious of his nakedness and her near-nakedness in the light nightgown.

Jake caught her arm and held her in place. "Did I hurt you?"

"No, of course not. I told you you didn't." Reluctantly, she met the honest concern in his eyes and some of her brittle control gave way. "Really," she added softly.

He wasn't convinced, but he let her go. To do what though? she wondered wildly, looking around. "Would you like something to eat? Or drink?"

"I want to get up."

"Oh, Jake, I don't think that's a good idea. You're bound to be weak."

"All the more reason to get moving," he snapped. "We can't stay here like this." He began pulling himself up, using the woven willow frame of the partition for support. Hannah hurried to help, only to be waved away impatiently. He swayed on his feet, but stood, defiance in every line of his body. He took a few tentative steps without releasing his hold on the frame, then let go and kept going.

"What are you trying to do?"

"Not trying, doing," he answered tightly.

"Jake, you'll fall."

But he didn't. Naked except for the bandage on his back, he headed for the door.

"It's still raining out," she warned, trailing him anxiously, hoping somehow to keep him from harm.

Bending to fit through the low door had to set his head reeling, but he did it. Left inside, Hannah called out to him. His answer was a terse, "I'm fine," that sounded forced between clenched teeth. Had he been able to get upright again? Should she follow?

Understanding his need for privacy, she decided, no, then changed the decision a dozen times before — after an eternity of waiting — she heard him bat the flap aside again. She met him holding out a shirt to serve as a combination towel and wrap.

"God, it's smoky in here. We've got to put out that fire."

"Why? It's not so bad down by the floor."

"Put it out, Hannah. It's a dead giveaway of where we are."

She knew some of his sharpness was a reaction to his effort and the resulting weakness; nevertheless, she felt hurt again. She was proud of the way she had coped, proud that she had even recognized dried buffalo dung as fuel and been able to keep the fire going. She found herself resenting his attempt to take over again just because he had regained consciousness at last. "When I was outside yesterday, I could barely see the smoke," she argued.

"It's just not a good idea. We are being followed, you know."

"So you keep telling me. But why haven't they caught up to us?" she asked, belligerently adding, "whoever 'they' are."

Jake gave her a baleful look, but his voice was mild when he said, "Make us some coffee first. Then we'll put out the fire. A few more minutes won't matter."

Mollified by his reasonable tone, if not his expression, Hannah did as he asked. While she waited for the coffee, she turned the clothes she was drying on every available prop near the fire. Finally though, the coffee was ready and she had nothing to do but join him on the blanket.

He held the cup without drinking to watch her over the rim. The intensity of his perusal made her uncomfortable, but what he said was worse. "I hope I don't seem ungrateful to you, Hannah," he began diffidently. "I know this has been hard for you and I regret any inconvenience you've suffered."

Like a hunted animal, her head snapped up. Inconvenience! She glared at him, ready to fling the coffee — and his gratitude — in his face. "You pompous —"

He grabbed her wrist and held on firmly, going up on his knees to tower suddenly over her. He didn't say anything, just met her angry gaze with his own stubborn one, waiting for her to relent. "Tell me what's wrong," he said. When he sat down, he was closer to her. Not touching her or threatening her in any way, just . . . closer.

"Nothing's wrong," she said. "Everything's just wonderful."

If she'd thought to provoke him, she failed. He sat, impassive, waiting for her to go on.

"What do you want me to say? We're out here in the middle of nowhere, chased by some people I've never heard of —"

"You've heard of them. You've seen them in action, Hannah. Twice. They're the men who burned your wagon train and tried to ambush my men. You know who they are and why they're doing it. I told you."

"But it makes no sense."

"When they understand that, it'll be over." He let that sink in, then asked, "Is that what all your temper is about?"

To object to his assessment would be to exhibit more temper, and she didn't want to do that. It was too revealing. If he found out what was really bothering her, he'd know she was jealous. Everything else — the hurt, anger, and resentment — was just a smokescreen for her jealousy of Caroline. Dear God, but she was a fool. He was a magnificent, virile man in his thirties. Did she

192

really think that in all those years no woman would put a claim on his heart?

She answered his question with another. "Isn't that enough?"

"I don't know," he admitted, frank to a fault. "In another woman it might be. But you're tougher than that."

He put down his cup to reach for the blanket, so he missed seeing the look on her face that would have told him how badly he'd hurt her again. He wrapped her slumping shoulders and urged her back into his arms.

"Come on and rest now, Hannah," he said, mistaking her dejection for fatigue. "Let's not fight. It's too tiring. We're both on the same side, you know."

As Hannah let him pull her down beside him, Jake would have given a lot to be certain that what he had said was true. He just couldn't make himself believe that Hannah was in any way allied with Daniel Veazie's men and their scheme to terrorize the frontier. Not knowingly anyway.

But Daniel Veazie was her husband, and she was here. If she knew what he was, why was she chasing after him? And if she didn't know, Jake was all the more certain that she was going after him in the attempt to win him back to her bed. Either way Jake would lose — had already lost, in fact. The Hannah he knew was too loyal, too strong to behave any other way. Look at all she'd done for him out of simple gratitude.

His arms tightened around her convulsively, refusing to grant her the chance to move away from him. With her back curled against his chest and abdomen, he clasped his hand just under her breasts so that their soft weight rested tantalizingly near. He moved her hair away from her ear with his chin and whispered, "I wasn't delirious all the time, you know. I remember how you held me. I'll never forget that."

193

Hannah made one last stand against the feelings he invoked. She stiffened and tried to rise. "I didn't put out the fire."

"It will go out by itself. Go to sleep, little one. You've done all you can."

Although true, that was no consolation to Hannah. Was it really just yesterday morning that she'd believed everything would be wonderful if only Jake would recover?

## Chapter Eleven

"Why is this village deserted?" Hannah asked. Having just won a major victory over Jake, she wanted to distract him.

He had been determined to go on today. Just as adamant that he needed at least two days to recuperate, Hannah had compromised on only one day of rest. Before he would agree, however, Jake had gone out alone to scout the encampment for signs of pursuit.

He had found none, or at least had admitted to none. However honest he was with her in most things, Hannah sensed that he tended to keep his own counsel when the issue was related to his job and their safety. For her part, she felt she had enough to worry about just trying to keep him from overdoing. She suspected that after getting wet again during his reconnaissance of the area, he was no more eager than she to leave their refuge.

Hannah's question brought Jake back to the moment. He was much more worried about remaining than he wanted Hannah to know. Instinct told him to go. He had found no evidence of Spotted Pony or anyone else in the area, but that didn't mean they weren't near. He hadn't expected to find them. He'd been testing himself more than searching.

What he'd learned about his stamina—or lack of it— had decided the issue. Hannah was right. Another day of travel in the rain might only bring on a relapse of his fever. Here at least they had shelter and relative safety as long as the rain kept up. That way it was likely that Veazie's men were also holed up somewhere. He and Hannah wouldn't regain the ground they'd lost by his illness, but at least they wouldn't lose any.

If only Spotted Pony didn't know this place as well as he did. . . .

Rallying to answer her, Jake put aside his worries. "It shouldn't be deserted," he told her. "Especially not at this time of year. This is the planting season, or rather, pretty much the end of it."

"It's a Pawnee settlement, isn't it?"

"It belongs to Many Buffalo's tribe, although perhaps not for long. If those men out there win"—he tossed his head to indicate their pursuers, carefully avoiding mention of their leader, Daniel Veazie, by name—"all this area will go to the railroad and the Indians will lose their permanent home."

Hannah wanted to protest, but knew it was useless. A village of Indians would not stand in the way of the railroad. "Then why aren't they here defending their land? Why give it up in advance?"

"They aren't giving up. They're fighting the only way they can, by helping my men. It's a gamble, but it's the only one that gives them any chance at winning. And even if we do win and the line follows the planned route rather than going through here, all that does is keep this spot safe for a little while. In time, white settlers will come and take it over anyway. Many Buffalo is only trying to buy a little time."

"It's so sad."

"It's life. Many Buffalo says he's thinking of changing his name to Many Troubles."

Hannah smiled, remembering his name change for her, from Fire Woman to Screeching Woman. "Before I met

196

him, I never even thought of Indians having a sense of humor. They do have one, don't they? And they need one to survive."

"They need more than that, unfortunately," Jake said, "especially since the buffalo are getting scarcer every year. That's the other reason Many Buffalo's tribe isn't back here now. They've had to go farther and farther each year to hunt the buffalo. The crops they plant aren't their real subsistence food. That comes from the buffalo. But since the Pawnee do plant crops, I think they have a chance of adapting to white civilization. Other tribes, like the Sioux and Kiowa, refuse to have anything to do with planting and reaping. They're warriors and hunters only. How can they survive that way when they're outnumbered and outgunned? Now that the war between the North and South is over, both sides have nothing better to do than to turn on the red man."

Their breakfast long gone, Hannah idly offered Jake more coffee. It was little more than barely flavored hot water, but neither of them cared. She was thankful he'd allowed her the small fire to heat it. A faint glow of embers flared up as she lifted the pot from the well-banked fire. With their supply of matches limited, Jake had taught her to preserve a small cooking fire that way. To Hannah, it was another skill to add to her growing list of accomplishments.

She had listened raptly while Jake talked about the Indians, not only because she was interested, but because she wanted him relaxed. Fascinating as the plight of Many Buffalo's tribe was to her, another subject interested her even more. And she wanted him completely off-guard before she brought up the name that had haunted her for almost twenty-four hours.

Keeping her voice elaborately casual, she glued her eyes to his face and asked, "Who is Caroline?"

If Jake's cup had been fine china, his grip would have

snapped it in two. His knuckles turned white. "Who told you about Caroline?" he demanded. "Zeb? *Colby?*" His tone of voice promised retribution for either guilty party.

Hannah's heart seemed to rear up in her chest like a rampaging stallion. Whatever she had imagined—hoped—his reaction would be, reality was worse. Much worse. He was angry. Or was that guilt?

"When you were delirious you called for her." It was hard to answer him when her mouth was dry as dust. "You seemed to mistake me for her once." She shrugged her shoulders to show it was of no concern to her, but her bleak expression gave her away.

It didn't matter though; Jake wasn't looking at her. He had gone away to the small place inside himself where he stored his feelings for Caroline. Since he rarely talked about her to anyone, he had no idea what to say to Hannah. Caroline was the reason he lived as he did, but he didn't like bringing her, even in conversation, into the daily struggle of his life. She was special, even sacred to him.

Jake's silence offended Hannah. She had laid bare her soul to ask the woman's identity. She wasn't going to be ignored, not when she'd gone this far. "Who is she?" she asked again, her voice insistent now that she'd given up all pretense of mere curiosity.

Jake's eyes wandered back to her face as if he'd forgotten all about her. He almost had. He sensed her urgency and knew he'd hurt her feelings by ignoring her. Recalling all she'd done for him, all she meant to him, he summoned his voice and said, "She's my daughter."

Hannah had no time to feel relieved. Instantly, her mind grasped the essential fact that where there was a daughter, there was also a wife. "Then you're . . . married." She didn't say "too," but the unspoken word hung in the air between them.

Jake was even less prepared to discuss Grace than he

was Caroline. Just by knowing Hannah, he had been forced to reexamine everything about his marriage to Grace, but the process was far from finished. He no longer knew what he thought or felt about her. Still, it was easy to see what Hannah implied: that he was no better than she, that he was also unfaithful to a distant spouse.

"I was," he answered, inadvertently putting more emphasis on the disclaimer of wrongdoing than he had intended. The rest of his stiff explanation didn't do much to mitigate the slightly self-righteous tone of his answer. "My wife died just after Caroline was born."

"Oh, that must have been terrible for you," Hannah said with quick sympathy. "But at least you have Caroline. Your poor wife though, she missed seeing her baby grow and become a little person. How sad for her."

Jake looked at her sharply, expecting to see some sign of insincerity. He had so often hated Grace for deserting him that he'd rarely thought to feel sorry for all she'd missed. Trust Hannah to give him a skewed perspective on his life, he thought ruefully.

"How old is Caroline?"

"Nine."

"Nine," Hannah repeated on a soft sigh. "That's wonderful. You must be so proud of her."

She hardly seemed to notice that he didn't answer. To acknowledge the obvious seemed absurd.

"Does she look like you?"

Jake considered not answering or telling her he didn't want to talk about Caroline, but he knew that wouldn't do. She would think something was wrong with Caroline, or with him, or her feelings would be hurt. Recalling how quickly most people became bored by a parent's talk about a child, he decided not to fight her curiosity. If he talked freely about Caroline and conveyed half of what he felt for her, Hannah would soon be satisfied.

"No. She's fair." An image of his young daughter formed in his mind, rebuking him for the inadequacy of his description. "She has blond hair and blue eyes. She's . . . fair," he repeated, finding it hard to choose the words that would express his meaning.

But Hannah wasn't put off. Not by anything he chose to say. Her appetite for details about Jake was insatiable. She gave him a blinding smile that was full of understanding. "Blue eyes. Like yours."

He shifted uncomfortably. "Well, yes, but she doesn't look at all like me."

"Like her mother then." Her smile became tender without losing any of its force.

Watching her, Jake was struck all over again by how beautiful Hannah was. Her features were crisply modeled, fine and pure. He had never seen her well dressed, yet she always looked appealing. Her eyes flashed with one emotion after another, changing like quicksilver from the dark brown of chocolate to the warm gold of honey. Her mouth always tempted his, whether she smiled and laughed or straightened her lips in stubborn anger. When she smiled as she did then, how could he help but smile back?

Hannah saw his smile as a tribute to Caroline's mother, not to her. "What was her name?"

Jolted back to their conversation, Jake was confused. "Who?"

"Caroline's mother." She could have worded it differently, but "Caroline's mother" sounded better to her than "your wife."

"Grace." He dredged his mind for a detail that would end this inquisition. "She was of German extraction, from Pennsylvania."

"Where did you meet her?"

"Back East. She wasn't the kind to travel far from home."

With anyone else Hannah would have become impatient by now, but this was Jake. She understood his reticence; she just wasn't going to accept the limits it imposed on her. After all, this was the man who had stormed her shaky defenses, angrily demanding answers about Daniel.

"Then you lived with her in Pennsylvania? Was Caroline born there?" Her questions were leading her to more questions. Suddenly she thought of a very good reason for Jake's unwillingness to talk about his family. Dismayed, she sat up straighter and leaned toward him. "Oh, Jake. She's all right, isn't she? I mean, where is she now? Who's taking care of her?"

Jake had to laugh. She was like a horse with the bit between its teeth, running headlong and headstrong. "She's fine. She lives with her grandparents near Gettysburg in Pennsylvania. They love her and are very good to her."

"Grace's parents," she said softly. "When did you last see her?"

"It's been almost three years, because of the war. I'm going there as soon as this is over."

Hannah couldn't doubt his quiet determination. "Will you stay there?"

Jake's mouth tightened. "No. I'm going back to get Caroline and bring her west. I belong in the West and the real opportunities are here, not back East. I'm going to have a ranch."

"And Caroline? Will she like that? Being on a ranch?" She was asking for information, not belittling his plans.

He smiled broadly for the first time since they'd begun this trying discussion. "Oh, yes," he said proudly. "She may look like her mother, but inside she's like me. She can ride and do anything a boy can do. At least she could before she went east."

Hannah hastened to remove the note of doubt in his

last statement. "Three years isn't so long," she assured him. "She won't have forgotten all you taught her in that time. And children are adaptable." She lapsed into a brief silence, then before he could wonder about it, went on, her voice warm with sympathy. "How did you manage with a small baby, Jake? It must have been hard."

"It was," he admitted on a harsh sigh. Then, like ice breaking up in a river, words began to come. The first were torn from him, chunks of himself that he gave up reluctantly, hating the exposure he felt as she listened. But then they poured from him, faster and easier.

He didn't intend to talk about Grace, and at first he didn't. But Grace was Caroline's mother. His failure to please her and keep her safe, if only for her daughter's sake, still ate at his heart. "I should never have taken Grace away from her home," he said haltingly. "She was too delicate for the life I wanted. Her father tried to warn me, but I wouldn't listen. I wanted her *and* the West. I should have known better. You don't get everything you want. But she was beautiful, all pink and white, with blond curls and shy, soft manners. I thought she was perfect, everything a woman should be. I couldn't believe my luck the first time she let me take her home from a church social."

Hannah listened, fascinated and horrified both by what he said and by what he didn't say. He was letting her see into his heart, whether he knew it or not.

"It was strange," he went on musingly. "Neither of us lied to the other. I told her my plans and dreams. She knew where I'd been, knew my background. I knew hers just as well. But she thought she could change my mind and I thought—not that she'd change her mind, but that she'd go with me and *then* we'd settle and have the nice things she wanted. But she didn't intend that, not ever. She meant to stay.

"Well, we stayed for a time while I tried to change her

202

mind. Once I saw that I couldn't, I forced her to choose by making my own plans. I was going and she could come or stay. Her father tried to talk me out of it, as I said, but I was adamant. I think she came with me only because she felt her life at home as a deserted wife would be insupportable.

"She wasn't a good traveler under the best conditions, but once she became pregnant it was terrible. She wasn't like you, Hannah, hardy and strong. Everything bothered her or made her sick. We tried stopping, but that didn't help either. The accommodations weren't right. No place was clean enough or good enough. So we went on. Caroline was born in Iowa. Grace felt more at home there than anywhere. There were German immigrants and farms, but it was too late to help either of us."

Afraid to break into his thoughts, Hannah didn't speak, and finally he continued. "Grace didn't die in childbirth. Everyone thinks so and I never correct them, but she didn't. She never recovered from the ordeal though. She . . . wasted away, you might say. Even then she was beautiful, like a china doll. She couldn't feed Caroline, so one of the women there nursed her. She was so kind to Grace. She would dress both of them, Grace and Caroline, as if they were sisters, two dolls . . ."

Jake broke off his narrative, still overwhelmed after all these years by frustration and thwarted anger. That woman—Margaret, her name was—had understood Grace as he never had. She had seen the child in Grace and accepted it, while he had been determined to make a woman of her. In his failure he had turned his anger back onto himself—or tried to. After all, how could he rage at someone so small and helpless? Someone who was also dying?

"After Grace died we stayed in Iowa until Caroline could travel. Then we hooked up with my father in Missouri. My mother was dead, but the woman with him cared for Caroline. Dad never married Anna, but she was good to him and to all of us. Once Caroline was old enough, about three, I took her with me. I worked as a cooper. She played with the shavings." His mouth curled up in a lopsided grin. "She could do more with curls of wood than you'd believe. She was such a good little mite, spunky and even mischievous, but good—if you can follow that."

Hannah could.

"I wanted her with me," he said in a voice as riddled with conflict as he must have been, "but I wanted her to have a better life than I was giving her. I wanted her to go to school. There wasn't any school for her out here." He waved his hand, indicating the emptiness of the prairie around them. "The Lunigs—Grace's family—could give her that and they were willing. With the war on . . . well, I could fight and she could have a real home, the kind her mother had and would have wanted for her.

"But now she's almost ten. I know that's not old enough to give up school, but I want her back. I stand to make enough with this job to stock a ranch, especially if I go where land is still cheap. I'll work and make a home for her. She won't want for the important things, Hannah. I swear she won't."

Hannah fought back tears. How different Jake was from Daniel. Everything Jake struggled for, Daniel had already thrown away: home, child, and wife. As far as Hannah knew, Daniel didn't even know his son was dead. Would he care?

Turning from such sorrowful thoughts, Hannah was quick to assure Jake that Caroline was a lucky girl to figure so importantly in his plans. That same impetuousness also made her ask, "In all these years, Jake, haven't you ever wanted to mary again? Then you'd really have a home for Caroline."

His response was quick and harsh. "Never. I don't need

204

a woman to make a home. I can do that myself. I'll hire a housekeeper, but that's all."

Having drawn his ire, Hannah decided not to argue the point. Now that she knew about Caroline, she understood Jake better. For the first time she saw the connection between his strange, risky job here in the wilderness and his dreamed-of future. She also saw that Jake had no thought of including her in his plans.

No matter how grateful he was to her for saving his life, gratitude would stretch only so far. She was not pink and white and blond. Her dark hair, mottled with more red than gold, was not what he dreamed of. What had he called her so far? Tough, sturdy, and strong. Wonderful words for an ox or a plow horse, but not the words a man uses to describe the woman he loves.

But then Jake had never pretended to love her. He had only *made* love to her, and that because she was available and so very willing. Even knowing all that, Hannah couldn't hate Jake. He was everything a man should be, everything she wanted. He was strong, caring, and kind, a man trying his best in a cruel and indifferent world to regain his child and make a home for her.

Whatever happened to them when they left this sod dwelling, Hannah knew she would give anything to be part of that home—impossible as that wish appeared to be. He might want her physically, but he didn't want a wife—certainly not one like her. When they reached civilization again, he would thank her and replace her—if at all—with someone like Grace. Someone delicate and feminine.

Hannah curled her fingers into fists in her lap. The backs of her hands were deeply tanned from their long exposure to the relentless Nebraska sun. She turned one hand to inspect the ruin of her nails while the other reached automatically for the small gold locket at her neck.

Because they weren't riding today, she wore her dress, such as it was, but only the locket had the power to assure her of her femininity. It told her that she was a woman, reminding her that she had been a mother—and a good one—to David. She often touched the locket before going to sleep or upon waking, using it as a talisman. She did so now, fingering it with such nervous intensity that her gesture drew Jake's eye.

"I've always meant to ask you about that locket you wear," he said. "Is it special?"

Surprised to have drawn his attention when he seemed sunk in reverie, Hannah dropped her hands away with guilty haste. He sounded hostile, not merely curious. She lifted her chin defiantly and glared at him. "Yes, it is special."

"I suppose Daniel gave it to you."

Hannah didn't know what to make of the contempt in his voice. She reacted to it defensively. David was always close to her heart, but never more so than at this time when she felt so alone. Jake had Caroline and his dreams for a home together with her. She, on the other hand, had nothing. David was gone. All she had of him—literally—were her memories and the curl of his red-blond hair she wore at her neck.

"No," she stammered with uncharacteristic uncertainty. In a way of course, Daniel *had* given her David, but that wasn't the way she thought of him. She considered David hers alone. "It's just . . . mine."

At another time Jake would have let her obvious attempt to deceive him—or herself perhaps—pass unchallenged. Why should he care that she loved foolishly? He told himself he didn't. His only concern was that her misplaced loyalty might endanger them, and he could prevent that, he believed, as long as he was in charge.

Her pretense annoyed him though. Her prying questions about Caroline had stripped away years of protective silence, forcing him to talk about Grace and Caroline when he hated the feeling of exposure. In the heat of his momentary anger, he conveniently forgot that telling Hannah had also soothed and relieved his conscience, especially about Caroline. Now he remembered only the guilt he still bore over Grace, and that this stubborn woman before him was the one who'd just stirred up all that dormant pain.

He lashed out at Hannah, blindly but with deadly accuracy. "Of course. You went to a jewelers yourself to buy that locket. What do you have in it? A photograph? Or is it a lock of your true love's hair?"

He hadn't meant to turn virulent, so when Hannah burst into tears, he was almost as distraught as she. He lunged for her, meaning to comfort her, just as she jumped to her feet, intent on escape. They collided with enough force to send both of them sprawling. Because Jake was heavier, he knocked Hannah back onto the blanket, then fell on top of her. She was too angry and upset even to worry about the damage he might have done to his wound.

She pushed his chest and struck out blindly at him, trying to get free from his weight. "Get off me!"

Jake made only the physical accommodations necessary to maintain his hold on her without hurting her. His right knee had landed between her legs, effectively pinning her to the floor by her skirts. He saw no reason to remove it. By propping himself on his right arm, he ignored the pain in his shoulder and used his less mobile left arm to hold her close.

"Hannah, Hannah, I'm sorry," he said earnestly. "I had no right to say that. I'm sorry, so sorry."

But she wasn't listening. "I hate you!"

If she'd had breath enough, she would have been shrieking. Jake had no trouble understanding that. "I know you do," he soothed. "That was a terrible thing to say."

"You don't know anything!" she raged, still not hearing him. "You think you're the only person in the world who loves a child. Well, you're not! You're not the only one! I have a child, too! Only he's *dead* and I don't have him anymore—"

"My God! Hannah . . ."

Jake was overcome. He rolled to his side, taking Hannah with him. There was nothing sexual about his embrace. He was motivated only by a deep need to comfort her. Even if he hadn't known loss and separation, he would have been moved by her sorrow. She was wracked by it and by the pain she was too incoherent to express. He could tell just holding her when anger left her and she experienced again the desolation of her child's death.

Jake held her to his chest while her tears soaked his shirt, marveling at all she had held back. Except for the days when she had been unconscious, he'd never seen her formidable strength and self-control breached. Even in the throes of passion she met him as an equal, countering every demand of his with one of her own. Her sympathy and warmth were qualities he considered uniquely female, like her lush and beautiful body, but he'd never before seen her so soft and vulnerable, clinging to him for her very support.

Lately, he had been the one doing the leaning and, yes, even the clinging. Between his injury and fever, his sense of himself as a man had taken a beating. Terrible as it was for Hannah, this emotional collapse of hers was vastly restoring to his masculinity.

He soothed and patted without stint, amazed that she felt so small and helpless in his arms. After her first strangled words, words he'd been unable to understand, Hannah gave up trying to talk and just cried until she was spent.

That process didn't take anywhere near as long as Jake

was willing to spend on it. He smiled to himself when he realized how strange that was. He had spent so much time soothing Grace that he'd vowed never to do it again.

How different Hannah was. And how different he was with her. Not exactly patient—again he smiled, thinking how furious she could make him—but . . . free. Yes, that was the feeling. With Hannah he could bellow out his rage and know she could take it. She wouldn't cower from him as if he'd suddenly become a rabid animal. She could give as good as she got, leaving him . . . free. With her, he didn't have to smile and pretend he wasn't dying inside. He didn't frighten Hannah. She wasn't a child; she was a woman.

She began to stir and make little withdrawing and composing motions as she tried to collect herself. Jake resisted, tightening his arms around her. He lowered his head to kiss the top of hers as he had been doing all along. This time she raised her face and looked into his eyes.

Her lashes were spiked with tears, her eyes luminous and wide. For a moment she looked at him blankly, as if she didn't know him, then recognition flared in the velvet depths of her eyes. "Jake," she whispered on a ragged sigh.

He knew it was wrong to take advantage of her emotional turmoil, but he didn't want to hear what she was going to say. He had wronged her again and again. What difference would one more time make? He took her soft mouth with his, fitting his parted lips tenderly over hers. *Forgive me.* His mouth silently begged of hers. *I need this.*

Hannah was startled at first. She hadn't expected to be kissed. He had been so comforting. She went rigid with surprise. Jake felt her resistance and eased his hold on her, persuading rather than forcing, but refusing to relinquish her mouth. Knowing he was unwelcome, he teased her gently with soft kisses at the corners of her lips.

Her stiffness softened, melting by barely perceptible stages to a wary kind of stillness that wasn't acceptance but wasn't denial either. Jake buried his fingers in the heavy silkiness of her hair and moved his mouth along her cheek, resting at the hairline above her ear. Her pulse beat against his lips, its steadiness a counterpoint to his own more pronounced beat. He sighed and told himself to back off, but when he did, Hannah brought her hand up to rest her palm against his face.

Jake had so thoroughly satisfied Hannah's need for comfort that it was easy for her to respond to his overture. Although it was sexual in nature, it didn't offend her because it was merely another facet of the tenderness he had been showing all along. She only needed time to adapt—and very little time at that. Already her body was shifting to accommodate Jake, subtly aligning her limbs to his. She stroked his whiskery cheek and rejoiced when he turned his face to nuzzle her palm with his mouth.

He groaned into her hand and let his head fall back to the blanketed floor. "God, Hannah, I'm sorry. I'm not even shaved—"

She laughed, but looked at him severely. "You're not even *well*, that's what you're not."

"I'm well, but I don't deserve to be," he said bitterly. He closed his eyes in apparent defeat.

"I don't know what you mean by that, Jake." She wished he would open his eyes so she could gauge his reaction to what she wanted to do. If she was wrong . . . well, it didn't bear thinking about.

To buy some time and perhaps incite a response from him again—at least enough to be sure—she touched his face again. Surely that was safe. She'd never invited him to make love before. She thought that was what he'd wanted minutes ago, but uncertainty made her touch

210

tentative. Why had he stopped?

He tolerated her caress, but that was all. His eyes didn't open and he didn't move. His stillness was complete. It reminded her of her own earlier and that gave her the heart to continue. "I like your beard," she offered softly.

He huffed in disbelief without looking at her.

"I do. It's long enough now to be soft." She rubbed her thumb up and down the ridge of his chin. "I like it," she repeated.

His eyes opened, the blue as bright as the hottest part of a flame, as he searched her face. "Hannah—"

Speaking at the same time, she said, "You've been sick . . . your shoulder . . ."

"It doesn't hurt."

"But it might."

His smile was pure masculine triumph. "No." He hauled her down to his chest with such alacrity that she could have no more doubts, at least about his desire.

"Jake, I don't want—"

He stopped in the process of kissing her and drew back to glare at her. His fierce expression stopped her breath. "Go on," he commanded.

"To hurt you."

Instantly, the tightness left his face. "You won't," he said against her lips. "I'll show you." He turned onto his good side and positioned her body along his side, her head nestled into the crook of his arm. Bending to her tenderly, he brushed her lips with his. She made a soft whimpering sound in her throat and rose to meet him, lifting her open mouth to his. The tip of his tongue ventured just inside her mouth, then withdrew. Hers followed and this time he moaned. He settled her back against his arm, kissing her thoroughly.

He touched her upper arm and let his hand close over the fullness of her breast. He felt her swift response as her nipple puckered against the warmth of his possession.

She moved her legs, seeking his body. He began to undo the buttons down the front of her dress. She had left the top few undone for comfort but enough remained to tax his dexterity, particularly when he preferred to fondle her softness than to work at the buttons.

He opened her chemise in the same fumbling, left-handed way, his very slowness contributing to the escalation of unendurable tension between them. Finally able to bury his face in the cleft of her breasts, he inhaled the sweet fragrance of her flesh. The scent was overlaid with smoke, the less pleasant odor that permeated the house, but he would have recognized her essence blindfolded.

Turning his head, Jake sighed, sending a puff of warmed air across the crest of one exposed breast. Hannah cupped the back of his head and directed his mouth to her there. However soft his whiskers were to her fingers, they were rasping and occasionally sharp against her breasts. She almost cried out once as he nuzzled her, rooting like a baby for her nipple, but then he found it and her cry was one of joy, not protest. Strangely, the slight scrape of his beard enhanced the sweet pull of his lips and the wet heat of his tongue.

Jake forgot about his bound shoulder and upper arm and reached for her skirt. He began to pull it up along her hip. When he had wads of material gathered there, he reached back farther and badly overtaxed his range of motion. He grunted in surprise at the pain. Hannah's head came up at the same time his did.

"Jake," she said, frowning in concern.

"Don't," he warned. "Just help me a bit."

"But you're hurt."

"Not as much as I'll be if we stop," he told her honestly, sitting up. He unbuttoned his shirt, his eyes fixed on the stubborn set of her mouth. "Please, honey."

She could never resist him when he used endearments. They were so rare from him. She scrambled up to help

212

him out of the shirt, completely unconscious of her own exposure until her bared breasts brushed against his chest. His shirt dropped behind him, unnoticed by either of them as he took her shoulders between his hands to prevent her from pulling back.

With his eyes steady on hers, blue as twin holes burned into the heavens, he drew her close again and rocked her gently from side to side so that the hardened tips of her breasts brushed lightly back and forth against his chest. Hannah's eyes drifted shut as she savored the almost stinging sensations. When they closed, Jake shook her slightly and ordered softly, "Look at me. Open your eyes."

It was hard to do, not because she was ashamed but because her emotions were so intense. Shutting him out visually let her focus on herself more. Or so she thought before she watched his pupils dilate with pleasure at the touch of her body to his.

"You feel like heaven to me, Hannah," he said in a voice roughened by excitement.

His hands moved to the bare skin on top of her shoulders, trying to work her dress down. With the waist still buttoned, she knew it wouldn't work. "Let me," she offered.

Jake caught at her hands and stilled them. "Help me first," he asked, rising to his knees. With his cooperation, that was quickly done. Since they both wore Indian moccasins, there were no clumsy boots or shoes to deal with. When he was naked, he caught her to his chest again and held her close, his hands lost in her long hair. He ran his fingers through it with rough combing motions that tangled more than smoothed. When she tried to move back, he held her in place. Something in the way he held himself communicated his tension to her. "What is it, Jake?"

He didn't answer immediately, but didn't flinch when she gazed inquiringly up at him. "Once," he began slowly, "you took your clothes off for me."

Although the light was dim, Jake had no trouble seeing her color rise as she remembered that day. He couldn't prevent her wash of shame, but he hoped to erase it. "I asked you in anger then and I've always been sorry for that," he went on. "If I asked you now—nicely—would you do it again?"

"I . . . don't know." That memory still rankled. "I never understood—"

"I know. I'll tell you, I promise. But later, Hannah. Not now." He touched her chin with his thumb, then framed her face with his spread hand and bent to kiss her gently. "Let me see you now. You're so lovely. Show me."

Quickly, while she could still feel his lips on hers and before she could change her mind, Hannah began to undo the rest of her buttons.

Jake grabbed her hands and held them while he backed away. He understood her haste. Sitting down, he leaned back, propping himself by his good arm. He smiled at her, his teeth showing as a slash of white against his dark beard. "Slowly, sweetheart," he cautioned.

Slowly.

The word seeped under her skin, melting into her veins like boiled sugar. Suddenly she was all thumbs, incapable of coordination. She put aside any of the feelings of shame or anger that had fueled her before and concentrated on Jake, on the way his eyes scoured her. She knew this was important to him and that asking had been difficult. She felt that her relationship with him had taken a giant step forward today. She didn't know yet what had changed, or even why. It had to do with the confidences he had shared with her and his promise that more would come.

It was enough. Hannah slid her dress down over one shoulder, then the other. She stroked her bare upper arms to ease the sleeves down, crossing one arm then the other

214

in front of her breasts. Without her petticoats, sacrificed for bandages, to impede its fall, the dress dropped free of her arms into a heap at her bare feet. She could have wished for beautiful underwear, but she knew Jake didn't care. He was looking at her, wishing away the thin cover of cloth hiding her body.

She bent over to lift her dress from the floor, first offering him a provocative look at her swaying breasts, then shielding them with an outstretched hand. Her hair fell forward, dividing over her shoulders, and she made sure it stayed when she stood up to face him.

Jake saw what she was doing and smiled. His pleasure was mixed with the pain of physical denial, but even that pain was welcome. Her hair was glorious, the burnished red glowing like the hidden fire of her passion.

Hannah couldn't help but return his smile when she saw the tightness in his face. She had no need of fantasy when she knew he was having to hold himself back. Although she was ready to throw herself into his arms, she restrained herself and took off her chemise with excrutiating slowness. Her hair shifted with each shrug of her shoulders, offering him tantalizing glimpses of white skin topped by dusky-pink nipples.

She undid the waist of her pantalettes and lowered them without turning to the side, her legs parted but not widely braced. She kept the darkened delta of her curls from him as she bent forward again and lifted one leg to free it. Her hair swung with the motion, showing him all of one breast. Then he saw the curve of her hip. He groaned as blood rushed to pool in his already aroused sex. The noise distracted her, but not enough that she dropped the pants. She held them up still, displaying all of one long slender leg.

"Drop it," he told her thickly.

She teased him for a few tense moments, then let the cloth slide down her leg. It went slowly, like a slithery cloth hand, caressing the length of her leg.

"Oh God, Hannah. Come to me." His eyes burned from his unwillingness to blink and miss a single glimpse of her glowing flesh.

She came, but first she tossed back her hair, the lift of her arms setting up sensuous ripples in her unconfined breasts. She folded onto one leg and gracefully sank down before him.

He took her hands in his and raised them to his mouth. "If I live to be a hundred, I'll never forget the way you looked, Hannah. I've never seen so much beauty before."

Hannah leaned forward and slid her arms around his shoulders. "Hold me, Jake," she pleaded, her voice husky with emotion.

He started to comply, then stopped. "Did I hurt you again?"

She shook her head, laughing. But there was an edge to her laughter that threatened to shatter her composure. Jake sensed it and drew her close. "You're the most wonderful woman in the world," he told her, meaning every word.

Now that Jake was holding her, Hannah let go of her emotions. She wanted him with a single-minded hunger that was like nothing she'd ever felt before. She gave no thought to his wound as she pulled him down on top of her.

He answered her wordless demand with his own wild hunger, possessing her mouth, running his hands over her body. She arched up from the blanket, following his hand and mouth. On his side, he lifted her leg so it draped over his hip. He left his hand there to stroke the soft skin of her inner thigh and the waiting heat of her womanhood. He pressed her there until she was sobbing with need, then filled her in one smooth, hard stroke.

"Yes, oh yes," she whispered brokenly.

"Hannah . . . oh God . . . I . . ." He began pumping

into her, his hands full of her, holding her in place, overcome.

*I love you.*

Collapsed on top of her, Jake didn't know whether or not he had said those words. For the longest time he didn't care, then he did. He could think of nothing more disastrous or hopeless than loving Hannah.

But he did. Totally.

He eased from Hannah, but continued to hold her. She seemed to be sleeping. He wondered how she could. He wanted to shake her out of her seeming indifference. Finally, he realized that he hadn't given himself away. He was glad — relieved, in fact.

Then he was sorry.

## Chapter Twelve

Hannah slept the rest of the morning. Jake spent part of the time dozing at her side, alternately holding her and withdrawing from her to wonder at his insanity. To pass the rest of the time and prepare for the next day when they would leave, he cleaned and loaded his weapons, checked on the horses, and packed what he could. The activities soothed him and made him feel they were making progress when he knew they were not.

He had been, by turns, surprised, amused, and finally, concerned by the way Hannah slept. It was the sleep of the exhausted. But when he thought about what she'd been through since the ambush, he realized that she had cause. Just caring for him during his fever would have put an ordinary woman to bed for a week.

Early in the afternoon Hannah began to stir, so he made more porridge and coffee, both things they wouldn't have time for the next day. Roused by the smell of coffee or some noise he made, Hannah came awake with a start. She sat up quickly and lost the blanket he had tucked around her. She grabbed it back, holding it to her chest while she looked around in alarm.

"Oh, Jake," she said in relief, finally realizing where she was.

Sensing her embarrassment, Jake didn't tease her. "How do you feel?" he asked, amazed at how much he cared. "You had quite a nap."

She tried to get up, still disoriented, and stepped on the blanket. "Is it time to go?"

Jake turned his back to let her collect herself in privacy. "Not till morning. There's a shirt of mine you can wear until you want to get dressed. It's still raining."

Hannah dropped the blanket and dived into his shirt. She suddenly remembered absolutely every detail of the morning, yet still she wanted to be covered now. It didn't make sense, but there it was. While Jake was still busy at the fire, she went to the door. "I'll . . . be right back," she told him.

"There's water for a bath if you like when you get back," he called out to her. It would have to be a sponge bath, of course, but the one he'd taken while she slept had renewed him. Again, he gave her privacy while she bathed by going out "to tend the horses."

By such ruses they made things as easy as possible until they were both restored. While they ate, Jake told her how he had passed the morning.

"Then you really are better," Hannah marveled. "It seems impossible. What could just go away like that and still have caused such a fever?"

"I don't know. As a child I had fevers. I remember my mother telling about them."

Hannah put her cup aside, uncomfortably reminded of David and of the way she had berated Jake earlier.

She thought Jake wasn't aware of her mood, but he was. He didn't understand the connection to what he had said; nevertheless, he hadn't forgotten that children were a sensitive subject for her.

"Would you tell me about your child, Hannah?" he asked quietly, noting the way her hand had again flown to touch the small gold heart. "I meant my apology this morning. I'm sorry for what I said."

"I know. I was . . . unhinged."

"With cause," he said. "What happened?"

"It was a fever. David, my little boy, was four. He'd just had his birthday three weeks before. He got a sore throat, then the fever." She spoke in a low voice she tried to control by keeping the words plain. "The doctor couldn't do anything. It was scarlet fever." She didn't tell Jake how she had held David to warm him, bathing him to cool him. If he remembered her efforts in his behalf, as he claimed, he would know.

"Do you have his picture?"

"We thought we'd do it when he was older," she said with a sad smile. "It was hard for him to sit still very long. I have a curl though. His hair was the most beautiful color, yellow with a reddish cast. And it curled. I never let Uncle Simon get it cut and David wanted a 'big-boy haircut' so badly."

Jake took her in his arms then as tears overcame her. They were gentle and sad this time, with none of the bottled-up fury and frustration of the morning. He felt nearly as sad as she did. Remembering Caroline at four, he could easily picture a rambunctious boy with a head of curls he would surely think were "sissy." No wonder she grieved, he thought, wishing he could stand between Hannah and all the pain the world could cause.

When Hannah stopped crying, Jake said, "Didn't you tell me Daniel had been gone for over four years? Does that mean he didn't know his son?"

"He came and went," Hannah answered. "We were never together much, even from the beginning. At first I considered it a sign that he was ambitious, which he was. Later I came to realize that he just didn't care. He was mildly pleased to have a son, but not enough to spend time with us. He said babies were for women. David was a good baby, hardly ever fussy, and he was a child any man would be proud to claim. But Daniel said he cried too much.

"He left us for good on David's six-month birthday. I had planned a party to celebrate," she recalled, her voice strained and weary sounding. "Oh, I knew it was silly, that it wasn't a real birthday. It wasn't much of a party either, just a little cake and some simple presents. It was more for Uncle Simon and me than for David. He was too little to know.

"Daniel laughed at me. Not fondly, you understand. He said I was a fool. He wanted me to leave David with Uncle Simon's housekeeper and go with him to New York. I was to be his hostess and impress the wealthy Easterners he wanted to separate from their money. Daniel had a scheme. He always had one. I don't remember what it was, only that my presence—as Uncle Simon's niece—was necessary. As near as I could figure it, I was supposed to make it seem as if Uncle Simon was another of Daniel's backers. That way people would think the scheme was sound. He was furious that I wouldn't go."

"Why wouldn't you?"

Hannah laughed sadly. "I would have gone. I didn't worry too much about Daniel's scruples then. But he wouldn't have David. He said he'd be in the way. I wouldn't leave David—not that way. Daniel screamed at me. I can still see the veins standing out in his neck. I would have done anything else, but not leave my child, not when there was no reason." She looked at Jake as if for verification. "Do you understand? Not for a man who cared nothing for his own son."

"He was the fool, Hannah. Not you."

"Thank you for saying that. I've never been sorry. Not really. Can you imagine how I would have felt if I'd been

221

off somewhere with Daniel when David died? I've thought about that so much. I had so little time with him, but at least I didn't miss anything about his growing, none of his smiles or tears. I was there."

Jake began to hope that what she'd told him originally was true, that she didn't love Daniel. She didn't sound like a woman in love. Still, she would have gone with him if he hadn't made her choose him over her son. What did that mean?

He poured himself more coffee, offering it to Hannah while he considered how to find out. When he sat down again, he took a place opposite her so he could look at her. Her face was so expressive he was sure she would give away her true feelings that way.

For a moment he entertained one last hope that he was wrong about Daniel Veazie. Perhaps he wasn't her husband. Her name could be something else — Veeder, maybe. There had been a Veeder family in Pennsylvania. Or . . .

No. The coincidence was too strong. And if he wasn't her husband, then the man who was might be a perfectly decent man who had simply drifted away from his family in search of adventure. Stranger things had happened in the West.

Ruefully, Jake rejected that notion. He *wanted* Daniel Veazie to be Hannah's husband. That way, once she knew what a thoroughly evil man he was, she'd have no compunction about divorcing him. She already hated the man responsible for murdering Willie and the rest of her friends from the wagon train. If she knew her husband had done that, she would give up any idea of pursuing him and reconciling their lives.

Impatient with himself, Jake finally decided to find out once and for all. He said, "Your husband's name is Daniel Veazie, isn't it?"

Hannah was startled. She had been thinking about David, not Daniel. The few memories of David she had shared with Jake had set off a chain reaction in her mind. How he had thrown back his head in laughter. How he had battled for his own way, legs braced, hands behind his back and pugnacious little chin thrust out. How she had loved him.

Wrenched back to reality by Jake's question, she wasn't able to keep her mental balance. She stared at him in confusion, wondering at his question for a few too many seconds. "Yes," she said cautiously, even as she herself wondered at that caution.

Then she remembered. She had never told him Daniel's last name. It hadn't seemed important. He wasn't well known like Uncle Simon or from Jake's area. "How did you know that?" she asked. "Did I tell you? I don't remember saying it."

"You didn't." Jake avidly studied the parade of expressions passing over Hannah's mobile features. She had been surprised, even confused, but more than that, she was suspicious of him and his motives. Or was that guilt? And if so, why did she feel guilty? Did she know what Daniel was doing after all? Was that why she was here?

Jake pushed away that old suspicion. It was unworthy of the Hannah he knew.

"Then how do you know his name, Jake?"

"I learned it a long time ago, when I sent Colby and Whitcomb to Columbus to try to find out who was behind the raids. They came back with his name."

For an insane moment Hannah grappled with his meaning. Then she found a way to make sense of it. Jake had told her he didn't know the identity of his backer. Maybe he was saying that Daniel was behind *this* enterprise. "You mean Daniel is the man who supplied the money for you to help the Pawnee?"

"No, Hannah. Daniel Veazie owns lands in Bellevue. If the transcontinental railroad begins there instead of in Omaha, he'll make a lot of money. To ensure that it will,

223

he hired the men who attacked your wagons to harass travelers leaving from Omaha. He's the man who paid Jethro to infiltrate my men and bring about the ambush. He's the enemy, Hannah."

Jake's words were all too clear. Perhaps if he hadn't spelled out the details of Daniel's guilt in such detail, Hannah would have been able to accept what he'd said. She knew Daniel was no saint. Hadn't she just told Jake how he had tried to work one money-making scheme after another? The land in Bellevue sounded just like what he would do.

But murder? Daniel was David's father, her husband. . . . She couldn't—wouldn't—accept that David's father was capable of such brutality. Those men had killed Willie. Daniel wouldn't have done that. He had *liked* Willie.

"No," she said, shaking her head in fervent denial. "I don't believe you. Daniel would never do that. He just wouldn't. Oh, I don't deny that he might own land in Bellevue or wherever. And he'd try to make money that way or any other. Legality wouldn't get in his way. I know that. But it must be someone else behind it. Daniel wouldn't kill people. Not like that."

"Hannah, I'm not wrong. Colby talked to him."

"Then he's lying to you. He just made that up. Or—" She was close to shouting at him now, close to tears, grasping at wild suppositions. "Or, Daniel could be *pretending* to be in charge. He's like that. He wants to be important, but he wouldn't kill people. I just know he wouldn't."

"Then you're saying I'm lying to you?"

"No . . . yes!" Hannah shouted. "You could be. Or Colby could be lying to you. Anyone can tell a lie sometimes . . ."

"The way you did when you told me Velma was your middle name?" Jake asked coldly.

*"What?"*

"That's why I was so bloody-minded to you after Colby told me the man behind all our troubles was your husband. If you hadn't slipped and started to call yourself Hannah *Veazie*, I would never have connected the two of you."

Hannah was having trouble keeping up with his accusations. "I can explain that. I was going to tell you I was married that night—"

"But instead you ran away. Were you trying to go meet Veazie?"

"Of course not! I didn't know he was out here. I was running away from you!" That wasn't strictly true either, as Hannah well knew. She had gone to get away from being a bone of contention between Jake and one of his men. She had wanted to give Jake peace to conduct his business as he needed to, to relieve him of the burden of protecting her.

"Then that story about your cousin in Fort Kearney is a lie, too?"

"Jake, I haven't lied to you. Except for my name being Velma," she added quickly. "And I only did then because that was hardly the time to tell you I was married."

"No. The time for that was when you first regained consciousness. But you didn't. You called yourself Hannah Hatch. Where did you get that name? From another man?"

"From my father!" Hannah all but shrieked at him. "It's my name. Mine! I took it back after David died. He was the only reason for me to use Daniel's name. I didn't want his name or anything else of his after that."

They faced each other angrily across the expanse of rumpled blanket where they had made love just hours before. Jake had pushed her, wanting answers to the questions that were, in his mind, the essence of Hannah. Who was she? Whom did she love?

225

Jake was afraid he'd found out the answer. He had expected her to deny Daniel. Instead, she had defended her husband and denied him, accusing him of lying.

For what reason would he lie to her? It made no sense.

"Oh, Jake," Hannah said mournfully, "why are you doing this to me?"

He had no answer to give her.

They didn't make up after their quarrel that day. For each, the hurt had gone too deep. Jake felt betrayed by Hannah's failure to believe him. He prided himself on his honesty. For Hannah—who wouldn't recognize truth if she sat on it—to question his word made him incoherent with fury. Even more grating was the knowledge that he loved her and that he had come within an eyelash of telling her so.

Hannah's feelings were more mixed. She didn't want to admit, even to herself, that Jake could be right about Daniel. She had accepted the fact that he was a shallow, self-serving man—a charlatan, in fact. She didn't love him now. Perhaps she never had. How could she have? She hadn't known him. He had been all surface charm, with courtly manners he left at the threshold of his own home—when he was there.

No. She had been wrong about Daniel. But that wrong? Could the man she'd married and borne a son to also be a murderer? Everything in her being wanted to deny the charge. If he were, would David have grown up to be like him? No, no, no!

She tried to sleep the day away, knowing she needed the rest. They would leave in the morning, rain or no rain. Neither of them could stand another day of this captivity. Even now, while she pretended to sleep, Jake paced the little house like a caged beast. She wanted to scream at him, but she'd already done too much of that. He had a

226

way of turning her into a virago, completely against her will.

While she didn't sleep, Hannah tried to think why Jake would lie to her. The only reason she could think of — jealousy — was absurd. For spite then? That made even less sense. Jake had shown her little but kindness and consideration. True, he had a temper, but it was no worse than hers. He had shown no inclination to spitefulness, even when she had goaded him.

As hard as it was to admit to herself that Jake might be telling the truth, it was even harder to admit that she wanted him to be jealous of Daniel. She was astonishingly jealous of Grace — and that poor woman was dead! But how could he envy Daniel? She didn't love her husband. He might be alive, as Grace was not, but he was deader to her than the sainted Grace was to Jake. He was the one carrying a torch, not she.

Round and round went her tiresome thoughts until Hannah decided anything would be better than this enforced inactivity. From the tempo of Jake's impatient strides, she was sure he would welcome her suggestion.

She sat up and said, "Jake, why don't we just go now?"

He turned on her, exhibiting the practiced reflexes of a gunfighter. Instead of shooting her, he merely accused, "You're supposed to be sleeping."

"With you stomping up and down next to my bed like a maddened bull?" she taunted. "You'll have a trench worn in the floor by morning." She cut off his retort with a raised hand. "Please, Jake. I don't want to fight with you. I can't sleep anymore. You're wearing yourself out just pacing. Why don't we put our energy to use? We can go now and have a head start on tomorrow."

It was what he wanted to do. But even though it made excellent sense, Jake shook his head. He told himself he wasn't rejecting the idea because it came from Hannah, and he wasn't. He was protecting her. Even if she wasn't sleeping, she was resting. He couldn't forget the way she had slept this morning. He blamed himself for overtaxing her.

Because she had, until today, shown him little of her softer, weaker side, he had fallen into the trap of treating her the way he would his men. Having held her weeping form and, yes, having made love to her so recently, he couldn't go back to ignoring her femininity. Besides, he loved her. He was going to keep her safe no matter what.

"Perhaps you've forgotten that it's still raining."

"Does it matter?" she asked. In fact, the prospect of wearing wet clothes again was daunting. Though she had joked that their clothes were smoked, not dried, they were at least no longer soaked.

"It would mean sleeping out in the open, in the rain," Jake argued.

But Hannah could sense that he was weakening. Determined to press her advantage, she went too far. "Anything would be better than being cooped up any longer in this hovel."

His voice stiff with wounded pride, he said, "You were happy enough when we first came here, as I recall."

He was right. She loved the house and would happily stay if only he would smile and say a kind word to her again. But she didn't say that. "As *I* recall, you can't remember all that much about that occasion," she said, feeling increasingly mean. All she'd done was make a suggestion, and here they were sniping at each other like children playing at war.

"Which is the best reason of all for staying," Jake said. "I don't particularly want to suffer through another bout of that fever."

Hannah was instantly contrite. "Oh Jake, I'm sorry. I didn't think—"

He waved off her apology. It wasn't needed. He'd only used the excuse because he knew it was the only one she'd

228

accept. Whatever her feelings about him, she put him first as selflessly as the most devoted wife.

"Why don't you try to rest," she suggested softly. "You can't be doing yourself any good pacing like that."

He wasn't, of course, but he was keeping himself away from her. He didn't trust himself near her, especially when she spoke like that. If he couldn't have distance from her, he needed his anger.

While he was thinking what to do, Hannah moved to one side of the blanket and patted the vacated spot invitingly. "Come on, Jake, sit down and talk to me."

He didn't move. "What about?"

"Oh, I don't know." Then her face lit up. "Yes, I do. Tell me about Jethro."

"Why? So you can call me a liar again?"

If Hannah had regretted her choice of topic, his sarcasm erased any need for remorse on her part. "Oh, never mind," she burst out. Pulling the blanket tight around her, she threw herself down, her back turned to Jake as if the sight of him was hateful to her.

Which left Jake no way to end his weary pacing until he was sure she was dead asleep. Although it took less time than he had expected for that to happen, he didn't lie down until long after her breathing was deep and regular, wanting to be sure he didn't disturb her.

As long as he was awake, he stayed carefully away from Hannah. He kept so far from her, in fact, that she had no sense of his presence beside her and so did not unconsciously move close in her sleep, seeking his warmth. As soon as Jake relaxed, however, all his restraint melted away. In no time at all, his arms were around Hannah and her head was pillowed on his chest, their legs wrapped in an intimate tangle.

In the early hours of the morning they began to reverse the process, as first one, then the other, became aware and withdrew. Thus, they woke with no conscious knowledge of anything except their quarrel and the need to go on.

Jake was up long before it was light. He saddled the horses and prepared everything he could. On an impulse, he moved the horses yet again, trying to hide them from anyone approaching the village. The rain was stopping, but because travel would still be a damp business, he let Hannah sleep as long as possible. Then she delayed their departure by insisting that she must check his bandage. It didn't take long because the wound was fine, but by the time she had finished, Jake was fretting at her impatiently.

The fact was, he was nervous. He sensed something—or thought he did. He was just about to escort Hannah outside when he decided not to. Instead, he moved the flap just enough to peer through it. He could see nothing amiss. With his peripheral vision obstructed by the thick sod sides, he had to lean out, but as long as he kept his head low, he felt safe.

Behind and above him Hannah hissed, "What's the matter?"

He started to answer her when he heard a high, patterned whistle and the fine hairs at the back of his neck stood on end. It could have been a bird, but instinct told him it was not. It was a signal. He had hunted and tracked game often enough with Many Buffalo to guess it was Spotted Pony signaling his men. A second trill, like an answering bird call, but different, convinced Jake it would be folly to walk outside normally.

How many men? He had no idea. Enough, he thought grimly.

He dropped the packs and thrust a gun into Hannah's hands. It was the one she had practiced firing, but she scarcely had time to recognize that fact.

"The men are out there somewhere," he said urgently. "Now listen to me and do *exactly* what I say." He gave her no time to respond, though she nodded. "This is loaded. Remember, it has five bullets, that's all. Make them count."

"But—"

"No matter what you hear out there, you *stay in here!* You'll be safe here. They can't burn you out, and to get in they have to come through this door. At this range you can't miss, so don't!" He kissed her once, hard, then fell to his knees and began to crawl through the opening on his belly. Before his head went through he added, "Don't let them lure you out. If it's safe, I'll let you know. Don't listen to any other voice."

Too stunned to comprehend the full scope of the situation, Hannah had no trouble understanding one thing. Jake was leaving a safe place to go and do battle with an unseen and unnumbered foe. Another woman might have been concerned about her own dilemma. Hannah could think only of Jake's danger.

Before his feet slid out through the flap, she had thrown down everything but the gun and flopped down on the floor in imitation of Jake. She had no clear intent beyond staying with him. Like Jake, who wore buckskins, she was dressed in the deerskins Bright Star had given her. Her hair was bound tightly and wrapped with leather thongs as a way to control its flyaway tendencies while they rode. The combination of clothing and hair wrapping made her no more noticeable than Jake against the sun-gilded grass that surrounded them.

The wet ground was spongy under her weight. As she tired to slither the way Jake was, she felt the cold wetness penetrate to her skin. She seemed to be gathering dried grass—*wet* dried grass, if there was such a thing—and an incredible array of matter in the front of her shirt. Crawling was hard work, especially with a heavy gun in one hand. She wished she'd had the presence of mind to put it down the back of her pants the way Jake had. Once in a while, as she mucked along, she lifted her head enough to see him. Lying flat, she could see the soles of his mocassins moving just ahead of her, a lure to keep her moving, like the proverbial donkey's carrot.

A few feet along the way she fell into a rhythm. She threw her left arm forward, pulled her body up to that point, and dragged the gun up last. She was more afraid of accidentally discharging the gun and shooting Jake than she was of anything else. She was too busy and too tired to think beyond the mechanics of her forward propulsion. As she grew more and more tired, it took her longer to complete each part of the cycle. She didn't realize what was happening until she lifted her head to check on Jake and couldn't see him. No feet. Nothing.

As soon as Jake had begun crawling, he'd been planning out what to do. Unlike the unnoticed Hannah behind him, he had the advantage of knowing where he was going. He also knew the camp well. Except for the dome-shaped houses themselves, there was no natural cover to hide him. No trees, no shrub. Just knee-high grass. There were paths around the houses and areas here and there where the grass lay in clumps, matted down by the recent rain and wind. Jake kept to the paths as much as possible, hoping to be obscured by the taller grass at the sides.

Inevitably, however, he had to stop crawling and make his move. If he had judged the signals correctly, the men waiting in ambush would not be able to see everywhere. The houses, at least seven feet tall, offered considerable protection if the men were where he judged them to be — and if there were not too many of them.

He hoped for no more than five or six. More than that and he would need incredible luck to survive. If he took down his fair share of those, at least Hannah would survive. He didn't doubt for a minute that she would be able to bring herself to shoot the men as they came after her. She wouldn't like it, but she would do it. Blessing her toughness one more time, he put her out of his mind to concentrate on his own task.

Still flat on his stomach, he worked a clump of sod from the ground. With that in his left hand and the gun in his right, he got up into a squat and prepared to run. First though, he lobbed the clump of grass and dirt into the air. His left arm was weak and less accurate than his right, but the toss was good enough to achieve his purpose. He wanted to create the appearance of activity in the grass well away from himself and away from Hannah's hiding place. As soon as his missile was in the air, he ran to the rear of the nearest sod dome.

It worked. He heard the cry *"Loo-ah! Go!"* from Spotted Pony, mingled with the yipping imitation war cries of the others. His ploy had made them show themselves, but they were on horseback while he was alone and on foot.

No sooner had Hannah discovered that Jake was no longer nearby than she heard the horrifying sound of attacking Indians. She froze where she lay, unable to think or act. The sound seemed to be all around her. Even the ground rumbled. For the moment, she was no longer in an abandoned Pawnee village with Jake. She was back at the wagon train, listening to Marcie Torvold's dying screams. With her eyes tightly closed, she saw it all again, the Indians, the horses, the flames. She burrowed deeper into the thick grass and tried to cover her ears.

As she brought her right hand up to her head, she nudged her cheek with the cold barrel of the gun. Frightened and disoriented, it took her several seconds to realize where she was and that it was her own hand holding the gun. She gasped and pushed it away, brought back to her senses by the improbable sequence. What if she had shot herself? she thought with disgust.

During the time she had been cowering in the dirt, the

233

situation around her had begun to change. She raised her head cautiously. She discovered that she was well hidden by grass, having unknowingly followed Jake off the path near one of the sod houses. She could still hear yelps and barking sounds from the circling attackers, but now instead of terrifying her, they made her angry.

She knew where Jake was now. She heard shots coming from the other side of the house next to her that had to be his. There were other gun reports, but those came from all around her.

She began to crawl forward on her hands and knees, sure that with Jake shooting at them none of the riders would see her. She was almost around the house when a horse thundered by her, so close she rolled to her left to avoid being trampled. Thinking to shoot the rider, she got up to take aim and saw that the saddle was empty.

Only in relief did she remember what Jake had told her about the gun. She had only five bullets. That meant she couldn't waste them. He had also told her long ago that her range with this revolver was limited—even assuming she could hit *any* target. The riderless horse, a big gray, plunged on, head tossing and reins flying out behind.

As she scooted around the house, moving quickly now, she saw Jake. He was crouched low to the ground, making himself as small a target as possible. She watched him fire once at a painted man who was shooting back at him as he rode by. Both of them missed, but then the unmanned horse careened into the other's path. The Indian had to pull up on his horse, giving Jake another clear chance. This time his shot knocked the rider to the ground. Instead of falling free, the man's foot caught in the stirrup. The horse reared, frantic to get loose, dragging the man under his hooves.

Hannah watched in fascinated horror as the horse pranced and danced, trampling the man to a bloodied mass before her eyes. Jake watched, too, she saw, but another man did not. Like Jake and Hannah, he was on foot. He saw Jake, but not Hannah, as he moved soundlessly forward across her line of vision, his gun leveled at Jake.

Without thinking, Hannah raised the heavy gun and aimed it at Jake's assailant. He seemed so close and loomed so big against the grassy background. Using all her strength, she squeezed the trigger and felt the report as an angry explosion of noise and pain. She landed on her backside, just as she had that first time practicing with Jake, her view of the world tossed and distorted in the action.

But when she looked again, the Indian was down and Jake was hurrying toward her. She saw him detour toward the fallen enemy to scoop up his gun, then he advanced on her. She saw his mouth move, but with her ears still ringing from the noise she couldn't tell what he was saying.

Which was just as well. She did recognize that he was angry and she began to cry. Not because he was angry. She cried with relief that he was alive.

"Oh, Jake, Jake, are they gone? I was so scared! That man . . ." Without thinking of the gun she still held clutched in her rigid fingers, she gestured wildly. Jake jumped aside and disarmed her.

"Dear God, Hannah! *You* were scared! What on earth were you doing out here?"

Hannah ran her hands over his arms and shoulders as he held her close. "You didn't see—" she choked out, trying to make sense out of what was incoherent to her.

"It's all right, sweetheart. You saved my hide again."

"Did *I* kill him?"

"One of us did for sure. With everybody shooting at once like that, it's a wonder we aren't all dead."

"Were there only two? It seemed like more."

"I think there were five."

"You killed *five* men?"

"The others ran away. One was wounded—I think."

"But won't they be back?" She kept sneaking horrified glances around Jake at the two mangled corpses, then shuddering with revulsion. All she could think was, that could be Jake. Her knees had begun to shake so badly that Jake was having to half carry her away.

He propped her against one of the houses—she was so turned around she no longer knew which one—and brushed off the grass and dirt on the front of her garments. "You came out right behind me, didn't you?" he said, noting the evidence before him.

"I just had to stay with you. I would have died in there."

He shook his head, but the corner of his mouth turned up in a wry grin. "Thank God I didn't know." Then he looked startled. "But I should have *heard* you. If you'd been one of them, I'd be dead. My God, I'm losing my touch!"

Hannah thought it best not to comment on that. To distract him, she pressed her unanswered question again. "The ones who ran away," she reminded him. "Won't they come back?"

"No. Neither of the dead is Spotted Pony, which means he's still in charge."

That was his answer? "I don't understand."

"He's an Indian, Hannah. He doesn't follow up after a raid. That's not the Indian way. They make a quick attack, then—win or lose—they retreat."

"But you said the others are white men." She didn't mention Daniel, but she thought of him. Retreat wouldn't be his way, she knew.

"They're supposed to act like Indians. It's what they're doing." He herded her back to the house they had used and urged her inside. "You'd better put on that uniform now. You're all wet. I'll get the horses."

He left before she could argue with him, so she argued with herself while she changed. It didn't make sense to her—none of it—but she hoped he was right. She never wanted to hear those high-pitched yelps of excitement again.

## Chapter Thirteen

When Jake brought their horses around, Hannah saw that he was also leading the big gray. "For a spare," he explained with a grin. "But I also wanted you to see the saddle."

It looked unexceptional to Hannah, who asked, "What about it?"

"Didn't you notice at Many Buffalo's camp that none of the horses were saddled?"

Hannah tried to think, but saddles hadn't been on her mind at that time. "I don't remember."

The look he flashed her was exasperated and something else that puzzled her. She couldn't misunderstand the stubborn way he set his jaw, however. "I wanted to spare you this," he muttered. Taking her by the arm, he began to urge her back toward the scene of their battle.

"I thought we were leaving," she protested. "And you have to change out of those wet clothes, too."

"I will, but first you have to see this. It's not going to be my word against your suspicions anymore."

"Jake, I believe you." Hannah tried to stop, but he pulled her along.

"I turned him over. It won't be too gruesome, but by

238

God, you're going to find out firsthand . . ."

He had indeed turned over the felled "Indian," but for Hannah it was gruesome beyond words. She had never seen a corpse at such close range, and this was the man she herself had killed. She tried to console herself by saying it might have been Jake. Just now, however, she was so angry at Jake that the words offered little comfort.

He held her by one hand as he bent to reveal to her the white skin just below the belt line on the body.

"You can let go of me now," she said in the iciest tones she could manage. As soon as he did, she walked away, her head high. She told herself she would never forgive him for that, but already she had. She was so stubborn— always—that she required proof, not words. Even Jake's words.

She didn't speak to him again until they stopped to make camp that night. She knew he thought she was punishing him for his "brutality," and maybe she was, a little. Mostly though, she was thinking about Jake.

In all of their dealings, Jake had been honest with her. If he had seemed to distrust her, it was for good reason. He had known for ages that her husband was his enemy and yet he had continued to treat her well. Wouldn't another man have set her loose to fend for herself in the wilderness, especially when she had already indicated that she wanted to do that by running away? Except for the fact that she hadn't left again, he had no reason to trust that she wasn't spying for Daniel. Even worse, the one man she'd unwittingly collected as a champion, George Jethro, had turned out to *be* a spy in the midst of Jake's men. With such an unlikely "coincidence," who could blame Jake for his suspicions? Only a fool would blindly trust her under those circumstances, and Jake was no fool.

She had—to her mind—proved her devotion to him over and over, not the least in caring for him under fire and in sickness. But—from his view—might not those acts simply be the smart moves of someone who recognized that, in her perhaps temporarily dependent state, her own welfare was tied to his?

Did he really think she was capable of being so devious and cunning? The thought appalled her. She considered herself the most straightforward of women—capable of lying in a tight spot certainly, but generally an honest woman. She *had* lied to Jake, but only once. Would she never gain his trust just because of one miscalculation?

With all day to contemplate Jake's broad back and uncompromising demeanor, Hannah rued again and again her reaction to his announcement that Daniel was his enemy. He had given her a chance then to repudiate her husband and all he stood for. Why hadn't she done so?

She told herself it was because of David, but it wasn't. Not really. Even if David had resembled his father in certain ways, as a son was bound to, she didn't believe for a minute that David would have grown up to be like Daniel. Daniel had been shaped by his family and by circumstances that wouldn't have been repeated in David's life. Hannah knew enough about Daniel's background to understand that he was driven by a need to manipulate others, something she had never seen in David. Like herself, David hadn't had a sly bone in his body.

No, David wasn't the reason for her rejection. She had been stung by her own pride. She saw that now.

Once she was clear in her own mind about what she had done, Hannah put the issue aside, determined to explain herself to Jake at the earliest opportunity. With her mind clear at last, she gave herself over to observation of the countryside. She didn't recognize the area as one she had traveled with the wagon, but the terrain was similar. They followed what seemed to her a "dry" streambed. It ran with water from the recent rain, but it was like none of the major rivers she had seen.

They stopped to let the horses drink once in late afternoon, but they didn't remain. Jake was pushing on as if he couldn't wait to get rid of her. Although she didn't object, Hannah began to regret each mile that brought them closer to civilization. To her, the word meant separation from Jake and everything she had come to care about. Jake was most of that, of course, but not all. How could she go back to Tennessee? Why should she? But could she go on to Fort Kearney?

She found no answers to those questions during the rest of their ride.

Making camp was so much an automatic process that no words were needed between them. They both knew their roles. Hannah's few attempts at pleasantries during their meager meal found no response in Jake. He barely looked at her.

She had one last way to get his attention before he slept and she was determined to make it work. "I need to check your bandage, Jake," she said, stopping him in surprise.

"You looked at it this morning."

"But not after all this effort today." When he didn't yield, she said, "Please, Jake. Let me see."

"It feels fine," he said, continuing to stand, as if in protest. But then he dropped to the ground in front of her, adding a curt, "Make it quick."

His sudden acquiescence worried her. Was there something wrong he wasn't telling her? But the wound was the same, healing as she was certain it should from the edges to the center.

Now that she had him trapped, shirtless and unbandaged, she couldn't remember all the fine phrases she'd assembled during the day to tell him. She began hesitantly. "Jake, about this morning . . ." He didn't help her. "About that man . . . I understand."

"What do you understand?"

241

"Why . . . you had to show me." She paused to adjust the bandage. For some reason she couldn't seem to work and talk at the same time. Both required concentration. "I believed you before. I really did. But I can understand why you don't think I did."

She waited for his response, her fingers poised at his uncommunicative back. When he said nothing, she rested her still-idle hands.

"Are you through?" he asked impatiently.

"Through?" Her hands fluttered up, then resettled, a sign of her confusion. "Well, I know you're not going to apologize," she said, trying to think what she meant to convey. "But I wanted you to know I forgive you anyway."

"How nice," he replied acidly. "I *meant*, are you finished fooling around with that bandage?"

Reminded of that job, she gave it a yank then. "I'm not fooling around with it!" she said, indignation making her final touches unintentionally rough. "If that's what you think, then go ahead and get gangrene. See if I care!"

"I think I'm safe from gangrene now," Jake said, reclaiming his shirt to stand. "You'll have to find some other way to poison me now. The truth is, Hannah, you missed your chance this morning. You should have let your husband's 'Indian' kill me off."

"I told you I believed you before. You won't accept anything I say, will you?" Rather than let him reduce her to tears of frustration, Hannah turned away and tried to leave. His hand on her arm stopped her. His touch was surprisingly gentle.

"I accept more than you think, Hannah."

"I'm sorry I sounded as if I didn't believe you, Jake. It was just . . . hard."

"I know."

"I thought about it all day. You have every reason to suspect me of being in on Daniel's scheme. I wasn't, I swear, but you can't know that and I haven't done

242

anything right. I lied to you—just once, but—"

"You saved my life—not just once."

Hannah couldn't think what to say next. He wasn't really arguing. Did that mean he understood?

"All day I thought you were angry with me about the body. I didn't blame you. That was cruel. I wouldn't be here now except for you—"

"Yes, you would. You saw him, too."

"Not until you fired, Hannah. I shouldn't have put you through that. I probably wouldn't have apologized. Around you I seem to be doing that all the time and I hate it, but I am sorry."

"I know you're right about Daniel. I just didn't want to believe . . ." She took a deep breath and started again. "He was David's father, but that wasn't it either."

Jake had pulled her down onto the blankets and now he was trying to kiss her. She wanted the kiss, but not before she had squared herself with him. She put her hand over her mouth.

He nibbled distractingly at her fingers, but she persisted. "I didn't want to admit to myself that I could have been so wrong about my husband. It was my pride. My mother used to tell me it would be my downfall. I do try to fight it. Just not very well." She let her fingers play over the soft growth of his beard. "It would have been easier for me if your wife hadn't been such a paragon," she mused. Now that he was listening, she was paying less and less attention to what she said.

"What?" Jake took her hand and held it away from his face to look at her.

Hannah heard his surprise but mistook the cause. Thinking that the word *paragon* was unfamiliar to him, she sought another way to say the same thing. "Well, think about it, Jake," she said, sitting straight up again. "How would you feel if I went on and on about how handsome and debonair Daniel was? What a perfect

243

gentleman he was? Wouldn't you begin to feel second best?"

"Is that what you think?" He seemed genuinely shocked. "But I've told you how wonderful you are—"

"Oh yes, wonderful," Hannah said scathingly. "You've thanked me for saving your life and for nursing you. You've told me how . . ." She faltered under the surprisingly heavy load of bitterness she felt. She was almost as stunned as Jake apparently was by the depth of her feelings. "Let me see, how was it you put it?" But she didn't need time to recall his words. They were burned into her brain. "I think you called me tough and hardy and . . . strong."

"I also said you were beautiful," he defended. "And you are."

"But not pink and white and yellow and beautiful." How foolish she sounded! Her attempt at jocularity was a miserable failure.

Jake took her face between his big hands as if to study it. "No, you're not," he said gravely. "Your hair is the color of dark fire. Your skin is rich, like heavy cream or ivory. You have molasses eyes. And your mouth is . . . soft but . . . fiery, too."

With his mouth just inches from hers, Hannah felt she was drowning in anticipation. She fought back by saying, "I felt like a draft horse, the way you talked."

"You're not listening, Hannah." He leaned closer.

She saw his lips twitch as he suppressed a smile. "Oh, of course, *now*," she chided. "You can trot out the fine words now, now that I've asked for them."

"If you're not careful, sweetheart, you're going to get exactly what you're asking for," he warned, taking her mouth in a thoroughly possessive kiss.

Hannah didn't want to respond. Even if she'd had to ask for the compliment, it was much more than "fine words." She'd tried to be dismissive because she was so touched. She'd never forget, but she was sure she shouldn't let him win her over so easily.

Jake slid one hand around her head to cup the nape of her neck under the Union-blue shirt she wore. The gesture, protective and possessive all at once, flooded Hannah with liquid heat. She flung her arms around his shoulders and pressed closer. He felt like a warm, hard wall to her.

He groaned and bit gently at her lower lip. His right hand slid down the outside of the shirt and settled over her breast. "Oh, woman, what you do to the front of an old army shirt."

Hannah's breath caught as his thumb worried the pouting fullness of her nipple. "I like what you do," she murmured, letting her head fall back.

"I thought I was tired."

"I knew I was."

Jake undid one button of her shirt and tunneled inside, where his hand encountered her chemise. He plucked at it. "Why do you wear this?"

"To protect me from the shirt," she answered without thinking. "The cloth is rough and with the horse's movement, I—" She stopped, suddenly aware of what she was talking about.

"Bounce," Jake finished for her with a wicked grin. "Why do you think I ride ahead?"

Hannah wasn't usually slow, but her ability to think was hindered by what Jake's hand was doing inside her shirt. "To lead," she answered promptly.

"Not really. Not with just two of us. I give you my back so I'm not tormented all day by the beautiful way you bounce inside this shirt."

She gave him a seductive smile. "That would torment you?" she asked, pleased. Then she laughed. "Funny. I wouldn't exactly call it *torment* to watch the way you . . . move."

As she had planned, Jake was disconcerted by what she'd said. He drew back to look at her, first surprised, then glaring fiercely when he saw her teasing expression. With her shirt fully open it was easy for him to slide his hand down to cup her bottom. "Careful," he growled into her ear. "I don't usually issue this many warnings." He lifted her onto his lap.

"Before what?" Hannah couldn't resist asking any more than she could keep from wiggling against his thighs and chest.

His chuckle was a velvet brush traveling the length of her spine. "Just keep pushing and you'll find out," he promised.

"Would it have anything to do with taking off the rest of my clothes?"

His laugh was a short bark. "It might."

"And taking off yours?"

"You want to check my bandage again?"

"If I have to. Anything to get you out of your . . . shirt."

Jake's chest rumbled with laughter. "Then that was a ruse. I thought so."

"You have a suspicious mind." Hannah pushed his shirt down over his shoulders.

"I need one to keep up with you."

She stopped undressing him and asked impatiently, "*Are* you going to keep up with me?"

Jake didn't react to her challenge as she had expected. Instead of helping, he sat back and held out his hands meekly. "I don't think so. The last time you undressed me I was out cold. This time I'm going to enjoy myself."

Hannah undid the cuffs of his shirt so it fell off. The idea of undressing him had great appeal, but she argued for effect. "You weren't out cold at all," she reminded him. "You were burning up."

"Then let's see if we can make that happen again."

"I thought you didn't want more fever."

"Cantankerous wench," Jake said without rancor, shaking his head at her.

Hannah avoided his attempt to draw her close. "There you go, trying to sweet-talk me again."

He stretched out on the blanket, lying back to watch her, only the glitter of his eyes and the small gleam of teeth showing his amusement in the dusky light. "Am I succeeding?"

"We'll see," she murmured, hungrily running her eyes over his length. The only male bodies she had seen that approached Jake's for beauty were in the museums she had visited back East with Uncle Simon. And those, like one or two of the handsome Indians she had seen at Many Buffalo's camp, had been hairless. She loved the dark, furry warmth of Jake's magnificent chest. She felt like a child turned loose in a candy shop. She wanted to touch him everywhere. Just knowing she could made her knees weak.

She leaned forward and put her face in the ruff of springy curls in the center of his chest. With her mouth open, she savored all the sensations that were Jake; the curve of muscle held by smooth skin, the thunder of his heartbeat when she found the dark copper coins buried in the thicket of hair, the wonderfully male scent of horse, leather, and fresh air.

Aware of her own pleasure as her tongue played with his small nipples, Hannah didn't notice Jake's hands clench to fists at his sides. He gave no sign of disturbance when her hair brushed his arms and shoulders. Her opened shirt and chemise also trailed over his skin as she moved, but it was the press of one bare breast against his ribs that made him close his eyes and begin to recite multiplication tables in his head. His self-control was so complete that Hannah, who had expected some response by now, was discouraged. She sat back and peered into his

247

face. He looked so much the stoic Indian that she almost gave up.

Then she remembered. Her pleasure didn't necessarily wait upon his, at least not this time. She was enjoying her freedom of his body too much to stop just because he was indifferent. At least he hadn't objected. Perhaps next time he'd tell her what he liked, but she wouldn't quit so easily.

She ran her hand experimentally down one leg, catching him so off-guard he almost yelped. She felt his muscles tense and ripple, but missed seeing his jaw clench in the dim light. Besides, she was looking at his legs, not his face. She took off his moccasins and tossed them aside while she considered the best way to remove his pants.

Inwardly, Jake groaned. He knew what she was thinking and knew, too, that as soon as she began unbuttoning his pants, his pretense of control would be shattered. He tried to put into practice every method of mind control he'd heard of, but none was as powerful as the image of Hannah's hands on his body. Still, he tried.

Hannah kept him in suspense for the longest time before she decided to approach the problem indirectly. She searched his waist for a belt first, then began to undo the top button. Because she was nervous, she was unusually awkward and slow.

Finally, Jake broke. "You're trying to kill me," he moaned.

Startled out of her trancelike concentration, Hannah jumped in guilty reaction. "Oh, Jake, you—" She fumbled even to speak. *Scared* wasn't the right word, but no other was strong enough to convey her meaning. "You surprised me," she finished lamely.

"Yeah, well, I'm still here, but I won't be for long if you don't stop torturing me."

When she looked back, she noticed that he had raised one knee and turned onto his side toward her. That change, plus his choice of the word "torturing," made her realize he wasn't as indifferent to her as she had feared. Another try at his pants proved her right. Forgetting the buttons, she clasped the aroused hardness of his sex and cuddled against his chest.

"You helped me more when you were unconscious than you are now," she complained softly.

He didn't move while she slowly stroked him through his clothes. "If it's help you want—" he said finally, taking her hand away. "That's not the way to get it," he finished when he had her hands corralled.

"I thought you were . . . indifferent," Hannah confessed, relieved enough to smile at him. "I thought I was doing it wrong."

"I wanted you to enjoy yourself."

"I was, but I couldn't bear to think I wasn't affecting you. Just your slightest touch excites me so. It didn't seem fair."

"My slightest touch?"

Hannah heard the smile in his voice and laughed. "Don't pretend you didn't know. I haven't exactly resisted you."

"Like this?" he asked, running one hand along her leg.

"Yes," she whispered, moving to give him better access. The warm pressure of his hand burned through her clothing to make her move restlessly. She reached down for his leg. "Then when I touched you, it didn't tickle?"

"What made you think that?"

"I felt your muscles twitch. I thought—" His kiss stopped her explanation.

"Don't think anymore, sweetheart," Jake urged between kisses. "Just love me. Please love me. And let me love you."

Hannah's heart soared. He had never spoken to her like that before. He had told her not to think, but she couldn't help it. She wanted Jake's love, she realized, because he already had hers. It was love, not fear or dependency, that had sent her crawling in the grass after Jake this morning. And it was love that gave that special magic to his touch. No matter what Jake thought, she could not give herself without reservation like this to a man she didn't love.

She wondered at her blindness. How could she have failed for so long to see what was obvious? She didn't worry that Jake would know, nor did she want to tell him. If he still didn't trust her, he certainly wouldn't want her love. Someday that would bother her, but not now. Now it was too new, too wonderful. She didn't want to expose her tender new feelings to his withering cynicism. It was enough right now just to feel love and know it for what it was.

Hannah let her love speak to Jake through her hands and mouth and body. As she had instinctively known, it was better to touch him when he was touching back, when he was responding. They helped each other out of their clothes without delay because the act of undressing was no longer paramount. Loving was.

Jake was tender and slow, all the things he had wished to be the last time. He was just as aroused, but being at peace within his own mind made finesse possible. Dusk had turned to darkness around them. Although he couldn't see Hannah clearly, her image was distinct in his mind. His hands touched and triggered a precise vision that was almost better than reality. She had become his ideal of beauty, and in loving her, he worshiped both his ideal and this one specific woman. Even the air around them was warm and moist, making the cover of a blanket unnecessary.

He wrung soft sounds of surrender from Hannah with his hands and drank them from her lips. Unable to tell her he loved her, he showed her.

"Oh, Jake, yes . . . yes," she cried when he entered her.

Her chant didn't change as he moved within her, giving and taking pleasure with her, body and soul. Because he was half afraid of what he would say, Jake contented himself with murmuring her name until he could say nothing for lack of breath. When he felt her legs tighten around his waist, he gave up his struggle for delay and joined her in a mind-blotting release.

When he could speak again, Jake asked, "Now do you believe that you're beautiful?"

"You make me feel beautiful, Jake. Once I didn't think I would ever feel that way again. I had decided it's not important," she told him, twirling a lock of his inky hair around one finger. "It isn't, really, but it's wonderful just the same."

"What you said before really stung me."

Hannah heard that with a sinking sensation of dread. Now what had she said? "What was that?" She tried a small laugh. "I've said so many things."

"No, no." He laughed. "Not the 'I hate you's' and the 'I don't care if you get gangrene's'. Those I can take. I just didn't mean to make you feel second best. You're not. I'm afraid I haven't been honest about Grace."

She held her breath, afraid even to sigh with relief. She had heard the smallest break before his wife's name, that telltale hesitation that revealed how hard it was for him to talk about Grace.

"She wasn't a saint, Hannah."

"No woman is," she told him gently.

"I've never told anyone about her. I used to think I was protecting her, but I guess it was really for my own benefit. I've never wanted to admit just how terrible it was."

Hannah thought he was referring to her death, and in a way, he was, but not entirely.

"The things I called you, sturdy and strong, those were compliments, whether you thought so or not. Grace

251

wasn't just delicate, she was childish and spoiled. She had been indulged until she didn't want to be a grown-up at all. She didn't want me and she didn't want Caroline."

Hannah tried to hide her shock. Perhaps he didn't understand. "But Jake, it must have been hard for her. You said she was sick—"

"She brought it on herself, Hannah, even her death. Believe me, I'm not exaggerating. I wish I were. I think she married me because no one locally would have her, in spite of her beauty. The people around her knew she wasn't going to assume an adult's responsibilities."

"I don't understand. Tell me plainly."

"Plainly?" He tightened his hold on Hannah. If he hadn't been too distracted for smiles, he would have smiled at the way she had cut to the heart of his problem. He had been trying to explain everything in "nice" terms—as if for Grace, he realized with a start. When would he stop doing that?

"Grace was small, not undeveloped really, just physically petite. No matter how gentle I tried to be, she never wanted to lie with me. In a way I accepted that, difficult as it was. What I couldn't accept was the fact that she didn't know how to keep house or even care for herself. I didn't find that out until we left Pennsylvania. Her father tried to send a woman along to be our maid. I didn't allow it, of course, because I had no idea Grace was incompetent."

"But you were married. How could you not know?"

"We lived with her parents. Her mother did everything. I urged Grace to be more helpful, but she told me her mother preferred it that way. Mrs. Lunig was rather domineering, so I could see the point. It never occurred to me that Grace didn't know how to boil water."

"How did she manage when you were on the road?"

"Badly. Very badly. Other women helped at first. They tried to show her what to do until it became clear that

252

Grace just didn't want to learn. She expected to be served, by everyone; it didn't matter that she was taking advantage of others who were already busy with their own families. I did most of the work. Grace just complained."

The picture he painted was terribly clear to Hannah.

"She began getting sick because she was pregnant, and that didn't help. She didn't want the baby. I think she may have tried to . . . abort . . . Thank God she didn't succeed, or couldn't. But her sickness never eased. I was very sympathetic then. I wasn't patient about the other things, but her sickness tore me in half.

"We stopped traveling in Iowa, as I told you, until after Caroline was born. Grace had all the help anyone could desire, but none of it mattered. She wanted nothing to do with Caroline. She couldn't feed her, nor did she want to. She didn't even want to live."

"But Jake," Hannah objected, "you make it sound as if she chose to die. You said she was sick. Couldn't she have had some disease you didn't know about?"

"I tried to believe that, Hannah. I really did. But she wouldn't eat. If I forced her to eat, she threw it back up."

Hannah grew excited. From being jealous of Grace, she had moved past that to pity for both of them. She wanted to restore Grace to Jake in memory so he could forgive and forget. She thought she saw a way for him to move past his bitterness.

"But don't you see, Jake? That couldn't have been willful. No one throws up on purpose. She must have been sick."

"I wish you were right," he said sadly. "But that's exactly what she did. I think she got the idea when she was pregnant and then afterward she just kept doing it. Maybe she couldn't stop. I know I couldn't stop her. If she didn't get sick naturally, she would gag herself, stick her finger down her throat."

"Oh, Jake."

"Yes. Well. Now you know."

Hannah had never felt so close to another person in her life. The death of her parents when she was ten had taken her only confidante from her long before she'd had more than childish woes to tell her mother. Except for Daniel, however, she had received love in generous measure since, notably from Uncle Simon, Willie, and little David. Their love had cushioned her disappointment in Daniel, which, although major, had not destroyed her or her capacity to love. Bad as it was to be cast off by an uncaring husband, what Jake had suffered was much worse.

She didn't have to ask if he had loved Grace. His love shone through every word he said about her. Yet she had given back so little, only the unwilling gift of Caroline, his daughter. No wonder she was the focal point of his life. Hannah's heart went out to both of them: to Caroline, who, like herself at ten, did not have her parents; to Jake, a loving man with no one to love him back.

But now he had her. He didn't know it yet, of course, because the time wasn't right. Yet. She wouldn't tell him. She would only show him by her every act. She would make him feel loved, perhaps for the first time in his life.

"One thing I've never understood," Jake said, breaking into her thoughts, "is how you can be so totally unspoiled when you have so much money. Why don't you complain and whine about these conditions?"

Hannah was so content at that moment she almost asked, "What conditions?" Jake held her lovingly close under the drawn-up blanket. What more could she want?

"Grace couldn't have put up with any of this. And she wasn't from great wealth. Her parents were just a comfortably provisioned farm couple."

"I was ten years old before I went to live with Uncle Simon, Jake. My parents were Ohio farmers, much like Grace's parents probably except that they didn't indulge me. I worked hard, helping my mother and my father. I

254

fed chickens, milked cows, fetched wood and water. Oh, I was no drudge, I can tell you. I had fun. I had cats in the barn and a dog of my own, a pony to ride. But I had chores to do and I did them. My parents wouldn't have let me shirk. Not that they were unkind. About all it took to discipline me was a stern look. I never expected to live any other life than some version of theirs when I grew up. But then they died."

"What happened?"

"My father's one indulgence was a fast horse. He had a red stallion he wanted to have pull a fancy carriage. He had seated by mother in it and was just getting up onto the seat when the horse took off. Maybe a horsefly or bee had stung it, no one knew. They were both killed. I never saw them, but I was told my mother looked like she was asleep. Her neck had been broken. My father was badly hurt by the road, the horse, and the carriage. People always said it was wonderful they died together because they loved each other so much, but I missed them badly. It was a terrible shock. All of a sudden I had nothing."

For a moment Hannah experienced that same feeling of desolation, then she rallied and said brightly, "But I did have something and it turned out to be much more than many others have. I had their love inside me and I had the training they'd given me. And then I had Uncle Simon and he was wonderful to me. He was totally inexperienced with children, so he treated me like a small friend. It was odd, but somehow it worked. It wouldn't have though, if my parents hadn't done their job so well, because he didn't know how to be a parent. That's a lot harder. I've been extremely lucky in the way my life turned out."

To herself Hannah thought, *And my luck's not over yet, because now I have you.* She turned and burrowed closer to Jake's warm length.

He kissed her brow and breathed deeply, taking the scent of her hair deep into his lungs. "Hannah, I—"

She kissed him, stopping his words. Settling over him under the blanket, she braced herself on her hands at either side of his head. They both needed sleep, she knew, because tomorrow was another hard day of travel, but right now they needed this more.

"Don't talk, Jake. Just love me, please. And let me love you."

# Chapter Fourteen

Jake pulled Victor to a halt to survey the area ahead.

"What is it?" Hannah questioned, stopping beside him. They were well into their third day of riding after the attack by Spotted Pony and his men.

That morning he had told her they were within a day of Omaha. At first she had been elated. Omaha meant safety. However often Jake assured her that they wouldn't be attacked again, she knew it was always a possibility. Because he didn't want her to be afraid, he had kept his concerns about the enemy to himself. Now and again—as on this occasion—his apprehension surfaced under the guise of extreme caution.

Hannah's greatest fear, however, wasn't for their safety. Not anymore. She was much more worried about what Jake would do once they reached civilization. He didn't consider his job complete, and she knew he'd never take her with him, even if he weren't going into danger—which he would be. The thought that in twenty-four hours or so Jake might leave her forever was infinitely more upsetting than anything else she could imagine.

She peered ahead into what looked to be an ordinary grove of trees. If anything, it was more inviting than the usual scenery, making Hannah wonder for a moment if Jake perhaps shared some of her unwillingness to arrive in Omaha. "It looks nice, Jake. Some shade for a change.

Or did you hear something?"

He shook his head. "That's the trouble. It looks too damn inviting, don't you think?"

"Could we go around it?"

"Not without a big detour. There's a ravine one way and a quicksand stretch by the river. That's another reason for my caution. It's the perfect place for an ambush."

"Why don't we separate—"

"No." Jake got off the horse, handing the reins up to Hannah. "I'm going to check this out on foot. Something about that path looks strange."

"Be careful."

"That's what I'm doing." He looked back at her long enough to warn, "And don't you *dare* follow me this time."

"I won't. I promise." She wasn't foolish enough to remind him that her following had saved the day before. She agreed with him anyway that that had been a fluke. Since she knew nothing about what he was doing now, she was willing to wait for his approval before moving.

Hannah watched without alarm as Jake worked his way into the shade. His care seemed exaggerated, but she trusted his instincts over her own. He had kept them from ambush before. Doubtless he knew what he was doing. She kicked her feet out of the stirrups and hitched around in the saddle, changing positions to rest from the strain of constant riding. The horses snatched mouthfuls of grass in the same surreptitious way.

For all of Jake's caution, his appearance in the grove of willows only sent up a few birds from the ground before him. Not even a squirrel scolded from a tree. Hannah let go of the reins and stretched, moving her shoulders in a circle to relax the tense muscles.

Jake looked back as if he were about to signal for her

to follow, then suddenly he went flying up into the air, feet first. His bellow of surprise was cut off just as quickly as it began when whatever lifted him let go, dropping him to plunge back to the ground. It happened so abruptly and was so bizarre that Hannah could hardly believe it.

"Jake!" she screamed.

It took forever to get off the horse and run to where he had fallen. She ran with no thought of caution, frantic to find him. It was as if, except for that brief time in the air, he had disappeared from the earth. Jake had cautioned her to keep her hat over her hair at all times while they rode so no one watching would suspect that she was a woman. Now she ran so fast her hat flew off, allowing her hair to fall loose and stream out behind her.

She found Jake in a heap among some bushes, unconscious again. She patted his face and called to him, sobbing his name in fright. She had no idea what to do for him. He was crumpled like a discarded rag doll and she didn't know where to start to care for him. She could feel his heart beat, finally, over the thunder of her own, but he didn't groan or move. She had thought nothing could be worse than his being shot, but clearly this was.

She thought of broken bones at last and began running her hands over his legs and arms. She couldn't be sure what she was feeling and she couldn't see through her tears. She patted down his legs again, more slowly, and then found on one ankle the loop of rope that had caught him. It was still there.

She was struggling to undo it, crying out to Jake hysterically, when she saw something else that made her blood suddenly run cold. Planted next to Jake's leg on the ground was a large booted foot. Her fingers failed her and she bowed her head in defeat, expecting the blow that would end her life. Jake was right. They had been

259

ambushed again by Daniel's brutal men. The boot next to Jake belonged to no Indian, but she had seen with her own eyes that the men were masquerade Indians. She had never felt so defeated. Jake was dying and she was as good as dead.

"Ma'am? He's not dead, is he? Oh, please tell me he's not dead!"

Hannah looked up in amazement as the tall figure beside her got down onto his knees. His voice, though deep at first, had risen in alarm and cracked under the weight of his concern.

"I didn't mean to hurt him. Honest!"

"*You* did that?" She looked up into the air, picturing again how Jake had been yanked up and then dropped. "What was it?"

"A trap . . . I set up a trap." He untied the rope from Jake's leg with big, deft hands. "I'm sorry. I thought you, I mean . . . *he* was someone else."

"So did we," Hannah said, staring stupidly. The "man" beside her was a boy, or rather a young man, grown like a large dog to nearly full size long before he was ready to be a man. He was raw-boned and awkward, with hands, feet, and shoulders it would take years for him to grow into. "I mean, we thought this was an ambush—or might be. That's why Jake—" She broke off in dismay. "Oh, God, what's wrong with him? Do you know? I can't tell."

"I think he hit his head, ma'am. The tree broke."

"The tree?"

"It was a bent willow trap. I bent a willow down with rope. When he stepped in it, the tree sprung up and trapped him. But he's so big and heavy the tree broke and dropped him. On his head, I'm afraid."

Hannah thought of her mother. "Do you think he broke his neck?"

They peered at Jake's neck together, one as ignorant as

the other. "I don't think so," the boy said. "It doesn't look broken."

"Oh, I hope not. But we have to move him. We can't stay here. Some . . . men are chasing us and I'm afraid they'll kill Jake."

"I can carry him if you think it's all right."

"Lift him to the path." Then she cautioned, "Gently."

He moved Jake as gently as possible, but Hannah had no idea if they were hurting or helping him. She greatly feared they were hurting him, but Jake gave no sign one way or the other.

When Jake was laid out on solid ground, Hannah went over him again for broken bones. She couldn't see his wound, but she put her hand on the bandage of see if the fall had caused him to bleed again. She could feel no wetness and had to be satisfied with that for now. She sat back on her heels and looked at him, wondering what to do.

"His shoulder looks funny to me," the boy said from above her. "Does it to you?"

"I don't know. I'm more worried about his head." She could feel a lump on the right side of his head. "He must have a concussion. I was unconscious for three days with one. What will I do if he doesn't come to?"

"If you're going to Omaha, I could help you. I was just hiding here awhile to be safe."

Hannah searched the boy's face. His expression was heartbreakingly earnest. "How old are you, son?"

"Almost seventeen."

"How almost seventeen?"

"It'll be a while," he admitted as a wash of red stained his face.

"Next year?"

"No. In February. I'm . . . big for my age."

"What's your name? How do you happen to be here by

261

yourself?" Hannah asked her questions out of kindness, not distrust. There was something terribly appealing about this boy.

"I'm Rory Talmage. I'm from St. Louis, Missouri. I was thinking I'd go back there."

"You just came from there?"

"More or less. It's a long story."

"I'm Hannah Hatch . . . Veazie," she said, holding out her hand. She couldn't have explained why she added the Veazie this time except for the fact that inside she was still stinging from Jake's accusations about her lack of honesty. "I'll want to hear your story, but right now I've got to figure out what to do for Jake."

"Were you in the Army, ma'am?"

Startled and amused by his question, Hannah almost laughed. She sensed, however, that he was serious and she controlled herself rather than embarrass him again. "No, but Jake was. He rescued me after my wagon train was attacked going west. I just wear these clothes to ride in and so I don't look like a woman."

"I've got a camp back here," Rory said. "I can carry Jake there."

"You're alone?"

"Yes, ma'am."

"Is it well hidden?"

"Yes'm. And I made traps around."

"So you did. Will I be safe going back for the horses?"

"Yes. The one your husband stepped in was the first. Bring them here and wait for me. I'll be back and guide you the rest of the way."

Hannah agreed and watched him lift Jake in his arms like a giant baby. For all his great size, Rory moved with surprising grace and surefootedness. She noticed that he rarely walked on the trail itself until he disappeared from view at a bend. She was careful to follow his instructions

262

as she brought the three horses in tow. Although she had taken no care in leaving them, they hadn't wandered except in search of tender new grass to eat. With all their travel, they had no desire to run anywhere.

Rory was quick to meet her. "Nice horses," he said approvingly, giving Victor's nose a pat before setting off again. As he went, he pointed out his defenses to her in an oddly detached way. Hannah couldn't decide whether he warned her out of concern for her safety or because he was proud of the traps. He had cause for pride, she concluded, for the entire stretch of path just beyond the entrance to the thicket was thoroughly booby-trapped.

His camp was well set up, both secluded and comfortable.

"He kind of groaned when I put him down," Rory told her when she was by Jake's side again on what was obviously Rory's bed.

"Maybe I should put a cold pack on his head. It might help keep the swelling down."

Rory went off for water, leading the three horses away. Hannah had both their packs to rummage for bandage material. She gave up her nightgown this time, knowing that with Rory around she wouldn't be wearing it anymore. By the time he returned, she had torn several strips to make pads to soak with water.

"How long have you been living here, Rory?" she asked, holding the cold cloth to Jake's head.

"This is my third day. Tomorrow I was going to undo the traps and go back to Omaha."

"Why the traps?"

"I thought someone might come after me."

Hannah could see the thought made him miserable. "Who?"

"My uncle."

"And you're afraid of your uncle?"

263

"Yes'm, I am. It's kind of hard to explain, but I don't trust him."

"Is he your only family?"

"He is now. My mother died early in the war; she and my little sister both got cholera. We all did, but theirs was worse and they died. My dad and I were all right after a while. Dad was in business with Uncle Joseph. They had a foundry, and business was real good during the war. We had a farm outside the city, not too far and not very big, but it was nice.

"Well, in May my dad had an accident at the foundry. Uncle Joseph took over everything. He said he was taking care of me. Dad died and Uncle Joseph sold everything, the foundry *and* the farm. He said I was too young to live there alone, that I couldn't manage. He . . . had papers he said left everything to him."

"Did you get a lawyer?" Hannah asked.

"He did. I tried to talk to one of Dad's friends, a Mr. Worthen, but he couldn't do much. He said my uncle was going to help me."

"But you didn't believe that."

"No, ma'am, I didn't. I think he killed my father." His deep brown eyes seemed to plead with Hannah for understanding. "I know that sounds crazy, but Dad didn't like what he was doing with the business. He didn't tell me much about it. He didn't want to worry me, and I know he thought I was too young to get involved.

"I heard them arguing one night just before Dad had his 'accident,' and I know Uncle Jospeh wanted him to sell the business. It had something to do with contracts they'd had with the Confederate government during the war. Uncle Joseph was on the losing side, you know. He and Dad always disagreed about the war. All I know is that Dad's accident was awfully convenient for Uncle Joseph."

"So he sold the business as he wanted to," Hannah said thoughtfully. She wrung out another pad for Jake's head, changing it to keep the temperature cool. "I'm not surprised that you were suspicious, Rory. Couldn't you get anyone to help you keep the farm?"

"Everyone said it was up to Uncle Joseph. He was my guardian. He tells everyone I'm like his own son to him, all the family he has in this world. He makes me sound like I'm ungrateful when I know I'm not. Or I wouldn't be if he really cared about me.

"Just about all I have left of my own is the horse I stole from the wagon train. It was *my* horse, but I didn't think I'd get to keep even that very long. Uncle Joseph is headed for Oregon. He has all the money from the farm and the business. I figured somewhere along the way to Oregon he'd arrange for me to have my own 'accident,' so I stole back my horse and left."

"And you've been hiding since then?"

"Yes'm."

"Please call me Hannah, Rory. I don't know if I can help you get back your property, but I'll try," she promised, thinking of Uncle Simon and the long arm of his influence.

"I don't care about the money, really I don't. I just didn't dare stay with him."

"Of course not. Have you eaten?"

"Ma'am?"

Hannah laughed. "That's the mother in me coming out. I wondered if you've had enough to eat here."

"I catch rabbits," he said, blushing again. "Not all the traps are meant for people."

If Hannah hadn't already decided that his story was too complicated to be contrived, she would have believed him seeing that blush again. She knew there were clever liars in this world, but Rory Talmage certainly wasn't one of them. With Jake disabled, she had little choice about accepting his help. They had to get to Omaha, where Jake would be safe and could be tended by a doctor, but Hannah couldn't decide whether to press on immediately or wait until morning. They had safety where they were, given the number of traps Rory had set for the unwary, and who could tell where they could stop once they left? They would lose part of a day by staying, but no more than that if they got an early start.

Hannah looked at Jake, hoping for a sign of recovery. There was none.

"Maybe by morning he'll be better," she said to Rory, her decision made. "I hate to move him when he's like this."

But in the morning Jake was still unconscious and they had to tie him onto Victor after all. Hannah watched in agony, trying to help Rory and getting in his way instead. She worried about Jake's head and the dislocated shoulder Rory had snapped back into position the night before when they had checked more thoroughly for broken bones. A thousand times she said, "Oh, be careful, Rory," knowing he was doing his best.

Rory knew Jake wasn't her husband now; but heaven only knew what he had made of the story she told him — highly expurgated, of course. She felt compelled to tell him something about Daniel and her uncle, not to mention a bit about Grace and Caroline. No matter how she emphasized her gratitude to Jake and his to her, Rory surely knew from the way she fussed over Jake that her feelings for him went far beyond ordinary gratitude. He was kind enough not to comment.

The ride to Omaha was worse than anything Hannah had endured on the entire trip. She couldn't stand to watch Jake and she couldn't look away for fear she might miss a chance to help him. She felt every jounce twice, once for herself and once for Jake. Rory tried to distract her with conversation, but finally he gave up the attempt and concentrated on getting them there.

Once they reached the outskirts of town, Hannah came alive. At last she could help Jake. She was indifferent, if not oblivious, to the stares they drew riding through the street to the hotel where she knew that Hannah Hatch, or at least her Uncle Simon and his money, would be remembered.

Even if the hotel clerk remembered Miss Hannah Hatch, he didn't associate that lovely lady with the disheveled, trail-worn, *dirty* creature before him. He did, however, recognize that the situation unfolding in the lobby required the manager's attention. That gentleman, sufficiently warned by the clerk, took one look at the lady's memorable red hair and confirmed Hannah's identity.

"My dear Miss Hatch," he said, offering his hand. "How may we help you?"

"We need three rooms and a physician for my friend. He was injured in a fall."

Rory carried Jake, doing whatever Hannah directed. If she'd had any attention to spare from Jake, she would have been pleased by the boy's aplomb. As it was, she was only grateful for his help. She waved aside the manager's attempt to show her to her room, insisting that he send the doctor to Jake at once.

When they were alone at Jake's bedside, Rory tore his eyes from the ornately carved chairs before the fireplace and said, "I can't stay here, ma'am."

Something in his desperate tone broke through Hannah's concentration on Jake and made her look at Rory. Now that she was so close to getting help for Jake, her impatience had grown rather than diminished. That impatience had made her forget that Rory was a person, not a pack mule to carry Jake for her. She felt deeply ashamed of her inconsideration.

She clasped Rory's hand and held it tight. "Please don't leave me now, Rory. I know this is difficult for you, but I'm afraid I'm going to fly apart any minute now. If you don't like your room, we can get it changed. I promise."

"No, no, that's not what I meant. I . . . I don't have any money."

"Well, neither do I, Rory, to tell you the truth." She laughed to think of it. "But my uncle will gladly pay for all of us."

"That wouldn't be right, ma'am, and I don't know how I'd every pay him back."

"You already have. You've helped me. That's all he'd ever ask of you," Hannah assured him seriously. "But you do have to do one more thing, and that's stop calling me ma'am. It makes me feel about a hundred years old. My name is Hannah."

Rory started to say, "Yes, ma'am," then he blushed. His blush only deepened when Hannah hugged him quickly and laughed.

"What do you think they'll make of our luggage?" she asked, distracting him from his self-consciousness. "I wonder if they've ever seen worse?"

"I don't think so," Rory answered. He edged to the chairs, apparently fascinated by them. "Do you think anyone ever sits in those chairs?"

Once Hannah would have thought them completely unexceptional; now she saw them as Rory did. "Not for very long, I'm sure. They look worse than a saddle right now."

"The horses!" Rory burst out, starting for the door.

"They'll be taken care of. Don't worry, the hotel has a fine stable."

With a perfect sense of timing, the doctor arrived then

to confirm Hannah and Rory's inexpert diagnosis. Jake had no broken bones. The bruises developing all over his body attested to his severity of his fall. He would be stiff and sore. When he regained consciousness, he would have a headache. Hannah remembered that and winced, thinking of Jake's temper. After Rory helped her bathe him, the doctor came back to strap his shoulder into a harness contraption. There was another one for his left knee. Dr. Bird assured Hannah that the braces would keep Jake immobile while his strained tendons healed.

Hannah devoutly hoped so.

She and Rory took turns sitting with Jake during his slow return to awareness. For Hannah it was enough like his bout with fever to be achingly familiar, but Rory didn't know Jake—and vice versa—so Hannah tried to do most of the nursing. After all, she wanted to be there when he came to.

Even when she was away from his side, she was too busy to rest. Her wire to Uncle Simon by way of his solicitor found him in St. Louis. He would be with her in a few days. By then, all of them, Rory and Jake too, would be well dressed and ready to present a good appearance.

While Jake slept—Hannah knew better than to do it when he was awake—a silent tailor discreetly measured him for his new clothes. Rory protested the expense, but he could not deny Hannah anything. He felt so guilty for hurting Jake he would have worn sackcloth and ashes if she'd asked. And his clothes were hardly that.

In deference to both male sensibilities, Hannah exercised a great deal of restraint in what she bought, for herself as well as for them. Her object was not to overwhelm them, but just to bring them up to standards they themselves would enjoy. Restraint was easier in Rory's case because he was awake and able to object.

269

Then, too, fond as she was of Rory, she didn't love him as she did Jake.

She couldn't help but picture Jake in each of the garments suggested by the tailor. He was so handsome and masculine. Why not fawn breeches and a coat of rich blue merino the color of his eyes? Or black to bring out the midnight sheen of his hair? If she bought too much, it was much less than she wanted him to have.

She was little more successful holding back on her own clothes. She had been so long without anything pretty to wear that she ached for exactly the kind of frippery she had once scorned. Jake had never seen her decently dressed. If she couldn't be blond and pink for him, she would be at her very best. For her, the dressmaker managed to find tobacco-colored watered silk to make a lovely afternoon dress that would show off the red high-lights in her hair. She found ecru lace and bottle-green lawn for other dresses as well.

So when Jake's eyes fell on Hannah for the first time as a fully rational person, he almost didn't recognize her. The wild abundance of her hair had been tamed and pulled back into fat curls at the back of her neck. Her dress was a forest green concoction that trailed a froth of lace from the sleeves and collar. The neckline, though more modest than some he'd seen, was not what he was used to from her. His eyes were immediately drawn to the swell of her bosom and from there he confirmed that it was Hannah by the tiny locket she wore.

"Hannah?"

She jumped up from her chair with a smile that lit every corner of the room. "Oh, Jake, you're really awake. How do you feel?"

He wished she hadn't asked. "Like hell. I can't move. What the hell have you done to me?"

Even his snarl couldn't dim her joy. "What do you

remember?"

He closed his eyes against a stab of pain in his shoulder. "Just tell me."

"You stepped into a trap in that little wood you were investigating. It . . . caught you by one leg and . . . tossed you onto your head when the tree broke."

That made as much sense as anything else in his life. "And you picked me up and carried me here?" He looked around without moving his head again. "Where are we?"

"Omaha. The hotel. And I didn't carry you, Rory did. He's the boy who made the trap. You'll like him, Jake. I don't know what I'd have done without him. He's so sorry about the trap, but his uncle had cheated him out of his farm and was after him, so—"

Jake raised his hand weakly. "Please . . ."

"Oh, I'm sorry. I know you're tired. I'm so glad you're better."

He wanted to argue, but asked instead, "Why can't I move?"

"The doctor, Dr. Bird—and he really looks like a bird, Jake. Wait till you see him. Of course, you *have* seen him or at least he's seen you—"

"Hannah!"

"It's a brace, he says. Your shoulder was dislocated by the fall. Rory put it back into place, but the tendons are stretched and you have bruises." She trailed off miserably, then rallied. "There's another harness on your leg. When the trap lifted you, it hurt your knee."

"This trap, what was it made of?"

"It was a willow tree bent down by rope. It snapped up when your weight released the rope. Rory was—"

"Sorry," Jake supplied, growing tired again. "Yes, I know."

"Well, he was, just as I said, but what I meant was Rory was—*is*—awfully clever. I think you'll really like

271

him."

"How old is he?"

"Sixteen, but he's big. You'll see."

Jake would, but not right then. He was already asleep.

Stunned to lose him again so quickly, Hannah sank back down in the chair, fighting tears. At first she couldn't think why she was crying. He was better. She had been hoping for exactly this recovery. So why did she feel so disappointed?

As she frequently did for reassurance, she reached up to touch her locket. Along with the gold heart, her hand brushed the exposed skin of her neckline and then she understood. Whenever she had played out this scene in her imagination, Jake had at least noticed the change in he appearance. In most of her daydreams, to be honest, he had more than noticed. He had been either struck dumb by her beauty—her favorite fantasy—or he had praised her dress or her hair or *something!*

Of course it was natural that he wanted to know what had happened. He'd also notice the way he was restricted—how could he not? But couldn't he have smiled at her once?

Evidently not.

The next time was no better. She wore gold taffeta with a brocade bodice and tapered panel to the floor at the front of a wide skirt. With gold ribbons threaded among her curls, she knew she looked elegant. But Jake only glared at her and fired questions at her. Questions she couldn't answer. Where were his men? Where was the damn doctor? And this young Rory?

He wanted, in order: the doctor to get him out of these contraptions, to get up, to meet Rory, and to get out of the hotel. Hannah knew he was in pain and she was prepared to do almost anything to please him, but she wouldn't put up with being yelled at. She yelled back and soon Rory came running. Once Hannah completed his introduction, Jake told her to go fetch the doctor. She wanted to send Rory, but Jake insisted, "I want to talk to him."

Hannah gave them both an indignant look and flounced out of the room. If she closed the door hard enough to jar Jake's head—too bad! The truth was, she was unwilling to leave Rory with Jake for very long. So far Rory had been her faithful ally, but Jake would subvert the boy to his own cause—whatever that might be. She knew it wouldn't be easy, because Rory was both loyal and devoted, but Jake had such authority that after a few words with him, Rory would begin to look to Jake for leadership, not to her.

It took her much too long to scare up the doctor, and when she did, Jake sent her from the room. Rory, of course, remained. Hannah could forgive Rory, but not Jake.

Driven back to her practically unused hotel room for lack of any other place to go, Hannah paced back and forth before the fireplace. She knew Jake was being impossible, but as she perched for a moment of thought, she was in complete agreement with him on one point. She hated living in the hotel. If she felt confined and out of place here, how much worse must it be for Jake?

Supposing she could find a house to rent? Then Jake could sit out in the yard or perhaps on a porch. It would be less expensive in the end certainly, and that would also please Jake. She could just imagine him adding up the cost of their rooms, meals, and services. It would make him decide that she was nothing but a spendthrift—not the way she wanted him to see her.

She got up from the silly chair, a duplicate of the ones in Jake's room, energized by her idea. If she got busy, she might find a place before Uncle Simon joined them. He would approve, she knew, because he preferred a homey atmosphere over the sterile luxury of even the finest hotel.

She was about to leave her room when a maid returned their laundry. Hannah took the beautifully done-up garments to put them away, full of appreciation for the work involved in cleaning them. At the bottom of the parcel she found her doeskin breeches and shirt, cleaned and folded along with her cast-off army uniform. She had rescued both from another maid, who had sniffed, "I'll have these burned, ma'am," after helping Hannah into her first real bath in weeks. She would never part with these reminders of her great adventure with Jake, she decided, placing them carefully in the clothes press before she left.

She came back late to find Jake awake and alone. Surprised, she asked, "Where's Rory?"

"Doing an errand for me."

"Oh. Then you like him?"

"He seems to be a sensible boy."

"Then you believe his story about his uncle?"

"Why not?"

"No reason not to. Not every uncle is as good as Uncle Simon," she answered carefully. She had worried that Jake would think her gullible. Although she was relieved that he wasn't going to chide her, something in his manner bothered her. It was as if he was hiding something from her.

"Where have you been all day?" Jake asked, raking over her costume with a jaundiced eye. "At the dressmaker's?"

She had changed from the gold dress to a more conservative dark skirt and white shirtwaist before going out. A reasonable move, she felt, doubly annoyed with him now because he had made her feel uncomfortable about something so sensible.

"Should I still be wearing my army uniform?" she fired

274

back to cover her flush. "I thought perhaps you'd enjoy a change of scenery."

Jake knew he should compliment her appearance, not carp at her, but the way she'd backed him into the corner made him unwilling. Besides, he had a pretty good idea what that quietly elegant outfit she wore had cost. Just thinking about it depressed him.

Hannah was hungry enough to accept any compliment from Jake, even the most grudging, but her own excitement about what she had just accomplished kept her from waiting, perhaps in vain. "Speaking of changing scenery," she began, too happy to hold back her news. "Tomorrow we're moving out of here. I found a house for us."

"A *house?*"

Jake's thunderous response was more vehement that she had expected, but in her delight she chose to look on it as pleased surprise rather than the total disapproval it sounded like. "Isn't it wonderful? When Uncle Simon gets here there'll be four of us, and a house is so much more practical. I was lucky to find what I did, especially since it's all furnished, even down to the dishes and linens. It belonged to an elderly lady who died back in the spring. They were going to hold an auction to sell the belongings, but I said we'd take it just as it is. There's even a lovely little yard where you can sit outside while you recuperate."

Jake closed his eyes against a pain that was worse than the throbbing ache in his shoulder or knee. Hannah's high-handed ways, applied to him in this instance, were not the least bit amusing. Not anymore. That afternoon when he had wrung the story of their arrival at the hotel from Rory, he had chuckled, seeing it all in his mind. Now he saw another picture just as clearly. He saw himself, carried like a helpless baby, to the "lovely little yard" while Hannah gave Rory directions about where he

275

was to be deposited. "No, no, not there," she'd say. "The sun will be in his eyes in a while. Better turn the chair the other way."

"Jake?"

Hannah's anxious voice broke into his brooding silence, the tone an extension of his darkest thoughts. He didn't know how to begin to explain how horrifying her happy plan was to him. He could thunder and rage for an hour and she would never understand.

*Let her think I fell asleep,* he thought. *It fits the vegetable she thinks I've become.*

Hannah touched his hand where it lay atop his chest, wondering how he could go so quickly from that incredulous boom into sleep. Had she said too much and tired him?

"Jake?" she called again, more gently, touched by the contrast between his strong, broad hand and this sudden exhaustion. Perhaps the doctor had given him laudanum, or perhaps he hadn't been able to get enough rest. After all, the hotel was noisy.

Yes, that was it, she decided, bending to kiss his cheek. The house would be good for them all. They'd have privacy. They'd be almost a family, living together and helping each other. She'd done the right thing. The move would help Jake get well.

As soon as Hannah tiptoed from the room, Jake let out his pent-up breath and added a few choice expletives. He would have to move, she'd see to that. Damn her. A house!

Then he smiled. Little did she know how much that move would help him. Leaving a house, any house, would be easier than getting out of this place. If Rory did his job and he played his own cards right, in two days he would be gone back to his men, back to his job and his own reasonable life.

He moved restlessly against his braces. For now he would tolerate being trussed up like a stuffed chicken. He'd had them off this afternoon, working his muscles. He had to concede one thing to Hannah — Rory Talmage was all right. He was a good kid, willing to help and still loyal to Hannah the way he should be. Knowing that she could rely on him would make leaving her easier. And she had her uncle arriving soon.

That made him laugh. Here he was worrying about Hannah! As if he needed to. If she'd been running the Confederacy, the war would have ended sooner and differently. She didn't need any man to take care of her.

Tired from his exercise and pain, Jake fell asleep wondering why he found so little comfort in that thought.

# Chapter Fifteen

Hannah opened the gate to the house she already thought of as home. She could have sent a servant to the market, but she'd wanted to do the homely chore herself. It had been too long since she had lived as an ordinary person. And the chance to pick out special things for Jake was too tempting to pass up.

She was playing house. She admitted that, if only to herself. In her mind, Jake was her husband and Rory was their surrogate son. She loved seeing them together in the yard. Jake bent his dark head to listen attentively to whatever Rory said. She wondered sometimes—well, actually, she wondered often—what they found to discuss so earnestly. Whatever it was, it was definitely man-talk. She had only to come within hearing and they both fell silent. Yet they were never displeased to see her. They welcomed her, in fact, never making her feel that she was intruding.

Rory did not look like either of them, Hannah observed, giving them a wave in passing as she carried her overflowing basket into the house. Rory had none of Jake's dark intensity and less of her fiery nature. He was steady and sensible, as Jake had first remarked, without being a bit dull. His features were more conventionally handsome than Jake's, more regular. His nose was rather high-bridged and aristocratic, for example, whereas Jake's was more of a knife blade. Rory didn't lack forceful-ness—certainly not with that strongly modeled chin—but the planes and angles of his face were more refined. If Jake seemed hewn from granite, Rory was chiseled from marble—and he was a long way from being finished. When he grew into the promise of his large bones and clever mind, he would be a formidable man.

Hannah left the basket in the kitchen for the cook-housekeeper, her only full-time help, and went to her room to freshen up. After she had lived so long without amenities, the pitcher of water and scented soap on her washstand were luxuries she would never again take for granted. She was careful not to fuss about such things, however, because Jake seemed to feel he had been person-ally responsible for her former deprivation. As if he could have done anything more for her than he had!

She peeked out the window to be sure Jake and Rory were still outside, then hurried into her coolest, prettiest dress, the bottle-green lawn. After the simplicity of put-ting on and taking off menswear, she found it a bother to struggle with rows of tiny buttons—something she had never done without a maid to assist her—but the charm of the final effect was well worth the trouble.

How she loved the way Jake's eyes coasted up and down her body when she pretended not to notice. She knew he did it, because she could feel the heat of his gaze; yet whenever she looked directly at him, his expression was always studiously bland. Probably he was inhibited by Rory's presence. He seemed to take his quasi-parental status with Rory as seriously as he took his real role with Caroline. Frustrating as it was to Hannah, it served to reinforce her already considerable respect for him.

She wasn't always as successful in schooling her own more expressive features, particularly when he wore his new clothes. Unlike Daniel, who had been fussily correct in his dress, Jake's inborn insouciance and superbly fit body gave extra dash to his wearing of the simplest garment. Which was all she had purchased—fortunately, given his reaction to the little she had bought. He had welcomed the new underwear and stockings as the necessities they were. Everything else he tried to decline, at first pleasantly and firmly, then with greater rancor.

Hannah would not hear of it. She had not been extravagant and she would not permit him to make her feel guilty about what she had done. Once he discovered that he still had his uniform and buckskins, cleaned and at his disposal, he pretended his concern had been for those and gave in. He wore only the darkest pair of breeches and one of the shirts, but Hannah was satisfied. None of the clothes fit over the braces, of course, so he used that excuse to discontinue their use except at night. It was a compromise, but one Hannah was happy to make. She knew he wouldn't have worn the braces long anyway.

This time it was Jake who was talking as she approached their chairs under the cottonwood tree. He broke off the discussion in midsentence when Rory got to his feet to offer her his chair.

She waved him back to it, teasing, "You're going to make me suspicious if you keep breaking off your conversations with such guilty haste every time I come near."

Predictably, Rory blushed scarlet, denying everything. "I was just on my way, Hannah. You take my place, please."

A look of complicity passed between Jake and Rory that Hannah didn't see. She felt it, however, in the watchful interest in Jake's eyes as Rory departed. "I hope you're not corrupting him, Jake," she said, her voice as airy as she could make it.

"Corrupting?" He matched her tone, but he had gone very still.

"That's the wrong word, obviously. I mean, you're not having him do something . . ."

"What makes you think that?"

He was wearing the look Hannah had come to think of as his Indian face. She would have to be direct. "I know you, Jake. You haven't given up. This business with Spotted Pony or Daniel or whomever is still on your mind. But it doesn't have to be." She leaned forward, unconsciously imitating his earlier earnestness. "I don't know how much money you were supposed to get for routing Spotted Pony, but whatever it was, I know Uncle Simon will double it just for bringing me back safely."

He looked so affronted that Hannah burst out, "Oh, don't look at me that way! It's no insult to you or to me. I know why you need the money and I understand. Besides, you've earned it. I just don't want you dragging Rory into something dangerous like this—and I know it is dangerous. He's only a boy!"

Jake had to call on all his inner resources not to explode in anger at Hannah. He told himself it was his own fault that she had such a low opinion of him. He had gone to such lengths to emphasize the fact that his motive for taking the job was monetary, but he could have throttled her for thinking that he'd harm Rory.

He was using Rory, but only as his eyes and ears and legs. And that only until tomorrow. There was no danger to Rory in that. None at all. But her outburst had given him a way to deflect her worries about Rory. He moved in the chair as if in protest against the hard surface.

"Do you think he's a good-looking boy? One a girl would find attractive?"

The question was so far afield from Hannah's thinking she could only stammer. "Of course he's good-looking.

281

What does that have to do . . . oh, I see. He's met a girl. Oh, Jake, tell me about her!"

He had counted on the eager leap of her mind to its own conclusions, but not on her equally eager curiosity. Since he was determined not to lie to her, he had to fall back on another of her quick responses. He pulled up, clutching at his shoulder as if he were in pain. It wasn't acting, just giving in to his constant discomfort in a way he would normally spurn. But it brought Hannah to her feet.

"Can I help you?"

"I think perhaps I'd better go inside."

"I knew you should still be in bed," she scolded. She reached for him, then drew back. "Perhaps I should see if Mr. Gilman is in the stable."

"I only need a hand, then I can lean on you." He didn't want her waylaying Rory, in case he had lingered there over the horse as he often did. It was his own horse, a mare he called Duchess, and he was especially fond of the animal. When she continued to look reluctant, he said, "For heaven's sake, Hannah, you did this all the time when we were traveling. Why not now?"

"I had no choice then. Now there's a strong man available."

He closed his eyes and heaved himself forward, knowing she would steady him.

She did. His arms felt so good around her that for several seconds she just stood and absorbed the sensation of Jake's nearness. She knew she was supposed to be helping him, but he felt so hard and strong that, as always, she felt sheltered by him.

Jake ran his hands over the thin material of her dress. "Umm. You feel different now." He bent his head to her neck. "And smell different. Like flowers."

"No more horse and smoke. This is lavender and it's just from the soap I used."

The scent was crisp and bracing as well as lovely, like Hannah herself, Jake thought. He couldn't help comparing it to Grace's favorite, lily of the valley. That cloying perfume had always annoyed him, but this was perfect. To break the mood gripping him, Jake tried teasing her. "And still no corset?" His fingers probed her waist for the telltale ridges.

Hannah's laugh floated out from under the tree. "The dressmaker was scandalized, I can tell you. Then she admitted I didn't need one. I've lost so much weight . . ." She cut off that line of thought abruptly lest Jake feel that she was criticizing his care of her. He was too sensitive on that score already. But Jake was busy investigating the flare of skirt below her waistline. He wouldn't have noticed a murder confession.

Nor would she. She wrapped her arms around his waist, one hand on the soft cotton of his shirt, the other on his breeches. She was echoing, more or less, the movement of his hands on her back. One held her in place while the other traced the line of her spine down over her hips.

"No great big hoop this time." He pressed her bottom.

"I didn't think you noticed."

"I noticed," he said next to her temple. He could feel her pulse throb against his lips. He moved his hand in a slow circle, creating friction among all the layers of cloth, and felt her pulse accelerate. "Someone else is noticing, too."

"Hmm?" Hannah noticed his response also, and moved to feel more of him.

"The old buzzard in the kitchen," Jake said lazily. "She's watching from the window. Has been since you laughed."

Mrs. Gilman. They came as a couple with the house. "Damn," Hannah said.

Jake administered a spank of reprimand he negated by

laughing when she only moved closer. "Come on, help me inside soon or I won't need you. I'll have my own crutch."

Laughing and trying to pretend shock, Hannah pulled back. "I can send her home," she offered. "Unless Rory will be back soon?"

"He won't be back for dinner. He's . . . eating out."

Hannah was too happy to ponder the small hesitation she heard. She linked her arm with his. "You'll have to tell me all about this girl later, but now lean on me as if you really need me. I have to make this look good for Mrs. Gilman."

He did it so well they almost toppled over, but Mrs. Gilman was not fooled a bit. She heard the laughter they tried to muffle and knew what they were about, just as she knew they weren't married. And with that fine young man living with them. All under one roof, no matter how many bedrooms there were. Harry said it was none of her business, but how poor old Mrs. Ambrose was resting in her grave with so much sin and corruption going on right in her own house, she never knew. And never was a better lady than Bessie Ambrose! She'd been a God-fearing lady who'd brought up four fine children all by herself after the Lord had seen fit to take her mister. And he'd been a fine man, too.

Mrs. Gilman stopped chopping onions to listen to their scuffles in the hall as they made their way to the stairs. Shameful creatures! She brought the chopper down into the wooden bowl hard enough to pulverize.

"Will you be all right?" she heard the woman ask.

Her chopping, vigorous again, kept her from hearing his answer, which was just as well. After a few minutes the woman appeared before her. Mrs. Gilman kept on chopping, although by now her eyes were running water so she could hardly see.

"Are you all right, Mrs. Gilman?" Hannah asked, then she smelled the reason for her tears. "Oh, the onions.

They always make me cry, too."

Mrs. Gilman sniffed, angry to be caught at a disadvantage when it should have been the other way round.

Hannah touched her arm. "That's fine, Mrs. Gilman. Mr. Farnsworth and I are the only ones dining here tonight so we won't need you to cook for us. Rory's the one who eats heartily, you know."

Mrs. Gilman wiped her eyes on her sleeves and objected. "But I have all this ready."

Hannah knew all about the provisions. She had ordered them before going to market. "I know and I thank you. Why don't you take the chicken along with you for Mr. Gilman's dinner? Mr. Farnsworth will enjoy the soup and salad and berries. His appetite is still not what it might be."

Mrs. Gilman sniffed again with disapproval. A man big as that needed meat and potatoes. She heard all about Mr. Farnsworth's arrival at the hotel from her cousin Lettie. Lettie was a maid there. It was her husband who had steered Miss Hatch to this house. Of course, Miss Hatch never called herself Miss Hatch here. She tried to pass herself off as Mr. Farnsworth's wife. But she knew better.

Of course, she couldn't say that, so she bobbed her head and said, "Thank you, ma'am. I believe I'll do that. Waste is a sin."

She was proud of that remark.

And Hannah was proud that she didn't laugh out loud. "Indeed it is, Mrs. Gilman."

Still, it took the woman fifteen minutes to gather up her belongings and leave. Hannah watched her waddle to the stable to speak to her husband. After a short time she came back out and went off toward her own house. Mr. Gilman had elected to stay behind. Hannah didn't blame him. The horses were good company. Hannah brushed aside a tear or two caused by onion fumes and hurried upstairs. She and Jake had not been alone in ages. She knew Jake was as eager as she was, but she couldn't forget that he still wasn't well. It had been only two days since he had nodded off during an argument. If he could do that, she was afraid he could fall asleep waiting for her.

Hannah was wrong. Jake was more than eager. He was impatient. He knew what she did not, that after tonight he might never see her again. Even if he hadn't needed Rory to set up things with Colby and Zeb, he would have found some way to be alone with Hannah this one last time. He had no idea how he would manage to forget her, but he would have to try. First, though, he wanted today. Something to remember—and to forget.

He sat on the edge of the bed. In deference to his size he had been given the master bedroom with the double bed. It was a handsome sleigh bed, wide but not long enough for his frame. Like everything in the house, it was scaled for pygmies. He pulled his unbuttoned shirt from his pants and bent to tug off his boots. Hannah reached them just as he did, slipping inside and kneeling before him.

"Don't," she admonished. "You'll hurt your shoulder."

"You'll get your hands dirty."

She turned her back and took the foot of his injured leg between her legs. "Does this hurt?" she asked over her shoulder.

"Not at all."

Seeing where his eyes rested, Hannah laughed and tugged the boot off. She did the second one with less care and washed her hands in the small basin by his dresser. "I was afraid you'd be asleep," she confessed when she turned to face him again. "Mrs. Gilman took forever leaving."

"Asleep?" Chuckling, he stood to take off the shirt. "Why would you think that?"

"You fell asleep the other day right in the middle of an argument with me. At least I thought it was an argument until then. But it's worked out well, hasn't it? This is a good place for us."

Jake remembered then. Wanting no argument with her now, he said, "I suppose renting a house does make more sense than paying for all those hotel accommodations."

Hannah completely missed the grudging nature of his admission. If he conceded that, she knew he'd be even more impressed by what she had really done — and she did want to impress him. "Well, yes, it does," she told him, "but I did something better. I bought the house. You see, with —"

"*Bought?*"

This explosion was so like the other that her pleasure evaporated, leaving her unsure of herself. "It was a very good move, I assure you," she said, putting all her conviction, plus some she didn't have, into her manner. "Omaha is beginning to boom. Once the railroad is under way, a house like this will be worth twice what it is now."

She had impressed Jake. He didn't doubt a word of what she had said. She had surprised him, but in a way he was glad. Because he loved her, he had been trying to conceive of a way they could live together. His mind told him it was impossible, but his heart was stubborn. He wanted her. He couldn't stand the thought of giving her up, even if he knew he wasn't good enough for her.

He turned away, ostensibly to put his shirt aside but actually to be sure he had himself under control.

"You don't approve, Jake?"

Did she care? One look at her face told him she did. "My approval isn't required," he said as gently as he could.

"But if it were," she prompted.

He shook his head and reached for her. She pulled back just enough to elude him and his rein on his temper slipped. "Hannah, I don't want to fight with you about a damned house."

"But it's important to me—"

"Good. You have it, don't you?"

"That's not what I meant! I—"

He hauled her to his chest and stopped her lips with his. At first the kiss was as rough as a hand clamped over her mouth, but when her hands settled on his shoulders for balance, it became a real kiss. His passion fired hers and she had to struggle to hold the thread of her thoughts. When his hand curled around her neck and his mouth opened hers, she pushed away as hard as she could. She succeeded only because he let her.

Seeing the flicker of surprise in his eyes, she hurried to make her point before she forgot it. "I want you to approve of what I do, Jake," she whispered urgently. "*That's* what's important to me."

Desire had replaced surprise, filling his eyes with sleepy fire. "I do." His solemn words were at variance with his expression. "And I'll approve of you even more when I get you out of that dress," he said, bringing the two into complete agreement.

"Jake!" But her protest turned to a laugh. How could she resist him? She didn't even want to try. "You'll have to help. Dresses are much more awkward than uniforms."

"I would have said graceful. You look like a willow wand." His fingers raced along the row of buttons at her back, freeing them with ease.

No sooner was she out of the dress than his hands were in her hair, sending pins flying every which way. She hadn't dressed her hair elaborately, but if she had, the result would have been the same. He wasn't satisfied until it flowed down her back. He sifted it through his fingers restlessly, watching it fall like a shimmering cloud around her shoulders. "This is better," he sighed, bringing it to his lips. "You have the most glorious hair."

"I'm too old to wear it like this in public," she said, laughing.

"Old?"

"Only girls wear their hair down."

He wasn't listening. His hands played with the silk of her undergarments, his touch through the slippery cloth making this one genuine extravagance among her new clothes worth ever penny. "You are so lovely."

"This is what I wished for at the sod house, beautiful things to take off for you."

He stopped untying a pink bow and looked into her eyes. "Did it matter so much to you?"

"Only that I wanted to look beautiful for you."

"You do. *You*, not the clothes."

Hannah nodded. "I know. I love the way you look in those breeches, but it's you who makes the clothes, not the other way around. But why not have both as long as it gives us pleasure?" She touched the hard ridge he made against the pants, startling a groan from him. He put her aside and shucked himself from his remaining clothes with no regard for the expense of their tailoring.

Before she could think of his shoulder, he lifted her to the bed. She seemed no more substantial than a butterfly, all shimmer and light. He had never loved her in full daylight, with sunlight pooled like honey around her glowing body. Her hair caught sparks from the light and sent it to him as fire.

He took her slowly, watching his body enter hers and retreat to do it again—and again—watching her face suffuse with passion. Hannah, Hannah, his body sang, and hers answered, giving him all he had ever known of love and all he would ever know of it. He soaked up every touch, every sigh and kiss, storing it inside him so that it would be there when she was not.

Hannah had never felt so worshiped and adored, so loved. He gave her love words and sweet names as freely as he gave his body. She gave them back, first crooning them and finally flinging them heedlessly into the room as she tossed beneath him. And when they were spent and satisfied, still clinging together, side by side, she stroked the dark shaggy head on her breast and murmured, "Oh, Jake, my love. How I love you."

Had he heard? She didn't care. The words didn't convey anything she hadn't already told him in other, more important ways. She kissed his damp brow and held him until he woke. "See?" she teased. "I knew you'd fall asleep."

"I wasn't asleep. I was just resting, conserving my energy."

Did he know then? *Had* he heard? His eyes seemed to say yes, but then he had always seemed to see right through her.

Jake saw her eyelids fall, veiling her golden brown eyes. Had he only dreamed what she said, or was it real? He wanted to believe he hadn't imagined that soft, almost reluctant admission. But did it really matter? He couldn't give her the life she was used to having. That she was plucky and determined was only a bonus of her nature. She was meant for a different life than his.

Hours later Jake carried her to her own room. He put her, beautifully naked and soundly sleeping, between crisp sheets. He folded her clothes into a neat bundle and put them on a chair before he gave her one last kiss. Even in sleep her arms circled his neck, forcing him to lift them away. He left without looking back.

In the morning, well before dawn, he dressed in his uniform and carried his pack past her closed door. His step slowed there, but then he walked on, moving with cautious haste to be on his way.

Rory had already eaten by the time Hannah came down for breakfast. She had been about to go to Jake's room when she heard Rory talking to Mrs. Gilman and thought better of disturbing Jake. Let him sleep, she thought tenderly, her mind and heart full of yesterday's love. On her way down the stairs she remembered that she had forgotten to quiz Jake about Rory's romance.

Rory didn't quite meet her eyes, she noticed as she greeted him. More evidence she would have to investigate. But later, not in front of Mrs. Gilman, she decided, being charitable. She helped herself to coffee and answered several of Mrs. Gilman's questions while she drank it. Seeing Rory edge to the door, obviously about to make his getaway, she forgot her good intention and asked, "Did you enjoy your dinner out last evening?"

He blushed as she knew he would and opened his mouth. She never heard what he was going to say, however, because Uncle Simon chose that moment to arrive.

Hannah rushed by Rory and ran to him with outflung arms, her voice thrown octaves higher by her excitement. He hugged her fiercely, then held her off to look at her, thundering, "Damn me, but you're blooming, girl! Here I thought you'd be all worn out and hollow-eyed from all that happened to you."

"I'm fine. I told you in the wire, didn't I?"

"Fine! You're better than fine! Oh, child, it's good to know you're safe!"

"You didn't hear about the wagon train, did you?"

"Not directly. But Calvin never wrote to tell me you'd arrived, so I made inquiries."

"I'm sorry about Willie, Uncle Simon. Those poor people never had a chance."

"Thank God you weren't where you were supposed to be. I've never had better reason to be thankful for your wayward behavior." His ginger mustache turned up again after its momentary droop and his eyes sparkled merrily. Wrapping her with one arm, he turned to survey Mrs. Gilman and Rory in the kitchen. Mrs. Gilman dropped a curtsy that he acknowledged with a nod, his eyes skimming over Rory to the room behind him. "Where's this young man I've heard so much about?"

"Well, Uncle Simon, this is Rory Talmage, and he's very special, too. He helped me bring Jake here safely."

"Good to meet you, son. Anyone who helps my girl here is a friend of mine." He took Rory's big hand in his, clasping it warmly.

Hannah touched Rory's arm. "Would you go wake Jake? I can't imagine how he's managed to sleep through all this noise, but he may need some help." The image of Jake lifting her in his arms contradicted her words, but she pushed that aside. Jake wasn't healed yet no matter what he had done last night.

If Rory was slow to leave, Hannah took it for reluctance to leave Uncle Simon's compelling presence. With his booming voice, however, Rory didn't have to worry about missing a word of their conversation. As it turned out, they had no chance to talk because Uncle Simon's man began moving him in. They left Mrs. Gilman to direct him and went to the parlor, Uncle Simon approving everything as he went.

"Damn me, girl, but you've done me proud again. This is a dandy setup."

Rory caught her eye at the door. Looking more crestfallen than she'd ever seen him, he hemmed and hawed, then admitted, "Jake's not in his room."

"Is he outside?" she asked sharply.

"No, ma'am, I don't think so. His . . . pack is gone."

"What's this?" Uncle Simon boomed.

"Check the stable, please, Rory. See if Victor is there." She didn't want to see the confirmation of her fears in Rory's eyes nor the sympathy in Uncle Simon's. She touched Simon's arm lightly and turned away. "Excuse me, please."

She nearly lost her nerve at Jake's doorway, assailed by

memories so fresh she could almost see the two of them together on the bed. It was empty now and neatly made. The wardrobe held every one of his new garments, even the shirt and breeches he'd worn. He had taken only the underwear, stockings and new boots. Without checking, she knew his buckskins and uniform would be gone, but she checked anyway. She wanted to scream and yell and bury her face in the one used shirt, knowing it would carry the scent of his strong, wonderful body.

She did none of that. She turned away and walked stiffly downstairs, her joy in this day of reunion with Uncle Simon extinguished.

She needed no more than a glance at Rory to confirm his finding. She concentrated on trying to school the hurt and betrayal from her expression.

Uncle Simon saw it and pinned Rory to the doorway with a look. "All right, young man, you know what this is all about, so tell us."

Hannah started to defend Rory, then saw that her uncle was right. Rory's unusual behavior, which she had attributed to embarrassment over a girlfriend, she now saw as betrayal of a different kind than Jake's. Her head snapped around from Uncle Simon to Rory. "Yes, Rory, tell us. You weren't having dinner last night with a girl and her family, were you?"

"Hannah, I'm sorry," he began. "He would have gone anyway, with or without my help. I . . . only kept him from doing too much for a day or two."

She nodded, accepting that he was right. "You found his men?"

"What men?" Uncle Simon cut in to ask.

Hannah took over the explanation, with Rory filling in a word or two as necessary. As their story took shape, Uncle Simon's expression gradually changed from suspicion to understanding.

"This Jake's last name wouldn't be Farnsworth, would

it?"

"Well, of course it is, Uncle Simon. I told you—" Then she remembered. She had told him *about* Jake without identifying him by name. "Why . . . do you know him?"

"Damn me, girl, came over here and sit down." As he did when he was nervous, he rubbed his palm over the wisps of hair atop his head. Most were gray, but there was still red among the strands now standing on end there. He drew her to the stiff little horsehair sofa beside him. "Not only do I know him—or at least *of* him—but I'm the man who hired him!"

"You!"

"Imagine that! And thank God I did, or who would have found you out there on the prairie?"

"Then you can stop him," Hannah cried. "Oh, Uncle Simon, you must! He's not well enough to be on a horse. The doctor prescribed complete bed rest for a week. It's only been three days! Tell him where he's gone, Rory."

Rory said nothing, only looking to Simon for guidance. Hannah was disgusted. As soon as Jake had revived, Rory had turned to him, deserting her. Now he was giving his loyalty to her uncle the same way. It wasn't fair. Didn't her desires count for anything?

They still counted with Uncle Simon apparently, because he nodded to Rory, eliciting the information she craved. The details meant little to her in her distracted state, but she understood the gist of his message. Jake had gone to reconnoiter with Colby, Zeb, and others at one of Many Buffalo's campsites.

"He won't be able to ride hard," she told her uncle even as she knew it wasn't really true. He had ridden hard with a bullet in his back; strained muscles wouldn't deter him—as she should have realized sooner. But she didn't want Simon to think Jake was beyond reach already. "You can send after him, can't you? If you hired him, you can tell him to stop." Her reasoning seemed unimpeachable to

294

her. Uncle Simon either thought so too, or he realized how much Jake meant to her. Although there were occasions when she hated his willingness to indulge her slightest whim, this was not one of them.

Simon patted her hand consolingly. "I'll see that you get him back," he promised. He gathered Rory under his arm as he left the room, already on his way again. Seeing their heads together, Hannah had a moment of unease, not only for herself but for Jake. She couldn't help believing that another male conspiracy had just been joined—one meant to benefit her, to be sure, but only insofar as the men in charge saw fit to pursue her interests. That was much less consoling to her than either of them would see.

She sat quietly, waiting for Rory to see Uncle Simon off and return to her. She planned no recriminations, but she wasn't surprised that he didn't hurry back to face her. She stopped his apology before it began. She had been thinking about what Uncle Simon had said—*I'll see you get him back*. It was well meant, but she didn't need long to realize how grating that would be to Jake. No matter how tactfully the order from Uncle Simon was phrased, Jake would immediately see—and resent—her hand behind it.

There could be no surer way to lose Jake forever than to have him dragged back from what he saw as his duty to dance attendance on Simon Sergeant's spoiled niece.

She asked Rory to repeat everything he had told Simon and this time she listened. "Could you find this place?" she asked finally.

Rory wasn't stupid. "Oh no, you don't, Hannah," he said, rearing back from her in dismay. "You're not roping me in on this."

She got to her feet, briskly brushing nonexistent dust from her skirt. "Fine. Then I'll go by myself. I still have my uniform and my pack. With the information you've already given me, I don't think I'll have any trouble finding the place."

"Hannah!"

She fixed him with a glowing smile. Did all males bellow in that wounded way whenever they were pressed?

"I'll go change," he said with a resigned sigh.

# Chapter Sixteen

Hannah left a note for Uncle Simon, telling him where she had gone and why. To her, the why was more important than the where, because she regretted asking her uncle to intercede in her behalf. It had been an impulse, albeit a protective one, and like so many of her impulses, she had had second thoughts about this one.

In spite of her concern for Jake, she wasn't looking forward to seeing him again. He would be angry. He wouldn't like being followed and he'd be furious that she had put herself and Rory into danger, especially after she had accused him of disregarding Rory's safety. But if he found out she had asked Uncle Simon to call him back — well, that didn't bear thinking about.

Somehow, she had to keep him from ever finding out. It wouldn't be easy though. Uncle Simon would keep her secret if she got to him in time and probably Rory would, too. A peek at his usually stern expression wasn't especially reassuring, but she thought she could get around him.

What she found amazing was the totality of Rory's

identification with Jake. Perhaps he'd needed to find a man to admire and ally himself with after the death of his father and his uncle's betrayal. If so, he'd obviously found the right man. But where did that leave her? Rory was helping her, but only because she gave him no choice. Besides, he wasn't so much helping her as he was delivering her to Jake. He certainly wasn't going to defend her good intentions to Jake.

The best way to keep Jake from discovering what she had done was to beat Uncle Simon's man getting to him, and that involved hard riding. It was the only aspect of the journey that didn't bother her. Ranger was fresh and lively after his rest and so was she. One thing she could say for life in the West, it wasn't dull.

It felt remarkably good to be back on a horse. She had had days to revel in her feminine garb—and she *had* enjoyed dressing up again—but there was a lot to be said for the simplicity of masculine apparel. This time her pack held some of the amenities she had sorely missed— bars of soap, hairpins, a hairbrush, proper towels and cloths, as well as a change of fine underwear and a pretty nightgown. She had also brought the doeskin clothes to wear at the Indian camp. All in all, she thought she had done well.

Hannah had just begun to consider what she would say to Jake when Rory indicated that they would stop. They had agreed not to bother with lunch in order to press on, so Hannah was surprised. She dismounted as he did and followed him, leading Ranger by the reins.

"The terrain after this gets rougher," Rory said in answer to her unspoken question. "I thought we'd better give the horses some water and a little rest. We won't have another chance until dusk."

With dusk hours away, Hannah didn't argue. She walked a bit upstream from the horses and bent, cupping her hands to drink. She spit out her first taste of water and looked up at Rory questioningly. It was bitterly alkaline.

"It's safe to drink," he assured her, smiling. "It just doesn't taste very good."

"Why not?"

"Something to do with the soils."

She got up and started to get her canteen, but Rory stopped her. "Save that for later. I told you it gets worse after here."

"But we never lacked for good water," she objected. "Are you sure?"

"Sure enough. I passed on a warning to Jake from Colby. Does that make you believe me?"

Hannah was contrite. "I'm sorry. I have no right to question you. It's just that water was never a problem before."

"Maybe it won't be, but I'd rather be sure."

"So would I." She went back to the stream and forced herself to slake her thirst thoroughly. The bitter taste conspired to make her crave more in order to wash away the bad taste, but without sweet water there was no accomplishing that. She patted some on the back of her neck and stood up.

"Are we making good time?" she asked when Rory had also drunk his fill.

He glanced up at the sun, well past its meridian. "Good enough."

"Am I holding you back? I can go as fast as you want, you know."

He laughed, shaking his head. "Jake was right. You are something else."

Hannah bristled. So they had talked about her! "I don't know what you mean," she said stiffly. "I'm sure your own mother would have done the same thing for your father." She didn't think how revealing that remark was. It was, like so many of her comments, the first thing that popped into her head.

Rory only laughed harder. "You can't know how funny that is," he said finally when her affronted look threatened to become permanent. "My mother never went outside without a parasol to keep the sun off her face. She wore gloves to bed!"

"Rory!"

"Well, that's only a guess," he admitted, still laughing.

"But surely she would have done everything possible to help your father!" Hannah had no idea why she was being so insistent. She just hated being thought of as an unnatural woman.

"Perhaps so," Rory allowed. "But are you sure that's what you're doing now? Helping Jake? I think I'll enjoy hearing you explain to Jake just how this adventure is benefiting him."

Hannah had no answer for him, so she glared at him imperiously. It was hard to keep that up when she needed his boost back into the saddle, but she tried—to his seemingly never-ending amusement. He was still chuckling when he started off again. She was already aware that Rory was a singularly self-possessed young man at times, but his reading of her situation was most disconcerting. If her motive was transparent to a sixteen-year-old boy, what would Jake make of it? And of her?

She shuddered to think of it.

She spent the remainder of the afternoon turning over—and rejecting—possible explanations for Jake. Finally, tired of the whole issue, she put it out of her mind, assuring herself that she'd think of something at the time. Didn't she always? That wasn't as comforting as it might be, but she was getting tired physically as well as mentally. Her layby had apparently taken its toll on her stamina. It was all she could do to keep her seat on Ranger and keep Rory and Duchess in her sights.

They were just emerging from the end of a long defile

when trouble struck. Coming from deep shade directly into the low rays of the dying sun put them at a disadvantage, as did their fatigue. The long, boring ride had lulled them into a dangerous complacency. Both of them should have known better, but she, being the older, had to bear the blame for their lack of caution. Although she had known that Rory was not Jake, not a wary, wily guide, she had succumbed to the usual feminine habit of turning over the responsibility for her well-being to him, simply because he was male. When would she learn?

Not in time to avert their present disaster.

Duchess was the first to sense that something was wrong. She danced sideways, rousing Hannah from torpor as she watched Rory work to regain control of his horse.

"Stop right there! Both of you!"

At first Hannah couldn't pinpoint the voice. It seemed to come from everywhere at once, but that was the effect of the defile behind them.

She wasn't armed, but Rory was. She sensed his cautious reach for his weapon, whatever it was, and wanted to warn him to forget it. She didn't have to. The voice rang out again, "If you touch your gun, I'll kill your horse. You, I *might* miss—maybe. The horse, never!"

"God, Hannah, I'm sorry," Rory said softly.

"They're probably robbers. Don't worry," she answered just as softly.

"Shut up!"

Two men separated from the landscape behind them, on foot but with horses nearby. She couldn't see their faces, shadowed as they were by brimmed hats and backlit by the setting sun. Hannah wished for her gun, even as she knew it would be useless. As long as they were on horseback they held a small edge, it seemed to her. If only she could distract them . . .

"Get down on the ground. One at a time. You first,

shorty!"

Shorty! Hannah almost laughed. It wasn't funny though. For the first time she considered her plight as a woman. How long would it take them to realize that she wasn't just a slight male? She could try to disguise her voice, but would that be enough?

"Hurry it up there!"

Far from hurrying, Hannah moved with great deliberation, trying to give Rory time. To do what? Dear God, she didn't know. He would try to protect her, but at what cost? She couldn't let him sacrifice himself for her.

She landed on tired legs that were shaking with nerves. Ordered away from Ranger, she complied, concentrating on slouching so that her feminine shape wouldn't be noticed. Her shirt was full, but they had the full glare of sunlight on them, and if the men ever touched her, her "disguise" would be worthless.

Rory joined her on the ground and moved to stand next to her as he was told. Clearly, she could not create much of a diversion now. With Jake she might have tried, but she didn't know if Rory was a good shot. If she tried a trick and he was no better than she, they would both be killed for nothing. Better to wait, she decided. Then her plan became academic when Rory's gun was taken from him.

The man in charge herded them before him, leaving the horses to his accomplice. When they had to raise their hands, Hannah was careful to keep her hands balled into fists for fear of revealing her sex. The posture had the added advantage of letting her shield her breasts with her elbows. It occurred to her, too late of course, that she should have wrapped her chest. But how could she have known?

They hadn't walked far when the man ordered them left onto a narrow trail. "Don't get any ideas," he warned. "The rest of my men are just ahead."

Now that they were away from the defile, the man's voice lost its eerie and frightening echo. She tried to look at Rory, but when she turned her head, the man behind them growled, "Eyes ahead, kid."

That gave her hope. Perhaps the men would decide they were a pair of kids and of no concern. She would keep quiet and let Rory speak for them. In spite of his manly size, his voice tended to crack under strain. That and her small stature might convince the men to let them go — provided they didn't look too closely at her.

Although Hannah tried to maneuver herself around so that the sun fell at her back, she wasn't permitted to move. Nor could she shade her eyes with her arms. Her attempt to do so only attracted attention to her, something she didn't want. It was disturbing enough to be surrounded by hostile men; not to be able to see their faces was worse. She was uncomfortably reminded of the time she had fallen into the midst of Jake's men. Then she had been safe, although she hadn't known it. Reason told her she wouldn't be so lucky again.

Someone to Hannah's left asked, "What'cha bother with them fer? Coupl'a kids!"

"Maybe," the leader muttered, then he shouted, "You there! What's your name, shorty?"

Hannah thought quickly. "Henry," she growled. It was a strange sound, reflecting more fear than masculinity. Henry was the first male name she could think of that was close to Hannah. Why she needed the similarity to her own name, she couldn't think.

"And you!"

"Talmage." Typically male, Rory had given his last name, while she had automatically thought first of her given name. How strange. At least Henry could also be a surname. Busy trying to think up another Christian name, she was caught off-guard again, this time more tellingly.

303

"Where'd you get the Yankee uniform, Henry?" she was asked.

Her brain began to buzz with frightening thoughts. Had they been stopped by these men because of her uniform? Did that mean . . .

"My father," she said succinctly.

"Where were you going?"

While Hannah's mind went blank, Rory found an answer. "To the dry lake, sir. We're looking for minerals and arrowheads."

She could have hugged Rory. It was a wonderful answer, totally plausible. Her heart lifted. They would be set free.

For a moment the men were quiet, then the man in charge said, "Bring their packs over here," and the world tilted sideways and began spinning away from Hannah. They would find her frilly underwear and nightgown!

She made an instinctive move of protest that earned her another warning, while their saddlebags were dragged over and deposited nearby. Hannah couldn't see which one was opened first. If not hers, they might yet be let go because, although Rory wouldn't have mineral-hunting tools with him, he also wouldn't have articles of feminine clothing.

She heard an almost collective grunt of surprise and tried to steel herself for attack, thinking they had found her clothes. "What's this?" one asked, holding up something shiny.

"It's a pick," Rory said. "I have a small shovel and a chisel and bags to put samples in."

It was true! She started to lower her hands as the men muttered comments she couldn't catch. They would be able to go.

"Look in the other one."

The skin at the back of Hannah's neck began to crawl. And this time her panic had nothing to do with what the men would find in her pack. She would not have believed anything could send her spirits lower, but this did.

She recognized that voice. Had she not been so frightened and disoriented, so disadvantaged by the sun in her eyes, she would have known it earlier. Daniel. The leader was Daniel Veazie. Her husband.

And these were the men who had killed Willie and Marcie Torvold and little Jonathan.

Now they would never go free. They would die without ever reaching Jake. Jake . . .

"Woo-ee! Lookee what we got here!"

She saw something white dance in a man's hand just before pandemonium broke out around her. She cringed back against Rory, expecting to be attacked. But it was her clothes they fell on. The men grabbed at anything they could reach, including each other, scuffling after her underwear like vultures after carrion. Men were punching each other and rolling on the ground.

She and Rory had the same idea at the same time, but before they could take more than a few steps toward freedom, Daniel fired his gun into the air. Everyone froze—especially Hannah and Rory. The men on the ground began to compose themselves.

"She's my girlfriend, all right? We're going to camp out at the dry lake. She's wearing her father's uniform so she won't look like a girl. It's for her own safety," Rory said. "To keep just this from happening." He looked around in disgust at the men. Some even looked a little shamefaced, others were grinning—especially the ones holding her clothes.

It was the right thing to say, but Hannah didn't hope for success this time. This was Daniel, not an unknown. The men might buy Rory's story, but Daniel didn't. She saw it in the set of his shoulders. She still couldn't see him well enough to catalog the changes four years had made, but she saw resolution in his stance.

"What's your name, girl?"

"Mary . . . Henry." She had almost said "Anna," the name she'd come up with earlier, but she didn't want anything to connect this girl in Nebraska with the wife Daniel had left behind. He wouldn't . . . please, God . . .

"Take off your hat."

Hannah's hands dipped, then rose again as if to ward off a blow. Her arms were tired from riding. Holding them up was wearing, but without the hat he might recognize her. At least she had pinned up her hair securely. It wouldn't tumble down around her shoulders. But he knew her with carefully dressed hair. . . .

"What for?" Rory demanded. "Leave her alone."

Daniel stepped closer, then swept the hat to the ground.

"Jee-zuz!"

"A redhead!"

"Hannah?"

She closed her eyes, momentarily shutting out not only Daniel's stunned gaze but also the way Rory drew back from her side in shock. Daniel's gun still pointed at her, but she ignored it to reach for Rory.

"You *know* this guy?"

She never got a chance to answer. Daniel jerked the gun, signaling one of the men forward. "Take him over there and tie him up," he ordered curtly. His other commands, to restore their saddlebags and "get on about your business," went in one of Hannah's ears and out the other. She watched Rory being dragged away and restrained, feeling helpless and responsible for his plight. As she was. He had done everything right. She was the one at fault. How would she ever make it up to him?

"Well, well. Hannah." Daniel's dry words sounded speculative.

She watched him slip the revolver into the holster at his hip and did some speculating of her own. He had changed in four years. Besides his neatly trimmed mustache, he now sported a natty little goatee. The pointed shape of the beard sharpened his features, giving him a decidedly feral look. Although she didn't know how old Jake was, he had to be about the same age as Daniel. Yet Daniel already looked dissolute. Lines of discontent bracketed his mouth, making deep grooves against the puffiness in his cheeks. His skin tone, once robust and healthy, now looked florid in the harshly direct light. Or perhaps that was just a reflection of the brilliant sunset behind her.

For some reason she couldn't fathom, she hoped it was only the light making him look villainous. He had been so handsome once.

"You're a long way from the nursery, madam." One side of his mouth curled up in an almost-sneer. "I suppose dear Uncle Simon could persuade you away where I couldn't."

Hannah's heart contracted painfully, then began to gallop in her chest. He didn't know about David. She had forgotten. She swallowed hard, then said, "David . . . died, Daniel."

"Died?"

"In early February. He got a sore throat that became scarlet fever. He was . . . four years old."

A look of raw hurt flared briefly in Daniel's eyes before he thrust it aside. He had no real image of David, just the vague notion of "son." On the few occasions when he'd remembered David, it had been with the idea of going back to claim him one day when he was grown. He'd also thought it likely that David would inherit the whole of Simon Sargent's empire. But that, like everything about David, was far in the future and thus not quite real to Daniel.

Hannah, on the other hand, was real and immediate. He'd learned one thing since coming to Omaha City this time. That was that the success his men had had along the Oregon Trail west from Omaha wasn't enough. Although the raids were blamed on Indians as he'd hoped, there hadn't been enough of them to make a difference to the railroad men in charge.

Like himself, those men had made investments in property along the established route. They stood to lose those profits if the planned route was changed. However troublesome the raids were, it was really a case of too little and too late. People expected Indian raids now and counted on the railroad to end them in the future.

Daniel wasn't ready to give up his plan yet, but having Hannah fall into his hands like this gave him other, equally intriguing options. If she was here, so was Sargent, although it hadn't been two days ago when Daniel had made inquiries.

He flicked his eyes over to where the men had tied her companion. "And now you're robbing the cradle. Is that it?"

Hannah's momentary pity for Daniel was quickly replaced by repugnance. She turned from him as if to stalk away.

"Not so fast," he said, grabbing her arm. "I'm in charge here, not you."

"That's right, I forgot," Hannah spat, turning back on him. "You're an outlaw now, aren't you?"

His eyes narrowed. "An outlaw? What are you talking about?"

She hadn't meant to reveal so much. If Daniel knew what she was doing here and whom she was going to meet, he'd probably kill them both. "Well, look at you!" She gestured around the camp. "If this isn't being an outlaw, what is? Do you make a lot of money robbing innocent travelers?"

"There's nothing innocent about you," he answered. "Why are you wearing that uniform?"

"For just the reason Rory said, to look like a man."

"Why? What are you doing out here?"

"I was traveling west. My wagon train was assaulted and Rory helped me."

"You're not going west now."

"This was an outing. I came back to Omaha. He . . . was going to show me about minerals. It's interesting."

Her story made no sense at all to Daniel. He'd stopped the two of them because she was wearing the uniform. Farnsworth and his men were out here somewhere. He could have trailed them, but it seemed simpler to stop them. If they knew where Farnsworth was, it would be easy to find out. But the kid was too young to be one of them.

Wasn't he? He was even younger than Jethro.

Then he remembered. Jethro had reported that Farnsworth had a woman with him. And Hannah was the one wearing the uniform.

What luck. He could use Hannah as a lure against Farnsworth. Then when he was wiped out, Hannah could be ransom bait for dear Uncle Simon.

"You're not a very good liar, Hannah, but then you never were." He watched her face carefully. "I suppose the dry lake is where you're supposed to rendezvous with Jake Farnsworth."

As he had expected, Hannah's surprised expression gave away her knowledge of Farnsworth and his hideout. She said nothing, but her look of utter dismay didn't need words.

"Good. We'll be going there in the morning," he told her, laughing at her distress. "Won't he be glad to see you again? Especially with me? Does he know you're my long-lost little wifey?"

Daniel's pleasure grew by leaps and bounds. Each suggestion added to her obvious misery, offering further opportunities for revenge. Determined to give the matter some concentrated thought, Veazie called over one of the men and ordered him to tie Hannah hand and foot. She tried to protest, but the man cut her off and began marching her to where Rory lay.

Daniel noticed and pointed to the other side of the camp, saying, "Over there. Not with the kid. I want them apart."

At first Hannah was relieved. She wasn't looking forward to explaining things to Rory. But if they were separated, they couldn't make plans to escape. His hands were tied behind him, as hers were, too. If they'd been together, they might have found a way to work on each other's bonds.

As soon as the sun set, the campsite was plunged into deep shadow. Hannah had seen enough of camps to know that this one was not of long standing. And Daniel had said they would leave in the morning. She wished she knew more about where they were in relation to where Jake was. She had listened to Rory, but her days of travel had taught her not to trust her somewhat unreliable instincts about direction. She had left the particulars up to Rory.

They had come out of the defile heading directly into the setting sun, but before that she thought they'd gone more north than west. And she didn't know anything about a dry lake. In all that Rory had told Simon or herself about where Jake was, the dry lake had never been mentioned. Obviously, that was an inspiration on Rory's part. Too bad it hadn't worked.

She counted six men besides Daniel, only one of them an Indian. If he was a Pawnee, as Jake said, he didn't wear his hair roached into that ruff the way many of the tribe did. Once she would have said she would recognize Willie's killer anywhere. Now she wasn't sure. She remembered a painted face, not specific features. Nevertheless, she was glad he wasn't the one who came to free her hands so she could eat.

Without anything to lean against, she had been forced to lie on her side, putting the arm under her to sleep. She took so long rubbing away the pins and needles in her arm and hands that, when she had eaten, the man gave in to her request that her hands be tied in front of her for the night. Since she was not brought anywhere near Rory, she would have to take advantage of the small concession by herself.

Daniel didn't come near her again. She made no attempt to stay awake, choosing to rest while she could. Tired as she was, she knew the discomfort of being unable to move freely in sleep would bring her awake soon enough. Then she would work on untying her ankles. It would be better to have her hands free, but she would take what she could get. Perhaps she'd be able to run away.

She had no idea how long she had slept; probably too long. She had also been overly optimistic about freeing her feet. Her fingers had little feeling in them. Even reaching her ankles was a chore. She managed best by propping her feet against a rock so she didn't have to hold them up to her bound hands by her tired leg muscles. If the knots had been tied tightly, she would have made no headway at all. As it was, it took her until dawn's earliest light to undo the first knot. She almost cried aloud in frustration when she felt no immediate lessening of pressure at its release. How many of the blamed things were there?

All too soon she had to abandon the effort because the men began to stir and waken. She pushed off from the rock and dozed where she landed, resting her tired arms and hands. When one of the men stepped too close to her, she yelled at him. It felt so good to vent some of her anger that she didn't even try to keep her voice down.

For a stunned moment after that, she almost believed

311

that her outburst had caused what happened next. The man she'd yelled at fell to the ground beside her. She heard him groan and rolled away from him, back to the shelter of the rock. By the time she got there, she recognized that the roaring around her was gunfire. They were being attacked.

A horse raced by her, barely missing the body next to her. She pressed back against the rock, flattening herself against it for cover. Bound as she was and without a weapon, she was totally helpless.

There was so much noise—guns shooting, horses pounding past, men yelling and cursing. Without a thought for the fact that by yelling she was giving away her presence, she yelled for Rory. He had been lying out in the open, tied the same way. She had to know he was all right.

Did he answer? She couldn't tell.

"Rory! Are you all right?"

Someone scooped her up from the ground and threw her over his shoulder, bounding away. At first she thought it was Jake. His men had to be the ones attacking Daniel's forces. Her scream for Rory had sent Jake to get her. She was safe. She didn't fight him, just resting her hands at his waist to steady herself.

As soon as she touched him, she realized he wasn't Jake. Jake's waist was lean and hard, not thick and soft with fat like this. Then she heard him panting with exertion. She began to struggle, bucking against his back and chest. The man—Daniel, she was sure—clamped his arm tighter around her knees, but his stride was badly off. He cursed—Daniel for sure now—but didn't stop. Neither did she. She squirmed around on his shoulder, using her hands as leverage, heedless of the precariousness of her perch. If he went down, so would she, but she didn't care. She screamed and gave another mighty buck.

Unfortunately for Daniel, her increased struggle caught

him severely off balance. He went down with Hannah on top of him. The weight of her body caught him with her knees in his midsection. Everything went black around him for a while until he caught his breath.

"All right now, Veazie. Just let the lady get up. If you make a move to stop her, I'll blow your head off."

Jake. Hannah nearly sobbed with relief. She began to collect herself for the awkward business of getting off Daniel. Without arms or legs for leverage, it would be hard.

Daniel's arm continued to hold her in place.

"We're going to get up together, Farnsworth," Daniel answered. "I have my gun right up against the lady's side. If you blow my head off, she goes too. She'll be just as dead as I am. Tell him, honey."

Hannah felt the gun barrel press her ribs. It was true. In the confusion of their fall she had not been aware of it, but there it was—a gun, not a rock, pressed hard and tight against her.

"Hannah?" Jake asked.

"Oh, God, yes. I'm sorry . . ." What could she do? "Daniel, I can't move. My legs are tied." She emphasized her predicament by leaning hard into his body. He wasn't strong enough to lift them both at the same time, and certainly not with her on top of him. She doubted even Jake could do that. If he pushed her off him, he would lose her body as a screen against Jake's shot.

Daniel made the only decision he could. He wasn't leaving without Hannah. She was his only hope of salvaging something from the wreckage of his plans.

"Throw down your gun, Farnsworth, and untie the lady. And remember, if I even *think* you're up to something, she dies."

Jake didn't believe him, but he couldn't take the chance. He had a derringer concealed in his boot, but he wasn't sure he could get it to Hannah. Her one lucky shot back at the sod village aside, it wasn't much of a weapon for her, especially since he'd never taught her to use it.

He threw the gun, not far, but far enough that Veazie couldn't object. By the look of strain on his face, Jake knew Hannah was doing her best to incapacitate her husband. He worked slowly, although it was remarkably easy to untie her ankles.

They made the most absurd group. It was two against one, and that one was on the bottom of the heap. But he held the gun, so he was the boss. For now.

Jake moved back slowly, willing Hannah to be careful. He didn't believe Veazie meant to kill her because she would do him no good dead. It wasn't hard to figure what he wanted of her. Jake had no idea what Hannah was doing here, but if she'd wanted a reunion with her husband, it obviously hadn't gone well. Some other time he'd laugh about that.

Hannah was making heavy work of getting to her feet. She was more concerned about Jake than herself. Daniel might kill her, but his more likely target was Jake—who was unarmed now. "My hands, Daniel," she gasped, playing at being helpless and weak. "I can't get up without my hands."

She didn't expect sympathy or help. She was waiting for the moment when she would feel the gun barrel lift from her rib cage. When it did, she planned to be ready. She was going to push Daniel back down and get her knee on his forearm. That would give Jake time to jump Daniel, even if he couldn't also get to his own gun.

Nothing worked the way she had planned. She did feel the gun move, but her lunge was misplaced. Perhaps Daniel sensed her move and compensated to avoid her. She fell heavily, more off him than on, and though she tried to scramble after him, kicking and rolling, he got free.

Hannah struggled to her knees, only to be knocked

flat. She saw Daniel make his getaway in a zigzagging dash. He wasn't shooting back at them, just running. As soon as the weight on her back lifted, Hannah tried to get up again. This time she tripped up Jake, sending him to the ground, half on top of her.

"God damn it, Hannah!" Jake exploded. "I almost had him! Can't you ever stay where you're supposed to?"

# Chapter Seventeen

Of all the men, only Zeb had a kind word or a smile for Hannah. Jake untied her hands, then stalked away without another word. She wanted to explain herself, but not until he cooled down. How could she have known she would trip him? She had been trying to help.

She tried to hold on to her feeling of injured innocence, but it kept slipping away. Jake was right. She had no business being here. She had foiled Daniel's attempt to take her hostage, but because of her interference, he had managed to escape. Surely Jake didn't think she'd done that on purpose! Or did he?

Hannah started back to the scene of the attack, rubbing her wrists and hands. Remembering Rory, she picked up her pace, looking around for him. But then she saw him talking to Jake and her concern for him turned into concern for herself. Nothing Rory would — or could — say would further her cause with Jake.

The camp itself was a mess. Horses and men milled about aimlessly in the shocked aftermath of battle, stepping over bedrolls and bodies with equal unconcern. Hannah decided to try to find her saddlebag and horse. Perhaps Rory would accompany her back to Omaha. Perhaps not, of course, but it was something to do.

She had just found the pack, right where she had last seen it, being fought over by the men, when Zeb found her. "Colby's hurt," he said. "Maybe you kin help."

Hannah didn't want to. Her reluctance had nothing to do with the fact that she knew Colby disapproved of her. That didn't matter. If she thought she could help him, she'd try, no matter how inept she felt. But she felt more than inept. She felt jinxed. If she tried to help Colby, she'd end up killing him. It was inevitable. And the man already carried a grudge against her.

"Oh, Zeb, I don't know anything about doctoring."

"That's not what I heared."

So Jake had told Zeb about her "operation" on him. That was good news. At least she hoped it was. But Colby wasn't Jake, and she'd vowed never to do anything like that again.

Zeb dragged her off anyway.

Then she saw Colby. He had been shot in the arm. He was holding his hat to his arm, while blood dripped freely from under his hand. His face was like bleached flour.

"Get some whiskey," she ordered. "And someone cut that sleeve off his arm."

Colby's eyes opened so wide in alarm that she could see the white all around his dark irises.

Hannah pried his hand free and spoke to him gently. "It's all right, Colby. We just have to stop the bleeding. The bullet went through and it's nice and clean. Just relax."

Once he fainted at the sight of a knife so near his bloody arm, the job went easier for Hannah. She made strips of her nightgown and poured whiskey over her hands and some of the strips. The exit wound was bigger, but it was the entrance point that pulsed with blood. She packed it with clean material and had Zeb hold it tightly in place while she found a stick to use to twist the bandage even tighter. With the stick in place, she or someone else could regularly release enough pressure to let blood flow down his arm and into his hand. She explained the principle to Zeb, wishing she knew more exact timing to tell him that "every so often."

She picked up Colby's blood-soaked hat, almost smiling that he'd chosen such an unlikely bandage. "When he comes to enough to swallow," she told Zeb, "give him some whiskey for the pain. Not too much though. He needs to have his wits about him. I'll get rid of this thing. He won't want to see so much of his own blood."

She backed up—directly into Jake. She gave Zeb an exasperated look, knowing he had seen Jake appear behind her and hadn't seen fit to warn her.

"Excuse me," she said, trying to step around his intimidating bulk.

"Is he going to be all right?"

"Zeb can tell you." She was almost as bloody as Colby, but Jake didn't let her by.

"I asked you."

"I hope so, but I'm not a doctor. He fainted just now, but Zeb will fix him up."

"I'd rather you did it."

"Well, I'm sure Colby wouldn't, so if you'll excuse me?" He stepped the same way she did, boxing her in. "Please, Jake. I want to wash!"

He took her arm then, scooping up her pack—recognizable by the remains of her nightgown adorning it—and went with her.

Because she had only been escaping and as long as she hadn't been successful, she paid no mind to where he took her. She sat where he pointed and simply stared up at him.

"Stop looking like a whipped puppy. I've never raised my hand to you yet, have I?"

"Why do I think that it's just a matter of time?"

He knelt before her and used some of her ruined nightgown to dab at her face. The cloth reeked of whiskey. He worked in silence and she suffered his attention in silence. People and horses parted around them like water slipping by two stones in a stream. When he held up her chin to look her face over, Hannah didn't want to meet his eyes.

She did anyway. "Go ahead and yell at me," she challenged, lifting her chin to get free of his hand.

"Would it do any good?"

"It might break the ice."

He sighed. "What the hell were you trying to prove?" he asked wearily.

Not sure precisely which of her many transgressions he meant, she only shrugged. "I'm sure Rory told you."

Rory's name relit the fire of indignation in his eyes. "And you said *I* was going to put him in danger!"

"I know, I know," she said mournfully. "I'm sorry about that. I really am. I don't want to do it. I just didn't see any other way to get to you. He wouldn't let me come alone."

He opened his mouth, about to roar at her. She put her hand on his mouth and said it all again—fervently. He pulled back and she followed until he was sitting back and she was kneeling before him. When she realized what she was doing, she snatched back her hand and got to her feet, on the offensive at last.

"You sneaked away!"

"I was coming back!"

"Sure you were!" He was towering over her again, so she turned away and tried to leave him standing there with no one to fight with.

He caught her arm and held it. "Don't you walk off on me!"

"You think that's *your* exclusive right?" She wrenched her arm free. "Well, it's not!" She never expected to be allowed to leave. Then she thought he'd follow her, if only to take up the argument. But he didn't. She was all the way across the camp before she realized he didn't care.

She wouldn't look back at her things until enough time had passed for him to have gone away. Then when she got there, everything was gone. Zeb came up to her, leading Ranger. Her pack was in place on his back.

Hannah looked to Zeb for direction, but he offered none. She wanted to go back to Omaha. Instead, she asked about Colby. Assured that he was fine, she let Zeb help her mount and joined the procession away from the camp. She saw Rory ahead of her, but made no attempt to reach him. Many Buffalo nodded to her gravely and she gave him a smile. In spite of his grim expression, his eyes seemed to laugh at her, but in a kind way. There were times she liked him a lot better than his cousin.

She wasn't surprised when they didn't enter the defile that led back to Omaha. She had known she wouldn't get her way this time. Besides, Daniel was out there somewhere and she had no desire ever to see him again. She overheard snatches of conversation among the men that told her he wasn't alone even yet. Spotted Pony hadn't been taken or killed.

It wasn't over yet.

The scene before Hannah was something few white men, never mind a white woman, would ever see. Seventeen men sat in a circle around the fire, smoking, telling stories, and in some cases, taking sips of whiskey from a bottle. If their activity, or lack of it perhaps, wasn't unusual, the men were. Eight were Indians from Many Buffalo's tribe. By the look on Rory's face, she wasn't the only one full of wonder. His eyes were so wide he looked as if he would never sleep again.

He was next to Jake, who sat just across the fire from Hannah and next to the Indian who was speaking. Hannah particularly appreciated this story because she could watch Jake as she listened.

The stories themselves were as varied as the speakers. Some were brief, some rambling and discursive. It didn't matter. No one interrupted or criticized. It had all begun when Whitcomb, one of Jake's men, told a ghost story. That led to a Pawnee story of a ghost bride, designed to reinforce belief in the existence of an afterlife.

Another Indian tale followed, one Hannah found particularly tedious. It seemed pointless, full of statements like, "So the next day the brave went out to hunt, but he found no game. He went back to the village." It was probably an honest reflection of what Indian life could be, but Hannah's mind wandered in the telling.

A quiet word from Many Buffalo brought her attention roaring back. He asked Jake to tell the story of "the baby in the basket." Jake's narrative style seemed a mixture of Indian and white. Like Whitcomb, he heightened suspense rather than maintaining a flat, prosaic tone, but he used Indian expressions he also translated. *Tirawa* was his name for the Great Spirit, and he used the terms interchangeably. Hannah was so fascinated by his story that it wasn't until he finished that she recognized what it was. It was the story of Moses and the bullrushes, referred to by him as "reeds." Jake ended by saying, "The baby grew up to be a great chief and a wise leader of his people."

Amazed, Hannah searched the circle of faces for a reaction, particularly among the whites. No one seemed aware of what he had done, or perhaps they'd heard it before and so had lost their surprise. Only Many Buffalo showed emotion, quiet satisfaction in a familiar tale well told again.

Now she listened to the broad-faced Pawnee next to Jake and studied Jake. The tale of a magical horse that brought riches and power to the poor Indian boy who saved it from slaughter was engaging, but Hannah preferred to watch the firelight flicker over Jake's rugged features. He was so dear to her. She could not imagine life without him.

She knew the life they had shared wasn't normal, even for him. He had fought for the Union and chased Daniel's men, but he wasn't a professional soldier. He didn't need adventure any more than she did. He wanted a ranch and a settled home for his daughter. Why did that goal have to exclude her? She loved him. She wanted the same thing—home, family, love. Daniel was no longer a barrier between them. Even Jake had to realize that now. She could help him, not with money but with her love and spirit.

She could not let Jake deposit her back on Uncle Simon's doorstep and walk out of her life forever. Somehow she had to make him understand—and she had only tonight to do it.

Tomorrow they would take the three captured men to the authorities in Omaha City. Uncle Simon would pay the men and they would disband. Or would they? She would try to find out from Jake. But even if they didn't disband, Jake would certainly take her back to Uncle Simon. She could never run after him again like this. Even she understood that.

She didn't know she had fallen from her dreamy contemplation of Jake into sleep until Zeb spoke to her. "Come on, Hannah. It's bedtime."

She raised her head and looked into his shoe-button eyes, confused by the laughter she saw there. His wiry arm supported her. He jostled it gently to rouse her.

"Oh, I'm sorry." She pulled away, rubbing her eyes and asking sleepily, "Whatever happened to the magic horse?" Everyone around them was leaving the fire for bed.

"He went to be with the Great Spirit in the sky, I 'spect," Zeb replied, grinning. "Actually, I sorta dozed off a bit myself there. Them Injun stories do that to me every time."

"I wanted to remember that one," she protested, then

322

laughed at the way she sounded, like a child whose bedtime story had been cut off. "Oh, well, thank you for the use of your shoulder, kind sir."

Zeb bobbed his head and scurried off, leaving her to make her way to her bedroll. As always, it was near Jake's, but carefully set aside — from him as much as from the others. She stepped around his empty spot, wishing she had the nerve to crawl into it and wait for him. He wouldn't lie down until everyone else was settled. Would he object to her presence? Would he kick her out?

She didn't dare chance his rejection. There were too many unresolved issues between them for her to be obvious. Using the blanket for a shield, she took off her outer clothes and put them aside. She would sleep in the pantalettes and chemise she had on and forget about the extras she had packed. They were no longer clean enough to wear after being tossed around and fallen on by Daniel's men.

She sighed and looked up at the tapestry of stars above her. What a day she had had — just one of so many strange and exciting ones since coming west. She wished she hadn't fallen asleep earlier. Now she was wide awake again, the edge of tiredness taken from her by that nap. She listened to the men settle for sleep, her attention attuned to the blanket nearest hers. Even when she heard Jake, she couldn't settle down. He didn't speak to her, nor did she acknowledge him. She pretended to be asleep, lying still in the vain hope that pretense would bring reality. It didn't, but it did enable her to hear Jake's every restless move.

She endured it all in complete silence, hoping, praying that he would speak to her. When he did speak though, it wasn't to her.

"Damnation!" he muttered fiercely, but only to himself. If she had been sleeping, or even resting normally, the sound would not have carried to her. It took her every

323

straining nerve to receive that soft sound.

Then he got up. He didn't dress. She would have heard the sound of his pants going on.

Hannah sat up. He was gone. She could see a faint gleam going away that had to be his bare back. Grabbing her shirt, she stepped to his bedroll and checked for his clothes. There was a shirt but no pants.

No one challenged her as she followed his path. Somewhere, someone was on watch, maybe two someones. She wasn't worried about being stopped, only about being prevented from saying what she wanted to say. If only Jake would listen and not be angry.

She had to stop once or twice to get her bearings. The moon was only a slim crescent in the sky, giving little light, and Jake knew how to conceal himself by staying very still. She found the guard before she did Jake. She waved to him and he answered by pointing out where Jake had gone. Another wave thanked him and then she was next to Jake, tongue-tied but there.

"I thought you were asleep."

She shook her head. "Pretending. I did my sleeping during storytime." When he didn't comment, she added, "I liked your story. Is that the way your missionary forebears told it?"

"It's just my version."

She took a deep breath. She hadn't followed him to make small talk. "Jake, I'm sorry I followed you here yesterday."

"Are you?" He didn't sound angry, just disbelieving.

"Well, not in some ways." She was determined to be honest. "I'm sorry about the way I did it. My first thought was that you weren't well enough."

"You can see that I am."

"That's debatable, no matter what you think," she pointed out. "Besides, you didn't let me see your progress. You hid—"

"You call the way I carried you around hiding?"

"I wasn't thinking then." She could feel her face growing warm. "Anyway, that seemed sort of . . . inspired . . . or—"

He laughed then, but it didn't make her feel better. "Jake, I don't want to go back to Omaha or back to Tennessee. I want to go with you."

He stiffened. "That's impossible."

"No, it isn't. You have this idea of what I am that's all wrong. You always have. Won't you just look at me the way I am? I'm not my uncle and I'm not my . . . Daniel. I'm me. Hannah Hatch from Ohio. Just a woman. I want what you want, a home and a family. Love."

The word hung in the air between them like the vapor from her breath. She wished she hadn't said it. It seemed to put a barrier between them. Another one.

"You'll have all those things again someday, Hannah. I know you will."

"I don't want them someday. I want them now."

The cry of a spoiled child? Oh, God. She wasn't helping herself.

She backed up quickly to try again. "Jake, think about the person you know me to be. No one has ever known me as well as you do. We've fought and loved and worked together. Have you ever heard me complain about hardships? Have I cried for the moon? Damn it, Jake. I don't want those things. I don't care about luxuries."

"Don't you?" His quiet challenge cut across her vehemence. "The first thing you did in Omaha was outfit yourself with enough dresses to last a lifetime."

"No! The first thing I did was get you a doctor!"

"Hannah, I'm not arguing that you neglected my care, or Rory's, or your uncle's. You're wonderful. You're a marvel. You can ride for days, shoot the enemy, nurse the wounded, and probably raise the dead! Damn it, that's just the problem! You're so far above me I shouldn't even be talking to you!"

"No, Jake, no." She shook her head, utterly miserable. She could feel the tears running down her cheeks, but they didn't matter as long as she could see the misery on his face. She reached for him, fighting his reluctance to let her near. "I'm not wonderful. I'm flesh and blood and bone. I'm just a stubborn, hardheaded woman with *nothing* in my life. My son is dead. You saw my husband. Do you still believe I want him? Uncle Simon is a dear, good man and I love him, but he's not mine.

"If I go back, I can be his hostess—when he's there. I can dress up and go to parties and balls—for a while. But that's not a whole life. I love it out here in the West. It's real and exciting. There's challenge and reward."

At last she had his attention without the accompanying skepticism. Or so she thought.

Jake was tempted, terribly tempted. He wanted her, heart, body and soul. But he couldn't forget the contrast between them. When she reached for him, he forced himself to remember that difference.

"I can't deny that you have an affinity for adventure and excitement. You can't deny, either, that everything about the way you live is different." She opened her mouth to protest and he covered it with one hand. "Hannah, you *bought* a house for us to live in for a few days! A *house!*"

She pushed his hand away. "That wasn't my money. It was Uncle Simon's and it was for him. He'll be in Omaha a long time. Besides, it was an investment."

"I'm sure it was—a wise one. But don't you see? I'll never be able to do that. I have nothing. No way to buy anything."

"But you'll be well paid for this job and Uncle Simon will reward you for helping me."

"Woman, you are making me furious!"

She could see that. "But why? Are you going to say it

was a pleasure to have my company? You know I was a care and an . . . impediment. I caused you trouble. I ran off."

As memories surfaced, recalled by her words, they lit fires in his eyes. He stepped back from her, but she saw his reaction. She put her hands on his shoulders. He took them down.

But he didn't let them go. He held her hands, looking torn and exasperated.

"Jake?"

"Let me be, Hannah. Just let me be."

"I can't. I know we're right together. I—" Could she tell him she loved him? Right out loud like this?

She decided she could, but that she shouldn't. In refusing her he wasn't thinking of himself, he was being noble, thinking of *her* good—as he saw it. And he was thinking that he had to go find Caroline.

Her eyes coasted from his closed, desperate face down his rugged chest to their joined hands. If he couldn't think of himself, perhaps—

"There is something else you may not have thought about, Jake." Before he could bristle with indignation, she squeezed his hands reassuringly. "Please, don't shut me off without listening."

He let her hands drop and folded his arms across his chest. He had to do something with his hands to keep from brushing aside that unbuttoned shirt and touching her. "Go ahead."

"I know you said you don't need a wife to make a home for Caroline, that you could hire a housekeeper, but I wonder if you realize how much a girl Caroline's age needs a woman to talk to. You know, I was just about her age when my parents died. I know how hard it was. Uncle Simon had housekeepers and cooks galore, but there was no one motherly for me to talk to . . . about my feelings and . . . about the way my body was changing."

Hannah knew she was being indelicate, but if it was hard for her to mention such things to Jake with all the intimacy of their relationship, how much harder would it be for Caroline? A flare of sympathy for the girl drove her on. He was clearly too embarrassed to speak.

"Caroline was a small child when she was with you. Now she's on the verge of womanhood. You'll be almost a stranger to her."

"And you would be a total stranger."

"But a woman," she put in quickly.

"Her grandmother is a woman."

She couldn't criticize Caroline's mother, but hadn't he as much as said that Grace had been spoiled by her upbringing? Was that what he wanted for Caroline? She knew it wasn't. "Didn't you say she was a bit . . . rigid? And she is older."

"She's a good woman who loves Caroline. I wouldn't have left her with anyone who wouldn't take good care of her."

"Of course you wouldn't. I'm not talking about care. I'm talking about adjustment and growing up. You're going to take her away from that care to live in a very different world, a world that's all male. Don't you think I know how hard that can be? It happened to me when I was Caroline's age."

"You were orphaned. I'm her father. I haven't deserted her. She still has me. It's not the same," he said stiffly.

"No, no, I know that. But the isolation from other females, Jake; that's different. I felt that in camp with your men. Why do you think I was so crazy to see those Mormons?" she asked. She hadn't intended to raise this issue at all. It sounded like criticism of his care again. "I wanted to talk to a woman. I lost my friend Marcie in that wagon train and I was on my way to see my cousin Elizabeth in Fort Kearney. Do you know, until a maid helped me bathe in the hotel, I hadn't talked to another woman in all that time?"

"I didn't think of that."

"If you'd been with only women, wouldn't you miss other men?"

"Of course." He looked thoughtful. "Then I'll make sure I find a good housekeeper for Caroline, one who's motherly."

How much clearer could he be? She did have some pride—didn't she? If she asked for the job—and wasn't that what she'd been doing?—he would refuse her.

Hannah straightened her spine and stepped back. "I . . . see," she said. She was lying. She didn't see now and she never would. Her eyes filled with tears and she turned to run away before she disgraced herself further.

Jake caught her hand and held her there. "Hannah," he said hoarsely. "Oh, God, Hannah, don't cry. I'm sorry, sweetheart. I am."

He was pleading with her, but for what? She couldn't tell him she understood and accepted. She just couldn't.

"It's not just me, Hannah. It's . . . so many things. I know it's hard, but it's better this way. You'll see."

She flicked her hand, tugging to free it. "Better? For whom? You don't understand anything!"

She ran then, back to the campsite and her bed. Sometimes she stumbled and sometimes she couldn't see where she stepped. It was amazing that she made it safely. She pulled her blanket and pack farther away from Jake's, far enough, she hoped, that he wouldn't hear her crying when he came to bed. She used the remnants of her nightgown as a giant sponge to soak up her tears, not even aware of when she slipped from misery into exhausted sleep.

Rory woke her late the next morning, following Jake's orders to let her sleep as long as possible. He knew something was wrong with Jake from his haggard appearance. That Hannah was no better confirmed his suspicions that they had disagreed. He felt vaguely guilty about their problem, although surely he had not caused it.

"Are you all right?" he asked when she only stared woodenly at him.

"Fine," she answered the same way.

Perhaps he should have explained things better to Jake after the attack. He wished now that he'd dared to warn Jake about who Hannah's uncle was. He'd tried, sort of, to take the blame for the way they'd followed Jake, but his explanations had sounded weak even to him. Probably Jake saw right through him.

One thing Rory didn't worry about. He knew Jake and Hannah loved each other. Whatever the problem, they would soon sort it out by themselves. He'd help if he could, but they would be fine.

"Can I bring you some coffee?"

"No. Thank you. I'll . . . get right up." She didn't want coffee. She didn't want to be any more awake than necessary. More than anything, she wanted not to feel the way she did—the way she would feel for the rest of her life. It didn't even help to see that Jake was hollow-eyed and gaunt. Nothing helped.

She did what she was told, mounted up and rode back to Omaha. Colby came near to thank her for helping him, a concession she appreciated somewhere deep inside, although she knew her response lacked graciousness. Zeb gave her a twinkling smile that made tears swim in her eyes. She would never see him again, and she loved him almost as much as she had loved Willie. He, too, cared for her, befriended her, but she didn't care that he was going out of her life.

She had room inside only for the ache in her heart for Jake. That was so immense it filled her. Every time she loved deeply, she lost. Her parents. Daniel at first. David, always. And now Jake. Nothing would ever hurt so much

330

again.

Hannah refused to take part in any discussion of arrangements once they reached Omaha. She didn't care that Jake and Rory pretended she was incapable of finding her way to the house by herself. She was being left behind like an unwanted parcel. Nothing else mattered.

In the end both of them escorted her to Uncle Simon, who confined his remarks in her presence to a few exasperated "Damn me, girl's," accompanied by the hard hugs that were his primary expression of love.

Hannah hugged him back, then headed for the stairs. With one last look at Jake, standing like an especially ill-made marionette with tight strings, she said, "I know you'll be pleased that Jake and his men have done their job so well, Uncle Simon. But Jake has done much more than that. I've been a particularly difficult charge, and he's saved my life more times than either of us care to remember. Please reward him generously."

Jake's half-expected bellow of rage never came and she made her escape to her room unscathed. There she stripped off her clothes and washed. She would have liked a bath, but didn't dare chance calling Mrs. Gilman for heated water. Not while Jake was still below.

Below. Hannah stood stalk still. Her room was directly over the parlor, something she'd never considered of importance before. Now she listened, her hand poised in indecision before an assortment of underwear. Jake was right, she thought irrelevantly. She had bought a lifetime supply of clothing. The array paralyzed her. The choices.

But she was really attuned to the rise and fall of male voices below. Not words—she couldn't pick up words or even recognize whose voice spoke. Not Rory's, she guessed. He wouldn't have much to say. She couldn't determine the tone either. It seemed steady and rational.

Her lips turned up in a scornful smile. Of course it was rational. Uncle Simon and Jake were two of a kind. Not

331

for either of them the kind of heated exchange she knew was appropriate to the moment! She pictured herself running down there and telling them what they could do with their cold, implacable logic.

But first she would dress. She grabbed up something — anything — then heard a different sound. The scrape of a chair? Oh, God.

Hannah pulled a cinnamon-colored robe around her. He was going . . . going . . . Jake.

She was at the top of the stairway, ready to throw herself down its length when she saw Jake start up. She stopped. He didn't. She backed up, matching him step for step. She backed past her open bedroom door. Seeing the bureau, she remembered she hadn't brushed her hair. She pushed back the untidy mass of hair from her face.

The hall was narrow, its walls hung with samplers and small, dark pictures in heavy frames. Wherever there wasn't a doorway, there was a chest or a high-backed chair. She almost fell into the one next to Jake's doorway. The door stood open as she'd left it after her inspection of the empty premises. She braced herself there and darted inside as if the sudden thought she'd had was sensible.

"You must take your clothes, Jake. They won't fit anyone else and you'll need clothes back East." She took them out and folded them, looking for all the world like a wife packing up her husband for a business trip.

He watched her as if she'd lost her mind.

He wasn't wrong.

"Hannah, I didn't come up here for clothes."

She finished the stack and held it out to him. He took her shoulders instead and stared into her eyes. He'd meant to . . . God, he didn't know what he meant to do. Apologize? Carry her off? He didn't know.

The look in her eyes, those dauntless, damn-you, beautiful eyes, would haunt him forever. He couldn't stay. He couldn't take her. He had nothing to give her but his love — and she already had that. It killed him that he had hurt her.

He touched his lips to hers. Just . . . touched. He couldn't do more or he'd never let her go.

He dropped his hands from her arms and backed away. She pressed the clothes, offering them urgently. He took them and turned away.

At the door he heard her say, "You'll be sorry."

He stopped and smiled sadly. "I already am."

# Chapter Eighteen

"You must be very happy today, Mrs. Veazie."

Hannah produced a tired smile. She was back to being Mrs. Veazie again, in deference to Uncle Simon's many friends and business associates who knew her by that name. "Yes, it's a historic moment," she murmured. Hoping her comment was sufficient, she edged toward Uncle Simon's private rooms. She needed to sit for a few minutes and rest her feet.

The woman's smile became especially avid. She sidled after Hannah as if she had become attached to her gown. "I understand that you were attacked by savage Indians not too long ago. You're so fortunate to be alive."

Hannah stopped and the woman, unable to halt in time, bumped her side. "I am indeed fortunate to be alive, Mrs. Gray, is it not?" Her trick for remembering names hadn't failed her — gray for boring. She had no idea where the story of her trials had come from, not Uncle Simon she was sure, but she was tired of hearing it.

Especially hearing it garbled this way. "I was part of a wagon trail going west that was attacked, but the savages in this case were white men, not Indians. The Indians were among my rescuers. In fact, Indians saved my life twice and perhaps a third time as well."

Mrs. Gray's eyes grew wide and excited. "Oh, my! Now why would they do that?"

"Perhaps because they're decent human beings, Mrs. Gray." Sweeping her with a cold eye, she added, "Now if you'll excuse me, I have to speak to my uncle."

She made her way out of the packed room by instinct. Wearing a fixed smile, she pressed forward, relentlessly filling any vacant space between herself and the door. Her feet hurt from standing, her knuckles were bruised from shaking so many hands, and her face ached from hours of unnatural smiling. Had she ever enjoyed this life? Did Uncle Simon?

She had her answer to that question in her first glimpse of him across the small parlor. His head was thrown back in laughter. He held a glass of port in one hand and a cigar in the other. Her smile relaxed and became natural. He was having a very good time, just as she would have once.

She was the one who had changed. She was happy for her uncle and proud of his part in opening the West to safe travel. She understood better than most what a boon the railroad would be to settlers. She had been deeply affected by the ceremony involved in laying the first bit of track out of Omaha, especially because of Jake's part in making it possible.

Jake had been gone a week. The week had taught her that, much as she might wish it, she wasn't going to die of loneliness. There were other people to think of besides herself. There were Uncle Simon and Rory, for example.

She knew Rory would have chosen to go with Jake, had he been asked. Like Hannah, he hadn't had the choice to make. Jake had decided to go alone for Caroline. Rory didn't admit to it, but Hannah was sure Jake had charged Rory with her welfare. Although in one way that annoyed her, in another light it could be seen as a sign that he cared for her. Not enough, of course, but in certain moments it was a comfort to her. Rory certainly was.

Rory had taken to Uncle Simon almost as easily as he had to Jake. They talked frequently long after Hannah had retired for the night. She knew her uncle was considering what Rory should do with the rest of his life. It was something Hannah gave a lot of thought to as well, although without coming to any conclusions. He could work for Uncle Simon, but she didn't favor that. She believed in education and wanted to send Rory back East to one of the universities there. If he wanted to work for Uncle Simon after that — fine. Both of them would then benefit from his education. In just the past few days she had seen Rory grow more and more poised as he met and mingled with Simon's associates. Uncle Simon introduced him around proudly, always telling people how he had helped rescue his niece and bring her safely to Omaha.

He was telling the story again as Hannah went to join them. Rory saw her to a chair, then bent and said, "I always want to explain that before I could rescue you, I had to trap Jake first. But I guess that would take away from your uncle's story."

It was easy to laugh with Rory. "Some people might not understand how heroic that was."

"Especially me," he answered, grinning.

That exchange, unless she counted shocking Mrs. Gray, was the highlight of her evening as Uncle Simon's hostess. That the reception had gone well gave her little joy. She understood now that she couldn't get joy from things like that. Joy could come only from people.

Once they were home, she accepted Uncle Simon's thanks and a goodnight peck on the cheek and went to her room to prepare for bed. Mrs. Gilman, much less disapproving of Hannah now that Simon was here and Jake was gone, had helped her dress, doing up the little buttons at the back of her gown, before she went to her own home and Mr. Gilman. Alone, Hannah struggled to undo her dress. She thought she had managed, then found there were also diabolically small hooks and eyes to unfasten as well. She took herself down to Uncle Simon for help.

He looked up from his chair and smiled at her. "You grow to look more like your mother every day, Hannah. And that's a compliment, girl. Except for Anne — God rest her soul — I've never known a woman who could touch Josie."

"I still miss her, Uncle Simon. She was special."

"And so are you." He undid the hooks for her. "When you get comfortable, come down again. I'd like to talk to you if you're not too tired."

Even tired, she would be back. She was curious to know what was on Uncle Simon's mind. Dressed in her nightgown, robe, and slippers, she sat down across from him and waited for him to speak.

He poured her a splash of brandy, then said, "You're not happy here."

It was pointless to argue. "It's not your fault, and it's not being here."

"Do you still want to go to Fort Kearney?"

"I don't know."

"It would be hard to send you off again this time, knowing what I do about the dangers. But Elizabeth and

337

Calvin would still welcome you, if that's what you want to do."

"I know what I want to do, Uncle Simon, but I'm afraid it's impossible."

"Farnsworth?"

She nodded and bent her head over the brandy.

"You love him?"

She nodded again and took a sip. The fiery liquid helped warm her where she always seemed to feel cold now, deep inside.

"Is Daniel the problem?"

"No. I didn't tell him, but he has to know I could get a divorce." She looked into Simon's troubled eyes and sighed. There was no use trying to spare his feelings. He would find out someday. "I'm the problem, really. He doesn't believe I could be happy without all this." She waved her hand to include the room, overstuffed with furniture, the drink, and her own clothes.

"He's a proud man," Simon agreed. "Do you know he wouldn't take any reward for helping you? He said you saved his life over and over and that you were even."

"I'm not surprised he said that."

"I offered him another job, short-term, and he refused. I'd have offered a permanent position too, but it didn't seem wise."

In spite of herself, Hannah was pleased by Jake's integrity. She smiled. "I can really pick 'em, can't I? Daniel, who only wanted my fortune, and now Jake. He'll only take me if I'm as poor as he is."

"Will he change his mind in time?"

"I doubt it. He has to be his own man."

"Then why don't you go back to Knoxville? I'm going to be here for another month and I don't think you can take another month of a place that reminds you of him."

338

Hannah shouldn't have been surprised by his perception, but she was. "I don't know," she said, reluctant to remind him of why Knoxville had been just as unacceptable only a short time ago. "You did pay Jake, didn't you?"

"I gave him cash and set up accounts for each of the men, Jake included. I intend to see that he gets more than he expected. I'm not the only one involved, of course, and I think he'll take from the others what he won't take from me. After all, he earned it."

"What about Daniel and Spotted Pony?"

"There are rewards for their arrest. They won't escape."

"Daniel was going to hold me for ransom. That was another of Jake's rescues."

"Damn me, girl. I wish I'd known that!"

Hannah smiled again. "It wouldn't have mattered. Jake is . . . just Jake, I guess. He's a pleasant change from Daniel."

"I wish I could help."

"You have. Did Jake find out you weren't the only one who hired him?"

"I don't know, come to think of it. Would it help if he knew?"

"Perhaps." She sipped her brandy and relaxed, pleased just to talk about Jake after days of trying not to think about him.

"He has family in the East?"

"A daughter. She's almost ten. She lived with his wife's parents while he was in the war. His wife died when Caroline was born—or just after," she amended, remembering his story.

"He thinks his daughter wouldn't like you?"

"He never puts the two of us together in his own mind, Uncle Simon. We're separate . . . problems, to him. I

339

tried to make a connection, but he thinks in a lock-step formation. First, he gets Caroline; then, who knows? Maybe he'll think of me then, maybe not. Next he'll have to get his ranch and his housekeeper." She sighed. "No. I'm pretty far down on the list. His marriage wasn't happy in spite of the fact that he loved his wife. I'm afraid he doesn't think much about his own happiness. He puts others first."

Simon grunted.

The noise might have meant agreement or disgust; Hannah couldn't tell. She put her glass aside and got up, intending to go to bed. She was pleasantly relaxed and sleepy for the first time in ages. It seemed a shame to spoil such a perfect state by fighting it.

Simon blasted her serenity to bits with his next words. "It looks to me, girl, as if you have to make the next move then. If you want Farnsworth, that is."

Hannah sat down with an audible thump. *"I've* got to make the next move!" She was irate. "I've done nothing but chase after that man and throw myself at him! No, sir. I'm done running after Jake Farnsworth."

"Well, I can understand how you feel. You do have as much pride as he does, and it won't be easy." He sounded—and looked—smug. "You did say you loved him, didn't you?"

"I did, but if you think that means I have no pride—"

"I just got finished saying you did, didn't I?"

He had. She had forgotten already. "Uncle Simon, you just don't understand. I'm not exaggerating. I chased him. I begged him to take me with him. I can't do more than that."

"No, of course you can't." He spoke to her in the soothing tones of her childhood. "It's just that unless you meet this girl of his pretty soon—say, before he takes her off out West somewhere permanently—you'll never have a chance to get to know her as a friend and not as a rival for her father's attention and love."

"But I wouldn't be."

"No? You'd be a stranger, an outsider, the mean old stepmother."

"I never thought of that." Hannah was stunned. Even Jake hadn't come up with that objection. "But she doesn't remember her mother. I . . . thought she'd *want* a woman to talk to."

"Because you always did."

It was impossible to hide her chagrin. She'd always hoped he hadn't known. "It wasn't your fault, Uncle Simon. You were wonderful to me."

"I tried, honey, but there were hundreds of times I'd have given anything to have a wife, just for you. I knew it was hard on you. Don't blame yourself for what you needed. It wasn't your fault any more than it was mine. We muddled through—and that's what Jake will do."

"He promised to find a motherly housekeeper," she said softly, aware of how much she was telling him about herself as a child.

"And he probably will, but you'd do the child a sight more good, especially if you can get in on the ground floor, so to speak."

"But how, Uncle Simon? Just show up and . . . what? Jake would *kill* me!"

"He won't be pleased," Simon agreed, looking grim, "but what choice do you have? Do you know where he's taking the girl? Does he already own land somewhere?"

"I don't think so. I think he would have told me. All he said was that he wanted a ranch somewhere where land is cheap."

"That could be a lot of places, and tracing someone out

341

in the territories can be a job. It's not impossible, mind you—especially if they make legal claim to land somewhere—but it can take a while."

"You really think I should go?"

"It isn't a matter of should and shouldn't. The situation is unusual."

"I'll say." She couldn't bring her mind to focus on the issue. Every time she tried, her thoughts skittered off on a tangent like a nervous horse. "You really believe he loves me, don't you?"

"I saw evidence of it, yes."

His words were a lot more judicious than Hannah liked, but she understood his caution. With Jake it didn't do to be too confident. "If he doesn't, then he'll be furious when I arrive uninvited."

*Judicious* was not the term for what he said next. The word for that was *scary*. "I'd say," Uncle Simon put forth in the same careful manner, "he'll be even worse if he *does* love you."

Hannah moaned aloud, but Simon wasn't done yet.

"In fact," he said, giving no quarter to her obvious dismay, "I'd venture that his reaction to your arrival will be a good measure, not only of how much he loves you, but also of how much he needs your help. The worse he acts, the more likely it is that he needs you. From what I saw of him, Jake Farnsworth isn't a man to enjoy needing someone else—for anything."

Didn't Hannah already know that? Hadn't she seen his misery when he was sick or injured? Did she really want to put herself in his path again? Especially when Caroline was concerned?

"I'd rather face Daniel again with a gun in my ribs, Uncle Simon," she said, answering her own questions.

Her uncle understood. "It's your choice."

342

But it wasn't really. "At least Rory will come with me. Jake *may* be happy to see him."

Knowing that Gettysburg, Pennsylvania, had been a major battlefield of the recent war, Jake looked for signs that Hanford, less than a score of miles away, had suffered damage. His own experience at Chickamauga told him that victory or defeat meant little to the land itself. To his eye, Hanford looked untouched by time. Both sleepy and prosperous, it was incredibly green and fertile. That undoubtedly accounted for the look of prosperity. After the gold-washed plains of Nebraska, the moist green of southeastern Pennsylvania looked unnaturally lush.

As he rode the last few miles, he thought about Hannah. He'd bought a horse—not to replace Victor, left behind with Rory, but just to have transportation. He didn't *want* to think about Hannah, but short of cutting out his heart, it seemed impossible to keep her out of his thoughts. He missed her, especially when riding like this. A dozen times he'd started to speak to her and sometimes he hadn't remembered his solitude until after he'd broken the silence. Then he was thankful there was no one around to hear his foolishness.

Jake never once considered it strange that he thought of Hannah, not Grace, in a place where he had courted and married his wife. Grace was truly dead to him now. He was in Hanford because of Caroline, not her mother. He looked around with interest, but without nostalgia. He noted that the general store was being enlarged and that the church had a new belfry, but those details had no personal significance for him anymore. That he had been married in the church and had once shopped regularly in

343

the store was of no importance. He noticed and rode on.

His plan, if it could be called that, was simple. He would present himself at the Lunig farm, collect Caroline, thank—and pay—her grandparents, and leave, taking Caroline with him. He knew their leave-taking would not happen today, possibly not even this week. Caroline would have possessions to pack and good-byes to say. He would give her time to do the things she wanted to do in the way she wanted to do them, within reason. They needed to travel in good weather, and it was already mid-July. But if they left before the end of the month, they would be fine.

Because Gustaf Lunig was a vigorous man in his sixties, still actively in charge of his farm, Jake had timed his arrival to fit as well as possible with the man's work schedule. He had, Jake remembered, worked around the barn and house garden in the morning, checking and overseeing the field workers in the afternoon. Jake had no reason to expect that Gustaf, always inflexible, would have altered his routine with age.

He had dressed in the plainest, most serviceable of the breeches and shirts Hannah had given him, and he carried the coat that matched in order to be proper. If Gustaf liked things simple, his wife Martha worshiped propriety. Thanks to Hannah, Jake was sure he could pass muster on both counts.

Nevertheless, he was nervous as he rode into the neat farmyard. He tied his horse to the railing by the barn and turned to confront the house—and the woman who stood in the open back door.

Martha Lunig was the same, yet subtly different. Spectacles, he decided. They were new. Everything else was unchanged. Her hair was an indeterminate color between ash blond and gray. Pulled back severely from her face, it formed tight braids that wrapped her head. Jake had always assumed that the tug of those braids kept her face so nearly unlined, but now he saw deep grooves beside her mouth to match the frown marks between her brows. She was neither tall nor heavy, yet she exuded strength and purpose. It came from the way she held herself, as if she resisted a strong wind, with set shoulders and a slightly compensating tilt forward.

It wasn't an easy face to smile at, but Jake tried. "Hello, Mrs. Lunig."

Would he have to identify himself? She pushed on the door, then let it fall back.

"Is Caroline here?"

"She's . . . what do you want with her?"

"I'm —"

"I know who you are. What I want to know is why you're here?"

"Why, to see Caroline, of course." Somehow, he knew it wouldn't do to use the word *get* or *fetch*. Although he was annoyed at her lack of welcome, he wasn't really surprised. As he would with a dog of uncertain disposition, he kept his voice and manner even and smooth, carefully doing nothing to rouse her protective instincts.

"She's well, I trust?"

"Perfectly."

"And you and Mr. Lunig?"

"The same."

Jake carried his coat folded over his arm. He stood within reach of the door, forcing himself to remain patient. "Is she here now?"

Martha seemed to debate some issue with herself before she answered, stepping back enough to let him enter. "Come in. She's at the spring house. You can wait in the parlor while I get her."

Jake's decision was much easier to make than hers. He took the door but didn't enter. The idea of waiting in the decorous fastness of the parlor like an unwelcome suitor was repugnant to him. "I know the way," he said, taking the choice from her. "Let me save you the trip."

He didn't look back to see her stare after him, her frown more fixed than ever, but he felt the weight of her attention like an arrow aimed at his back. The path was well worn and familiar to him. He remembered the spring house as one of the most pleasant places on the farm. More shed than house, the structure was as close to being frivolous as anything of the Lunigs could be.

By training and habit, Jake made almost no sound as he approached the building. He wasn't consciously hoping to catch Caroline unaware, yet he welcomed the idea of having a few seconds to observe her before she knew he was there. He wanted—needed, perhaps—time to absorb the changes he would see.

He saw two pails of water next to the door of the spring house, but no Caroline. Then he heard a small sound, soft as a sigh or the fall of a leaf, and he followed it to the back of the shed. There sat Caroline, like a cat in the sunshine, curled against the warm shingles. She was reading intently, oblivious to her surroundings.

Jake soaked up the sight of her, her smooth brow and cheek, the wisps of pale hair escaping from her braids, the peek of petticoat under her skirt. Her knees were drawn up to support her book, revealing scuffed black shoes and the bottom of her underwear. She turned a page, then sighed gustily, swiping at a tendril of hair the breeze teased at her forehead. As soon as her hand fell to the book again, the hair drifted back to her brow and resettled there, undisturbed.

Jake lifted his hand, and the movement, involuntary

346

and unconscious, brought him to Caroline's attention. She jumped to her feet. Her face burned with embarrassed color as she fought to find her apron pocket and store the book away. Startled though she was, Jake could tell that she was only embarrassed, not fearful. It made him enormously curious about her choice of reading matter, but that was an issue for another time.

"Oh! You're not— You startled me."

"Caroline." Jake had to swallow hard before he could speak. "It's . . . I'm your papa."

Her eyes grew wide, then with a shrieked "Papa!" she hurtled into his arms. He dropped his coat to catch her, hugging her slender body to his chest. She hung on his shoulders with her feet dangling at his knees. He swung her in a circle, then back and forth so her legs made a pendulum, hugging, holding. She made incoherent sounds and he didn't do much better.

Long before Jake was ready to relinquish her, Caroline squirmed for release. He set her down gently and went back to looking at her. "You've grown up, mite." His voice was rough with emotion, for he was close to tears.

"I'm almost ten," she said proudly.

"On August seventeenth, the happiest day of my life."

Caroline beamed, showing handsome white teeth that seemed almost too big for her face. Those teeth had only been started when he'd brought her to Hanford. They reminded him of how much he had missed. He couldn't help noticing with relief that they were beautifully spaced and even, for all their size. She would grow into them, he knew, and he would miss no more of her growing.

"I have your letters in a box in my room," Caroline offered shyly.

Jake wanted to be pleased—was pleased—but he was also overwhelmed by a terrible sense of guilt. He had

347

labored for hours over each letter, managing to produce only the poorest few lines imaginable. What could they have meant to her, those stilted assurances that he was well and thinking of her? Only that he was alive.

Her letters, on the other hand, had given him quicksilver glimpses into her heart and soul. She had heard about a battle in the war and worried that he was involved. She had found an abandoned robin's nest with the broken egg shells that looked like fallen pieces of sky. The barn cat had four kittens, one with beautiful blue eyes.

"I have your letters in my saddlebag. I've read them so many times I know them by heart. I tied them with one of your hair ribbons."

"Really?" Her smile stretched wider. "What color?"

"Blue. Like your eyes."

Her eyes lowered demurely, then she started as they fell onto the water buckets. "Oh, Gramma will be needing the water. I forgot."

Before she could pick them up, Jake hoisted them. Their weight was nothing to him, but to Caroline they would have been heavy. He frowned in annoyance that she had been sent to perform such a chore. "Do you always fetch the water for your grandmother?"

"If Grampa is busy, I do. It's hard for her. She needs a lot of help sometimes."

Her lack of resentment was apparent to Jake, yet he couldn't help remembering her pampered mother. Had Grace's parents simply become sensibly aware that children needed chores, as Hannah said, or had they taken advantage of Caroline's obvious good nature, using her as unpaid farm labor? He intended to find out.

Caroline skipped ahead of him, carrying his coat, then ran to her grandparents, who stood like a pair of avenging angels before the gates of paradise. "Grampa! Gramma!

348

My papa came! See? He's here just like I said."

Jake put down the pails and held out his hand to Gustaf. "Mr. Lunig," he said formally. "You're looking well."

There was no warmth in the narrowed eyes that met him. "So are you." His voice carried the faintest trace of an accent, a slight singsong inflection entirely missing from his wife's speech.

"And Caroline is blooming," Jake said, forcing himself to be gracious. He had meant it as a compliment to their care of her. In any case, he couldn't keep his eyes from her after such a long separation. When she smiled back, he glanced at Martha and asked, "Where would you like these?"

Gustaf stepped forward. "I'll take them."

"Just tell me where," Jake insisted, taking them up again.

"In the kitchen," Martha said, adding belatedly, "Thank you."

Caroline bounded to hold the door for him and followed him inside. "How long can you stay this time?" she asked eagerly.

When the pails were dispatched, he surveyed her gravely, feeling the tight bands of tension around his chest easing. With her welcome indisputable, he could admit to himself how worried he had been that she had forgotten him. "That depends on you, punkin'."

She threw her arms around his waist and buried her face against his chest. "Then you'll stay forever and ever," she said extravagantly.

Jake folded his arms around her but didn't answer because Gustaf and Martha had followed them inside. One look at those closed countenances took away all thought of his reply. Even his smile faded as Gustaf spoke pointedly to Caroline.

"You were going to gather the eggs next, weren't you?" His voice was gruff, although Jake could discern no harshness in the suggestion.

A balky frown quickly replaced Caroline's recollection to her duty. "Oh, but Grampa, my papa is here!" She grabbed Jake's hands and held on tightly, her pleading look directed to Gustaf.

A quick flush darkened her grandfather's weathered face. "Don't be impertinent, miss."

Jake squeezed Caroline's hand. "I'm not leaving, honey. You do your chores." He nodded as her eyes swung up to read his face. "I'll still be here when you're done."

Assured at last, Caroline left slowly, but tension remained in the room, thick as molasses. Jake had won no points by backing up Gustaf's authority when just his presence had caused Caroline to question it. For that alone, Jake would not be forgiven.

Just outside, Caroline waited by the door, straining to hear what they would say. She was not a sly child, but she knew that what was being said in the kitchen was important to her. She would gather eggs as she had been told, but first she would listen.

The words came to her clearly. "Why did you come here?"

Grampa.

"Caroline is my daughter. I love her."

"And a fine way you've taken to show it! Going off and leaving the poor child!"

Gramma.

"The country was at war, Mrs. Lunig. I brought her here to your fine care while I did my duty."

"Duty! You're a barbarian! You went to war because you love fighting! Other men had substitutes—"

"Would you have paid for my substitute, so I could've kept Caroline, Mrs. Lunig? I don't think so, but never mind that. I came back as I said I would, for Caroline."

"The war's been over for ages! What kept you?"

"Getting my pay—so I can pay you for Caroline's keep." Jake kept a sharp rein on his temper. "Mrs. Lunig—"

But she sputtered like an overfilled teakettle. "Pay! If you—"

"Caroline is my child, my responsibility. Just as I sent her money all along, I want to reimburse you for what it's cost you to have her. That's not an insult, just fair and right. You've been good to her, as I knew you would be."

The Lunigs rejected his sop by ignoring it. "You're not taking her away," Martha went on righteously. "I just won't—"

"Mrs. Lunig—"

"Martha!" Gustaf's voice overrode the others briefly. Insofar as anyone had any authority over Martha Lunig, her husband did. It was slight, however. He backtracked quickly as she turned on him, her glasses emphasizing the flash of her eyes. "He's only come to see the girl," he said placatingly. "It's his right."

"No, Mr. Lunig," Jake contradicted. He would not deceive them about his intentions. "I've come to take Caroline with me."

"No! You can't! This is her home, the only one she's ever had!"

"She'll have a new one. With me."

"Where!"

It wasn't a question, but Jake answered as if it were, ignoring the implicit accusation. "Texas." He spoke firmly, although he could as easily have said Colorado. Texas, to his mind, had the advantage in that it was a state already and thus would sound safe to the Lunigs.

They were not noticeably relieved. Appalled was more like it.

Outside, Caroline's heart skipped up to her throat. Texas!

Her grandmother's next words dropped her heart back into her chest where its thud slowed until it was only pounding in muffled terror. "You're not satisfied that you killed that poor child's mother—our daughter!—dragging her all across the country. Now you've come back for Caroline! You're going to kill her, too!"

"I did not kill Grace, Mrs. Lunig. I loved her and cared for her—"

"I know what you did to her! I've got her letters! I know!"

"Mrs. Lunig, I know how you feel—"

"You know nothing!"

"Martha, Martha . . ."

"I loved Grace. I tried to make her well. I tried . . ." Jake struggled to keep his raw emotions under control. "You knew this was temporary," he insisted, fighting desperately back to the issue at hand—Caroline. "I told you I'd be back when I brought Caroline here. She's my daughter . . . I love her."

"The way you loved Grace," Martha spat at him bitterly. "She doesn't need that kind of love!"

"Mrs. Lunig—"

But Caroline didn't wait to hear anymore. She clamped her hand across her mouth and ran to the hen coop.

Jake found her there, the egg basket empty at her feet. This time she wasn't reading. He took one look at her tear-streaked face and gathered her into his arms. The stiffness in her shoulders as she resisted his comfort made him long to weep with her.

"You heard."

She nodded and sniffled.

He sighed. How to explain? "Do you remember the way we lived together?"

Her pause told him more than any words could say.

"It was nothing like this. This is . . . settled and orderly . . . secure. We moved around. I made barrels and worked odd jobs. We didn't have a farm or even a horse. It probably wasn't good for you, but it was the best I could do then and I wanted you with me. When the war came I brought you here so you could go to school and have a home. But now I can do that, too. Only not here."

"In Texas," she said in a voice still quavery with tears.

Jake hesitated; he wanted to be honest. "Or someplace like it. Out there in the West the land is open and there aren't so many people."

"You don't like people?"

"I like people, but I can't afford to buy land where there are lots of people, and it takes a lot of land to raise cattle. Or horses. I'm good with horses and I could raise them in Colorado where they still run wild. Either place would do for me. You could help me choose."

"You want me to go there with you?"

"Yes. I want that more than anything in the world."

"Would we have a house?"

"Oh yes. I've earned money and saved it all this time. Our place wouldn't be as big as this one, not at first anyway. But we'd have a house—and a housekeeper." Hannah's urging came back to him, reminding him of his promise. "Do you remember Anna?"

Caroline thought, then she laughed. "A big lady? Soft and warm . . . yes, I remember!"

Jake smiled. That was Anna, his father's love, big and soft and warm. "We'll have a housekeeper, like Anna was.

How does that sound?"

It sounded wonderful to Caroline—and scary. "I have to think," she said. That was what Grampa always said to her. *Think, Caroline.* This time she would. Hard.

If Jake was disappointed in her answer—and he was—he was also proud of her. He had painted the best picture he could for her. She had listened and, he hoped, been tempted. But she had not given in. She showed maturity and wisdom beyond her years. He could ill afford to give her time to think, but what else could he do? He wanted her happiness even more than his own.

"That's good, sweetheart. You're a wonderful girl. Don't ever forget that I love you. I'm just so darned proud of you!"

She felt his love, felt the depth and warmth of it. It was as big and soft and warm as her memory of Anna—whoever she was. But she had heard Gramma, too. And she had to be sure.

She would find the proof, she was sure, in the letters her grandmother had. Somehow she would find those letters and read them. She didn't worry about reading letters that weren't hers. Gramma had read the letters her papa had sent her. She would read these. They were from her mama, so in a way they were hers, too. Weren't they?

# Chapter Nineteen

It wouldn't be hard to find Jake in Hanford, Pennsylvania, Hannah decided after her first look around. The town was so small it had no hotel.

There was a boarding house, however, and there Hannah arranged with Mrs. Bergen for the rental of three rooms on the second floor. She wanted a fourth as a sitting room for Rory, but that room, the only other, was already let to someone Mrs. Bergen called "a very quiet widower gentleman."

"You probably never even see him," she confided. "He spends very little time here." Nevertheless, Mrs. Bergen decided to assure Hannah of her privacy by putting Rory in the single room on the same side of the hall, segregating her guests appropriately by gender.

Since the rooms were scrupulously clean and, if anything, overfilled with furniture, Hannah was content with her arrangement, which included two meals a day, breakfast and dinner. Judging from Mrs. Bergen's ample body, Hannah expected just those two meals would be more than sufficient for her needs, but because Rory was still growing, she would avail herself of the woman's offer to prepare a boxed lunch any day for an additional fee.

While Rory unpacked their trunks from the carriage, Mrs. Bergen brought refreshment to Hannah in the parlor. The room, in fact the whole house, rather reminded Hannah of the house in Omaha with its handsome parlor stove and the riotous array of chairs, tables, bookcases, and shelves, all groaning with accessories.

It was there in that littered room, while plied with tart lemonade and sweet, crisp cookies, that Hannah began to tell lies. The first, unsurprisingly, was the easiest. She corrected Mrs. Bergen's assumption that Rory was her son. She was too amused to be offended, thinking of the nine-year-old she would have been at his birth.

"Well, of course you look too young to be his mother," Mrs. Bergen said by way of apology, "but elegant ladies like you do manage to keep your youthful looks long after the rest of us lose ours. And, of course, he looks nothing like you," she added, still probing for an explanation.

"He looks like his father," Hannah said finally. She didn't like pretense, but she was unwilling to leave it up to this woman to assign them a relationship, not when there was a chance that anything untoward about her might ultimately reflect badly upon Jake and perhaps cause him problems with Caroline's grandparents. Hanford was too small, and too conservative, for her to play at shocking Mrs. Bergen. "He is my dear sister's son and all the family I have left in this world—except for my aged uncle," she added, mentally apologizing to Uncle Simon for consigning him to premature decrepitude.

"Your sister passed away?"

Quickly Hannah decided to stick as closely to the truth about Rory as she could for fear of tangling them both too deeply in this web of deception. "She and Rory's younger sister died of cholera early in the war."

"How sad," Mrs. Bergen commiserated. "And the boy's

356

father?"

"Mr. Talmage was killed in an accident at his foundry," Hannah said, pleased to be able to provide the truth again. She would have to think to tell Rory that she was now his aunt, but remembering that wouldn't tax either of them.

If she hadn't been so pleased with herself, she would have stopped right there. But when Mrs. Bergen wanted to know what had brought them to Hanford, a deceptively innocuous question, Hannah gave in to her powers of imagination. She wished she had thought to provide herself with a covering story for her arrival in Hanford. During the long, boring trip she would have had time to consider the ramifications of her story and select one that contained no hidden flaws. Instead, she had to make do. Hearing about the elderly widower upstairs seemed to give her a perfectly plausible explanation.

"My husband was killed at Gettysburg, Mrs. Bergen. I'm here on a sentimental mission, to visit his grave and say a last farewell."

"That was a terrible time, my dear." Mrs. Bergen was instantly solicitous. "I'm so very sorry for your loss."

Too late, Hannah remembered Jake. What would this woman think of her if she managed to reconcile with him? She had to make a quick correction. "It was a blow, but I believe now I'm nearly ready to go on with my life. I have Rory and I have the comfort of knowing that Daniel gave his life willingly in a cause he believed in deeply. You see," she added, inventing as she went, "he was a career military officer. He prepared me well for his passing."

"Oh, my dear. How brave you are!" She patted Hannah's hand repeatedly, and when Rory came to the door looking for Hannah, it was she who jumped up to intercede. She drew him back to the hall, whispering in a peculiarly carrying voice, "Just give your aunt a few minutes to collect herself. She's quite overcome with grief now, but in a bit she'll be her usual brave self."

Hearing Rory's surprised "Oh?" caused Hannah to be nearly overcome with giggles. She fought them down and composed herself enough to join them in the hall. She didn't, however, quite dare to meet Rory's eyes. She felt mean that she had played upon Mrs. Bergen's sympathies and only that discomfort kept her sober until she and Rory were alone.

Although he'd been surprised, Rory took Hannah's confession in stride. "I should have thought of it earlier," he said. "You couldn't be my mother, and we have to have some kind of story for why we're together. That will do, provided we tell Jake in time."

Hannah didn't even want to think about telling Jake!

Rory grinned, understanding her perfectly when she groaned at that and asked him to make her excuses to Mrs. Bergen at dinner. She was too tired to eat and the idea of facing Mrs. Bergen so soon again made her quail.

On his way out, Rory turned and said, "By the way, you ought to know that your sister was named Louisa and your niece was Betsey."

With her mind already on the delightful look of the tester bed in the next room, Hannah could only stare blankly at the door where Rory had been. Sister? Niece? Then she remembered and grimaced. Being a liar was going to take concentration—and for that she needed a nap.

Rory was explaining to Mrs. Bergen that his "aunt" was too tired to eat and begged to be excused from dinner when he felt a prickling at the back of his neck. He knew it was Jake before Mrs. Bergen turned to welcome her other boarder.

"Ah, Mr. Farnsworth," she greeted cheerily. "We have company for you!" Then she laughed, "Well, not *for* you exactly, but—"

Jake cut through the pretense Rory struggled to preserve by offering his hand. "Rory, good to see you."

His tone said it wasn't, but Mrs. Bergen was too surprised for subtlety. "You *know* each other? Well, isn't that amazing?"

Unsure what Jake might say, Rory rushed to offer his version of the coincidence first. "In a way it is, but we all met back in Nebraska when Jake and I helped Mrs. Veazie's uncle."

"Why, that's just wonderful!"

"I should have known," Jake muttered. "I saw the carriage . . ."

Rory winced. He'd argued against buying the carriage, but Hannah had been adamant. In the circumstance, speed mattered more to her than the chance of offending Jake—who would probably be offended anyway. She would have chosen a humbler equipage, but no other was available. Given no real choice, Hannah typically made do with elegance. "It was that or ride horseback," he said grimly. That was as much of an apology as he could offer Jake.

Mrs. Bergen saved the moment by being scandalized. "Oh, my laws! Imagine a lady like your aunt on horseback!"

Having to choke back laughter did a lot to keep Jake from mayhem. "And how is your lovely aunt?" he asked Rory.

Mrs. Bergen shooed them to the table, oblivious to his sarcasm. "And how would you expect her to be, having to rattle over the road for days?" she asked, pointing Rory to a seat. She fanned herself with one hand and exclaimed, "Men! Why the poor dear lady is too exhausted to come to the table for dinner. But don't you worry, young man. I'll fix up a tray you can take up to your aunt after we eat."

The meal was much quieter than Mrs. Bergen would have liked, but she made allowances for the taciturnity of men. Mr. Bergen, dead for over fifteen years, had been a man much like these two. They talked of the roads, boats and trains they had traveled on, touching not at all upon their reasons for traveling.

Although she respected their right to privacy, she was too taken by Hannah not to brag a bit about knowing her reason for coming to Hanford. She was sure Mr. Farnsworth would be as touched as she was by the delicacy of Mrs. Veazie's sensibility. She knew he, too, had served in Mr. Lincoln's army. Perhaps he had even known Mr. Veazie. But any man would like to think of a woman journeying so far to visit her husband's final resting place.

Since Hannah had not thought to tell Rory about Daniel's elevation to war hero, the story was as new to him as it was to Jake. To his credit, Jake managed a polite response to Mrs. Bergen's suggestion that he might like to accompany Hannah on her pilgrimage to Gettysburg. His thoughts were anything but polite.

When the meal was finally over, Jake stalked blindly from the room. Rory found him pacing furiously up and down the side veranda. It was a lovely summer evening, but Rory was as indifferent to the breeze and the softly dying light as Jake was.

Rory started to speak, but Jake cut him off. "Don't bother. I don't blame you. I know exactly who's responsible for this . . ." Then words failed him and he stomped off into the shadows of the porch.

Rory waited without comment, knowing Jake needed this outlet. While Jake took out his anger on the floorboards, Rory blessed Hannah's surprising and unlikely fatigue. Had she experienced some premonition that accounted for her unusual withdrawal tonight? He could think of no other explanation, but he wasn't going to second-guess their luck—his as much as hers, because if Jake and Hannah quarreled too badly he would have to mediate. If he could. Perhaps by morning Jake would be cooled down.

Jake was at the far end of the veranda when Mrs. Bergen called from the door, "Mr. Talmage? I have your aunt's tray ready now."

Rory bit back a curse, then answered politely, "Thank you, Mrs. Bergen."

Jake was quickly back beside him when she called again. "She's a little bit deaf," he told Rory, who—all unwilling—went to get the tray, calling out in a louder voice as he went. His unwillingness had nothing to do with the food. He simply didn't want to have to tell Hannah that Jake was their housemate. He had to warn her, although, given Jake's demonstrated temper, he didn't know what good warning her would do.

But when he came from the dining room, Jake took the tray from him. Rory opened his mouth in token protest, then shut it without a sound.

Jake smiled at him grimly as he eyed the stairs he was about to climb. "You might want to go talk to Mrs. Bergen awhile. Even if she's a little hard of hearing, she'll be able to hear the noise Hannah's going to make when I get my hands on her."

Rory watched Jake's purposeful march up the stairs and glanced at the closed dining room door. Mrs. Bergen's quarters were on the opposite side of the house from Hannah's. He quickly decided that she was deaf enough not to need his company as she did the dishes in her solidly built house.

He went for a long walk instead.

Jake was quite familiar with Hannah's room. The door had stood open every day but the one last week when it had been let to Miss Bagly. A door connected it to the second room to make a suite. Like his small room on the

361

other side of the house, the second room had a single bed she could use as a settee. Every night since his arrival he had cursed his similar too-short, too-narrow bed and wished he could afford the larger so he could at least spread out diagonally. It was one more thorn in his side that Hannah had hired an extra room just for sitting.

Fueled by his indignant trek up the stairs and by the tray he carried—even if she hadn't requested the indulgence—his knock on her door was sharp and short. He didn't wait for her to respond. Before she could, he was inside with the door closed behind him. She had not tried to shut out the summer breeze or the light, which now tinted the room with lavender streaks of sunset. The lacy canopy of the tester caught in the play of air around the bed as Hannah slowly sat up and looked at him.

He had been angry—livid—ready to throw down the tray and do her bodily harm. Arming himself with the tray had been a way, he hoped, to slow him down before he gave her the thrashing she deserved. What *right* had she to come here? What—

But that was before he saw her.

Framed by the lace and linen of the bedclothes, her hair fell in tousled waves that danced like firelight around her shoulders. Her nightgown, a flesh-colored satin he had never seen before, had twisted in her sleep, revealing most of one creamy breast as she sat up. She wasn't aware of it, he could tell.

Some barely rational part of his brain was noting each change in her expression. Her first reaction was not surprise. That came second, as if she had been dreaming of him and had to wake up before she could be surprised.

"Jake!" It was a soft rush of emotion, more pleasure than surprise. Then she saw the tray and took in his stance. It was all bluff, but she had no way of knowing that. She became wary and started to move.

He could have put the tray down and gone to her, but

he chose not to. As long as she didn't know the tumult in his breast, he could continue to hide behind his Indian face.

"What are you doing here?"

He wanted to shout with laughter. He knew her so well. He heard the tiny quaver she tried to suppress, hiding it behind challenge. His smile was fleeting. "I think that's supposed to be my question."

She flounced with what looked like annoyance or dismissal. He knew she was trying to straighten her gown without drawing it to his attention. As if he hadn't noticed!

"I could give you two answers. I live here and I've brought your dinner."

"I didn't ask for dinner."

"I know that. Mrs. Bergen sent it by Rory. I intercepted it."

He saw concern for Rory flit over her features, chased away by a healthy regard for her own self-preservation. "Jake . . ."

He put down the tray and moved toward her. He saw her fight down a desperate desire for flight, and he chuckled. "Is this where you throw yourself on my mercy and beg forgiveness?"

Hannah's head snapped up. "Certainly not. It's a free country. I can go anywhere I want to."

"Even to visit your late, lamented husband's grave one last time?"

She almost laughed and so did he.

"Hannah, I am very angry," he said, reminding them both. He took another step.

"I know you are." Her tone attempted to placate.

"I came up here intending to tan your hide." Another step.

"I'm sure you did."

"You don't sound worried." He was right beside the

bed.

"I'll worry another time," she whispered, holding up her arms, open and inviting. "Oh, Jake, I've missed you so."

He sat down and closed his eyes briefly, still not sure he dared touch her. "Do you suppose you could pretend to be worried? As a sop to my pride?"

She wrapped her arms around her drawn-up knees. "I'm shaking in my boots."

"You have on boots?" He drew the sheet aside to uncover her feet. Even her toes were pink and beautiful. "I have it on very good authority that a lady like you never wears boots or rides horseback or does anything strenuous."

"But you know me better, Jake." She offered her hand, palm up. It showed her recent care, but it was still the strong little hand he knew. "I was terrified to come here. It's the hardest thing I've ever done."

He brought her palm to his mouth and she followed, moving into his arms the way she did every night in his fantasies. It wasn't only the inadequacies of his bed that kept him from sleep night after night. It was Hannah, the loss of her softness and her strength.

Her mouth opened under his, drawing him into her, stealing his will. His hands found the boundary between satin and skin, rejecting the cloth, sliding under it to stroke her hot softness. Her eager hands stripped away his clothes so she could rub against him, catlike, skin to skin.

His control stretched to a thread as she pressed her breasts to his chest and tempted his throbbing hardness, brushing from side to side against him. He settled his hands around her throat, lifting her chin with his thumbs. He traced the opening of her lips with the tip of his tongue and bit softly on her full lower lip. The quick intake of her breath drew him into the hot wetness of her mouth, and when she moaned, he felt the sound in his

364

own throat.

Jake reached behind her and looped her knees out from under her so she slid along him as they sank down together to the bed. His tongue traced patterns on her breast, touching the smooth flesh but avoiding the erect crest. She tried to direct his mouth, her hands tunneled into his hair, but he slid away down her chest to her abdomen, leaving a trail of moist skin quivering with each new touch. He paid homage to her triangle of fiery curls, burying his face there. He exhaled in a gust of heated air that made her cry out in passionate need.

Needing control, he sought his anger, but it was gone. He would have to send her away, but not before he fed his terrible hunger for her. He stretched himself out above her, letting her take his partial weight, while he hovered, aching and full. Her face was so beautiful, flushed and soft, her eyes half-closed in passion. What did she see behind her eyelids?

Jake bent to bring his mouth to her breast, taking the pouting fullness deep into his mouth, pulling on the nipple, then tonguing the button hardness against his teeth. When she cried out he left that one, still wet from his mouth, and sought to suckle the other. He lifted his head to find her eyes closed, her head thrown back over his nestling forearm. With his weight supported on that arm behind her neck, he touched the soft slipperiness at her center. Her heat, her readiness, was like a blow to the back of his head. He stroked her because he had to, poised to enter that sweet enclosure.

"Look at me, Hannah." His command was husky, forced through his constricted throat.

Her eyes fluttered, opening to reveal dilated pupils that were softly unfocused. As he thrust home, her eyes widened with wonder. "Jake," she breathed. "Oh, Jake . . ."

She was his . . . his . . . his . . . his body said with

each driving, possessive stroke. He watched her absorb the sweet shock of each thrust, and when he knew she would cry out, he took the sound into his mouth. The force of his repeated plunges into her drove them up against the headboard and rocked the bed.

He didn't care. He didn't stop. She rose to meet him, pushing up from her heels planted by her hips. He felt her stiffen and hang suspended, clutching his shoulders, while coils of tension wrapped and unwrapped inside her. Within seconds, he found his own satisfaction in a potent, pulsing release.

They fell so fast and so hard that Jake didn't know how long he had been collapsed atop her. But when he shifted his weight to relieve her, Hannah protested. "No. Don't leave me." Her arms tightened, too weak to hold him but strong enough to make him stay.

In time he lifted his head and looked into her face. He brushed back a damp strand of hair and smiled ruefully. "I certainly told you off, didn't I?"

Hannah winced. Were they back to that? She nuzzled into his hand. "Don't."

Jake rolled away, taking more than the comfort and warmth of his body. "You can't stay here, Hannah."

He didn't look at her so he didn't see her desolation. She didn't know he didn't dare look. She saw only his utter rejection of her. She had no defense against such devastation. She didn't move or cover herself as he dressed, pulling on his clothes with angry determination.

She didn't know she was crying until Jake said, "Don't cry, damn it. It won't work. You have no business being here."

Her only response was to put her hand over her eyes; her tears were beyond her control. She didn't think about her nakedness, but he pulled the sheet up and tucked it around her shoulders with rough tenderness that was lost on her. Like a small child hiding her eyes, she felt invisible as long as she didn't have to see the way his hard face shut her out. Even when he was gone, she didn't move.

From Hannah's room Jake went to his own, staying just long enough to realize that he couldn't stand being there. It was too early to go to sleep, and how could he sleep anyway after what he'd just done?

He raked his hand through his hair, then brought it down over his face as if he could wipe away what he still saw. He was a bastard. A total bastard.

With no prospect of sleep in store, Jake decided on a long walk. He took the rear stairway to avoid passing Rory's closed door. Thus, he also missed seeing Rory on his return up the front stairs.

Rory moved cautiously past Hannah's door, noting the silence from within. He wondered if Jake was with Hannah or in his own, equally quiet room. As he prepared for bed, Rory hoped the stillness around him was a good sign.

It was still quiet two hours later when Jake returned. His walk had restored him somewhat, but the bed looked no more inviting than before. He pulled back the covers and started to undress. He got as far as taking off his boots before he knew he had to go to Hannah. He made the bed look slept in, then left, carrying his boots with him.

Little had changed in Hannah's room. Moonlight had replaced dusky sunset, but she had scarcely moved from her bereft position. The hand she had used to cover her eyes lay beside her face, as if to ward off a blow. She had turned enough to uncover one shoulder.

He turned the locks in the two doors and undressed again, this time folding his clothes neatly over a chair-back. He got into bed beside her, prepared to muffle her

367

outcry until he could apologize. She didn't wake or resist when he drew her against his chest. Her only response was a deep, weary sigh, like a child's after a long, exhausting cry. Grateful for her acceptance, he held her that way until he, too, felt peaceful enough to sleep.

Jake came awake in a hurry when Hannah suddenly pulled herself from his side. He sat up and instinctively reached for her, letting his arms fall only when he saw the way she fended him off with one hand while holding the sheet around herself with the other.

"Hannah, I'm sorry."

She looked wildly around the room. It was morning—early, but morning. She wanted to throw his meticulously folded clothes at him and order him out. To do so, she would have to give up the sheet. She felt around the bed with her feet, searching for her nightgown and wanting to cry. Last night she had been beyond tears, but here they were, welling up in her eyes. Everything numbness and shock had saved her from feeling last night came rushing back, threatening to oppress her. She couldn't find her nightgown, but fortunately her temper was very much at hand.

"How could you! I don't—"

Jake put his hand over her mouth, firmly but gently. "I had to come back, Hannah. I had to tell you I'm sorry. I would have told you last night, but you didn't wake up. I thought you needed your sleep." He started to remove his hand, then thought better of it. Her eyes still shot golden sparks at him. He couldn't say it, but he was glad to see her behaving normally again. "Please, let me explain. I feel like such a brute."

When her eyes closed, Jake knew he'd won. He didn't like to think in terms of winning and losing with Hannah, but he was grateful that she would give him a chance. He moved his hand to her chin and raised her face to his. "Don't look at me like that. It kills me."

The soft huskiness of his voice undid Hannah. She held herself stiffly, but her voice was soft. "Tell me then."

He sank back to the bed, taking her with him. "My gown . . ."

Jake held her tighter. "You're the most beautiful creature God ever made, Hannah. You don't need clothes." His big hand nestled her head into the hollow of his shoulder and stayed to stroke her hair from her face.

"I'm ashamed of what I did last night," he said.

His flat statement didn't encourage comment, but she had to know. "All of it?"

"It would take a saint to resist you, Hannah, and God knows I'm no saint."

"I don't understand."

"I should never have come near you."

"I see." She tried to move away, but he wouldn't let her go.

"You don't see. You don't see anything."

His bitterness persuaded her to try again. "Then make me see. Tell me. You haven't yet, you know."

"Everything is a mess."

This was an explanation? Hannah bit back a resigned sigh and guessed. "Caroline?"

"The Lunigs don't want to let her go. I can understand it, but I don't know how to fight them. They blame me for what happened to Grace and see Caroline as some sort of . . . replacement for her. Oh, they know she's different." He laughed, showing his pride. "Believe me, she's different, but I think even they see that as an improvement. They love her."

"What about Caroline? What does she want?"

"It's hard for her. She was happy to see me and sometimes I think she'd choose me if I forced her, but I don't want to do it that way. I thought the Lunigs understood that the arrangement was temporary. I told them I'd be back and they agreed. Now they say it's not right to tear Caroline from everything she knows. Perhaps I should have gone west first and settled. *Then* I'd have something definite to promise. I could tell her what she'll have and where it will be. Everything I say sounds like a . . . fantasy. I don't have anything to point to, just what I think I'll have. What if I'm wrong?"

"You won't be." Hannah's voice was dead certain. "Does Caroline love you?"

"Yeah. I know she does. I couldn't let her go now. She's really wonderful, bright and good. I can see how hard it will be for the Lunigs."

He had told Hannah much more than he realized about his problem. "You're not staying with them."

Jake sighed. "They didn't offer and I wouldn't ask."

"How much longer can you wait before you have to leave?" She put his dilemma in terms of time rather than money for the sake of his pride.

"I don't know. I wanted to leave this week, but that's impossible now. Caroline asked for time to think and I didn't want to pressure her. The trouble is she seems to be getting *less* willing to leave every day."

Which meant the Lunigs were playing on her natural fear of the unknown to plead their case in private. She didn't say that because Jake would probably defend them. For a hard man, Jake was remarkably soft-hearted.

"How do you spend your time? Do you see Caroline?"

"I spend most of the day there."

"Doing what?"

"Well, I work around the way I used to when I lived there. Caroline has chores. They've done that right. At first I thought maybe they were using her as cheap labor, but they're not. They're good people."

But not too good to fail to take advantage of Jake's greater goodness, Hannah thought acidly. She wanted to scream at him, but she knew that wouldn't help. "Does Mr. Lunig pay you?"

370

"Of course not. I wouldn't take it anyway." He fell silent, deep in thought, his hand idle in Hannah's hair. "I have to try to talk to Caroline again. Maybe today."

Her head came up abruptly. "You can't even talk to her alone?"

"Well, I can. I just haven't pushed it. But I need to know what she thinks. I've wondered if it would be best if I waited until spring before we left. I could find work here and give her more time to be sure."

"Oh, no, Jake. You've waited so long and worked so hard. That would be giving up."

"In a way, but I'd still have Caroline."

"No, you wouldn't. The Lunigs would have her. You'd have nothing but leftovers. You don't deserve that."

Jake laughed. "My fiery Hannah." He kissed her forehead indulgently.

She narrowed her eyes. "I didn't come here for a toss in the hay and a pat on the head, Jake."

His affable expression snapped off. "You had no business coming here at all."

"I came because I wanted to get to know Caroline."

"No!"

Hannah put a hand over his mouth. "Jake, please!" She looked at the door nervously, torn between laughter and embarrassment. "This isn't the prairie."

"No, it's my life you're playing with and I won't have it!" His attempt to keep his voice down was a failure. The low rumble carried like thunder.

"I'm not playing, Jake. This is my life, too."

"You will not go near Caroline," he ordered, holding her forearm as if to break it.

Hannah winced. "I won't promise that. I can't. But I will promise not to do anything to harm your cause."

His grip on her arm eased, only to refasten at her waist. "It's not too late for me to spank you," he said in a deceptively conversational tone.

She toppled onto his chest, laughing. "I can't believe you thought that would do any good."

"It probably wouldn't improve you, but it might do me a world of good."

She put her arms tight around him. "Better than this?"

"Hannah, Hannah," he whispered, taking her mouth in a kiss. "You don't play fair."

Someday, she vowed, he would realize that she didn't play at all.

# Chapter Twenty

Caroline sat behind the spring house with her knees drawn up, in her favorite position and place for reading. She took out her reading material with more than her usual stealth, for this time she wasn't just reading the forbidden dime novels Becky Winn brought her from her father's ever-changing collection. Because Gramma disapproved of just about all reading except from the Bible, saying this activity was a waste of time, Caroline had formed the habit of hiding her interest in books. But this was worse than just reading, because Caroline had stolen her mother's letters from Gramma's bedroom.

She hadn't wanted to steal them. First she had asked about them, pretending a careful indifference she hoped would disarm Gramma. But that wasn't easy to do. Gramma had been startled to be asked.

"Letters?" she had replied in her gruff way. "What letters?"

"The ones you told Papa you had from Mama."

"Oh, those letters. What do you want with them?"

"I'd like to read them," she had said bravely. "I've got

Papa's letters, so I'd like to read hers, too, since I don't remember her."

"You have her dolls and baby clothes, miss. You can remember her with those," Gramma said, turning away. "Besides, I don't have them anymore."

Caroline had known that was a lie even before she found the package hidden away in the bottom of Gramma's underwear drawer. The lie had made her more determined to find the letters and read them, because Gramma disapproved of lying. She said it was a terrible sin.

It had taken Caroline almost a week to ferret them out, because now that Papa was here, she had very little time to herself. Not that he pursued her—he didn't. But Gramma and Grampa had become much more watchful of her. They kept her busy more than before, usually within their sight. It made her feel bad. It was as if they no longer trusted her. And now that she'd actually sneaked the letters away to read them, Caroline felt somehow deserving of that distrust.

She hadn't taken all the letters, just a few from the ribbon-tied parcel, hoping to be able to put them back unnoticed. She took one from its envelope, carefully putting the envelope in her pocket before she started to read. After a while she looked up at her surroundings and peered around nervously. Sneaking was hard work, she decided with a sigh. Her mother's handwriting was delicate and spidery, much harder to decipher than even the sometimes smudgy print in Becky's books.

She hadn't read many personal letters, just her father's straightforward ones, and with no idea what to expect, Caroline found herself puzzled by what she read. Whatever she expected, it wasn't this. Gramma was certainly right about one thing: her mother hadn't had a good word to say about Papa. Or about anything, in fact. The trip they were taking was awful. The weather was hot and dust got into everything. She couldn't eat the disgusting food and she hadn't been able to bathe in days. Caroline grinned at that, then she sighed and replaced the letter in its envelope, not sure she wanted to read another.

She listened for footsteps on the path, ready to jump up and start filling the pail. Gramma rarely came here after her, but Grampa would. Both of them, however, had heavy treads that warned her in plenty of time to look busy. With no sound but the birds to distract her, Caroline took out another letter.

This one was worse. "Oh, Mama," it said, "why didn't you *make* me stay with you? Everything is so terrible and Jacob isn't even *kind* anymore. He makes me carry heavy loads and he gets so impatient when I burn the biscuits even a little. I hate this trip and I long for my beautiful home with you and Daddy."

Caroline let her hand drop to her side, too upset to keep reading.

"So you are here, after all," Jake said, appearing suddenly at the corner of the shed.

Totally flustered, Caroline leaped to her feet, almost forgetting the incriminating letter she held until the last second. In her concern about her grandparents, she had forgotten how silently Papa moved.

"I didn't hear you," she said. She slid the letter beneath her apron, but not before Jake's sharp eyes saw the movement.

"Sometime I'd like to know what it is you like to read," he said with an easy smile.

His smile always invited confidence in Caroline, but today she was too rattled to be influenced by its charm. "I just like to read," she defended stiffly.

"That's wonderful," Jake replied. "I always wondered why some people went to all the trouble to learn to read and then never used the skill. Do you like stories?"

Caroline was confused. Her mother's letter said Papa

wasn't kind, but here he was saying exactly what she'd never been brave enough to say to Gramma. And he looked so kind. What if he only looked that way, but wasn't really? She knew that was possible; just as the reverse was possible, too. Grampa and Gramma were gruff and spoke sharply to her, but they loved her. She knew that now, although she remembered being afraid of them at first. Did that mean Papa had been kind to her always or not? She didn't remember much except playing around his feet while he worked. She remembered hugs and rides on his shoulders and how he once made her ice skates out of wood he curved especially for her feet. Wasn't that kind?

But Mama said he wasn't kind to her *anymore*. Maybe he was only kind here to win her over. Gramma said he killed her mother and would kill her. How could she understand or figure it all out? He didn't *look* like a killer, and in stories the killers always had small, mean eyes and nasty laughs.

Caroline decided on a safe answer to her father's question. "My teacher, Miss Plummer, loaned me some of Mr. Dickens stories and I read *Uncle Tom's Cabin*." Even Gramma had read that, although after the terrible battle at Gettysburg no one here had felt the same way about the war to end slavery.

"Did you like them?"

"Oh, yes. They made me cry."

Jake nodded. His interest in her reading obviously hadn't put her at ease and he wondered why. Perhaps he'd sounded too much like a teacher. "Are you supposed to be fetching water or can we talk awhile?"

"I just . . . came here. I'll take back some water though."

He smiled. "Then let's sit down."

Caroline sat, still too nervous to enjoy his company. All the while he'd been gone she had daydreamed about his

376

return. When Mr. Lincoln was shot and killed, she had wondered if he was sad, too. Sometimes she had minded having only grandparents to live with, especially when they disapproved of things Alice and Becky could do. But now that he was here, she didn't know what to do about him.

He wanted her to go away and leave Gramma and Grampa alone. But they needed her. It made no sense to her that the very things that bothered her, their age and their old-fashioned ways, were reasons why she felt she should stay with them. Every night they sighed over her education and said how out in the harum-scarum West she would never see another classroom. They made the harem-scarem part sound almost attractive. But then there was her mother's view of it all, too.

"This is peaceful," Jake said, trying to help Caroline relax. "This was always my favorite spot here."

"Was it?" He had snagged her interest in spite of her defenses. "I like the barn loft, too, but Gr—" Too late she realized she was about to complain about Grampa.

"But your Grampa is usually in the barn," Jake finished, grinning. "I know."

"I get in his way, is all," Caroline said, being loyal. "Or I might."

"Tell me about your friends."

"I have two best friends, Alice and Becky. We call ourselves the ABCs. I'm the oldest and the tallest. When we walk we always put Becky in the middle because she's kind of small and her brother picks on her. He's older."

"Do you see them very often?"

"Only at church in summer, but we sit together in school."

Jake wanted to ask why the girls didn't come to play once in a while, but he didn't. "Do you still ride horseback?"

"Not very often. Grampa doesn't have a gentle horse

for me. If I'm at Becky's I can ride her mare, but nobody lets me ride astride anymore. It's not ladylike."

"Some very nice ladies ride that way sometimes," Jake said, thinking of Hannah. "Not just Indians either. Your other grandmother was just such a lady, and her parents were missionaries."

"Really?" Caroline perked up. "Could I meet her someday?"

"I'm afraid she'd been gone a long time," Jake answered sadly. "She'd be so proud of you."

Caroline tried to think of some way to fill the silence that ensued, but it stretched on and on. She knew he was going to ask her what she wanted to do, when it seemed she knew her own mind less and less every day. Finally, he did, although he phrased the question indirectly. Had she thought about his question?

She nodded, unable to find words. She searched his face hopefully. His eyes were bright blue, startling against the darkness of his complexion. There were no hidden tears there as there were in Grampa's watery eyes. "Couldn't we just stay here?"

"You could, honey, but there's nothing for me to do here. This is your Grampa's farm. I have to have my own place."

"I just always thought you'd come live here."

"No, I can't do that." He didn't say the Lunigs wouldn't have him. That didn't matter, because even if they wanted him, he didn't want their life. He never had.

"But you lived here before, with Mama."

"Just while I was trying to persuade her to go west with me."

"She didn't want to go?"

"It wasn't right for her. I know that now."

"Did you then?"

"No, not really. You see, she wasn't like you."

"Like me?"

378

"Well, I remember how you loved our life before. You took to it like a deer takes to a salt lick. Your mama was brought up differently. She never got water for her mother, for example. She didn't learn to cook."

"I can't either, except for oatmeal and pan fries."

"Not together, I hope."

Caroline knew she was being teased, but Jake did it so gently it didn't hurt. He was like Becky's father that way. She stared at him, trying to make his reality fit with the picture of him she had carried in her heart. In so many ways he was better than that. She didn't want to hurt him. "Can I think about it a little more, Papa?"

"Of course you can, punkin'."

He smiled at her, but Caroline wasn't reassured. He didn't cry or sigh the way Gramma and Grampa did, but he looked sad. When he helped her up, he gave her a hug and filled up the pail for her. He carried the water to the house then and, for the first time, left early.

She watched him leave, worried that his shoulders were slumped in discouragement. Gramma came to the door and watched with her, then bustled off to the barn to tell Grampa he was gone. Caroline couldn't help resenting the suddenly youthful spring in her grandmother's step and the satisfaction in her grandfather's eyes.

The picture Hannah made sitting on the veranda with Mrs. Bergen brought a smile to Jake's face, the first since he left the Lunigs' farm. She was wearing the dark greeny-blue dress he remembered from Omaha. Her presence, he noted, had persuaded the energetic Mrs. Bergen to pause in her round of labor for a chat.

Hannah noticed his tired smile, as did Mrs. Bergen. She got to her feet and offered Jake her place while she brought another glass for him. As she bustled away, Hannah said, "You look tired, Jake." It was an expression of concern, not a coy reference to their lovemaking.

He took it that way. "I am. I'm losing ground every day, Hannah. I can see it happening, but I don't know what to do about it."

"Did you talk to Caroline?"

He nodded. "She asked for more time."

"Did she say why?"

Jake smiled sadly. "She didn't have to. She's trying to get up her nerve to tell me no. She doesn't want to disappoint me, but she doesn't want to hurt the Lunigs either. She asked me to stay."

"Have they ever asked you to stay?"

His mouth twisted. "No. But I couldn't anyway."

They had fallen into a depressed silence when Mrs. Bergen returned. She poured lemonade for Jake, which he drank appreciatively. Under ordinary circumstances she would have left them alone, because she was not a woman to intrude where she wasn't wanted or needed. In this case, however, she believed she had something to offer.

"How is Caroline, Mr. Farnsworth?" she asked, taking the seat opposite him.

"She's fine," Jake answered, surprised by the question and by Mrs. Bergen's manner. She had never initiated a conversation with him before.

"While I was in the kitchen I had a thought. Now that Mrs. Veazie and her nephew are here, I know you'll want to introduce them to your daughter—" His shocked expression made her laugh. "Oh, come now, Mr. Farnsworth! I may be a country woman and a widow too long, but I recognize love when I see it."

Hannah opened her mouth, then shut it without a sound. What could she say?

Mrs. Bergen addressed her then. "Yes, I know you came to say good-bye to Mr. Veazie—as you should. But the coincidence is just too much. Naturally, your intended here"—she gestured to Jake—"wants you to meet his

380

daughter. The important thing, now that you're rested from your trip, is to do it the right way."

Jake couldn't have said anything sensible if he'd tried. He had lost control of his life—totally. Was it Hannah's fault or his own? He wanted to blame her, but he hadn't been doing any better before she arrived.

Sensing that Mrs. Bergen needed permission to go on, Hannah asked, "What do you suggest?"

Mrs. Bergen relaxed. "I've known Martha Lunig all my life. She's not an easy woman. She's made her mistakes and paid for most of them." She turned her gaze to Jake. "I remember you courting Grace Lunig. A lovely girl, God rest her soul, but not a strong one. Now, your girl Caroline, on the other hand, she's made of sterner stuff. I've seen her grow up here. She's brought a lot of joy to the Lunigs, but it's been hard on them, too."

"Hard on them?" Jake blurted in surprise. "What do you mean?"

She was surprised in return. "What do I mean? Why, Mr. Farnsworth, think of it! They're sixty years old. She's a lovely child. She's been a help to them, too, but mostly she's a care."

"But they want to keep her."

"Because it's *you* who wants to take her. Martha Lunig is not a forgiving woman. She doesn't want Caroline to go off with you and live the rowdy life that killed her daughter. She thinks it's her duty to keep Caroline safe. She's been telling that child what an irresponsible wretch you are ever since you left here."

"Jake is not irresponsible, Mrs. Bergen."

The woman smiled at her—beamed, in fact—pleased by her loyalty. "Of course he's not. Anyone but Martha can see that. And Gustaf. He sees what she tells him." She looked from one to the other. "My suggestion is that you take that handsome carriage and team of horses and drive right back out to the Lunigs'. The three of you—"

"Where is Rory?" Jake asked, suddenly reminded of him.

"In the stable, I believe," Hannah answered. "He'd have to change his clothes."

"You, too, Mr. Farnsworth," Mrs. Bergen said, treating him the way Hannah did Rory. "You make a formal call on the Lunigs and bring Caroline back here for supper. She'll be thrilled to ride in that carriage and meet your intended family. When Martha Lunig learns that a fine lady like Mrs. Veazie will be bringing up her granddaughter, she won't be able to refuse you."

Jake sought Hannah's eyes, feeling helpless. "But —"

Mrs. Bergen got to her feet. "That's my suggestion," she said briskly, then before she had quite turned away, she added cryptically, "My sister Hattie is Martha's best friend. I won't say Hattie is a gossip, but she doesn't have a real grasp on the word *confidential,* if you know what I mean. Hattie knows you're here, Mrs. Veazie. I wouldn't be surprised if Martha knows by now as well. If you don't want a lot of complications for Caroline, you'd do best to make yourself known now."

When they were alone, Hannah was afraid to meet Jake's eyes. "Jake, I didn't mean to cause you trouble. I wouldn't do that for the world."

Because he knew it was true, Jake saw no need for a direct reply. "I didn't expect opposition; that's where I was foolish," he said, his mind caught on the barbs Mrs. Bergen had pointed out. "But I can't use you this way. It wouldn't be fair, to you or to Caroline. How could she ever trust me again if I lied to her in this?"

"It wouldn't be a lie to change your mind later," Hannah told him softly. "Those things happen." She was opening herself wider to the possibility of hurt, but she was willing to take the chance. Was losing later any worse than losing now?

"But —"

382

"Would it be so hard for you to pretend to want to marry me?"

Rather than let her know it was his dearest wish, he was gruff. "Of course not."

"You don't have a choice, except to give up Caroline without a fight. Is that what you want?"

"You know it's not."

"And you know you'll make a good life for her. She's being manipulated into staying because, like her father, Caroline has a soft heart. I will tell her as few lies as possible, Jake. We have to explain Rory and Daniel. Other than that, we'll be honest."

"But it's unfair," he protested.

"No more unfair than what the Lunigs are doing. You're her father, and a good one. Don't give up."

"I can't. I hate this, but I can't let them keep her. I can see her spirit being squeezed out. If I leave her here, she'll become as close to an imitation of Grace as they can make her."

Hannah got to her feet. "I'll find Rory and freshen up. Wear your black coat, Jake. It's so handsome with the fawn breeches."

"I'll find Rory. You shouldn't go into the stables like that, and you don't need to change a thing. You look beautiful."

Neither of them had to find Rory, for he appeared just at that moment. Hannah told him what to wear and went to thank Mrs. Bergen.

"Thanks aren't necessary, Mrs. Veazie, not for doing what's right. Mr. Farnsworth is a fine man. I thought so years ago and I know so now. He just needs a little help. Good men like that are helpless against women like Martha—and like me sometimes!" She was already scurrying around the dining room, beginning her preparations. "Oh, yes," she called out as Hannah departed, "tell Caroline we're having cherry cobbler. She always wants me to bring my cobbler to church suppers."

As a woman, Hannah couldn't help but sympathize with Mrs. Lunig. She was caught unprepared by immaculately dressed people on a formal call. Forced into being gracious when she surely didn't want to be, Mrs. Lunig led them into a well-kept parlor. Because, in a way, they were calling on Caroline, not herself, she couldn't send the girl to the kitchen for the refreshments propriety demanded she offer. And when she was absent from the parlor, she couldn't monitor the conversation as she wished. All in all, Hannah decided, watching Mrs. Lunig, the afternoon was a trying one for her.

Upon meeting Caroline, Hannah understood, as she knew she would, Jake's single-minded concern for her. She was everything he had led Hannah to expect. Her lively blue eyes were the only obvious physical link between father and daughter, but in every intangible, Caroline was Jake's child.

"Papa didn't tell me about you, Mrs. Veazie," Caroline said hesitantly.

"Please call me Hannah, Caroline. I'd like it so much."

The girl darted a quick look at her grandmother, saying nothing more. She didn't seem jealous or upset, just surprised and curious. Her eyes went willingly to Jake's when he began to explain. "I didn't know myself until today, punkin'. We had never made things clear before . . ."

"You see, Caroline," Hannah put in, "I'm a widow and although I knew I loved your father, we weren't sure this was the right time for us. But I wanted to meet you . . ."

"How long have you been alone, Mrs. Veazie?" Martha Lunig asked.

"As Mrs. Bergen will tell you, I came here to visit Gettysburg, where—"

"Oh, that was so terrible, Mrs.—Hannah," Caroline said with ready sympathy. "I worried so much about Papa after that. I did before, too, of course, but that made it all so real!"

Martha spoke again. "Do you have children?"

"I had a son, Mrs. Lunig. He died of scarlet fever just after his fourth birthday. Except for Rory, I have only my uncle, Simon Sargent. You may have heard of him. He was one of the men responsible for the westward expansion of the railroad from Omaha. He decided to stay on there for a while until the first sections of track are laid. There are always so many problems to be dealt with in a beginning venture like that."

"And you're going to marry Mr. Farnsworth?" She sounded aghast.

"If he will have me." Her sincerity was obvious as her eyes met Jake's across the room.

"Have you lived in the West, M—Hannah? I mean, have you?" Caroline asked.

"Oh, yes. It's a wonderful part of the world, at least as far as I've been."

"And how far is that?" asked Gustaf, speaking for the first time.

"I've been on the prairie well beyond Omaha. That's where Jake and I met. He saved my life."

Caroline looked at Jake with excitement shining from her eyes. "Oh, Papa! You never told me!"

While Jake looked uncomfortable, Hannah smiled knowingly from one to the other. "Your father is a very modest man, Caroline."

"What were you doing out there that Jake had to save you?" Gustaf wanted to know.

Hannah almost felt sorry for the Lunigs. They wanted so much to discredit Jake—and her. Her sympathy didn't survive the memory of how disheartened Jake had looked earlier, almost rejected by his daughter because of them.

385

They didn't realize that the naked jealousy of their questions set him up as a hero. "I was traveling to Fort Kearney to be with my cousin when our wagon train was assaulted. Jake was working for the railroad, chasing down the very men who attacked us. He rescued me and brought me back to my uncle in Omaha."

"Indian attack?"

"Actually they were white men masquerading as Indians, but thanks to Jake they have been brought to justice."

"And you want to go back there?" Martha asked incredulously.

"Oh, yes. That was only one mischance. It's magnificent land, as endless as the sky."

"And you, young man," Gustaf asked Rory, "where do you come from?"

"My father owned a foundry outside St. Louis. My mother and sister died of cholera in the war. Then after my father was killed in an accident, I found my way to Hannah. She and her uncle, and Jake, are my family now."

Hannah decided it was time to issue their invitation for dinner. She phrased it as if it had come from Mrs. Bergen and included mention of the cherry cobbler.

"Oh, Gramma, may I?"

What could she say except, "You must wear your blue dress, miss."

When Caroline had scampered from the room, Hannah issued more invitations, one to the Lunigs to join them for a carriage ride at another time, and another to Caroline to go with her to Gettysburg on a picnic. "I'm not ghoulish, Mrs. Lunig, I assure you. After two years I am quite ready to put the past behind me. I understand that Gettysburg is quite lovely. We will not make a mockery of the scene. We just want a family outing."

When they didn't object immediately—which was all

the time she allowed them—she asked Jake, "Would tomorrow be all right with you? I'm sure Mrs. Bergen will prepare a fine picnic."

"Whatever you say, my dear," Jake answered.

Hannah didn't betray her inner laughter at his docility. Nor did she dare look at Rory.

Caroline came back in a dress the shade of her eyes, her face scrubbed and her hair neatly rebraided. She had taken the opportunity to replace her mother's letters back where they belonged, too smart not to make the most of this chance. The letters seemed less threatening to her now, for now she had a real person to quiz about the West and about her father.

"How pretty you look in that dress, Caroline," Hannah said. "The color is perfect for you. Did you make it, Mrs. Lunig? The workmanship is exquisite."

Pleased by the compliment, Martha's somewhat square face grew pink.

"My mother was skilled with a needle, too, Mrs. Lunig," Hannah continued, aiming a warm smile at her adversary. "Could I perhaps call you Martha? Jake has spoken of you both so often I feel I know you already." She included Gustaf in her attention with another smile his way. "It was such a comfort to him while he had to be separated from Caroline to know that she was loved and well cared for. He spoke of you both with such gratitude."

Across the room, Jake concentrated on keeping his face blank. He had agreed to come back and introduce Hannah and Rory only out of a desperate need to put the best face on the potential ruin of his plans. He'd hoped to keep Hannah's appearance here from becoming a scandal. He would have counted the day a success if they had only avoided disaster.

But this? This was a rout. Hannah had scouted the opposition, fired a few big guns for effect, and won the day. He had spent nearly two weeks patiently courting

387

Caroline and her grandparents. After one social call, Hannah was graciously collecting the flutter of white flags from them. She would call them Gustaf and Martha. He would forever be Mr. Farnsworth, the roughneck who had carried off their princess to her death.

The remainder of their mercifully short stay passed in a blur. Jake smiled and nodded on demand, seeing only Caroline's revived sparkle. Hannah, with her charm and her wealth, was giving him back his daughter. He no longer minded the deception, but he bitterly resented the need for it. Why was his love and care not good enough?

He drove the team of matched chestnut horses with Caroline perched beside him. "Do we have time to go through town?" she asked.

"I don't know why not."

Although Caroline didn't wave and shout for attention, the prancing horses and shiny carriage made heads turn as they circled the small bandstand in the center of town. Rory lowered the window and asked Jake to stop at the general store, a suggestion Caroline met with glee. Pleasing her was so much fun he put aside his resentment and enjoyed the moment.

He and Rory followed the ladies inside while Caroline helped Hannah pick out a present for Martha. After excessive deliberation, they fixed on a delicate pair of embroidery scissors shaped like a stork. Urged by Hannah, Jake remembered that Gustaf had enjoyed an occasional cigar. When they had selected six of the finest available, they completed their purchases with a fancy box of bonbons for Mrs. Bergen. Jake was prepared to battle with Hannah about paying for the gifts, but again she surprised him, yielding with such a sweetly submissive smile that he found himself nervously awaiting her next trick.

It never came.

Or was it possible that everything she did here was the

trick? She wanted to marry him. He knew that. He had been scorched by the statement she'd made in the Lunigs' parlor. It was what he wanted too, in spite of all their differences. Seeing her with Caroline made him achingly aware of what a good mother she would be to his daughter. Her interest in the girl was genuine and warm. Was she trying to use Caroline's expectation of their marriage to force the reality onto him?

It would be so easy to give in to her. But how would he feel later when he couldn't provide the horses, carriages, and clothes she was accustomed to having? Then she would be like Grace, tearfully accusing him of failure.

The specter of that failure haunted him all during dinner. Mrs. Bergen had killed a fat hen and made plump, tender biscuits. Caroline was in her glory, almost too excited to eat. Jake's lack of appetite stemmed from worry that, after all, Caroline would yet be snatched away. Would she understand that the trappings of wealth that were seducing her young heart belonged to Hannah? Would she understand why they weren't going to marry?

Rory sat next to Caroline on one side of the table, cementing what looked like a very promising friendship. Caroline shyly admitted that, Becky Winn's brother notwithstanding, she had always wanted a brother. She speculated that his six years of seniority were just right, because Becky's brother was three years older and still a tease. "Besides," she said, shooting a laughing glance at her father, "then I can meet all your friends and have a better pick of a husband someday."

Jake had opened his mouth to quash that notion when Hannah touched his arm, signaling restraint. His reply wasn't needed anyway, because Rory was equal to the challenge.

"My sister Betsey always thought I'd be useful that way someday, but I told her it wouldn't work. Because I know my friends, I know none of them are good enough for my little sister."

"That seems to be the way it works, Caroline," Hannah added. "All my friends said so. Nevertheless, like you, I always envied them their brothers."

Hannah's hand slipped from Jake's arm amid the general pleasantries that followed, leaving him feeling strangely bereft.

How easy it was for Hannah, he thought, looking at her briefly. She met his gaze serenely, sending him one of her patented smiles. She came. She smiled. She conquered. Everyone. Everything. Every barrier fell to her.

He, most of all.

And what was he going to do about that?

## Chapter Twenty-One

The day was an exquisitely designed torture for Hannah. Once again she was part of a family—almost.

She remembered her days in a happy family, until death had robbed her of her parents. That was the loving unit she had tried to construct for David with Uncle Simon. David had been too young for outings like this trip to Gettysburg, although he had loved short rides that didn't tax his patience. Even now, she looked at the lush green farmland and pictured him running pell-mell, his sturdy little legs churning over the gentle slopes of meadow.

As David had been the focal point of that almost-family, so Caroline was of this. Each of them related principally to her. Rory was her new big brother, protective and gently teasing. Hannah played stepmother-to-be, not the choicest role perhaps, but one she found remarkably fulfilling because Jake was the father. Just as she never resented Caroline's supremacy with Jake, the girl never seemed to mind her father's occasional attention to Hannah.

And his attention was most occasional. If anything, Jake went out of his way to ignore Hannah. She told herself she understood. Certainly she didn't blame Caroline for what she saw as her own failure.

In spite of her hopes, Jake had not been happy to see her. He had come to her in anger and stayed only to slake his passion. She hadn't realized that a man could be so unforgiving of himself for a weakness of the flesh. But perhaps he was angry because it was she who tempted him. And satisfied him. Then too, perhaps he blamed her and not himself. With Jake, who could tell?

Jake wasn't the only unhappy person. Gustaf Lunig continued to be hostile. Stiff with disapproval, he had handed Caroline up into the carriage. His contradictory remarks, that "going to stare at a battlefield graveyard was pure foolishness," and that "if Caroline had ever wanted to go, *he* would have taken her," made perfect sense to Hannah—unfortunately. She didn't want to feel sympathy for the harsh man.

Nor was Martha completely won over. She accepted Hannah's invitation to ride to church with them on Sunday with reluctance. It was obvious she agreed only because she knew Caroline would accompany her father without them, should she decline. She added another hamper so loaded with food that even Rory's appetite would be challenged.

It seemed sadly fitting to Hannah that the day was full of tensions. They *looked* so wonderful together, a family of four handsome people out for a day's excursion. Yet the cross currents were sharp. Jake confined his attention to Caroline, becoming expansive only when they shared the driver's seat. Rory continued to be Rory, keeping his own counsel, but always there when Hannah needed him.

Before they reached Gettysburg, where they planned to rent horses, they stopped to make a small dent in the food. Even Hannah ate heartily, inspired beyond her usual appetite by the fresh air. She packed away the remaining food for another picnic on the way home.

Their mounts turned out to be quite ordinary except for Jake's. His horse was called Max, which he soon told them was short for Maximum Trouble.

"Rather like Jay perhaps?" Hannah asked with a teasing laugh. The look he sent her in reply asked not to be reminded of that time. Hannah at once fell silent, dropping back to put distance between them.

Before long, Caroline maneuvered back to her side to ask, "Who was Jay?"

"Just a difficult horse I rode once," she answered. She did not make little of her reply to put Caroline off. She was hurt because Jake had been unwilling to be reminded of their past.

When she realized that Hannah would not elaborate, Caroline sighed noisily. "That must have been exciting."

Hannah heard her unspoken request for details and slowly began to tell the girl about her father. For that was what she wanted to know. Although she was interested in Hannah's story—the little Hannah would tell her—she was desperate for information about Jake. Implicit in all her questions was her need to know what manner of man her father was. Was he good? Kind? Could she, a young girl, trust herself to his care?

As she spoke, Hannah slowly stopped feeling hurt. Her stories not only went straight to Caroline's heart, where they found a home, but also served to remind Hannah of how much she and Jake had shared. In living on the edge of their nerve and wits, they had learned more about each other than ordinary people learn in years of companionship. Certainly she had not known Daniel so well. Nor did she still.

Caroline was their guide to the battlefield at Gettysburg. She had an amazing grasp of the details of strategy employed by each side and encyclopedic knowledge of the results. Here was where General Lee's men had massed, and there they had been repulsed, she said, pointing. Her descriptions were so real that Hannah saw the bloodied fields and heard the screams of the wounded and dying.

Looking at Jake, Hannah felt the color drain from her face in concern. She, who had never seen a battleground before, had been moved, but Jake had been at Chickamauga. For him, seeing this was like returning to hell.

She was about to go to him, intending to touch his arm and remind him that he was well and whole, when Caroline interrupted herself with a cry of alarm. "Oh, Hannah, I'm so sorry! I never thought of how this would affect you!"

Hannah turned in surprise. "Me?"

"I forgot your husband died here. Please forgive me."

Jake turned his horse away, abruptly leaving Hannah to cope with her lie.

"There's nothing to forgive, Caroline. The truth is stark. It shouldn't be softened for any of us, I think." She looked around, restored to the now-placid scene. "How do you have so much knowledge of the battle? You weren't here, I trust." The words would have sounded silly another time. After what they had just heard, no one thought to smile.

To Hannah's surprise, Caroline blushed hotly and dropped her head. "I . . . I read about it. A lot," she admitted. The first person she dared glance at was Rory. When he didn't seem to censure her, she looked at Hannah. "I know it's not very feminine, but I wanted to know. People said such strange things, depending on which side they supported. I know that sounds funny, but some people here came from the South. Becky's mother had a brother fighting for the Confederacy."

"What did people say?" Hannah wondered, hardly aware she said it aloud.

"That the Southern 'crackers' turned tail and ran. That

the Yankees in blue did the same."

"I'm sure they all wanted to," she murmured, looking out again at the scene of devastation. When she looked back at Caroline, her gaze was full of respect. "I think you're very wise," she said gently.

Hannah wanted to tell Caroline the truth about Daniel. The story she had thought up so lightheartedly in Mrs. Bergen's parlor seemed twice the travesty here. Not only was she deceiving Caroline, but she was also claiming undeserved honor for Daniel.

She would gladly tell Caroline the truth—or the part of it relating to herself—if doing so wouldn't imperil Jake's plan to win her from her grandparents. She could admit that Daniel was not a war hero, but then she'd have to explain that he wasn't dead either. Then how could she go on pretending she and Jake were about to marry? Confession might be good for the soul, but it raised doubts in the deceived. Once raised, Hannah would have no way of keeping Caroline's doubts confined to areas where they applied. Her trust in both of them would be shattered.

Turning away from Caroline and Rory, Hannah consoled herself that at least Daniel would not profit from her lie. She had noticed Jake's direction and purposefully avoided it, choosing instead to climb a small knoll that offered shade.

When Hannah was beyond the range of her voice, Caroline said to Rory, "Papa should be with Hannah now. To console her."

Rory was amused. She sounded so fierce. "You're sure about that? I would think"—he paused to remember his mother's expression for such sentiments—"the *delicate* thing to do would be to give her time alone."

He knew Jake was not ruled by delicacy—nor was Hannah—but from his glimpse of the Lunigs' parlor he was sure Caroline was. His own mother and sister would have felt right at home there.

His offer of brotherly affection to Caroline was sincere enough, for all that it had been easily given. He saw little difference between Caroline and Betsey. She was boyishly slim where Betsey had been plump, her hair an almost silver blond rather than the tawny gold that ran in his family, but she was a girl—a young girl—and thus of little interest to Rory.

"Maybe I just don't know enough yet to understand what people *should* do. Gramma tells me stuff, but it doesn't stick."

Her statement, and the windy sigh that went with it, caught his attention. He'd heard her sigh before, and now he wondered what it meant. Was she a complainer? Someone who'd fuss over a bit of discomfort. Hannah had become his standard of womanhood, but experience with his mother and Betsey told him she was unusual. Jake assumed that Caroline was as adventurous as Hannah. What if he was wrong?

Rory decided not to mention her sigh, believing that he would learn more by watching rather than asking. "What does your grandmother tell you?"

Caroline braced the slender shoulders above her straight-as-a-board chest, rolled her eyes, and treated him to a rapid fire list of do's and don't's that began with, "Sit with *both* feet on the floor," and ended with, "And a lady *never* blows her nose without a handkerchief."

Responding to Rory's roar of laughter, Caroline confessed with a grin, "I did that once. Just to try it."

Rory wiped the tears from his eyes with the back of his hands and found that Caroline was offering him her handkerchief. "Whatever for?" he gasped, still trying to picture this pretty girl doing something so . . . indelicate.

"I can see you're no lady," she teased him, withdrawing the handkerchief like a magician whisking away a scarf.

She shrugged. "I saw one of Grampa's hayers do it and I thought it was pretty awful."

Rory looked at Caroline with new respect. Betsey would never have tried such a thing. Perhaps Caroline would suit them after all.

She sighed again, making Rory aware this time that it wasn't a complaint but an expression of her yearning. She looked in Jake's direction and said, "The stuff about manners is the easy part—if you just hold your nose and do it." She grinned to show that was a joke and went on, quickly serious again. "What I don't know about is the part about the way people feel."

She alluded to more than Jake's indifference to Hannah's "suffering." "You mean the question of leaving your grandparents?"

Caroline nodded. "They say they need me."

"What do you think."

"Well, I do some things to be helpful, but really Gramma likes to do things her own way. Lots of stuff I do, she goes around later doing over. She can't help it, Grampa says. And I know I make work for her. She makes my clothes. And I worry her. If I stay at the spring house, she thinks I've fallen in the well and sends Grampa after me."

"Then why do they say they need you?"

"They don't like Papa."

"Do you know why?"

"Because of Mama."

"He took her from them, you mean? Well, that's normal," Rory assured her. "No married couple wants to live with parents. I wouldn't, if mine were still alive."

"But Mama did. Do you suppose there was something wrong with her? Or is there something mean about Papa?"

"Mean? Jake?" Rory was surprised. As angry as he'd

seen Jake, he had never seen a sign of meanness in him. "No, Jake's not mean, I can tell you that. Oh, he gets pretty mad and sometimes he yells, but he's never mean."

Caroline eyed him doubtfully. "Did you ever know anyone really mean?"

"My uncle," he answered promptly.

Caroline swung around to look in Hannah's direction. "You mean . . ."

Rory remembered who Hannah was supposed to be and laughed. "No, not her husband. My father's brother. He was mean enough to kill my father and steal everything left to me."

Caroline couldn't doubt his sincerity. "That is mean!" she said, impressed. "Are you going to get him for it?"

He could have laughed, but he didn't. "I've thought about it. First, though, I have to be older. Hannah's uncle, Mr. Sargent, wants me to work for him someday, and Hannah says I have to go to college."

"Would you mind?" Caroline could barely contain her excitement.

"I don't know. I was always going to run the foundry. That's hard work, but it's gone now. I'm going with Jake and try ranching."

Rory didn't know it, but he had just given Caroline another powerful incentive to accept her father's plan for her life. She started to ask him more when she saw Hannah returning. She nudged Rory's arm. "Go tell Papa to be nice to Hannah. I think she's sadder about him than she is about her dead old husband."

Hiding a smile, Rory did as she bid. Caroline might doubt her understanding of people's feelings, but Rory did not.

Jake greeted him with a sour "I don't see what's so funny," which didn't brighten when Rory's chuckle became a laugh.

"It's just your daughter. She's . . . all right."

"All right?" he huffed, offended by the lukewarm compliment. "Of course she's all right."

Rory couldn't resist teasing him. "Well, she has some doubts about you."

"Evidently," Jake responded bleakly.

Rory was instantly sorry for his too-direct hit. "She thinks you should be paying more attention to Hannah." It was more explanation than apology, but he thought it would do. "She's not jealous at all, is she?" he went on thoughtfully. "Don't you think that's remarkable?"

"Maybe she just doesn't care about me."

"No, that's not true. She's heard a lot of criticism of you though, so she has some questions. I don't think that's surprising."

"No, it's not, but I don't know what I can do about it."

"Treat Hannah well," Rory said bluntly.

Predictably, Jake bristled. "What's wrong with the way I treat Hannah?"

He couldn't say "everything," so he was specific. "You ignore her. You don't act like a man about to marry the woman of his dreams." When Jake started to protest, he held up his hand. "Caroline's heard about your mistreatment of her mother—true or not—and all she has to offset that is the way you treat Hannah."

Jake heaved a great sigh that reminded Rory of Caroline. With his mouth twisting up in a parody of a smile, Jake asked, "How did you get so damn smart?"

"Talking to Caroline," Rory answered. "She's a good kid."

As Caroline and Hannah walked slowly toward the grazing horses, distantly trailed by the men, Hannah asked again about the girl's intriguing knowledge of the battlefield. "Are there books about the war already?"

"I don't know," Caroline told her. "I only read newspaper accounts."

"Newspapers? I wouldn't have thought the Lunigs would subscribe to newspapers."

"They don't, but my friend Becky's father does. He lets me read them. Gramma and Grampa don't have much use for reading."

"Do they object?"

Caroline's head had sunk to her chest. "Gramma thinks it's sinful. Even the books my teacher loans me."

"I thought they saw themselves as sponsors of education," Hannah said thoughtfully.

"Only in school and as long as it doesn't interfere with practical things. They want me to behave well. That's their real concern. Grampa reads some in German, but they haven't had much need for book learning."

Hannah wanted Caroline to understand that Jake was different without being obvious about it. "Perhaps in this, too," she said, smiling, "you resemble your father. He likes to read. It's a love instilled by his mother, who was brought up by missionaries. They were the first teachers in the West, you know. He knows some wonderful Indian tales, some of them remarkably like *Bible* stories. They're moral fables, but with a charming twist."

"I love Western stories the best of all," Caroline said, her step quickening with her enthusiasm. "My favorite, favorite book is called *Stella Delorme; or The Comanche's Dream*. It's by Ned Buntline. Becky's father reads all those books and she brings them to me. Mr. Buntline wrote one about a cavalry scout, too. *Life in the Saddle*. But *Stella Delorme* was the best."

"I don't believe I've heard of Mr. Buntline," Hannah said.

"Becky says her mother calls them trash, and Becky doesn't like them either. She says they're stupid, but she doesn't like adventure and she only wants to read about

400

nice people, not outlaws and bandits and pirates."

Suddenly Hannah understood that Caroline's Mr. Buntline was the author of dime novels, those luridly popular tales of adventure and romance. Her discovery made her even more determined to help Jake win his spirited daughter away from the stultifying grasp of her too-conventional grandparents. How Jake would enjoy knowing that Caroline already embraced the world he loved.

"If your Gramma disapproves of reading, how do you manage it?"

"Becky brings me a book each Sunday to exchange for the one I've read. I take a candle to bed and read at Becky's or at the spring house. And at school when I finish my work early. Miss Plummer loans me her books there."

Hannah didn't miss the note of pride or the hint of challenge in what Caroline told her. "Good for you," she said, wanting the girl to reap some probably long-overdue approval for her diligence. "You would love my uncle's library—and he would love you for using it."

Absorbed in her discussion with Caroline, Hannah didn't notice Jake and Rory until she reached for the reins of her mare and found Jake already there. "Let me help you, my dear," he said, lifting her to her seat by the waist.

She was so surprised that she missed hooking her knee over the always-awkward sidesaddle. Jake did it for her, giving her an intimate pat and a scorching glance that brought heat to her face. She hardly knew what to make of him. After acting like a bear trapped by one foot, he was suddenly—suspiciously—attentive to her. And it didn't end there. He chose to let Rory handle the reins of the carriage with Caroline so he could sit inside with Hannah.

Never one to mince words, she almost asked him for an explanation. Afraid of what he might say though, she didn't. Instead, she chose a safe topic. "Caroline is everything you said she was."

"Rory seems to like her," he answered mildly.

"Is that what you're doing? Putting them together?" It was an explanation—not the one she wanted—but a possible one.

"He's told me he wants to go west with me. He thinks he'd like ranching."

Hannah looked out the window quickly to hide her flare of pain from him. So that was the way of it. Jake and Caroline would also take Rory. She didn't blame Rory for wanting to go. Nor could she blame them for wanting him. It would be wonderful for everyone except her. She would be left behind, alone.

"I'm sure he'd like it, and he'd be a great help to you. He's very level-headed."

Jake knew she wasn't happy, but he didn't know what to do about it. He was supposed to be mending his fences with Hannah, but the way she acted, nothing short of a marriage proposal would make her smile. He couldn't pretend to be something he was not. Not even for Caroline would he tie himself to a woman who would end up unhappy with the lot he could give her in life. And nothing had happened to change his circumstances for the better.

Quite the opposite, in fact. Courting Caroline was costing him both time and money. With every passing day the money he had allotted to this project diminished. Because of Hannah and Rory, it now appeared that he would win Caroline in the end, but because of them his expenses had more than doubled. He'd paid Mrs. Bergen for the extra meals, bought presents, and paid for renting horses. Little things, perhaps, but they added up quickly. If he wasn't careful, he would soon be using money set aside for the purchase of land just to pay for their passage west. Hannah might have paid for their trip out, but getting them west again was his responsibility.

Most galling of all, he might have to ask Hannah for a loan. The thought of it made him feel physically sick. He would do it, but only as a last resort.

To distract himself from that prospect, Jake asked, "Do you think Caroline will choose to go with me?"

Hannah winced at the way he said me, not us. But she also understood his insecurity, his need for reassurance. "I'm sure she will. It's what she wants to do. She has only to convince herself that it's not wrong. She has a strong sense of duty and a kind heart. The combination is especially difficult to deal with, but it's one of the fine things about her."

"I know. I just wish I could be sure."

"I think it will be obvious on Sunday."

His eyes narrowed. "Why Sunday?"

"She'll say good-bye to her friends then, at church."

"And be ready to leave by when?"

"Is your schedule so tight, Jake?"

"Damn it, of course it is." He struggled to hold his temper. "I never expected to be here so long."

"You could have told her rather than asking. She doesn't understand your problems, you know. She only knows her own. Why don't you explain?"

"I don't want her worrying. She has to feel secure with me or the whole thing is wrong."

"Secure?" Hannah frowned, unsure of his meaning. Then, suddenly, it hit her. His problem was money, not time as such. She had been thinking about travel time that might extend into early fall storms on the plains or the mountains beyond. That could be a problem, but his was more pressing.

It didn't help that she had the solution. He was sick of her solutions already. But she had to offer. "Uncle Simon would loan you money," she said diffidently.

His teeth gleamed white as he gave her a savage-looking smile. "You mean *you* would."

"I can't think of a safer loan to make," she snapped. "I know you'd crawl through fire to repay it."

"Crawling isn't my favorite posture, but I seem to have to do a lot of it."

Hannah bit back her tears, unsure whether they were for his pride or her own. She had to be insane to dream that two such stiff-necked people could ever get together. "I'm sorry I can't be poor enough to suit you."

The remainder of the trip passed in silence, except for their second, rather strained picnic. Jake was physically attentive, strangely so, but otherwise quiet and withdrawn. Caroline's ebullient spirits lifted them anyway. She had never had a picnic before, she confessed, and now she'd had two in the same day! She hugged them all good-bye, promising to be ready early for church, and skipped inside, carrying the lunch basket.

Jake took over the horses on the way to town, relegating Rory back to Hannah's side. He took one look at her face and said, "I see it didn't go well."

"What?" she asked, suspicious.

"You and Jake."

"Does it ever go well?"

"Oh, well. At least Caroline didn't notice. I'll have to talk to him again before Sunday."

So Hannah had her explanation after all. It was for Caroline.

Much more of this, Hannah decided, and she would indeed become jealous of Caroline. But how could she? She loved her already.

"Becky, this is Hannah—um, Mrs. Veazie." Caroline

sent Hannah an imploring look that apologized unnecessarily for her butchered introduction. Seeing that she had it, she went on. "Anyway, Becky, she's going to be my new mother."

Hannah couldn't keep herself from hugging Caroline. She sounded so proud. *Hannah* was certainly proud to be presented so warmly to Caroline's friend. "Just call me Hannah," she told Becky. "I'm pleased to have a chance to meet Caroline's best friend."

Caroline lowered her voice confidentially. "I told her about the books, and she's *glad* I like to read."

They were a family again — this time at church. Mr. and Mrs. Lunig accompanied them, their martyred air gradually giving way to something like acceptance as they were congratulated over and over by friends who were genuinely pleased that they were about to be relieved of their responsibility for Caroline.

No formal plans had been announced, yet everyone seemed to accept the legitimacy of Jake's claim to his daughter. Hannah suspected that Mrs. Bergen and her sister Hattie had prepared the way for the community's acceptance by telling everyone about Jake's new family. Hannah understood why. The Lunigs were conventional people. They would find it hard to oppose what people expected of them.

The Lunigs were not going to lose totally in this exchange. They were being as well praised for relinquishing Caroline as they had been lauded for taking over for Jake in the first place. And although Hannah knew that Martha and Gustaf had said harsh words about Jake in the past, no one alluded to that now. Jake was just as well received. People remembered him and thanked him for his war service. He was also praised for being responsible to his small family. If the Lunigs didn't realize that not every man in his position did his duty so thoroughly, everyone else seemed to.

Seeing Jake and Caroline by the carriage, Hannah broke free from some well-wishers and went to join them. She arrived in time to hear Jake ask, "How long will it take you to pack up, punkin'?"

For a moment Caroline's eyes darkened. "Do we have to hurry?"

"We don't have to hurry, but we shouldn't linger here either," Hannah said. She was speaking out of turn, but she wanted to save Jake from seeming to push her from her home. "It takes a long time to travel so far, Caroline, and your father doesn't want to court danger by delaying. There can be sneak storms in the early fall on the plains. It doesn't do to take chances like that."

All trace of hesitation disappeared, swept aside by the girl's excitement. "Do you think we'll see Indians?"

Jake and Hannah laughed together, unwittingly presenting exactly the picture of unity Caroline craved. As they sought each other's eyes, sharing their amusement, they privately acknowledged it was what they wanted too. "I can guarantee it," Jake said. "I plan to show you off to my friends along the way. We'll seek out one tribe of Pawnee Indians especially. You'll like them, but you might not want to mention it to your grandparents. They might not understand."

Caroline suppressed a knowing giggle and went to tell the others they were leaving. Watching her, Hannah said to Jake, "She doesn't know she has Indian blood, does she?"

"Who'd believe it, looking at her?"

"You'll tell her, won't you?"

"Of course. It's never been a secret, although the Lunigs don't know. Grace was ashamed of it, so I didn't volunteer the information. It wouldn't have helped anyone."

"Caroline won't be ashamed."

Jake frowned. "Not now anyway. Who knows about later? Believe it or not, I wasn't too happy about it myself once."

Hannah was surprised. She knew the prevailing sentiment against all Indians, but had assumed that Jake was too strong to be influenced by it. "When?"

"When I was nicknamed Breed."

"Oh, Jake."

"Then my father sent me to live with Many Buffalo's family. I hated the idea."

"Because of the way you'd been treated?"

"They were kind enough to put that face on it. In fact, I was pretty poor stuff compared to the Pawnee boys my age. They'd been riding and tracking from birth. Many Buffalo saved my hide a time or two, although looking back I don't know why he bothered. I acted terribly superior. In time, of course, I got caught up in the adventure of it. My father was right. It was what I needed."

"Maybe you can send Caroline there for a similar visit," she suggested. To her surprise, Jake didn't see the joke.

"God, no!" he exploded. "One look at her hair and some brave would offer his string of horses for her."

"Oh, Jake, she's too young."

"That wouldn't matter. Indians marry young. Some buck would wait years for her."

"Are you going to be one of those terribly possessive fathers, Jake?" She was teasing him, but warning him, too. "If you are, you should know there's no better way to lose your child's love."

"Don't worry, about it, Hannah," he said, stalking away angrily. His expression told her she had again stepped over the line he drew around himself and Caroline.

When would she learn?

Right now, she decided firmly, watching Jake prepare them to leave the churchyard. In this small leave-taking she saw the beginning of the larger ones to come, leaving Hanford with Caroline and then the three of them leaving her behind at Knoxville.

It would happen—unless she found a way to erase Jake's image of her. She would start by keeping her big mouth firmly shut. She would offer him no more unwanted advice. None. And she would smile.

She began immediately, all the while groaning inwardly. This would take some work, but she would do it. She had no choice. She had only the time it would take them to reach Knoxville to make herself indispensible to Jake's happiness.

# Chapter Twenty-Two

Hannah kept her resolution all the way to Ohio. There she began to panic. Nothing had changed. Jake kept his distance. They stayed in inns and small hotels, getting two rooms that kept Caroline and Hannah together, allowing her no opportunity to talk to Jake in privacy. He treated her chivalrously, rather as if she were his aging grandmother, helping her in and out of the carriage and taking her elbow on the street.

She had been keeping herself distant from Caroline as well, as distant as possible given their travel arrangements. She believed it was unfair to both of them to forge strong bonds between them that were doomed to be severed. If Jake intended to leave her behind—and he clearly did—she didn't want Caroline to be hurt. She knew that in Caroline she had a potentially powerful weapon to use against Jake, but she couldn't do that. Using Caroline was beyond her. She was too fond of her.

But she had to do something. Smiling and being quietly ladylike was getting her nowhere.

"I think we should camp out tonight instead of finding an inn," she said as soon as everyone was eating lunch. "We have enough food here for supper. We won't need provisions until tomorrow." Every day they bought food to eat along the way, to Caroline's continued delight.

She spoke up immediately. "Oh, could we, Papa? I've *never* slept outside."

Jake shot Hannah an irritated look. "You have too, you just don't remember it." Because he was annoyed with Hannah, he spoke too harshly.

Caroline wilted. "I'm sorry. It just sounded like fun. Not that I don't like where we've stayed," she hurried to assure him.

His frown deepened. Caroline's frequent rush to apology was the only trait he dislike in her. He knew she had been taught by the Lunigs to be biddable, but her willingness to accept blame for things completely out of her jurisdiction bothered him.

Seeing the frown, Rory spoke up for once. "Why not?" he asked. "We'll be doing that later anyway. Why not start now?"

Caroline gave him a grateful look but said nothing. Begging her grandfather had only made him less willing, and she had no way of knowing that Jake was more flexible.

Hannah, too, said nothing more. She knew Jake's scowl was meant for her and that it was because she had surprised him, not because her suggestion was unreasonable. Jake didn't like ambushes, and he suspected one now.

"Maybe we can," he said, pretending to be won over. Actually the suggestion was wise. It would save them money and give Caroline a taste of the future in surroundings that were unthreatening. The Ohio countryside was very much like Pennsylvania, green and friendly.

"Oh, thank you, Papa!" Caroline's eyes sparkled engagingly. "Where shall we camp? Do we have to look for water?"

"Just bears," Rory deadpanned.

She wasn't fazed at all. Only Jake could upset her, it seemed, and that always unintentionally. The rest of the meal passed quickly amid teasing speculation about where they would sleep.

When Caroline began to help Hannah repack their food, Jake sent her off to help Rory with the horses instead. She didn't resist, just looked to Hannah for confirmation. Hannah smiled easily, secretly delighted both that Jake was seeking her out—even if to scold her—and that Caroline was loyal to her. She, like Hannah, sensed Jake's mood; but unlike Hannah, Caroline distrusted it.

Jake's word was brief. "I don't know what you have up your sleeve, but it won't work."

She faced him calmly. "When do you plan to tell her the truth about us?"

"Not yet." He answered as calmly, but Hannah knew she had landed a telling blow. He had been surprised again.

She softened the blow by asking, "Would you like me to explain?"

"No."

"You know I wouldn't speak against you. I'd take the blame myself. I can tell her about Daniel."

"No. It's my duty, but I'll do it when I want to. Don't try to force me."

"Just don't leave it too long. You weren't planning to wait till Knoxville, were you? I think she needs time to adjust. She's had a lot of changes." She was giving advice again, but why not? She had nothing to lose now.

He left before she could say more, taking with him the small glow his presence cast over everything they did together. Hannah hadn't expected him to shirk the job of telling Caroline they would not marry—that wasn't Jake. She had only wanted him aware of how hard it would be. She wanted him thinking of Caroline's welfare. And she

411

wasn't finished yet.

Although the days were perceptibly shorter now, there was still plenty of light left after they had cared for the horses, eaten, and set up their beds. So Hannah made a second suggestion. "I'd like to practice shooting again, Jake. It's been a long time since I've fired a gun and I'm not sure I remember how to load it anymore."

Caroline was agog. "You know how to fire a gun, Hannah?"

"Not very well, I'm afraid. Jake tried to teach me, but I was a poor marksman. Perhaps you'll have a better eye," she said innocently.

"Me?" Her eyes flew to Jake. "Would you teach me to shoot?"

He leveled Hannah with a glance, but his answer was mild. "If you wouldn't be frightened."

Rory spoke before Caroline could. "We're the ones who should be frightened, not them."

"That's right," she chimed in. "Maybe Hannah and I will get to be such good shots we'll go off and form an all-female outlaw gang!"

Rory groaned, but Jake laughed and forgot—for now—his annoyance with Hannah. He began teaching Caroline by using Hannah as his model. Once she had renewed her acquaintance with the steps involved in loading, Caroline took over. She was an apt and dexterous pupil. Unlike Hannah, she had no misgivings about the use of weapons. She saw only the adventure, not the danger.

But she wasn't wild or foolish either. Jake would not have permitted it. Over and over, he stressed safety and care, and Caroline listened. She was more child than woman, but she was as strong as Hannah and had far better judgment about distance. With her eye, her cool head and her enthusiasm, she made an ideal student. Even Rory admitted to being impressed.

After that they camped out every night except one

stormy night when Jake overruled the ladies' insistence that a little rain wouldn't hurt them. On the last night before they were to sell the carriage and team, Hannah considered with wonder just how far they had come—not only in miles but in spirit. There were, she knew, "real" families with far less unity. They had everything: love, respect, and fun. But they didn't have a future, at least not together. Not the way she wanted it.

She wasn't pretending to be asleep; pretense wasn't necessary. With everyone else asleep, who was there to impress? They were sheltered in a thicket of oak and maple trees where every leaf was being stirred by breezes almost strong enough to be winds. Clouds scudded overhead, unseen because of the trees but still there. She heard Jake's breathing in her mind, deep and even, broken now and then by an endearing vibration that was almost a snore. She was so attuned to him. How could she live out the rest of her days without him? Was she doomed to listen for him in vain from now on?

Unable to bear her own thoughts, Hannah folded back her blanket and got to her feet. She made no more noise than a ghost, which she resembled in her pale nightgown. It was soft, of cotton so delicate it was almost transparent in daylight. In the dark, however, it concentrated the feeble light, gathering it in and giving it back like moonlight.

Sure of her way, she went quickly along the path that led to the pond that had attracted them to this resting place. Here the breeze was stronger. It flattened her gown to her front and billowed it out behind her. Her skin tightened and grew goosebumps, but still she didn't move.

She wiggled her toes into the thick grass that sloped down to form the bowl of water. Whenever the rounded but not quite full moon slipped from behind the veiling puffs of cloud, it laid a silver path over the surface of the pond, a path so inviting she wanted to follow it, certain it would lead to enchantment. Even shimmering as it did, it looked almost solid enough to support her weight.

If only she could swim, she thought again. She had always wanted to ask Jake to teach her. Now there was no time left. Tomorrow they would board the train. Tomorrow they would begin the last phase of their trip.

Without thinking, she cast off her gown, letting the breeze take it from her hand behind her. She wouldn't try to swim, but she knew from her earlier bath that the water was warmer than the air. She walked down the slope and kept going until she had to gather her hair and lift it to keep it from getting wet. The slope was gentle so far, with no dips, hollows, or stones, and with the water lapping at her breasts, she decided to go just a step or two deeper. She would be warmer when she was more completely submerged. Still holding her hair, she dunked a bit and stepped cautiously forward.

The silty sand and mud gave way under her foot and pitched her forward. Still trying to keep her hair dry, she slid below the surface of the water, taking her cry of surprise with her. It rose to the surface as a bubble, carrying no sound.

Hannah knew she was in no danger. All she had to do was stand up, but she was so disoriented she couldn't find the bottom. She reached out, struggling for air and for substance. All she saw were bubbles of air rising around her, released from her hair. She was angry and frustrated. Wasn't she supposed to rise? To float up? She tried, straining against the press of liquid around her, kicking, reaching, her lungs bursting.

Her foot bumped something and then she was lifted, dragged up to the air.

Jake.

He was moving, carrying her, dropping her to the grass, pressing on her back. She gasped and pushed the mass of her hair back from her face.

414

"Oh, Jake. Thank you. I . . . thought you were asleep. I thought . . . I thought I would die." She leaned on the warmth of his chest and clung to his shoulders. "It was so stupid."

Jake didn't trust his voice. What if he'd really been asleep? What if he'd been strong enough not to follow her? He'd debated with himself and lost, knowing he was too vulnerable to her to be alone with her in the moonlight. If he'd waited longer . . . God! His hands tightened on her shoulders.

"I'm so sorry," she whispered. She welcomed the pain of his clasp. It was real, reminding her that she hadn't died.

"You idiot!"

"I know." Hannah lifted her head and found his mouth waiting for hers. His skin was cool, like hers, but his mouth was hot and sweet. He had not kissed her since he left her bed the morning after she arrived in Hanford. He told her now it had been too long for him as it had been for her. Crushed to his chest, she couldn't raise her arms to hold his head to her. It wasn't necessary. He turned, angling his kiss to deepen the contact, his tongue thrusting to fill her soul. She wrapped her arms around his waist and sighed with contentment, letting the drugging power of him chase away the last of her fears.

His hands slid down her back, under the weeping weight of her hair, leaving her flesh soothed and warmed. As one, they sank back onto the grass facing each other on their sides.

"I tried not to follow you," he said into her ear. His voice sounded rusty and unused. "What if I hadn't?"

"You did," she assured him thankfully.

"I didn't want to." He kissed her neck, moving her hair aside with his palm. "I was never going to do this again."

Hannah's hands drifted down his back. He was as bare as she was. "But you didn't put on your pants." Looking up at him under lowered eyelashes, she saw his grim expression and regretted teasing him.

"They're over there with your gown. I took them off as soon as you went in the water."

"Then I was safe all along. I didn't know."

He smiled then. "Only you would feel safe with me chasing you."

He put her onto her back, holding her in place almost roughly. When she reached for him he put her hands, one by one, on the ground beside her. Although his face was shadowed, she felt the warning in his eyes, felt it heating her, and didn't move. He moved her legs apart with one hand to make a place for himself between them, and with his arms around her waist, pressed his face to her abdomen.

His skin was hot now, too, as hot as the inside of his mouth. The hint of beard on his jaw was an erotic counterpoint to the moist smoothness of his tongue as he licked away the drops of water from her body. Her skin heated and she writhed, wanting to thrust up to meet him. He held her still, moving down to the slim roundness of her thigh. He nipped at the soft skin at the inside of her thigh, then soothed and smoothed the flesh with his tongue before drifting across her openness to the other thigh.

"Jake, oh, Jake," she moaned, filling his ears with the sounds he wanted to hear. When he couldn't wait to take her, he made himself delay, pressing, then withdrawing, teasing himself to distraction. She wrapped his hips with her legs, fierce and demanding, as he slid home. Filling her with his heat and his hardness.

Never again, his mind told him, while his heart sang a different song—mine, mine. Savor this. Remember, taunted his intellect, but his body was already lost. He could never keep this moment. How could he? The feelings were too intense. They were beyond his control.

Her body took and gave back, pulling him away from his mind.

Hannah, too, was beyond thought, dying a little in Jake's arms. She still wasn't sure she hadn't dreamed it all. "Maybe I really died and I'm in heaven now. It feels like heaven."

"What on earth were you thinking?"

She laughed. "I didn't want to get my hair wet and I lost my footing. There was a drop-off, I guess. I kept telling myself I would rise—like the bubbles. But I couldn't. All I could think was, how stupid to die like that after surviving so much worse. And without ever telling you I love you." She added that softly, reaching up at the same time to cover his lips with her fingers.

When he drew back as if he would answer anyway, she shook her head and rolled away from him. She truly didn't want to hear whatever he thought he should say. "I always wanted to ask you to teach me to swim. I meant to."

"I should have." He put on his pants, watching as she bent to wring the water from her hair.

Hannah concentrated on the chore, noting his mild regret. Nothing had changed—again. He had saved her because she needed saving and made love to her for the same reason.

"What will you do about your hair?"

She shrugged into her gown and smiled. "Be glad I can feel that it's wet. Thank you, Jake. Again."

Jake let her go. What else could he do? She didn't want to hear that he loved her unless he was also willing to marry her. The words didn't matter, even to him. He ached with the knowledge of the love between them. But it wasn't a solution. She was still Hannah and he was still Jake.

\* \* \*

Jake had known explaining his inability to marry Hannah would be hard. Just how hard, he badly underestimated.

He woke the next morning knowing he'd already put it off too long. He lured Caroline up onto the driver's seat with the promise that he'd let her handle the reins. She had done it before in her usual capable way, adapting nicely from her occasional experience with her grandfather's more modest wagon and single horse. It didn't help that Hannah was particularly subdued this morning, looking as if she could read his mind.

To complicate matters, the horses were skittish, either because he had communicated his nervousness to them or because of the weather. Probably the latter. The wind had become brisk and the air hummed with prestorm energy.

All in all, the setting wasn't conducive to an earnest father-daughter chat, but time was running out. His own fault, assuredly, but he had not wanted the turmoil his announcement would bring.

When the dancing horses were under control enough that he dared divert his attention, Jake made his announcement. It came out too baldly, but because it was much rehearsed, his statement was clear and unequivocal. It was a decision he would not change, he told her, and although he knew it would make her unhappy for a while, the decision had also been made with her best interests at heart as well as his own.

He was prepared for some quiet tears and some pleadings on behalf of Hannah. He wasn't prepared for Caroline's cry of outrage and fury. Or for the fact that she would immediately try to get down from the carriage—while it was still moving along smartly.

Jake lunged for Caroline. He caught her, but in the process let the reins go slack. The frisky horses needed no other invitation. They bolted, taking off at a racketing pace that soon had Caroline clinging to Jake and the seat for dear life.

While Jake fought for control of the runaway team and for the preservation of his daughter, Rory and Hannah bounced around inside the carriage like kernels of corn in a hot pan. Rory braced his feet across the seats and held on to Hannah.

"Jake must have told Caroline!" he shouted, grinning from ear to ear.

Hannah clenched her hands and exhorted heaven for the child's safety.

Slowly, inexorably, Jake reasserted control, aided by the horses' fatigue once their frolic had begun to run its course.

As soon as the horses stopped, Caroline extricated herself from Jake's weakened grasp and climbed down unassisted. He should have been able to stop her, except that his muscles had turned to jelly in the aftermath of the crisis. Caroline appeared to suffer no after-effects at all. Except for one.

"I hate you!" she shouted up at him from the ground.

Jake stared at her helplessly, still too frightened to function.

Rory popped out of the carriage, immediately followed by a white-faced Hannah. Caroline dissolved into tears in Hannah's arms, and together they walked back along the road.

Jake secured the reins and bounded down, finally mobile. He was now as furious as Caroline had been when she tried to leap from the moving carriage. She *hated* him? All his terror and anxiety had become temper. He faced off against the embracing females, ready to charge after them.

To Rory, he was as lathered as the horses. He threw all his weight against Jake and barely managed to hold him back. He succeeded only because Jake was still too stunned to be entirely sure of his purpose.

"Let Hannah talk to her."

Jake continued to glare at their backs. "She almost killed us all!"

Rory understood the "us all" really stood for Caroline. "She'll be all right."

"*All right?*" He took steps to follow that Rory diverted.

"Let's take care of the horses," he urged, turning Jake around.

"I ought to shoot the pair of them!" He was looking at the horses, but the exact object of his ire was unclear.

As was Rory's reference when he answered, "But you won't. Think how placid they'll be from now on."

Hannah and Caroline didn't go far. A small dip in the road gave them instant privacy and a fallen log provided seats. When Caroline's storm of tears abated, Hannah handed her a handkerchief without taking away her supporting arm.

"Rory said he wasn't mean," she hiccupped between swipes at her eyes and nose, "but he is!"

"No, no," Hannah soothed. "Rory's right. Your father is the kindest man I know."

"How can you say that? I thought you loved him," she demanded hotly.

Hannah almost smiled. However bizarre her words sounded, Caroline's inner logic was clear. "I do love him. I can say it *because* I love him, and hard as it is, I understand and accept him, too. He just can't believe that I could be happy living in a modest way with him. He's wrong, but I can't make him see that."

"But it's not fair!" Caroline cried. "We were going to be a family. I was going to have a mother."

Now Hannah had to fight tears. "You make me feel so honored, Caroline. You're a wonderful girl and I already love you. That won't change, believe me."

"I'll make him change his mind. I'll tell him he has to take me back to Gramma and Grampa."

"No, you can't do that. He loves you and needs you. Getting you back, making a home for you, is what kept him alive during the war and afterward. You'll like your new home and you'll have Rory besides."

"But I'll be the only girl," she protested. "I'll have to cook and do all the work like Mary Ann Bellows did when her mother died."

"Jake is going to hire a housekeeper. He promised. She'll do all that and be a mother to you as much as you want."

Although some of her worst fears were soothed, Caroline wasn't willing to be completely placated. She was too much Jake's child to overlook his affront to her moral code. Narrowing her eyes, the same startling blue as Jake's and still glittering with tears, she said harshly, "He lied to me. He said we'd be a family."

"That was my fault, Caroline. And if you think back, you'll understand it, I think." Hannah went slowly, choosing her words carefully. "Your father came for you alone. He left me in Omaha, saying good-bye forever. After he was gone, I decided not to accept that and I chased after him. It's not the kind of thing a woman usually does and I don't recommend it." She gave Caroline a thin smile as she thought about the horrendous example she was providing the girl.

"Jake wasn't happy to see me. Not at all. You see, I'd put him in a difficult position, one I hadn't even stopped to consider." She paused and sighed. This was harder than she'd imagined. "Then Mrs. Bergen, who had no trouble figuring out how I felt about him, told us that now your grandparents would have no reason to keep fighting him for you. They were afraid of him, but they'd trust a lady like me. And they did. She wasn't wrong."

"But that just makes it worse," Caroline exclaimed. "He just used you to get me, then when he did, he refused to marry you!"

"But *I* did that. I put myself in that position. I offered, and in the circumstances, he had no choice. I had compromised his position with your grandparents. He never deceived me. And he didn't want to deceive you. That's what this is all about. Jake is like you are—very, very honest. That's why he had to tell you."

She didn't say anything while she considered all that Hannah had said. It was a lot to absorb.

The wind lifted the edge of Hannah's skirt and drew her eye to the sky. It would rain soon. She was about to suggest that they go back to the carriage when Caroline asked, "How can you love him when he doesn't love you back?"

"It's not something I have any control over, honey. Even if I never see him again, I'll always love him. But I believe he loves me, too. He doesn't say so because he thinks it would be cruel to admit it and not marry me, but I can feel his love as easily as I can feel my own." She rushed on to add, "Maybe I shouldn't tell you that, but I'm being just as honest as I can be. Grown-up problems with love are never simple, you'll find. In a strange way, he's being noble to refuse to marry me. He wants what's best for me and he can't believe a life with him would be good enough. And he doesn't want an unhappy wife."

"Like my mother was."

Hannah was surprised. "What do you know about your mother?"

Caroline made a face. "I read some of her letters to Gramma. They were one of the reasons I couldn't decide to come with Papa. She made it sound awful."

"Your father blames himself for taking her away from the comforts she loved and needed. It made a big impression on him. He knew you were different though, more like him."

"But so are you. Why doesn't he see that?"

"He does, but he knows I'm used to money and he

422

thinks I'd miss that." She got up and brushed off her seat. "Let's go back now. I haven't given up hope, you know."

Caroline's face had an almost comical look of determination. "I bet I can change his mind."

Hannah touched her arm in warning. "Gently, dear." She smiled, but Caroline's stride back to the carriage was militant.

Jake was up on the seat, holding the horses, and Rory offered to hand Caroline up beside him. She directed her answer to her father's unflinching profile. "No, thank you," she announced loudly. "I'll ride inside with Hannah."

Hannah and Rory exchanged exasperated looks as he helped her inside. "It's going to rain," she reminded him. "See that Jake has a wrap, would you?"

"We both do," he replied. "We'll be fine."

The rest of the trip was more difficult than it had to be. Caroline didn't soften toward Jake, revealing a stubbornness that was so like his that Hannah found her company—and her rather aggressive sympathy—tedious. More and more, as a result, Caroline spent her time with Rory, for only with him did she behave normally.

Consequently, Jake and Hannah found themselves thrown together by default. For Hannah, at least, it was a mixed blessing. If she'd been capable of feeling jealous of Caroline, Jake's attention to his daughter would have destroyed her. Even at a distance, his eyes sought her constantly and lingered on her protectively.

"She's a good traveler," he said with a rueful glance that seemed to refute a charge she had made. "I wasn't wrong about that."

Hannah agreed, waiting for his point.

"How can she be so stubborn though? Who would have thought it?"

Her laugh brought his eyes to hers. At his puzzled

look, she laughed harder, but didn't explain. "She'll be better when I'm gone." Sad to say, it was true.

Jake didn't comment. When she went, would she take the ache in his heart? Or would it be worse when he was alone? Although he was leaving her behind, that was how he thought of the future. He would be alone. She would have friends and a social life to resume. He would have only his odd little family group—minus the woman who was its heart and soul.

"What if your uncle isn't home?" he asked.

Hannah shrugged. "He's frequently away. The house is staffed."

He had been about to suggest taking her on to Omaha, and now he wondered how he could have been so crazy. With one word—staffed—she brought him back to reality. How could he have forgotten? She would want for nothing.

The thought failed to comfort him.

Across the aisle, Caroline brushed soot from her sleeve and sent her father a hostile look. "He's not going to change his mind, Rory. Hannah's not even *trying* either."

"What would you suggest she do? Hit him? Cry?"

"It's not funny."

"No, it's not. Why don't you give it up? You're not doing anybody any good."

"I just *hate* giving up." She considered his stolid expression. "How do you stay so calm? Don't you care?"

"Not the way you do, I guess." Wearily, and just a little warily—they'd had this discussion before—Rory tried to explain. "I just recognize that I don't control the world."

She snorted inelegantly. "Of course not."

"Right. But you see, the way you act, you think you do."

"I do not!"

"It's being a kid," he said, ignoring her indignant interruption. "When you're little, you think you're the center of the world. Everything that happens, happens to you. I've just learned that life isn't really that way. What I want doesn't figure very big in the world."

"Because of what happened to your father?"

"I suppose so. I don't know. But I know this much. People—older people—do what they do and there's not much kids can do about it. This thing with Hannah and Jake is like that. Maybe they'll get married. I always thought they would, but maybe they won't. The world will go right along either way. And so will you."

Caroline had never before been exposed to cynicism and it affected her profoundly. She sat in complete silence for the longest time. What he said made sense to her. Rory was her friend, her brother, and for the first time she thought about his life, not hers. She and Papa were all the family she had left.

She forgot Hannah and Jake. She had a new problem to think about.

"You're going to get him someday, aren't you? That uncle of yours? How will you do it, do you suppose?"

# Chapter Twenty-Three

"Oh, Hannah, it's so big! And beautiful!"

Hannah dredged up a smile for Caroline. She didn't add, "and empty." She would not belittle Uncle Simon's home, her refuge heretofore, for any reason. It was everything Caroline said, lovely and dauntingly large. "But Uncle Simon isn't here, and I so wanted you to meet him."

"How do you know already?" Rory asked. They were coming up the drive in the handsome carriage Jake had insisted they hire, complete with driver, to convey them to the door.

Hannah's smile became normal. "See the flagpole? If Uncle Simon is home, he flies a flag. It's more of a pennant than a flag, really. He got the idea from reading about the Middle Ages. He loves stories about knights and castles, so he had his own flag made. It tells his friends he's at home so they'll all come visit. He's a most hospitable man."

Caroline sent Jake a pleading look. "Maybe we can stay until he comes. I'd like to meet him."

Hannah spoke up before Jake had to. "Unfortunately, that could take weeks."

"If he's in Omaha, we'll visit him," Jake promised,

ending the discussion which had been their sprightliest in days. Now that their parting was imminent, no one had much to say.

They were not expected but, as Hannah had assured them, that was not a problem. Uncle Simon came and went without warning, bringing guests and business associates who were far more demanding than they would be. Hannah's welcome was warm, even teary, because of the time when Uncle Simon had worried over the fate of her wagon train. When she told everyone proudly that Jake and Rory had rescued her, their reception was similarly assured. They were ushered off to handsome rooms, to baths, and the offer of refreshments to tide them over until dinner.

Elspeth, the stately Scotswoman who managed the house for Uncle Simon, personally escorted Hannah to her room. It was not the one she had shared with Daniel, but stood next to the still-empty nursery. After taking one look at that desolate space, she couldn't decide if she was happy or sad that it remained untouched.

Elspeth gave her a few moments of tactful silence before she asked how long they would be staying. When Hannah explained the situation, Elspeth expressed pleasure that she was home, then added in a hopeful voice, "Mr. Farnsworth is a fine man, I'm thinking. Mr. Talmage, too, of course. He has a Campbell look to him, like the clan chieftains of old."

It was Elspeth's finest compliment, for she was proud of her Campbell blood. Hannah smiled. "Yes, he's a fine boy."

"Boy? You'll not be calling a man like that 'boy'!" she exclaimed. "Not one with Campbell blood."

Hannah did not dare laugh and insult Elspeth, but it took all her self-possession to school her features into blandness. That Elspeth, who only minutes before had brushed aside Hannah's story that white men and not

427

"savage Indians" had murdered poor Willie, should now elevate a man with undisputed Indian blood to the ranks of a Campbell nearly too much for Hannah. Because of her struggle for composure, she nearly missed the rest of what Elspeth was saying. She heard only the name *Mr. Veazie*.

"I beg your pardon, Elspeth. What did you say about Mr. Veazie?"

Elspeth was clearly upset. "You didn't know, Miss Hannah?"

"Know what? I didn't hear what you said."

"Oh, but I thought you knew. I shouldn't be the one to tell you."

"Tell me what, Elspeth? Please." Then seeing the woman's determination to be proper at all cost, Hannah added, "Perhaps I do know. I . . . saw Daniel in the West, you know."

"Oh, my dear, then this will be terrible news to you. He was murdered by another one of those heartless beasts. Just like poor Willie."

"No, I didn't know that, Elspeth. Murdered?"

"Mr. Gordon said it was because of the railroad. I never understood that, but I did hear him say an Indian killed him. I don't see how one of those could have been mixed up with the railroad and I surely hope it's nothing to do with Mr. Simon's railroad."

Hannah thought immediately of Spotted Pony. Was he dead, too? To compose herself, she walked to the door of David's room and opened it. Daniel had been as good as dead to her for so long she couldn't pretend to grieve for him. Still, there was something in her that hurt. She touched the locket at her throat and put a name to the feeling. With Daniel gone, she had lost her last link to David. It had been the weakest kind of link, but losing it saddened her nonetheless.

She paced into the nursery, seeing it as it had been. The

cradle, then the small bed David had been so proud to sleep in. It was all gone.

She felt helpless and lost. There were so many "if only's." And what was more useless? Now she was free of Daniel and it no longer mattered. Jake would not have her.

She crossed the room swiftly and closed the door, leaving it behind. She would not tell Jake about Daniel's death. It didn't make any difference now. Perhaps it never had.

Elspeth waited by the door to the hallway, her hands twisted together at her waist.

Hannah gave her a small smile. "I'm glad you told me now, Elspeth. Daniel wasn't a good man, but he gave me David." Her voice faltered and she had to wait for the power to go on. "Still, I'm glad I was . . . with him in Omaha. He didn't know about David and I know it saddened him. In spite of his disregard, he cared for David at some level."

"Of course, he did, Miss Hannah. He was a precious scrap."

"That he was," she agreed, smiling now like her old self as Elspeth left her.

She had told Caroline she hadn't given up on Jake, but that was now true only in part. She knew he would leave, but seeing David's room and learning about Daniel had given her a new kind of hope. If she couldn't have Jake, perhaps—if God was kind—she could have his child? She had given only the slightest thought to the possibility of pregnancy before. She had been too busy trying to stay alive to consider the consequences of their lovemaking. But why not?

She had conceived before. Jake had a child. She might, in fact, already be carrying his child. The chance was perhaps slight, but there was tonight, wasn't there? She didn't want the child to try to bind Jake to her—that wasn't her way—but for herself. She had already laid the groundwork for acceptance of any possible pregnancy by telling Elspeth she had been with Daniel in Omaha. The world would think she and Daniel had reconciled briefly before his death and accept her child as his.

If only . . .

This was the biggest "if only" yet, but it gave her hope. Perhaps she would not be alone when Jake left tomorrow.

"I thought perhaps I'd find you here."

Hannah looked up in surprise. Hearing Jake was like having her thoughts suddenly materialize to flesh and blood. She had come to the paddock to watch Lucky Jim cavort for the mare of his choice, a lovely thoroughbred called Marjorie Daw. Caroline had retired with a book from Uncle Simon's library, and she had announced a similar intention, leaving the room to Jake and Rory.

"Where's Rory?"

"He went to bed."

Hannah accepted him beside her without comment although her heart thudded against the confines of her chest at his presence. She had gone to her room, only to discover she couldn't breathe there. She had meant to dress for bed and wait for Jake to go to his room. She hadn't changed her mind about going to him, but deciding on a course of action was one thing. Doing it was quite another. She hadn't expected him to seek her out.

"I used to dream I was riding Lucky Jim."

"A handsome horse," Jake said.

They had spent the afternoon on horseback, touring Uncle Simon's acreage, stopping only to walk the gardens and to throw crusts of bread to the ducks, geese, and swans on the pond. Jake had not commented on the splendor of the estate, but he didn't need to. She knew everything he saw only confirmed his belief in the rightness of his decision to leave her behind.

"Will the horses stay out all night?"

"I don't know; probably not. I'm not familiar with what the stablemaster does anymore."

"Are you cold?"

Hannah looked up again. Was her nervousness showing? She fingered the shawl she'd thrown about her shoulders. "No. The air is lovely."

He took her hand. "Walk with me?"

She nodded, unable to speak. His hand was so big and warm, so familiar, as it folded over hers, drawing her along. They followed the fence, then entered a stand of trees near the gardens. A small bridge arched a pebbled stream. They stopped at the crest to look down at the water.

"I'll think of you here," he said after the silence between them had stretched to the point of tension.

"Will you?" She didn't look up.

"You know I will."

Again she nodded. He would—at least sometimes and for a while. When he moved on she followed, her hand still in his. "Do you know where you'll go?"

"Not really. I told Caroline Texas or Colorado, but I don't know."

"I wasn't asking because—" She started again. "I won't follow you again, Jake. You needn't worry about that. I can't say I'm sorry I did this time, but I'll never do it again." She tried to smile. "You're safe from pursuit."

He stopped along the gentle slope of grass next to the stream and captured her other hand. "Even if you don't see it now, Hannah, this is right. It's as much for your good as mine."

"My father said that once when he punished me," she answered, trying for a light touch. "I didn't believe it then and I don't believe it now."

He dropped her hands to drag his fingers through his

hair.

She laughed at the familiar gesture of exasperation. "Poor Jake. You're surrounded by stubborn females." She put her hand on his chest. "I'm being honest. It's all I have left to give you. I know I've been a trial to you, taking things into my own hands. I can't say I believe you're right, but I understand that you do. And I love you. In all my life, all I've wanted was someone to love who loved me back. I have that even now. You'll go, but you'll take my love and leave yours with me. I'd give everything just to spend the rest of my days at your side. If it's not to be, it's not to be. But I have love and so do you. Nothing can change that."

"Hannah . . ."

She put her hand over his mouth, stopping the strangled sound of his speech. "No. Don't." She put her arms around his shoulders and stood on tiptoes to touch her lips to his lightly, dropping down as soon as he responded.

His hands went around her back, but he didn't draw her into his embrace when she stiffened to hold him off. He was not pressing her.

"I came outside tonight to wait until you went to your room," she told him in an even tone. "I was going to come to you then. Would I have been welcome?"

He crushed her to his chest and let his mouth answer hers directly. It was the hungriest kiss she'd ever known. She melted against him, making every adjustment within her power to mold her body to his.

Jake was overcome, physically and emotionally. He had been about to follow Rory to bed. Instead, he'd been drawn to the open window in time to see Hannah reach the paddock. He had not expected her to welcome him. Quite the opposite. Even if he'd known which of the many imposing doors led to her room, he wouldn't have dared go to her later, feeling that he had no right. It was a

432

feeling he still had.

Powerless to prevent his surge of desire, Jake neverthe-less slowly brought himself back from the edge and ended the kiss. He drew back far enough to say in a raw whisper, "This isn't why I followed you."

Hannah's breath caught. "Would you deny me this last time?" To ask like that meant giving up her pride, but with Jake she had none left.

He bent his head to her neck. "Not like this, Hannah. Not here." He wanted to honor her, not take her in the woods like an animal.

She laughed and drew his head up, her hands framing his face. "We've had only two nights in a bed, Jake." She gave him little stinging kisses all around his mouth. "Why won't you recognize that I'm not the elegant lady you think me?"

"You're the finest lady alive."

"I'm a woman first, Jake, and I want you. Now."

Groaning, he gave up and pulled her down to the carpet of grass. He wanted to be tender and slow and gentle, but Hannah had other thoughts. Her bald state-ment of desire had roused him to a fevered pitch that, wonderful as it was, wasn't enough for her. She wanted him desperate and needy. She wanted to imprint her image and her passion upon Jake so completely that he would never be satisfied with another woman. And she wanted his baby. Above all else, she wanted that.

Jake spread his coat and her shawl to make a nest for her. The wide neckline and buttons at the front of her dress yielded her breasts to his eager hands and mouth. Hannah opened his shirt and pants.

He tried to stop her once, protesting, "No, love, let me —"

It was too late. She was touching him and he couldn't wait. She showed him no mercy except, finally, to help with her skirts and underwear.

In his arms, Hannah felt she was part of Jake, joined to him by more than the passion of their embrace. When he moved in her, he *was* her body, the best part of it. She wrapped herself around him, rising to meet each strong thrust, crying out with the joy of it. She found her release only seconds before his, then fell into a dreamlike state that was, to her, better than sleep.

Jake moved before Hannah wanted to and she tightened her hold around his back.

"I'm squashing you.

"No. I love it. Please don't move."

He gave her more time, then gently eased away to pull his clothes together. She made a few adjustments without rising, determined not to be rushed. He did up the buttons on her dress, smiling at her pleased expression. "How can you look like that?"

Hannah turned toward him and rolled up onto one elbow. "Very easily." Her answering smile was tender as she traced his lips with one finger.

He didn't want to apologize for giving her what she had obviously wanted, so he laughed. "What am I going to do with you?"

"You're going to love me."

"Again?"

"Again. In my bed." She had decided on that, knowing that ever after she could remember him there.

"I still have to go, Hannah."

"I know that. I also know you need your sleep, but you have the rest of your life to sleep. Tonight is mine — if you will have me."

He would.

Jake knocked softly on Caroline's door and waited for her to unlock it after he identified himself. They were in Independence, Missouri, their last stop before beginning

434

the final trek west. Here they would join a wagon train, the larger the better in Jake's opinion, for the Santa Fe Trail, and indeed their destination in New Mexico, was plagued by the threat and reality of Apache attack.

Inside, he looked quickly around Caroline's room to see if it was comfortable. It was small and impersonal, but clean. She had not unpacked.

"I have to go out on an errand and Rory's not back yet. So promise me you'll stay right here with the door locked. I'll be back in, oh, an hour at the most."

Caroline hurried to the bed and came back carrying her reticule. "I'll come with you. I don't want to stay here alone."

"I'm just going to the bank, Caroline. You'll be bored. I'm sure I'll have to wait and there'll be nothing for you to do."

"There's nothing to do here."

"You have books to read, don't you?" Jake knew she had already read the books Hannah had given her from her uncle's library. He intended to find a bookstore — if he could — after he finished at the bank. That was why he didn't want her with him.

"I've read them."

"Caroline, you knew there would be times you'd have to put up with boredom. I can't take you with me every-where."

"I won't be bored at the bank. I'll just look at the people and everything. I won't say a word."

For the hundredth time since leaving Hannah behind, Jake wished her with him. He had expected to miss her, but not like this. He hadn't realized until he was alone with Caroline how many times Hannah had smoothed things between them. She had put in a few words, some-times explaining and sometimes offering a diversion, that had satisfied Caroline in a way his peremptory orders did not. She wasn't flatly disobedient, just stubborn and determined to have her way.

Knowing it wouldn't work, Jake tried one more time. "Rory will be right back. You can talk to him."

"He'll just go find Zeb and the others. He won't come back here for ages, and I don't like to be here all alone."

Exasperated, Jake gave in. She was also as subtle as a blacksmith's hammer. If Hannah were with them, read the unspoken accusation, she wouldn't be alone in her room. Jake hated the necessity of that also. And it worried him—which Caroline knew and played upon at will. Like now.

Because he disliked her defiance, if that was what it was, Jake didn't make any effort at conversation as they walked through the hotel and outside. He didn't mind the expense of the hotel, which was entirely for Caroline's benefit. Zeb and Percy, an old friend of his, were staying in a boarding house outside the center of Independence. Although Rory stayed at the hotel with them, again for Caroline's sake, he spent his time with the men whenever Jake was free to chaperone Caroline.

As they walked the busy street, Jake told himself he had no regrets. He would never stop missing Hannah for himself, but he hoped Caroline would soon forget her. Special as Hannah was, it didn't make sense to Jake that the girl should have come so completely under her spell. He knew she had been careful not to get too close to Caroline on the trip. But it had happened anyway. Maybe just *because* Hannah hadn't been pushy or tried too hard to win her affection. That had to be it, he decided. Caroline was just contrary enough that if he'd wanted her to love Hannah, she would have been jealous.

Still, he was proud of Caroline and enjoyed her company. She kept up with his long-legged pace and took in everything she saw on the streets, her head craning this way and that so as not to miss anything of interest. Usually, she asked questions, but now she didn't because she knew he was irritated. That made Jake feel guilty all over again. He wanted her to feel close to him.

"Papa?" Caroline caught at his hand, interrupting his tiresome thoughts. "Do you know Mr. Colby's wife very well?"

The Colbys were to be the final members of their group. They had not yet arrived in Independence, but were scheduled to travel with them to the territory of New Mexico. Jake frowned, trying to think how to answer her. Colby's wife would be the only other female with them, and as such, she and Caroline would be thrown together a great deal. "I've never met her, honey, but I've known Frank Colby for years. He's a good man, so probably she's nice, too."

In fact, Jake was worried about Ellen Colby. Frank had married her just before the war broke out, over the strenuous objections of his three grown children. Although it could be said that after losing his first wife, the children's mother, so long ago, he deserved another chance at happiness, the truth was that Ellen Colby was only two years older than his oldest child. Frank's picture showed a lovely young woman with a lively expression and dark hair and eyes. Frank said she wasn't as dark as the photograph, that her hair was mink brown, not black, as it appeared there. The description worried Jake as much as anything else; Colby wasn't the kind of man for poetic phrases. That his wife inspired them could mean trouble for them all.

"Does Zeb know her?"

"I believe he's met her."

"What did he think?"

"I don't remember him saying much," Jake answered cautiously. Actually, Zeb had predicted, "That one will lead him on a merry chase." But Jake temporized that Zeb knew little and cared less about women, choosing to forget Zeb's alliance with Hannah and his outright affection for Caroline.

Caroline executed a jiggling little hop to keep up with him, saying only, "I wish he said he liked her. I *know* he liked Hannah."

Jake refused to comment and they walked the rest of the way in silence.

The bank intimidated Jake. It was dark and quiet, with well-oiled wood panels and uncomfortable benches in the lobby. No matter how legitimate his business, he always felt that any banker could tell that he was an imposter who could be refused with impunity. It had been one thing to trail after Simon Sargent to the Omaha bank and quite another to come here by himself, attempting to take out a loan for the money they needed to outfit themselves for the trail to New Mexico. Sargent had supplied him with what he called a letter of credit, but Jake had little faith in the piece of paper he had been guarding so carefully all the way down the Missouri River.

He stood just inside the door, waiting for his eyes to grow accustomed to the inner gloom. He tried to remember what Sargent had done, where he had gone and whom he had asked to speak with. But that had been another bank. Sargent had known those people and known his way around whereas Jake did not.

Once again he wished Caroline had stayed behind. If he was refused—and he expected to be—he didn't want her to witness his embarrassment. Or his anger. Because what would he do then? How would they go on without money?

Jake's fog was so deep he was hardly aware of Caroline pressed to his side in the shadow of the door and even less aware of what was happening right before his eyes.

A man, dressed in black the way he himself was, in black coat, black breeches and boots, stood just ahead of him in the middle of the bank. He said loudly, "Everybody do what I say and no one will get hurt, do you hear me?"

One woman gave a small, frightened squeak, like a rusty hinge moving, but otherwise there were only murmurs and mutterings of assent.

"You there," the man yelled at a man behind the counter. "Get the money from every teller and put it in a bag. And be quick about it!" He waved his gun then so Jake could see it.

Jake began to try to edge back to the door, blocking Caroline's body with his. But she didn't move. He chanced a glance down at her, afraid she didn't realize their danger.

She was looking straight up at him, her eyes bright and fearless. He tried to move again and this time she nudged him with her shoulder. Then he saw that she was trying to reach his hand. Thinking she wanted to hold his hand out of fear, he groped for her. His hand closed on the cold metal of a gun. He was so surprised he almost dropped it.

Caroline grinned at his shock and mouthed the words, "It's loaded."

After that, everything that happened seemed to involve someone else. He had no intention of halting the holdup, but that's what he did. Everyone told him later, Caroline included.

He walked up behind the gunman with his usual silent tread. One of the bank employees, thinking him the robber's accomplice, gasped at seeing a second person, but since his cage was being emptied of money then, the bandit thought nothing of the noise.

Jake pressed the gun Caroline had given him to the man's neck and took the gun out of his suddenly limp grasp. Jake didn't need to say a word until after a stunned few minutes passed and no one came forward to help him. Quickly, Caroline appeared at his side to take the thief's gun from him.

"Take off my belt," Jake told her. When she had it free,

he forced the man to the floor and tied his hands at his back.

Then and only then did the bank employees and customers come forward to congratulate and thank him. Someone, he was told, was going for the sheriff.

"We thought you were with him," they said, one after the other. "We didn't see the girl at all."

"The girl," Jake noticed, was in her glory. "That's my papa," she told everyone. "We came here to get our money to go on the Santa Fe Trail to New Mexico. We're going to have a ranch there and raise cattle and horses."

Jake didn't relax until the bank robber had been taken away, then he headed for Caroline, intending to whisk her away, back to the hotel. She was surrounded by people asking her questions. What bothered him was that she was answering them. He couldn't see her, but he could hear her. Not the words, just the rise and fall of her voice, going on and on. He had to get her away.

Getting through to her was difficult until someone noticed who he was and said in a booming voice, "Here he is now, Caroline. Here's your papa!"

The sea of people around her divided and she jumped to her feet and hugged him. "Come on, honey, let's get out of here fast."

She started to resist, then grinned as if she suspected that he had devised a clever new game for them to play.

At first everyone stood back, making an aisle to the door, but as soon as their intention became apparent, a large man stepped in front of them, blocking their way. "Come now, Mr. Farnsworth," he chided. "Caroline said you came to get your money. You mustn't run off without doing business here. Why, people might think you don't consider this bank a safe place!" He led the laughter that followed, chuckling delightedly at his joke.

He was well dressed and, despite his jollity, obviously in charge of the bank. All Jake's anxieties about such people forced him to stop. No matter what service he had rendered, this man could still turn him away from his money if he chose to be offended.

"Is there a place where I could talk to my daughter for a minute?"

"Of course there is," the man answered, flinging out his arm in an expansive gesture. "You may borrow my office. I'd be honored."

Caroline took his hand and walked meekly inside with him. Jake barely took in the paneled walls and massive desk. He sank to the first chair he came to and asked, "Are *you* all right?"

The question was patently silly. She was glowing. "Are you all right?" she asked in answer, obviously struck by his agitation.

"What did you tell all those people?" he demanded.

"Just that we came here to get our money for New Mexico. Was that wrong?"

Jake didn't know. He couldn't think. He didn't want the world to know that when he left he'd be carrying a lot of money. What if he was robbed? "No, no. That's all right, honey." He wanted to reassure her. She had been cool and clever, and above all, he wanted her to know that he approved of her.

Then he remembered the gun. "Was that gun really loaded? And why did you have it with you?"

"I feel safer with it," she answered. "It was loaded because I didn't think it would do me any good unloaded."

She was so reasonable—and so unreasonable at the same time. She seemed to have no idea she was a child. "Did you tell those people it was your gun?"

"Oh, no. They wouldn't have understood. I did say I nudged you because you didn't seem to notice the robber. Was that wrong?"

"Lord, no, but I just wanted to *leave*." He couldn't

shake the terrible feeling that Caroline had been in danger. How would he manage the trip to New Mexico? All he could think was that coming west even this far was foolish and wrong. If Caroline were hurt, he'd never forgive himself.

"Well, I thought about leaving," she said, bringing him back to the holdup. "But we couldn't do that. The door opened *in,* and if we opened it, the robber might have turned and shot us."

Jake groaned and she went to sit on his lap and comfort him. After they hugged a few minutes, Caroline laughed and said, "And you thought I'd be bored coming with you!"

A discreet tap on the door reminded Jake that they were occupying someone's office. When he answered it, a man shook his hand and introduced himself. He was a newspaper reporter who wanted to interview and photograph them. They went back out into the spotlight, where Jake sat, looking stiff and uncomfortable, with Caroline, proud and composed, at his side.

He answered question after question, as did Caroline, but he remembered only one of them — and that because it produced gales of laughter from the people still lingering to savor the excitement of the aborted crime. When asked why he was dressed all in black, he said, "I wanted to impress upon the banker that I'm a sober and dependable person." Only after he heard the reaction did he recall that the bank robber had been dressed the same way. It was a relief to be able to join their laughter.

After all his ordeals, conducting business was almost easy for Jake by comparison. The president of the bank, the man with the booming voice whose office they had used, took Jake there again and personally served him. His fears of refusal allayed, Jake was able to enjoy the experience.

Thanks to Caroline, he was treated here the way Simon

Sargent had been treated in Omaha. His letter of credit was as good as Hannah's uncle had promised. Mr. Melbourne, who invited Jake to call him Ed, even helped him make his travel arrangements without cash once he understood his concern about carrying money with him. All in all, Jake was well pleased.

They bought extra copies of the next day's newspaper. Their picture was on the front page side by side with a reproduction of a wanted poster provided by the sheriff. Their bank robber turned out to be a man with several aliases and a string of successful bank robberies. "Kid" Belasco had been caught so easily because, as he told the sheriff, he, too, had thought the man behind him in the doorway was his accomplice. That man, known as Baltimore Blackie, was still missing.

Caroline took three of the newspapers away with her in her bag when they left four days later. She wanted to send one clipping to her grandparents or, failing that, to her friend Becky back in Hanford. Jake convinced her that hearing the story would only cause those people to worry about her safety.

Instead, Caroline wrote letters. The one to the Lunigs was purposely bland and reassuring, but to Becky she told the full and exciting story. She held back nothing, not even the fact that the loaded gun her father had used was hers and that she had learned to shoot it. She ended the letter by condemning the bank for not offering her father a reward and, in the true cliff-hanging style of her favorite writers, by speculating whether or not Baltimore Blackie would follow them to New Mexico to take his revenge on them.

Jake, posting the two letters for Caroline, eyed the relative heft of the two envelopes with suspicion. If she had told her friend about her adventure, might not the Lunigs find out? And try to get her back? He decided they were safely beyond the reach of Grace's parents at last and sent both letters.

He had no idea that when Becky read Caroline's letter, she would not believe a word of it. Caroline was known for her imagination, but this time, Becky decided, putting the letter in her drawer for safekeeping, she had gone too far. Indians, Becky could believe, even if they couldn't have been her friend's cousins; but her own gun?

That was preposterous.

# Chapter Twenty-Four

Hannah sat back on her heels and blew out a tired sigh. The room was a mess.

"Why don't you let me finish up here, Miss Hannah?" asked Sadie. She was one of the day maids sent to Hannah by Elspeth to help her pack. "You want to keep these dresses here?"

Hannah brushed the hair from her eyes and stared distractedly at the pile of clothes Sadie indicated. "No. Those are the ones to give away. I'm only taking these." She pointed to a much smaller stack.

"Oh, but, ma'am! These are so beautiful!"

"Perhaps there's something there you'd like for yourself." She took in Sadie's florid complexion and got up to rescue the dress she thought would most flatter her coloring. "Why not this?" she asked, holding it up to the flustered woman. "It would look lovely on you."

"Oh, I could never wear that!"

"No? Just see how pretty you look, Sadie." She drew her to the mirror. "I think you should have it — or if not this one, then any that catches your eye. As you wish."

"No, I mean, ma'am, I can't fit into it."

"Well, let's look at the seams." She turned the gown to the inside. "I had to have this taken in, and all the cloth is still here. You see? I'm sure it could be let out to fit you.

Are you skilled with a needle?"

"My sister is," Sadie said eagerly. She was holding the dress as if she'd never let it go.

"Well, there. Then the problem is solved. Is there something here to suit your sister too? Elsie, isn't it?" Hannah smiled, cheered by Sadie's pleasure. "It wouldn't do for her to have to fix a dress for you and not have one for herself as well. Does she look like you?"

"Her hair is browner, Miss Hannah."

Together they selected another gown and put the two aside for Sadie to take home. Hannah brushed off her palms on her skirt as she looked around the room one more time. Tired of being cooped up inside, she decided to take Sadie up on her offer to finish for her. A fresh breeze was stirring the curtains and Hannah wanted to be outside.

She met Elspeth in the lower hall, but she only smiled and waved her on. "Yes, I know. You'll be at the paddock. Well, it's a nice afternoon. What there is left of it."

Outside, Hannah pulled her wrap closer. The breeze was really a wind out here, for spring had come reluctantly to Knoxville this year. The ground squelched under her feet in places, but Hannah didn't care. After tomorrow she'd probably never have the pleasure of watching Lucky Jim's family again.

She knew she was sentimentalizing the horses, but as long as she never admitted it, no one would know. Marjorie Daw had produced the prettiest foal ever, chestnut brown with three white socks and a blaze. Uncle Simon had said she could name him. The only name she wanted was Lucky Jake, but so far she hadn't had the nerve to suggest it.

Her obsession with Jake was no secret. Everyone knew she had not recovered from being left behind. She doubted she ever would. She would, however, go on with her life, such as it was. Ironically, Daniel had given her a start. Because he had no other family, she had inherited the land he'd bought in Bellevue in hope of affecting change in the railroad route from Omaha to that settlement. She had decided to go to Bellevue and begin a new life there as a school teacher. Uncle Simon told her the town was small and friendly, practically ideal for her purposes.

Lucky Jim came to the fence and whickered into her palm. Not satisfied with her pat, he pushed against her shoulder, looking for a treat.

"I'm sorry, Jim. I didn't bring you a carrot today. Wasn't that thoughtless of me? But I will tomorrow."

As if he accepted the promise, the horse trotted away, his own white socks flashing just above the newly green grass. The wind tossed his mane as he circled the maternal pair, watchful dam and awkward foal. He was showing off, almost the same way he had when he had courted Marjorie Daw. Or maybe he ran because it was spring and he was alive.

Hannah understood. Something green and vibrant had welled up inside her as well. It wasn't the new life she had hoped to be bringing forth soon, but it was life nonetheless — her life — and she refused to spend any more of it mourning for what she didn't have.

"I should have guessed I'd find you here."

Absorbed in her thoughts, Hannah had not heard Jake's soft approach behind her. The sound of his voice, so often imagined, made her cry out and turn too quickly. Only a quick grasp at the railing saved her from falling.

Jake.

The wind blew her hair across her eyes. She brushed it away, expecting the apparition to be gone when she could

447

see again.

"You're . . . real?"

He laughed softly, another sound from her dreams. "Absolutely. And you? Are you real too?"

She tried to laugh but couldn't. "I don't know. I don't feel real right now." She continued to cling to the fence, needing support. *Why are you here?* her mind screamed. Then she remembered that she had loaned him money. He would repay it, but why not by mail?

Jake walked closer, watching her face intently. Was he looking for a welcome?

"How are you, Hannah?"

"Fine, and you? How are Caroline and Rory?"

"We're all well." His scrutiny didn't ease. "Forgive my sudden arrival like this. I came right here"—he looked down at his somewhat travel-worn clothes—"just as I am."

Hannah turned in order to rest more fully against the paddock. She had such conflicting needs, to throw herself into his arms and to pummel him with her fists. Her mind was filled with her question to the exclusion of everything else. Until she knew why he had come, she couldn't talk to him.

"Your housekeeper sent me here. She said I was just in time. What did she mean?"

If his voice was rough, Hannah was too distracted to notice.

"Hannah?" he prompted.

She rallied, raising her face and smiling up at him. "Oh, that. Well, I'm leaving here . . . the day after tomorrow."

"Where are you going?"

Should she tell him? "To Bellevue in Nebraska. You may remember that Daniel owned land there." He proba-

448

bly didn't know that Daniel was dead.

He looked surprised. "Why Bellevue?"

"Why not?" Her look challenged him to object.

"Why not indeed?" He gave his attention to the horses without saying more.

"Tell me about your home. Where did you settle?"

"In New Mexico."

"New Mexico!" Her stomach contracted at the thought of him so far away. She would never have found him there. Then she remembered that she had promised them both that she would never pursue him again. It was a promise she was determined to keep.

Jake smiled then with honest delight. "I'm nearly as surprised as you are. It was Zeb's idea."

"Zeb is with you, too?" The unfairness of it all made her voice sharp and accusing. She'd had months of aching loneliness and depression to live through, while he had spent his time surrounded by friends and loved ones.

"Zeb and a friend of his and Frank Colby and his wife Ellen. We're all neighbors, or as much neighbors as people can be out there."

"Are you in the desert?"

"No. There is desert in the territory, but not where we are. We're on plains somewhat reminiscent of Nebraska. It's more arid, but very beautiful, especially with the mountains just off in the distance. It gets hot in summer, I'm told, but we had snow and winter just as you do here."

"You have cattle and horses?"

"Horses to run the cattle, but I want to build up a herd and sell them. People need horses and many don't dare raise them because of the Apache threat. They steal horses more than cattle."

"You don't fear the Apaches?"

449

"I have no understanding with them, if that's what you're thinking. They wouldn't be impressed that I have Indian blood. I just hope we're enough off their path to escape their attention. So far that's been true."

"Have Caroline and Rory adjusted well to life there?"

"Both well but differently." Jake emulated her stance, leaning against the fence and looking at the horses instead of at her. "I don't know which of them has the harder time, to tell the truth. Caroline is trying to be a boy and Rory doesn't know whether he's family or hired help. But apart from that, they both love the outdoor life even when it's hard—which it is."

"And you, Jake? Are you happy?"

"Yes." His voice made it a more qualified statement than it might have been, but he didn't hesitate with his reply.

Hannah didn't know whether to rejoice or despair that he sounded unsure. One part of her wanted him to be as miserable as she was, but if he were, then what was the point of their separation? One of them, at least, should be happy.

"I never expected to see you again."

Instead of commenting Jake asked again, "Why are you going to Bellevue?" When she showed no inclination to answer, he added, "I know Daniel is dead, Hannah."

"How did you find out?"

"Simon told me. He was in Omaha when we arrived there."

"He never told me."

Jake shrugged. "You're not answering my question."

"I'm not sure I can. I need something to do, some way to be useful. I thought of setting up a school here, but the need isn't as great. I'd be in competition with others. When I found I owned land in Bellevue, I asked Uncle

Simon to see if it would do for me. He thought it would. It's neither a backwater nor a boomtown and it's new to me." Satisfied with her accounting, she smiled. "Who knows? Maybe I'll get to Fort Kearney after all."

"If you do, you'll have friends there. Some of Many Buffalo's tribe are there. They're replacing the so-called Galvanized Yankees who manned the fort during the war."

"I've never heard of them."

"They were Confederate soldiers pressed into duty there to guard against the Sioux. Now Pawnee Indians are replacing them."

"Is that where your cousin is?"

"He's guarding the railroad workers against the Sioux."

"He doesn't mind fighting other Indians for the whites?"

"The Pawnee have never fought the white man and they've always fought the Sioux. It's not a change. I just hope his trust in the government isn't misplaced. The Bureau of Indian Affairs only makes tribal distinctions when it's to their advantage. Now it is. I'm afraid that when the railroad is finished and people swarm into the West, the government will find it convenient to forget the Pawnee's service. But for now they're safe."

"Except from the Sioux," Hannah added, as realistic as Jake.

They stood without speaking until Hannah suddenly remember her manners. "I'm sorry, Jake," she said, turning to him. "You told me you just arrived and yet I haven't even let you go to your room. I'm sure you must want to rest. You surprised me right out of my senses."

They didn't resume their conversation until after dinner in the library. Hannah poured brandy for Jake and sherry for herself, feeling terribly at odds with everything. Although she'd told him she had never expected to see him again, she had dreamed of this encounter endlessly.

No, not this encounter, she corrected. She had imagined a vastly different one, one as passionate as their last night together. She had fed on that for weeks. He had not been so bloodless then.

She took a seat facing him and studied his appearance. He was as compelling as ever, his body hard and fit. He seemed more at ease than she remembered, yet with a curious inner tension at odds with that ease.

"I answered your question, Jake," she began after a period of quiet watchfulness, "now I'd like to know why you're here."

"I needed to see you again."

"Why?" She was relieved that he didn't pretend that he had come to repay her loan, but still his answer didn't satisfy her.

"To know that you're . . . happy, I guess."

"And am I?" she asked softly.

He put down his glass with a sharp clink that resounded like a rifle shot in the quiet room. Surging to his feet to lean over her, forcing her back against the chair, he said, "I hope to God you're not."

Blood began to sing in her veins, staining her cheeks with color. "But you're happy. You told me so."

"There's happiness and happiness," he said flatly. His hands braced on the arms of her chair prevented her from rising—if she'd wanted to. She didn't. "I have everything I wanted and planned for so long to get. In that sense I'm happy. I'd be a fool to complain, but I miss you. I've never stopped wanting you from the day I met you—and distance didn't change that. I want you with me."

"I'm still rich," she said just as flatly.

He backed off and stood up to rake his hand through

452

his hair. "I know." His eyes were so dilated they looked black, their blue mere rings around the dark centers. It was a look she had heretofore seen only when they made love. "You didn't take up your old life."

It wasn't a question. "Which old life?" she asked. "The one I lived as a practically single parent of a small child? Or the one in your imagination?"

"The one with cotillions and balls and dinner parties."

"I've always been Uncle Simon's hostess when he's at home. That was my only social life after David was born," she told him. "Oh, I have women friends I see and a few other friends who didn't give up on me. But you forget, Jake—I was married. Deserted, but married."

"I never forgot that," he said, pacing away.

He was right. He had never forgotten. "And never forgave me either," she said with surprising bitterness.

His head snapped around so he could look at her. "Is that what you think?"

"Shouldn't I?"

He came back to stand before her chair, only this time he dropped down onto his haunches to bring his face level with hers. "My God, Hannah. Have I lost you after all?"

His agonized expression pierced Hannah's heart, sharp as an Indian arrow. She was too confused to speak.

Jake took her hands. "Hannah, I love you. Leaving you here was the hardest thing I've ever had to do, worse than burying Grace or leaving Caroline in Hanford to go to war. I know I thought some harsh things about you in the beginning, but that was before I understood what you are. I wanted to take you with me and there hasn't been a day since that I haven't missed you and wanted you and hoped to find you free when I came back."

"You *planned* to come back?"

"Always."

453

She couldn't doubt him, but somehow that made the misery of the past months worse. "Then what was the point of going? Why didn't you tell me? Or take me with you?"

"Because I had to give you a chance to find out what you wanted."

"I always knew what I wanted. I told you and told you!"

"You thought you knew, but you were so removed from your regular world, how could you be sure? And I couldn't be positive until you had the chance to live that way again."

Tears came to Hannah's eyes. She was angry and hurt and ecstatically happy, all in a jumble. "You fool! I'll never forgive you for this. The only thing that kept me going after you left was the hope that I was carrying your child. When I found I wasn't, I wanted to die."

Her anger surprised him, but the possibility of a child shocked him to the core. He had never given conception a thought. He got up and scooped her into his arms so he could take her place and hold her on his lap. When he had her close, he said, "Tell me you still love me. I need you so much."

Hannah answered him with a kiss, showing him instead of telling him. She used all her love and all her lonely hunger to make him understand once and for all what he was to her. Then, to make doubly sure, she said the words he wanted to hear. "I love you, Jake. All I want is to be your wife and have your children."

Jake smiled. "And to think you could have been pregnant." He shook his head ruefully. "What would you have done?"

"No one would have known it wasn't Daniel's child. Oh, I would have told Uncle Simon, I suppose. Or he

454

would have guessed, but he wouldn't have minded."

"You wouldn't have told me?"

"How? I didn't know where you were."

"Simon knew."

"He wouldn't have gone against my wishes. I told you when you left here you were safe from me. I wasn't going to chase you again."

"But you will marry me, won't you?"

"Whenever you say." They sealed that vow with another kiss that Hannah ended by pulling back. "If you're still worried about my wealth, there's something you should realize. Uncle Simon could get married again, you know, and have his own children. Stranger things have happened."

"I don't worry so much about that. It was never the money that concerned me as much as it was that you might be unhappy without it. I didn't want you to regret not having a house like this and clothes like what you're wearing."

"I saved this dress because you liked it." It was the bottle green lawn she had worn in Omaha. "I was giving most of the fancy ones away."

"You might want to keep them now. We have occasions to dress up, more than you would as a school teacher in Nebraska."

"Tell me about your ranch. Is it big?"

"It's getting bigger. Zeb and his friend Percy sold me their land. Zeb wants to stay but Percy didn't like working cattle. Zeb will work for me and own shares in the cattle besides. Neither of them wanted to manage, Zeb especially, but I'd hate to lose him. I thought maybe someday Rory could have that land for his own operation if he wants."

"Do you have a house?"

"The original one is becoming the bunkhouse. We're building an adobe house to replace it. You'll be able to decide how you want it arranged and it can be added on to as we need room."

"Did you get a housekeeper for Caroline?"

"I did, and she's a gem. Her name is Lupe Martinez. She's a great cook and a warm-hearted, motherly woman. What made her attractive at the start was the fact that she had a daughter." He laughed, thinking about that, then explained. "Her daughter turned out to be more interested in Rory than in Caroline, but that's settled now. You'll love Lupe and she'll love you."

"You've done so well, Jake, but I knew you would."

"I had a bit of luck—and some help." Laughing, he moved her to reach inside to the breast pocket of his coat. He pulled out a folded piece of newsprint. "This will tell you."

Hannah opened the clipping to a picture of Caroline and Jake. The headline read, "Girl and Her Father Foil Bank Holdup."

"Jake! When was this?"

"On the way to New Mexico. Caroline sent you this clipping."

"She knew you were coming here?"

"She and Rory gave me no peace about you, so when we found out about the rewards, they knew I'd come back for you. I warned them not to expect you to be waiting, but they never doubted."

"And you did?"

"Constantly. I was so afraid. I had the loan to repay as an excuse to see you, but I didn't dare expect to be welcome." He smiled at her expression, urging, "Read the article. Caroline said to tell you it was just like something out of her favorite book. She wouldn't tell me more than

456

that. Do you two have women's secrets already?"

Jake looked so disgruntled that Hannah decided not to tell him about Caroline's choice of reading matter. If Caroline trusted her to keep her secret, she would. "That's exactly what it is," she told him, giving him a kiss to make up for the slight.

She read the article with delight, chuckling over the quotes from Caroline. Called "the girl who's not afraid of Indians," she sounded as proud as Jake was modest. "Oh this is wonderful, Jake. Did you say you got a reward?"

"Two of them. One from the bank and one for catching a wanted man. That money has made the difference for us and I owe it all to Caroline."

"We can put aside the money from my trust to educate the children. Rory, too."

Jake approved with a nod, but drew her attention back to the article. "What this doesn't say—because Caroline was smart enough not to tell them—is that *she* was the one carrying a loaded gun, not me. She had your gun in her bag. While I was busy with my own thoughts, she saw the gunman and handed it over, prodding me into action. The rest was so easy it was unbelievable. She could have done it herself—and probably would have if I hadn't been there."

"Imagine the headline—'Gun-toting Girl Foils Bank Holdup!' She'd be famous. Oh, Jake, it's marvelous. It is just like something in a story, and I have books to take to her. I couldn't resist buying things I thought she'd like even though I never expected to see her again."

"I think you did. You must have known I'd be back, just as you knew I loved you."

"I did know that. I just didn't think you knew it."

"We can be married here so Simon can be with you."

"But what about Caroline and Rory? Won't they

457

mind?"

"We'll have a party instead. I'm not waiting any longer." He got up and began to carry her to the stairs. "Just wait till you see the view from our bedroom. I faced the house so we can see the mountains right from the bed. The sky is endless there and the mountains look different in every light. You'll love it *and* the bed I'm having made just for you."

Hannah put her arms around his neck and snuggled close. "I don't think you ever doubted me at all."

"I hoped," he said. "Next to love, hope is the most powerful force on earth."

# Author's Note

Although the characters and events of this story are fictional, the background is not. The Union Pacific Railroad route was in dispute, particularly as to its point of origin, right up to the actual laying of track, begun on July 10, 1865. By September 22, 1865, ten miles of track led from Omaha, Nebraska, not from Bellevue. By August of 1866, the railroad passed Fort Kearney, 190 miles from Omaha.

Pawnee Indians were enlisted to serve as guides and guards for the railroad workers against the Sioux, their traditional enemy. Besides serving along the route itself, they were installed at Fort Kearney to replace the "irregular regulars," a number of former Confederate soldiers called the Galvanized Yankees, when those men were withdrawn from the fort after the end of the Civil War. The Pawnee were more peaceful and accommodating to the white man than other tribes of the plains; nevertheless, Pawnee men customarily wore their hair in the fierce-looking style we now call a Mohawk.

# MORE TANTALIZING ROMANCES

**SATIN SURRENDER** (1861, $3.95)
by Carol Finch

Dante Fowler found innocent Erica Bennett in his bed in the most fashionable whorehouse in New Orleans. Expecting a woman of experience, Dante instead stole the innocence of the most magnificent creature he'd ever seen. He would forever make her succumb to . . . *Satin Surrender*.

**CAPTIVE BRIDE** (1984, $3.95)
by Carol Finch

Feisty Rozalyn DuBois had to pretend affection for roguish Dominic Baudelair; her only wish was to trick him into falling in love and then drop him cold. But Dominic had his own plans: To become the richest trapper in the territory by making Rozalyn his *Captive Bride*.

**MOONLIT SPLENDOR** (2008, $3.95)
by Wanda Owen

When the handsome stranger emerged from the shadows and pulled Charmaine Lamoureux into his strong embrace, she knew she should scream, but instead she sighed with pleasure at his seductive caresses. She would be wed against her will on the morrow—but tonight she would succumb to this passionate MOONLIT SPLENDOR.

**UNTAMED CAPTIVE** (2159, $3.95)
by Elaine Barbieri

Cheyenne warrior Black Wolf fully intended to make Faith Durham, the lily-skinned white woman he'd captured, pay for her people's crimes against the Indians. Then he looked into her sky-blue eyes and it was impossible to stem his desire . . . he was compelled to make her surrender as his UNTAMED CAPTIVE.

**WILD FOR LOVE** (2161, $3.95)
by Linda Benjamin

All Callandra wanted was to go to Yellowstone and hunt for buried treasure. Then her wagon broke down and she had no choice but to get mixed up with that arrogant golden-haired cowboy, Trace McCord. But before she knew it, the only treasure she wanted was to make him hers forever.

*Available wherever paperbacks are sold, or order direct from the Publisher. Send cover price plus 50¢ per copy for mailing and handling to Zebra Books, Dept. 2244, 475 Park Avenue South, New York, N.Y. 10016. Residents of New York, New Jersey and Pennsylvania must include sales tax. DO NOT SEND CASH.*